Silent
Revenge

Silent Revenge

LAURA LANDON

Text copyright © 2012 Laura Landon
All rights reserved.
Printed in the United States of America.

Published by Montlake Romance
P.O. Box 400818
Las Vegas, NV 89140

ISBN-13: 9781612184777
ISBN-10: 1612184774

This book is dedicated to my editor Eleni Caminis.
Thank you for everything, especially for making me laugh.

Chapter 1

*J*essica Stanton sat alone against the far wall of the ornate ballroom and watched her host and hostess, the Duke and Duchess of Stratmore, greet another guest. As usual, few even noticed she was there, and the people who gave her more than an occasional glance were greeted with her usual unapproachable air of aloofness.

She was, without a doubt, the only female in all of London society determined to be a wallflower.

With her hands folded properly in her lap and her back uncompromisingly rigid and straight, she ignored the four young debutantes who twittered past her. They stared curiously and whispered rude comments, then made a wide circle to avoid her. Let them think what they wanted. That she was a recluse. An oddity. Any description they cared to use was better than the truth.

She turned an envious gaze to the scores of elegant ladies dressed in silks and satins swirling across the dance floor in the arms of fashionably tailored gentlemen.

She would never be one of them.

With a graceful turn of her head, she dismissed the thought, then smoothed the pressed pleats of her slightly outdated, pale green bombazine gown. Her gaze focused on the arched entry as Baron and Baroness Littlebrook began their descent down the wide stairs. They were not the couple whose arrival she awaited. Nor was the baroness wearing the gown she'd waited all evening to see. Her gown. The gown she'd designed.

Jessica breathed a heavy sigh of disappointment and touched her hand to her perfectly pressed lace collar, determined to wait a little while longer. Patience had never been one of her mastered virtues, but she refused to leave until she glimpsed Lady Penelope Drummond's gown. She had dreamed it, sketched it, and pictured it in her mind's eye a thousand times over. She would not leave until she saw it.

The silk moiré would be the softest shade of peach, a color perfectly suited to the newlywed viscountess. The design would be ornamented with rows of beautifully hand-sewn ivory lace trim, the décolletage dipping just enough to be enticing, but not so low as to be vulgar. Jessica closed her eyes and envisioned how the young beauty would look in her creation, and excitement raced through her veins.

The designs. The colors. The parade of magnificent fashions worn by the cream of London society. Many of them were hers. Her creations were the reason she risked coming, her motivation for sitting unnoticed in the crowd, ignored for the most part, while a world of gaiety and laughter revolved around her. A world in which she could never be a part.

Over the years, she had become an invisible nonentity. Never without an invitation, for it would be a major breach of etiquette for society to ignore her, considering her late father's influence with the queen and her deceased stepmother's claim to nobility. Yet never was Jessica a part of their circle, either. But that was not why she braved society discovering her secret. She came only to see her creations.

Jessica lifted her gaze to the top of the empty stairway. Where was Lady Drummond? She only intended to stay long enough to see her gown, and then she could be gone.

Suddenly, three raucous young men in long tailcoats came toward her, hampering her view of the stairway. Obviously emboldened by drink, they moved in her direction, snickering as two of them pushed their friend toward her.

"Would you care to dance, Miss Stanton?" he said as he wove back and forth like a wave on a churning sea.

"Perhaps," Jessica answered with a regal lift of her chin and a faux smile pasted on her lips. "If a gentleman who possessed at least a modicum of maturity and who could stand upright without assistance were to ask me. You, unfortunately, possess neither."

Uproarious guffawing followed from his two friends as the red-faced young noble backed away, executing a low bow that threatened to topple his unsteady figure to the floor.

Jessica averted her eyes, dismissing all of them with a turn of her head.

She kept her gaze focused on the other side of the room only long enough for the three men to move away, then turned her attention back to the ballroom. Lady Drummond was nowhere in sight, but Jessica's cousin, Melinda Wallace, Duchess of Collingsworth, walked toward her with a slight grin on her face.

"I see you have dashed the hopes of yet another fine young nobleman seeking to gain the attention of the unapproachable Miss Jessica Stanton," her cousin said, sitting beside her.

Jessica breathed a heavy sigh. "I only wish their futile attempts would stop."

Melinda laughed. "I would not hold out too much hope for that to happen. James says your name has been associated with wagers taken at White's."

Jessica sucked in a harsh breath and stiffened her spine even straighter. Why couldn't everyone just leave her alone?

Melinda covered Jessica's hand fisted in her lap. "Your attempts to become a nondescript wallflower have only created more of a challenge to see who will be the first to break through your icy facade, Jessica."

Jessica looked at her friend and saw a mixture of compassion and understanding. Melinda wasn't only her cousin, she was her friend. Her *only* friend. Friends since they were old enough to talk. From that time on they were as close as sisters. Melinda was one of the few people in all of London who knew her secret and did not care.

"Has Lady Drummond arrived yet?" she asked. There was an expectant look on her face that indicated she was as excited as Jessica.

"No. And I don't know how much longer I can stand the wait."

Melinda's understanding smile showed off pretty white teeth and deep green eyes that glistened with happiness. "I've already received three compliments on my gown, Jess. Lady Smithson wouldn't give up until I told her where I'd found such a stunning design."

Jessica returned her smile. "Did you tell her it was an original? Designed especially for you?"

"Yes," she said with a giggle. "Then I just happened to let slip the dressmaker's name. Accidentally, of course."

"Of course." Jessica tried to hide her grin.

"I'm sure that by tomorrow afternoon Madame Lamont will have another customer, thanks to you."

Melinda gave Jessica's hand a reassuring squeeze. "Why don't you come with me and we'll sit over by the window? It's terribly stuffy here against this wall, and there's such a nice breeze coming from the garden. I'm sure you'd be much more comfortable in the open."

Jessica shook her head. "It's enough that I'm here, Mel. There is no need to take unnecessary chances."

"No one will notice, Jess. I promise I'll stay right beside you and make sure—"

"Please, Mel," Jessica murmured, touched by her concern. "I'm used to being alone. I prefer it that way."

"It would help stop the talk, Jess. Then everyone would not think you such a recluse."

"I don't mind." Jessica turned her face toward the empty doorway, then tried to change the sober expression on Melinda's face with an impish grin. "Would you like to hear all that I have discovered as an unnoticed wallflower?"

Melinda's eyes widened in anticipation. "Yes, you devious little spy."

Jessica laughed. "I am, aren't I? Well, let's see." She propped a dainty finger against her cheek and lifted her eyes thoughtfully. "The very prim and proper Lady Drucilla Englewood is, even as we speak, meeting quite clandestinely in the greenhouse with a man whose nearness makes her 'fairly swoon with the vapors.'"

"No!" Melinda gasped. "Who?"

"Lord Ducannon."

"They are in love?" Melinda asked, her eyes wide in disbelief.

"Yes. Very."

"But she's promised to the Duke of Eddinton."

"Only because Drucilla's father has his cap set on a duke for his daughter, or a marquess at the very least. Ducannon is only a baron."

"Poor Drucilla. And she is so sweet."

"It's too bad someone doesn't ask to see our hostess's azaleas. I hear they're simply beautiful this time of year."

"Oh no, Jess. That would compromise the two lovers in a scandal."

"Scandals are forgotten. Marriage to the wrong husband is an agony that lasts a lifetime."

She and Melinda exchanged serious glances.

"How astute you've become, Jess. And without anyone knowing. I didn't realize you were such a romantic."

"I am hardly a romantic. I only see two people in love who are being kept apart. All of society knows how desperately Drucilla and Ducannon love each other. Everyone knows it would be a sin to force Drucilla to marry Eddinton."

Melinda worried her lower lip. "Do I dare?" Melinda asked, eyeing the doorway leading to the greenhouse.

Jessica gave her friend's hand a gentle squeeze. "I see Lord Parley straight ahead talking to Lady Munster's widowed sister. I hear his fondness for flowers is almost obsessive. Perhaps he would enjoy showing the widow our hostess's azaleas."

Melinda nodded and then stood. "I think I'll get us a glass of punch, and perhaps…"

Jessica gave her friend a satisfied look, then sat back in her chair. "And if you see your husband, tell him to avoid any involvement in a new company Lord Mottley is forming. He's recruiting investors for a new trading firm. I fear the men connected with the venture cannot be trusted. Not only is the plan's legality questionable, but the words *smuggling* and *illegal cargo* were mentioned in their discussion."

"How do you discover all this?"

Jessica shrugged her slim shoulders. "It's amazing what people say when they think no one is around to overhear them."

"I'm going to get us that punch. I'll be right back."

Jessica watched her friend cross the ballroom and then looked again at the empty entryway. Lady Drummond obviously preferred to be fashionably late in the extreme.

Jessica breathed a sigh of frustration, then scanned the crowded dance floor. A myriad of muted rainbow shades twirled hither and yon, bold and vibrant with the movement, captivating her until Melinda returned with two glasses in her hand.

"Lord Parley seemed very interested in seeing the Duchess of Stratmore's azaleas. And James said to tell you thank you. He knows the new company to which you are referring and is grateful for the warning."

Jessica lifted the glass to her lips and sipped. "Have you noticed Lady Ellis this evening? Someone should really take pity on her and tell her how absurd she looks in that dress. She's entirely too buxom to wear something so revealing, and a woman her age should never wear pink. She should only wear—"

Mel grabbed her shoulder in silent warning, and Jessica instantly quieted. The cautionary look on her friend's face gave her pause, and she became even more concerned when Mel placed a silencing finger against her lips. Jessica turned around, her gaze taking in the suspended stillness that covered the ballroom. She'd never seen anything so odd. Anything so astounding.

Wide-eyed servants stopped where they were, balancing teetering trays of glasses in their hands. Musicians held their horsehair bows awkwardly above the silent strings of their violins. Hundreds of shocked dancers stood frozen in transfixed amazement, like marble statues in a garden. Every mouth of London's nobility gaped in shocked disbelief, as if the incredulous sight crossed so far over the line of comprehension that it paralyzed them in midmotion.

Jessica looked at Melinda in confusion, and her friend squeezed her hand in a death-clenching grip. She studied Mel's serious expression, then followed her gaze to the man poised at the top of the stairs.

Every nerve in Jessica's body tingled with a charge that came from somewhere beyond the here and now. His presence captured her and refused to release her. She tried to shift her gaze from his imposing form, but could not look away from the tall dark stranger who towered above them from the entryway. The scorching look on his face as he stared out into the crowd sent a cold shiver down her spine.

She was fixated by the daunting figure, waiting for him to move. The power he exuded engulfed her in an uneasy mixture of vibrancy and fear.

He stood ramrod straight, his shoulders back, his chin high, and his long, muscular legs braced for battle. The broad expanse of his shoulders filled out his midnight-black dress tails to perfection. The snowy cravat at his neck glowed in contrast to his bronzed skin. His impressive height and extraordinary stature dominated the entire room. But it was his deadly glare that caused her heart to skip a beat. The lethal glare he cast over the ballroom defied any of London's elite to challenge his presence.

No one did.

No one moved. No one breathed.

No one dared.

With overt certainty, he allowed the gaping nobility to drink their fill, and then slowly, deliberately, he followed one step with another until he stood at the bottom of the staircase. As if he didn't care that all eyes remained riveted on his every move, he greeted his host and hostess with unquestioning self-assurance and aplomb.

Not wanting to miss even the slightest detail, Jessica leaned a little to the left to see around the portly gentleman blocking her view. She stared in fascination as the broad-shouldered stranger reached to kiss the duchess's hand. The duchess's mouth dropped, and her complexion paled.

Jessica held her breath as she waited for tragedy to strike.

The intriguing stranger executed a low bow. His unsmiling eyes did not soften, nor did the stony expression on his face relax. When he straightened to his full height, the Duchess of Stratmore clenched a trembling hand to her throat in obvious discomfort.

As if he realized how close his hostess was to losing her composure, he nodded curtly and squared his shoulders, then walked away as the duchess crumpled in a heap at her husband's feet.

The foreboding stranger seemed oblivious to the chaos he'd left in his wake. He took a few steps into the ballroom and lifted a glass of champagne from the tray of a benumbed servant, then stopped. With slow deliberation, he turned to face the gaping crowd.

As if some mysterious force controlled her destiny, Jessica felt compelled to get a better look at the handsome stranger before he disappeared. She stepped into an opening where she could get a better view.

His gaze caught her movement, and his haunting intensity locked with hers.

A shivering awareness ran through her, heightening the sensation that prickled at the back of her neck, tightening the pronounced confusion that struggled deep within her breast.

His frown deepened, and his brows narrowed to a thick, formidable line. His telling expression warned her that he was as aware of her as she was him.

All stability ceased to exist while he held her captive with his concentrated look. Her blood blazed hot as a raging fire. The air she needed to fill her lungs vanished.

He held her captive, and then, with a brutal jolt, he released his grasp of her. Her heart lurched violently as if she'd just fallen from a very great height. With a final commanding look at the crowd parting before him, he strode through the open double doors that led to the garden.

The nighttime darkness enveloped him as if he was one of its own, swallowing him into an inky blackness.

Melinda sank down in the nearest chair and stared at the empty doorway. "He's come back."

"Who is he?" Jessica watched the doorway, hoping he would reappear.

"Simon Warland. The Earl of Northcote."

"His entrance caused quite a commotion." Jessica looked at the stunned faces in the ballroom. No one was dancing. The more curious of the *ton* flitted from one group to another as they discussed the appearance of the Earl of Northcote with growing animation.

"I cannot believe he's here."

"Why not?"

"The scandal. His father was found dead three years ago. Everyone believes Northcote killed him."

"You don't?"

Melinda lifted her chin. "James refuses to believe he did. They have always been close friends, and James says the earl is incapable of murder."

Jessica looked at Melinda, amused at the unquestioning confidence she placed in her husband's opinion. "Why do you think he's come back?"

"There can be only one reason," Melinda said decidedly. "He has come to find a rich wife."

Jessica raised her eyebrows and gave her friend a skeptical look. From the expressions on the faces of the eligible females in attendance, a dark grave would be a more pleasant alternative. "A wife?"

Melinda nodded. "It must be so. The earl is bankrupt, and James says that without a miracle, he'll lose everything. The creditors will have control of all Northcote properties by the end of the month."

Jessica looked again at the empty doorway. She let her gaze focus on the darkness beyond the patio door and the shadowed figure that had walked through its portals. "I pity the unfortunate female forced to become the sacrifice. It doesn't seem the most pleasant of futures," Jessica said.

Although she couldn't explain it, Jessica sensed a connection to this stranger. Like two threads woven through a piece of fabric. Each thread separate, yet both necessary in order to make the pattern complete.

Perhaps it was because society thought of both of them as oddities.

Jessica looked back to the top of the stairway. Lady Drummond stood at the entrance in all her regal splendor, wearing the dress Jessica had waited all evening to see.

Her heart pounded in her breast, excitement rushing through her veins. The gown was stunning, beautiful, absolutely divine. The most magnificent creation she had ever designed. She couldn't wait for society's reaction to it.

She looked around the room, anticipating the smiles of admiration, the exclamations of wonder. But not one person looked toward the entrance. All in attendance stared at the terrace doorway, at the spot where the stranger had been swallowed by the darkness.

Her heart fell. No one gave Lady Drummond or her gown a second glance. No one even noticed she was there.

* * *

Simon Warland tried to relax the muscles that bunched across his shoulders. Bloody hell. Coming back had been harder than he'd anticipated. He took a healthy swallow of Stratmore's excellent liquor and stared out into the darkness. The sound of footsteps approaching caused his muscles to knot. He didn't relax until the stranger spoke.

"Without a doubt, Simon, when you make an entrance, it's one society will talk about for weeks."

His longtime friend, James Wallace, the Duke of Collingsworth, crossed the lantern-lit patio and stopped beside him.

"How could I think of missing tonight's ball? It's always one of the most coveted events of the year." Simon fought the hollow pain in his gut and swirled the amber liquid in the crystal snifter. Perhaps downing the whole amount would help. He lifted the glass, but James's words brought the glass to a halt halfway to his mouth.

"You just missed her. Rosalind left not even ten minutes ago."

Simon clenched his fingers around the fragile crystal and squeezed. "How unfortunate. And I so looked forward to seeing my stepmother." Releasing a controlled sigh, he lifted the glass to his mouth and took a swallow.

"I'll admit I was surprised to see you, Simon, but not nearly as shocked as the Duchess of Stratmore. I'm afraid she's still crumpled on the floor at her husband's feet."

Simon tried to smile. "I'm sorry I didn't let you know, James. I wasn't sure until the last moment whether or not I'd be able to attend. An invitation was not exactly waiting for me when I arrived."

"Do I dare ask how you acquired one?" His Grace asked, crossing his arms over his chest and leaning his hip against the carved railing.

"I have my solicitor to thank for tonight's pleasure. He knows a man who knows a man who…" Simon laughed. "You get the idea." He lifted his head and breathed deeply. "I hope it didn't tax his bank account overmuch. I'm afraid with my limited funds I will never be able to pay him back."

Simon lifted the glass and took another long swallow. It lit a fire all the way down to the pit of his stomach. He welcomed the feeling.

"Whatever the cost, it was well worth the fits and vapors you caused. I haven't seen such a commotion for years. Too bad Rosalind wasn't here to see it."

"Yes. Too bad." Simon took another long swallow. "I had hoped to shock them all at once."

Collingsworth threw his head back and laughed out loud. "Well, if that was your goal, you accomplished it well enough. Did you see Baron Woolsley? To hold himself up, the pompous old fool groped a statue of the goddess Venus in a most improper place. The poor red-faced baroness couldn't release his grip. And I thought they were going to have to carry the Earl of Carlysle out on a board. Luckily, the countess is twice his size and she managed to keep him on his feet."

Simon was tempted to smile, but that wasn't what he remembered. He remembered the shocked looks of abhorrence and embarrassment. The disbelief, and tainted looks of repulsion.

"They're convinced I killed him. I saw it on their faces." Simon's words hung in the air like a heavy yoke across his shoulders.

"You know London's elite," his friend said, his voice flat, his tone factual. "The more impossible the story, the more embellishment it receives." Collingsworth paused. "Why did you come back, Simon?"

Simon took a deep breath and digested the question he knew was utmost on James's mind. The same question he'd asked himself a thousand times over.

Simon shook his head. "I don't know. Perhaps just to see Ravenscroft one more time. To ride through the gate and climb the steps and walk through the rooms. To relive the memories and let the earth sift through my fingers before it's lost to me forever. To say good-bye."

"There is nothing you can do?"

Simon's chest tightened painfully, and he swallowed past the lump in his throat. "The creditors sent me notice just before I left India. The estate is bankrupt."

"Perhaps if you had returned sooner?"

Simon hesitated. "That was not possible." He lifted the glass to his mouth and let the potent liquor warm the ice water that ran through his veins. "Do you think my father killed himself?"

James shook his head. "I don't know. His body was found at the bottom of the cliff the morning after you left. It's possible he'd had too much to drink and lost his balance."

"But you don't think so?"

The duke shook his head. "I'm afraid we'll never know. There were no witnesses, except for your stepmother. She claims not to have seen anything."

For a long time, Simon said nothing. He only breathed in the cool night air and let the warm liquor seep to every part of his body. "It's funny," Simon finally said, abandoning the empty snifter to drag his hands through his hair. "There was nothing I could do to stop him from wasting my inheritance while he was alive and nothing I can do to save it now that he's dead."

He closed his eyes and let the air fill his chest. Maybe it hadn't been wise to come back. To see the home that had been in the Northcote family since the reign of King Edward VI, knowing it would be lost to him forever.

"Let me help. I could—"

"Don't, James."

"But the money is yours. Your father was unbelievably drunk that night, making astronomical wagers. I thought it best if he lost the money to me. I was going to give it back when he sobered. But they found his body that next morning at the bottom of the cliff."

Simon stared out into the darkness.

"Simon. The money is yours."

"I'll not take blood money. If he did kill himself, it was because he'd sobered enough to realize what he'd done."

"Then let me help you. A loan. I'm as rich as Croesus. I would never even miss it."

"No, James. I'm not desperate enough to accept charity, even from you."

"It isn't charity. Consider it a loan."

"Enough!"

There was a slight pause, and then James turned and stood with firm determination. "There is another way."

"No." Simon held out his hand.

"Hear me out, and consider what I'm saying before you reject my suggestion." He paused. "You could take a wife."

"A wife." Simon's laugh was bitter. "I will never offer my name to another woman again. Even if I did, what woman would accept the offer of a man the *ton* thinks murdered his own father?"

"Surely—"

Simon set his jaw. "No."

"But what of an heir?"

Simon lifted the corners of his lips into a sardonic smile. "An heir to what? By the end of the month I will no longer have anything to leave a son. And even if there were someone who wanted my name, what father would consider Simon Warland, the disgraced, bankrupt Earl of Nothing, a suitable husband for his daughter?"

"Not everyone would turn you down, Simon. There are many eligible—"

"No!" Simon turned away from his friend and clasped his hands behind his back. "I would rather watch my home be placed on the auction block than take a wife to save it."

"That may well happen."

"Let it! You will see me beg on the streets, James, before I will prostrate myself before a woman ever again."

An uncomfortable silence breached the darkness before Simon finally turned back to his friend. "Forgive me, James. I suffered from a momentary bout of self-pity. I promise it will not happen again."

The Duke of Collingsworth leaned back against the railing. "Have you been to Ravenscroft?"

"No. I intend to go tomorrow. It's been three long years, so I'm not sure what I'll find. Perhaps there's something left that hasn't been pawned or sold off to pay their debts."

"Your father…" James cleared his throat uncomfortably. "Your father is buried in the family graveyard at Ravenscroft."

Simon swallowed past the lump in his throat. "Did anyone come to bid him farewell? Any of his old friends?"

James paused. "A few. And a handful of servants staying there to close the house."

"And you."

"Yes, me."

"Thank you." Simon looked at his empty glass, wishing there were more. Thankful there was not. He'd spent enough days in a blind stupor both before and after his father's death. He would need a clear head to get through the rest of the night. Tomorrow he could drink to forget.

"Come," James said, turning toward the ballroom. "I'll introduce you to my wife. We'll have another drink, then take our leave to let the wagging tongues of society devour the rest of your shattered reputation."

"Did you marry that pretty young innocent you were considering when…" Simon paused. "Before?"

"Yes," James finished, smoothing the uncomfortable gap. "Melinda Everston. Now Melinda Wallace, Duchess of Collingsworth."

"And are you happy, James?"

"Yes, Simon. I couldn't be happier."

Collingsworth clapped Simon on the shoulder and squeezed tight. "I wish you could meet someone half as wonderful as my Mel. You would see."

"Then lead me to this love of your life, friend, while I still have the stomach to face the curious onlookers."

"I must warn you. Melinda will probably have you tamed before I finish your introduction. Your entrance left even the strong trembling at the knees, but she will do her utmost to soften you and prove to all that you are harmless."

"I was that intimidating?"

"The Duchess of Stratmore's palm leaves trembled."

Simon smiled. "Good. I do not care in the least what society thinks of me. Fear is as good an emotion as any."

Chapter 2

❦

*J*essica woke early and couldn't go back to sleep. She couldn't forget how Lady Drummond had looked standing at the top of the stairs of the Stratmore ballroom, ready to make her entrance. All eyes should have been fixed on her. Each and every one of society's elite, frozen in statuesque stillness as they stared in open adoration at the magnificent gown Jessica had created.

But they weren't.

Instead, their attention was still focused on the Earl of Northcote's surprise appearance. Jessica, however, couldn't forget the expression on the Earl of Northcote's face. An expression that mirrored a tortured soul. Was she the only one who saw it?

The tall, imposing stranger loomed before them with anger blazing from eyes that had bored into her with unrelenting intensity. Lady Drummond in her beautiful gown was nothing more than an intruding illusion.

Damn him!

She threw the covers back and bounded from the bed. With a moan of frustration, she stomped to the washbasin in the corner of the room, then scrubbed her skin with rose-scented bathwater. When the cool water hit her warm flesh, she came alert with a startling revelation.

She would create Lady Drummond another fabulous design, equally as stunning. Only this time when she wore it, *he* would not be there to steal everyone's admiration.

Without looking, Jessica grabbed a dress from the clothes chest and slipped it over her head. It didn't matter which gown she wore, because there were only four day dresses from which to choose, besides the two better dresses she kept for the balls she chose to attend.

She wore only plain, simple gowns. She wanted to draw no attention to herself, nor did she want her clothes to reveal that she was the mysterious designer everyone clamored to have create a gown for them.

She pulled her long chestnut hair back into the same severe chignon she wore whether day or evening, then smoothed the starched lace collar to perfection. She took her first step toward the door but stopped when Martha, her childhood nurse and personal maid, walked into the room.

"Oh, I'm glad you're up, mistress. Mr. Cambden is downstairs in the morning room to see you."

"Ira is here?" Jessica frowned. "Oh dear. I hope he hasn't come for the design I promised to create for his wife's birthday. It isn't done yet. I haven't found the right shade of satin edging. Madame Lamont promised to send over more samples. Did Ira say he'd come for the design?"

"He didn't say, miss."

Jessica checked her appearance one last time, then turned toward the door. "Would you have Mrs. Goodson ready a tray of hot tea and some of Mrs. Graves's biscuits?"

"Right away, miss."

Jessica raced from the room, skipping down the stairs as if she were still an eighteen-year-old. It was always like this when Ira came to visit. He'd been her father's longtime friend and solicitor, and since her father's death ten years ago, he was as near to any family as she had left. Aside from Melinda and James, Ira was one of the few people she'd allowed to get close enough to her to become a friend—to know her secret.

"Good morning, Ira." Jessica swept into the morning room with a bright smile on her face.

Ira turned from the window to face her. Behind him, a heavy drizzle fell from an ominous-looking sky, coloring the room in a dreary gray. Jessica fought the urge to rush over to him and wrap her arms around his portly body as she often did. Something about his expression stopped her.

"I wasn't expecting you," she said, her smile wavering. "I don't have Esther's design done yet. Is that why you've come?"

He shook his head. "I haven't come for Esther's design."

Deep worry lines etched the dear man's forehead, and the fear she saw in his eyes caused her heart to stir in her breast. For the first time, Jessica noticed the death grip with which he was clutching a brown leather folder to his chest.

With a sigh, he placed the folder on the table and opened his arms. Jessica stepped into his warm embrace. "Something is wrong, isn't it, Ira?" she said when she'd stepped away from him.

Ira kept hold of her hand and wrapped his soft, cushiony fingers around hers. He brought her hand to his chest and cradled it there. "Yes, something is wrong. Perhaps you should sit down, Jessica."

A feeling of wariness stole its way through her body, and she sat in the chair while she waited for him to give a reason for the troubled look on his face.

"What is it, Ira? Surely it can't be as bad as all that."

The friend who'd been like a father to her since she was fifteen looked down on her and shook his head. Another apprehensive shudder stole through her.

"There's no easy way to tell you this, Jessica," Ira said, dabbing at the perspiration on his forehead, "but…" He paused. "Oh, Jessica. I have just learned that your step-brother, Baron Tanhill, isn't dead."

Jessica's breath caught and she clutched the arms of the chair to steady herself. She couldn't breathe. This could not be happening. "What?"

"Lord Tanhill isn't dead. He is on his way back to England."

Jessica felt the blood rush from her head. "No. That can't be."

"It is, Jessica. He's alive. A friend of mine just returned from India and saw him there. I made sure it was true before I came to you."

Jessica shook her head. "He's dead. We were told he was. He drowned when his ship went down ten years ago."

"That is what he wanted everyone to believe, but it wasn't true."

Jessica rose to her feet and stood on trembling legs. Her skin turned cold and clammy while her jagged breathing came out harsh and labored. "I don't believe it. Why would he want everyone to think he had died? What purpose would it serve?"

"Lord Tanhill owed some very dangerous people an incredible amount of money. His death created a convenient escape from his debts."

"Then why would he risk coming back now?"

The look on Ira's face became even darker. "He's coming back for your inheritance."

Jessica laughed. "My inheritance? I have no inheritance."

"Please, Jessica, sit down." Ira led her to the sofa, then picked up the folder from the table and sat down in a chair in front of her. She leaned forward so she would not miss one word he spoke.

"I didn't think anyone knew besides myself," he said, hugging the folder. "I was certain I could take the secret with me to my grave. But it's too late. Somehow he found out."

"What did he find out, Ira?"

He sighed and took out an official-looking document. "This is your father's will. It states that your town house and everything in it is to go to your stepmother, the late Baroness Tanhill, and consequently to her son, Lord Tanhill, as her surviving heir."

Jessica clamped her fist into the folds of her dress. She could not lose her home. It was her security. Her haven. Her refuge from all the curious stares and prying eyes.

Loud waves roared against her ears until she feared her head would burst. "I cannot lose my home," she said, fighting to keep the tears from spilling down her cheeks.

"There's more, Jessica," Ira said, taking her hands in his.

Even though she was seated, the room felt unsteady around her.

Ira dropped her hands and leaned back in his chair. "After your fever, your father refused to face what had happened. He still saw you as perfect. He never thought you would not marry. To ensure your future, he married Lady Tanhill. With her title to introduce you into society and the money he'd provided in your dowry, he was positive you were assured of a credible husband."

Jessica's heart skipped a beat. Just thinking of the woman her father had allowed into their home after her mother had died turned her stomach. "I wish she had never married my father, Ira. She didn't love him."

Ira shook his head. "She was destitute. She married your father for his money."

"So what does this have to do with her son? What are you worried Colin will do when he comes back?"

The expression on Ira's face remained grave. "According to your father's will, on your twenty-fifth birthday, Lord Tanhill will gain possession of your house and everything in it. And your husband will receive your entire wealth."

Jessica stared at Ira in stunned disbelief. "My husband! But I do not have a husband!"

"Your father thought that you would. He expected to live long enough to make sure you married someone who would always take care of you."

Jessica slumped back against the sofa. What would she do? If her stepbrother got the house, where would she go? Venturing out into the world was unthinkable. It took every ounce of courage she had just to accept the invitations to the balls. And she only went on those occasions if Mel would be there and if she knew someone would be there wearing one of her gowns.

It suddenly seemed too much. She stood and walked away from Ira, distancing herself from his words. The facts he presented to her were inconceivable. She would lose her home and whatever small inheritance her father had left her unless she found a husband.

She paced back and forth across the room, then stopped. "What will happen if I don't have a husband, Ira?"

Ira wiped his hand over his face. "If you have no husband, then the inheritance becomes yours."

Jessica stopped. The inheritance would become hers. *The inheritance would become hers!*
Hers!

She wanted to laugh. She took in a deep breath and released a quivering sigh of relief. "Then everything will be fine," she said, rushing across the room to give Ira a quick hug. She muffled a near-hysterical giggle behind a trembling hand. "Oh, Ira. There is nothing to worry about. Don't you see? Between my small inheritance and the money I receive from my designs, I'll get by. I don't require much. If I'm sure to always live within my means, I'll be able to live quite comfortably." She didn't know how much money she would have, but it did not matter. She had her designs. She could support herself.

Another thought entered her mind and she raised her hopes expectantly. "Oh, Ira. Perhaps Lord Tanhill will not even want the house. Perhaps you're worrying for nothing."

One look into his face told her Ira did not think so. Jessica only knew she had to do everything in her power to make it so. This house meant too much to her.

Ira's reaction was not encouraging. He shook his head, then walked over to the small writing desk and placed his folder on the top. With slumped shoulders, he picked up the stack of papers and shuffled through the documents until he found what he was looking for. He handed her the single sheet of paper.

"This is what you are worth, Jessica Stanton. This is the *small* inheritance your father left you."

Jessica skimmed down the page until she reached the number at the bottom. Her face paled. Even though she had never swooned before in her life, she feared she might now.

"Is this right?"

He nodded. "Yes."

"But…" She looked at the staggering sum again. "Where did Father get all this money?"

Ira poured a cup of tepid tea and took a swallow. "A small portion he inherited from his father. A great deal came from his profits from the East India Company. Your father was a very astute businessman. He was very frugal and invested wisely. Some of his wealth can be attributed to luck, but most of it was sheer genius. He had the Midas touch. Our queen even called on him for financial advice more than once."

Jessica looked again at the figure at the bottom of the page. "I had no idea Father had so much money. I thought I would be fortunate to be left a small inheritance that would provide for me until I died."

"I wish to God your father had indeed left you a small inheritance," Ira said deliberately. "I wish more than anything that on your twenty-fifth birthday you would not become one of the wealthiest, if not *the* wealthiest woman in England. I wish that I had the power to protect you from your stepbrother."

Jessica frowned. "What do you mean?"

"I don't know how he found out, but Lord Tanhill knows about your inheritance."

"How do you know?"

"Because he has already contacted Percival Westchester, one of the foremost solicitors in all of England. I have a very close friend who works for Percival. As soon as you receive the money, your stepbrother intends to start proceedings against you."

"Against me? Why?"

"To prove you incompetent. To prove that you cannot manage such a large amount of money by yourself." Ira ran his fingers through his thinning hair. "Tanhill is beginning preparations to have himself placed as your legal guardian. He intends to prove you mentally incompetent. To have you put away. In an asylum. He wants the money and knows he must have you committed to get it."

Jessica couldn't stand by herself any longer. Her knees gave way beneath her. If Ira hadn't reached for her, she would have fallen to the floor.

An asylum.

A place where they locked away people society did not want to look upon, people who were different. Where abuse and mistreatment were common, and compassion and caring did not exist. Where society hid those who were blemished, and forgot them until they died.

The thought of living amidst such squalor, filth, and disease scared her to death. The idea of being locked in a dank, dark cell of cold, gray stone with bars on the windows evoked enough fear to give her nightmares. Jessica had been plagued with them while Lord Tanhill lived in her home.

"Can he do it?" she asked, even though she already knew the answer. Of course he could. He knew her secret.

God help her, she was scared.

She swallowed hard. "What can I do? How do I fight him?"

"There's only one way, Jessica. You must marry. You must find a husband who is strong enough to stand up to Tanhill."

Jessica shook her head. "I cannot marry!" She knew her voice was too loud. She knew she sounded like the crazy person her stepbrother, Colin, would have everyone believe she was. "Who would have me, Ira? Who in all of London would consent to marry a freak?"

"You are not a freak."

"Explain the difference to the people who would walk on the other side of the street if they ever found out about me. Explain that to the people who would believe just as my stepbrother. That I should be put away."

"Marriage is your only solution."

She could not keep the despair out of her voice. "Don't you understand? That is not a possibility. No male in all of England would take me as his wife."

"I'm afraid you're wrong. There would not be an end to the number of men who would take you. If only for the money."

Jessica paced back and forth, voicing each concern aloud as if putting it into the open lessened its hopelessness. "Even if I could find someone who would agree to marry me, how would I know he wouldn't put me away himself once he has the money?"

"You don't. You must choose someone strong enough to stand up to Baron Tanhill, and honorable enough to never betray you."

"I can't do it, Ira. I can't sell myself for money. I can't trust any man enough to put my life in his hands."

"You have no choice. You cannot fight your stepbrother on your own, Jessica. He is the essence of everything evil. He will destroy you. I'm afraid only someone equally as ruthless can protect you from him."

"Are you certain Colin cannot harm me if I marry?"

"Colin cannot touch your inheritance once you marry. Without your money, you are of no use to him. And, you will have a husband to protect you."

Tears streamed down her cheeks and she swiped them away. "But I don't want to marry," she whispered.

"It's the only way, Jessica."

She was loath to admit it, but this was the first time since the day she'd been locked in her imperfect world she had to admit she was helpless to survive alone.

"I'm afraid, Ira."

"I know. I'm afraid too."

Jessica took a handkerchief and wiped the traitorous tears that trickled down her cheek. "Ira, I don't have much time left."

"I know," he answered.

She steeled her shoulders with all the determination she could muster.

She would be twenty-five in six days.

* * *

Jessica paced the drawing room like a caged animal. She knew what Colin was like. She knew firsthand the cruelty that came naturally to him. She knew the meanness that was a part of his personality. There wasn't another man alive who was strong enough or intimidating enough to hold his own against him.

She sat down on the sofa and dropped her head to her hands. She was exhausted. It had been hours since Ira had left her, reemphasizing the need for her to find a husband as quickly as possible.

The shadowed figure of the tall, imposing man who'd dared to face the *ton* flashed before her. Jessica forcefully pushed it away. She refused to let his image become a reality. He may have had the courage to stand up to the *ton*, but that didn't mean he could withstand the deviousness of which Colin was capable.

She walked to the window. There was nothing but blackness out there. Nothing but the quiet silence of a town gone to bed.

Mel said Northcote was her husband's closest friend. She said the Duke of Collingsworth would trust him with his life. Surely if Collingsworth thought so highly of him, he was honorable enough to protect her. And, she knew he was desperate for enough money to pay his creditors and save his estate.

She closed her eyes and the Earl of Northcote appeared again. This time she let his formidable stature and blatant strength envelop her. She let her mind focus on the challenging glare in his eyes and the unyielding force in his gaze. She let his power and dominance cover her and for a moment she felt at peace. She felt safe.

Was it possible?

A stab of frantic indecision clutched at her insides. He had, after all, evoked terror in all of London's nobility. She'd seen it. Colin would not dare challenge him.

Jessica rationalized that question using the same sense of order with which she solved every problem. Hadn't Mel told her how desperate he was to find a rich wife? Wasn't he about to lose everything if he didn't marry someone with enough money to save his inheritance? Marriage to her would be a perfect solution with no risk to either of them.

She would be safe from her stepbrother, and the earl would gain back everything that belonged to him. She would never make any demands of him, and upon thinking of it, she was confident he would never expect her to publicly play the role of his wife. Especially when he found out her secret.

She sat on the edge of the sofa, digesting the decision she had just made. It felt right. Placing her life in his hands terrified her, but not as much as knowing what her stepbrother was capable of doing to get the money. Not as much as being certain of the hell she would live locked in an asylum.

With determined resolve, she turned and reached for the bell rope. "Hodgekiss, have the carriage brought round."

Chapter 3

Simon stretched his long legs before the fireplace and leaned back in the large burgundy leather chair. The comfortable wingback happened to be one of the few pieces of furniture that remained in his London town house.

He fingered the three-cornered hole in the leather, thankful for the flaw that had saved it from being pawned. He was also thankful for the mar in the headboard of a bed upstairs as well as the loose leg on his desk and the imperfections of a few other damaged pieces scattered throughout the house.

He looked at the meager belongings in his study, then lifted the bottle from the table beside him and tipped it until the last of the amber liquid filled his glass. He brought the glass to his mouth and swallowed, then dropped the empty bottle to the floor. It teetered precariously, then toppled.

He wanted to get drunk. He *needed* to get drunk. He needed to forget today.

As if his Indian manservant, Sanjay, could read his mind, the small, dark-skinned man crossed the room. In his ever-so-silent manner, he placed a second bottle on the table, then reached down to pick up the empty.

"Before this is over, Sanjay, you will wish you had not been so foolish as to insist on coming back with me to England."

"That will never be, master. My mother and sisters are alive because of you. I am alive because of you."

"But not Sarai."

"That is because it was her time to be taken from this life, master. You did all you could. And I am thankful. To serve you in this one lifetime alone is not enough to repay you for what you have done."

Sanjay lit another candle branch and placed the brightly glowing flames on the far side of the room. The study shone with the brightness of day, as if the light could ward off the gloom.

"I fear I will have to find you in my next life, too," Sanjay said, turning up the one lantern so it burned brighter. "So that I may complete the task I have started. Perhaps I will come back as a donkey. To ease your burden and carry you where you wish to go."

Simon rubbed his hand over his eyes and lifted his mouth in a slight grin at his proud young friend's loyalty. "Somehow I don't think you would make a very good donkey." He filled his glass with the liquid from the new bottle and took a deep swallow. His head fell back on the cushion, and he closed his eyes. "I'm afraid serving me will not count as such a noble achievement for you in this life. You did not realize you would be asked to serve such a weak master."

"It is only when the evil spirits attack your body that you are weak. In time you will destroy their power." Sanjay opened the heavy drapes and let the light from the full moon fill the room. "The fever has not come to plague you for a long while, master. Perhaps it has found a more agreeable soul to torment."

Sanjay placed another log on the fire, and Simon watched the flames dance while he lifted the glass to his mouth. He doubted if he would ever destroy the evil spirits' power.

Even the strong whiskey he'd been drinking for the past two hours did not have its desired effect. He was becoming numb, but he was not that drunk. He had not forgotten.

He had ridden to Ravenscroft earlier today, most of the way in the rain. He'd entered through the ornate wrought iron gate, no longer shiny and black but tarnished by the weather and lack of care.

He'd turned down the long lane that led to his family home with an odd mix of dread and anticipation. His chest tightened painfully as he stared in dismay at the overgrown lawn riddled with thistles and weeds and broken tree limbs.

His childhood home seemed vacant and forlorn. After taking a deep breath, he'd climbed the seven steps to push open the heavy oak door of the home that had been in his family for almost three hundred years. With slow, leaden steps he'd walked through the empty rooms, each stripped bare of what had for generations belonged to his Northcote ancestors.

The Gainsborough paintings that used to hang above the fireplace and behind the desk in the study were gone, as were the two Reynolds paintings, and a painting by a new artist, Millais. Gone, too, were all but a few items of furniture, each room devoid of everything except one or two of the older, less valuable pieces.

As he walked from room to room, his footsteps echoed on the bare oak floors. Not that many years ago, beautiful Turkish carpets would have softened his steps. Their rich colors and thick texture had transformed the massive architectural wonder into a warm, luxurious home.

The marble statues and Greek vases he was used to seeing in each room were gone, as were the delicately carved tables on which they'd sat.

The silver, the china, the glassware—gone. The jewels—gone. Every drawer, cupboard, and secret hiding place—empty. Every floor and wall stripped naked. Everything. Gone.

The last place Simon forced himself to enter was his mother's favorite room. The room where her collection of priceless Chinese vases had been displayed with pride—eighteen in all.

Gone. All of them, gone.

Simon took another sip from his glass, then rose from his chair to escape the memory. He braced his hands against the mantle of the fireplace and lowered his head between his outstretched arms.

The flames twisted and turned in mesmerizing configurations, forcing the hazy recesses of his mind to recall the last glimpse of Ravenscroft he'd seen as he'd ridden away. The memory would have to last a lifetime. After today, he would never go back again.

"I should have gone with you to your home, master," Sanjay said as he stood hidden in the shadows. "Perhaps I could have helped."

It had taken Simon a long time to accustom himself to knowing the man was with him. Sanjay was always there, even when Simon did not see or hear him.

"I could walk through the empty rooms and the vacant stables, Sanjay. But I could not bring myself to visit the place where my father was buried. He rests in a quiet meadow a short walk from Ravenscroft Manor, next to my mother, but I couldn't go near it."

Simon eyed the glass, the ache in his chest tightening with a haunted desolation he could not make go away.

"Do not trouble yourself so, master. Someday your desire to find peace with your father will be stronger than the anger that eats at you."

Simon shot his friend a cynical smile. "I don't think there will be enough days in my lifetime for that to happen."

Sanjay stood in silence, then walked to the door. "Do you desire anything else, master?"

"No. Go to bed. I can manage by myself."

A knock on the front door, timid at first, then growing louder, interrupted Sanjay on his way out of the room.

"Whoever it is, send them away," Simon instructed. "I don't wish to see anyone."

"Very well."

Sanjay closed the study door behind him and left Simon alone with his anger. Heaven help him, if his father were here right now, he would be tempted to do what the whole of London was convinced he'd done three years ago. He'd be tempted to kill him for squandering his inheritance. For losing everything he loved.

Simon ground the heel of one hand against his eyes to clear his blurring vision, then heaved his glass into the flames, smashing it into hundreds of slivered pieces.

Bloody hell, but he hated giving up! He hated watching the money-hungry creditors stand in line, prepared to pounce on the few remains of the Northcote estate. All because of his father's foolishness.

All because of *her.*

He fisted his hands until his knuckles ached, then took in harsh gasps of air to ease the tightening in his chest. It was good she was not here right now either, or he'd wrap his hands around her neck and squeeze until—

"Master."

Sanjay's tentative voice brought him out of his nightmare, but left the anger simmering close to the surface. "What?"

"There is a young lady here to see you. She says it is of the utmost importance."

"Send her away. I don't wish to see anyone."

"But I think—"

"I don't care. Doesn't this young lady realize the hour? It's hardly the time to pay a social call, and I'm not interested in anything else she might have in mind."

"The lady is most insistent, master. I think it would be unwise of you to send her away."

Simon turned his back to his loyal servant and slammed his fist against the wall. "I said—"

"Please, Lord Northcote. It's very important that I speak with you."

Simon turned and glared at the woman with the soft, feminine voice, then bellowed with all his might. "Out!"

He expected her to jump with fright. His booming voice could do that even to grown men, but she did not run. Instead, her eyes flashed with a spark of emotion that wasn't quite clear. Determination? Desperation? Simon couldn't tell.

She closed the distance between them as if she didn't fear him in the least, her steps sure, poised. Then she faced him with a confidence he found irritating.

To his further fury, Sanjay backed out of the room and closed the door behind him, leaving him alone with her.

He walked to the table to get another drink. "Who are you?" he asked, filling his glass. He steadied himself against his chair while he waited for her reply. She didn't answer.

He turned and looked at her, the depth of emotion revealed in her eyes an unreadable confusion. Her eyes were not just dark and mysterious, but a deep blue that defied comprehension. Her skin was clear and radiant. Her lips full and lush. Enticing. Kissable.

He'd seen her before. But where?

He looked closer. Ah, yes. The Stratmore ball.

He shifted his gaze away from her, not wanting to notice the way she looked, but he found himself unable to turn from her for long.

She was not young. Twenty-three. Perhaps twenty-four. Neither was she overly tall, but trim and quite pretty. Even though she tried to hide her softness by stripping her dark hair back from her face and tying it in the most hideous knot Simon had ever seen, she didn't achieve her goal.

She stood with shoulders braced and a proud lift to her chin. Her regal bearing seemed in contrast to the desperation in her gaze.

His first reaction was a certain curiosity about her, an interest in her. But he quickly squelched that emotion. He just wanted her gone. "I asked your name," he demanded louder.

"Miss Jessica Stanton, my lord."

His mind reeled in confusion. That name. Did he know her? Simon studied her more closely, trying to remember if he'd known her or her family. His mind clouded without giving him an answer. Obviously, the liquor was finally taking hold. "What do you want? You shouldn't be here. Not at this hour. Not alone."

Her breasts rose as she took a deep breath. "I've come to make you a proposition."

Simon raised his eyebrows and stared at her crisply pleated dress with its dainty lace collar. The gown was not of the latest fashion by far, but worn, practical, nondescript.

"A proposition?" he asked behind the glass he'd lifted to his lips. He couldn't quite stop the smile that tugged at the corners of his mouth. Her look was more fitting that of a vicar's daughter than a woman attempting to seduce him.

He slowly lowered his glass. "How interesting. I'm not accustomed to being propositioned by a woman. It's usually the other way around."

Simon watched an appealing scarlet blush darken her cheeks as a blatant look of indignation filled her eyes.

She bulleted him with a determined glare. "Let me assure you that you have made a grave error. The proposition I have come to offer is strictly business. Nothing more."

He held the mocking grin on his face as he tried to ignore the heat that warmed his blood. "My mistake," he said, lifting his glass to salute her.

Bloody hell, she was intriguing. She lifted her chin in a defiant manner, as if that simple act allowed her the degree of confidence she needed. Hidden beneath that awful hairstyle and plain gown, she was a beauty waiting to be revealed.

"It is rumored, my lord, that you are in dire need of funds. I have come with an offer that will solve your financial problems."

Simon felt like he'd been blindsided, her words hitting him like a blow to his pride. Anger flared within him. Damn, James! Damn him for thinking he could trick him into taking enough money to cover his debts.

"For a certain favor," she continued, "I am willing to give you all the money you will ever need."

"A favor?"

She looked around nervously and wet her lips. "Perhaps you should sit down while I explain."

"I'm perfectly comfortable where I am," he answered, bracing his arm against the back of the leather wing chair. His lack of compliance seemed to leave her at a loss for words. "Who sent you?" Simon demanded.

She looked shocked. She obviously did not think he would catch on to her scheme so quickly.

"Tell me. How much did James pay you for your little charade tonight?"

"James?" She stared at him with a surprised look of wide-eyed innocence. "I was sent by no one. I have come on my own."

He should have known James would make another attempt to give him the money. After he'd refused his offer last night, his friend had undoubtedly thought of another way to help him. He had found a very willing accomplice who would ask him to perform some minor service for her, for which she would no doubt be so grateful she would reward him handsomely.

Perhaps James thought he had a better chance to get Simon to accept the money if he felt he had earned it. Simon looked at her face. Such an open, honest face. James had been clever in his choice. The woman he'd selected certainly had an appealing look. With the flushed glow to her cheeks and her tiny upturned nose, she was quite pretty.

Simon shook his head to clear it. "And what exactly is the price you demand, my lady?"

For the first time, she looked more than a little uncomfortable. She opened her mouth to speak, but the words died on her lips.

"The favor?" he repeated when she did not answer. "What favor do you desire?"

"Your name."

Her voice was soft, and Simon strained to hear. When he finally realized what she'd said, he stared at her as if she'd suddenly grown two heads. Bloody hell! What kind of joke was this?

"Get out! Take your twisted scheme to find a husband, and get the hell out of my home."

He thought he saw a fleeting look of panic in her eyes. A look quickly replaced with determination.

"I cannot. Not until you listen to what I have to say. Please, my lord. Hear me out. That is all I ask."

Simon glared at her long and hard. There was no mistaking the resolve he saw in her expression.

"You are about to lose your inheritance, Lord Northcote. I have at my disposal all the wealth you will need to pay your creditors, and more."

Simon knotted his hands into tight fists and held them at his sides. He silently cursed the girl for playing such a cruel joke, Collingsworth for tempting him, and his father for putting him into such a humiliating position. How much more would he have to endure?

She took a step closer. When she spoke, her voice held a hint of desperation. "You would never have another financial worry. All your problems would be solved."

He leveled a lethal glare in her direction, daring her to stand up to him. She didn't back down. "Really?" Simon said, slamming his glass on the corner of the marred desk. "And all this money is mine for the taking?" He walked to the fireplace and looked into the brightly dancing flames. "Why do I have a hard time believing that?"

"What did you say?"

He turned toward her. "I asked why I should believe you."

"Because it's the truth."

The way she stared into his face was most unnerving. As if she were evaluating him. Studying his features intimately. Hanging on to his every word.

Simon couldn't quite believe this was happening. He sat down in his chair and rested an ankle atop the other knee. He was not going to make this easy for her. And he sure as hell wasn't going to accept her offer. He had not come back to accept charity. Not even from James.

He propped his elbows on the arms of the chair and steepled his fingers. "Sit down," he said, indicating a tattered chair on the far side of the room.

The girl walked to the chair and pushed it so near him their knees almost touched.

She seemed confident enough, and yet, he swore her hands shook as she placed them in her lap.

"You wish to sit this close to me?" he said with a deliberately provocative smile. He would let her play this out.

"I...I would like to sit where I can see you clearly," she said, and her voice trembled.

"Very well, Miss Stanton. Is there anything else you wish to offer me?"

She stared at him with a puzzled look on her face. "Anything else? I'm afraid I don't understand. What else do you need?"

Simon stood and leaned forward. He touched his hand to the soft skin on her face, then skimmed his fingers down her throat, then moved downward. "Perhaps your company for the night? Was that part of your bargain?"

She slapped him.

Before he knew what had happened, she reached out with amazing speed and smacked him hard on the side of his face.

Simon pulled back and watched her eyes open in alarm. Her hand flew to her mouth to cover a muffled cry when she realized what she'd just done.

"I guess not," he said with a shrug. "'Tis a shame."

She squeezed her eyes shut as if to block out the sight of him watching her. In the glowing candlelight, he could see the scarlet coloring of her cheeks.

"I'm sorry," she whispered.

The words seemed sincere, but her voice sounded harsh, barely believable.

Simon sat back in his chair and smiled. Somehow he wasn't convinced she regretted slapping him. He gave her time to compose herself, waiting for her to recover and look at him. "And how much money did you come to offer, Miss Stanton? I will wager it's just enough to cover my debts and pay off all my creditors with perhaps a little left over to get me by until I can get back on my feet. Am I correct?"

"I do not know, my lord," she said, the defiant gleam back in her eyes. "I have no idea how much you are in debt. I only know how much money I have to give you."

The girl lifted her hand to reach into the small reticule hanging from a cord around her wrist. He heard her breathe a heavy sigh as she lifted out a folded piece of paper from her cloth bag.

"I'm quite sure it will be enough," she said, holding on to the note she'd taken from her bag.

"Yes. I'm sure it will be enough." Simon watched her intently as he fingered the three-cornered tear in his leather chair. For a moment he thought she wouldn't give him the paper. "May I see how much my friend thinks it will take to cover my debts?"

She hesitated another second, then placed the folded paper in his hands. Simon opened it and stared at the number at the bottom of the page.

He looked again. Then blinked and looked once more.

He glared at the woman who gave the harmless impression of innocence, then in a blinding rage, crumpled the paper and threw it to the floor. "Bloody hell, woman!"

Simon bolted from his chair and towered over her. "Is this a joke? What kind of fool do you think I am?"

Her eyes grew wide with alarm, and this time her trembling was unmistakable.

She jumped from the chair and reached down to pick up the paper, then clutched it to her breast.

At least she had the common sense to get away from him. He wanted to strangle her.

"I want to know who put you up to this and why!" His gaze raked over her, from her plain clothes and lack of jewels, to the frayed cuffs on her gown. How did she expect him to believe she possessed that kind of money, looking like she did? "Look at you. You barely look able to feed yourself. And that dress." He stopped long enough to look at the confusion written on her face. "Well?"

"I'm sorry. What did you—"

"I want you to go back and tell whoever sent you that I didn't fall for your scheme." Simon tightened his fingers around the corners of the chair where she'd been sitting. "Did you honestly think I would believe your lies?"

He watched as a look of desperation filled her eyes. "Answer me, dammit!"

"I'm telling you, it's the truth. The money is mine, and I'm willing to give it to you if only you will—"

"Will what, woman?"

"If only you will—"

She stared at him with an unblinking gaze and swallowed harshly. "Marry me," she whispered in a voice so soft he barely heard her.

He stepped back from her as if her nearness offended him, and stared at her in abject disbelief.

When he could stand her look of desperation no longer, Simon turned away from her. Who would dare to play such a cruel trick on him? Surely not James? Rosalind? The thought that it might be Rosalind turned his stomach, and he swallowed the bile that threatened to choke him.

"Get out."

He didn't wait to see if she moved. With his back to her, he braced his arms against the mantle. The logs in the fireplace crackled with a soothing, comforting sound, so opposite the rage and turmoil boiling within him.

"You don't understand, my lord. Please, turn around so I can talk to you."

He clutched his fingers tight against the mantle and gritted his teeth. He couldn't bear to look at her. "Did you honestly think your little scheme would work?" he whispered.

"Please, sir. You must look at me."

"Did James know you were going to try to force marriage on me? Or was that your own idea?"

"I don't know what you're saying."

"Do you have any idea how cruel your little joke is?"

"Look at me."

"Do you?"

"Look at me!"

"Answer me, woman."

"You must look at me!"

"Damn it! Answer me!"

Simon spun around to face her. In two long strides he reached her. "Bloody hell, woman," he shouted, holding her firmly at arm's length. "I said, answer me! What is the matter with you? Are you deaf?"

She stood rigid before him, her expression pale and frozen with shock. Simon stared at her for a long, tense moment, then dropped his hands from her shoulders and let his arms fall limply to his side.

"Bloody hell. You are."

Chapter 4

❧

*J*essica swallowed against the lump in her throat and answered the horrified expression on the Earl of Northcote's face with a determined glare of her own.

She would never get used to that look.

"If you are truly deaf, how do you know what I'm saying?"

"I can read your lips. As long as you face me when you speak, I know what you are saying."

She lifted her chin and straightened her shoulders, bracing herself to battle his prejudice, his disgust. She could not fail. She was far too desperate to let him intimidate her.

She studied his face closely. Such a fierce look in his eyes. Such...

She looked again, expecting to recognize a loathing expression, the repulsion she usually saw, but she saw neither. What she read was his explosive anger. A mistrust that bordered on betrayal.

This was worse than the look she would encounter if society ever found out. Heaven help her. He was the most formidable man she'd ever seen.

The perfect man to face Colin.

The earl paced back and forth near the fireplace as if he needed the movement to clear his confusion. Or to control his anger. "Sit down," he ordered, pointing to the chair. The hard look in his eyes said that refusing to comply was not an option.

Jessica sat in the chair and waited while he searched for another glass to replace the one he'd smashed against the wall. When he couldn't find one, he tipped the bottle and drank, then wiped his mouth with the back of his hand. The flames behind him outlined his powerful physique, emphasizing his long, muscular legs and the massive width of his shoulders. Heaven help her but he was intimidating.

"Who are you?" he asked, pinning her with his foreboding glare.

"My name is—"

He held up his hand to stop her. "I know your name! I want to know who you are!"

Jessica wanted to tell him it did no good to yell at someone who was deaf. Instead, she concentrated on his lips. He talked so fast it took all her ability to keep up with him.

A vein stood out on the side of his neck, and the muscles in his jaw worked furiously He swiped a hand over his jaw in frustration while he waited for her to explain.

She took a fortifying breath. "My father was the late Sir Henry Stanton. His—"

"Bloody hell."

Jessica stopped short. His blackened gaze focused on her face, impaling her with a frown so ferocious it caught the breath in her lungs.

"Who did you say was your father?"

"Sir Henry Stanton. He founded Stanton Shipping and Stanton Mining." Jessica studied the questioning look in his eyes. Something she said caused an obvious reaction. "Both companies seem to have been quite successful. Perhaps you knew of him?"

"Yes," he answered, but there was animosity written on his face. "Then that would make you Baron Tanhill's…" He stopped as if he could not finish the sentence.

"Stepsister," she answered, watching for a sign of recognition. She didn't have long to wait.

"That's impossible. Henry Stanton had no daughter. I may be drunk, but I'm not so sotted that I wouldn't remember if Stanton had a daughter."

Jessica clenched her fists together in her lap and held tight. "He did."

His eyes narrowed, the glare in them as black as midnight, as deadly as a double-edged rapier. "*If* your father was Henry Stanton," he said, making it clear he did not believe her, "I met him once when I was younger. He did not mention you."

"He wouldn't," she answered. "Because of my…my deafness, my father did not ever talk of me. He was very protective. He thought it best to shelter me from the public."

The effort to remain focused on him was difficult as his black gaze stared at her with blatant disbelief—and revulsion. It was not surprising that he saw her as society would. Lacking. Not quite whole.

The earl tipped the bottle to his mouth again and paced the length of the room. His lips moved and his hands fisted at his side. Heaven help her. He was talking.

"Excuse me, my lord," she interrupted. "I don't know what you're saying unless you look at me."

He stopped his pacing and stared at her, then looked at the chair that sat opposite her. When he reached the chair, he sank onto the cushion.

The negative impact of what she'd just told him was evident. The extent of her disability was a huge barrier.

For a long moment he kept his gaze lowered. When he raised his head, his black glare riveted her with his anger. "Why are you here?"

"According to my father's will, I will soon come into a great deal of money. For the last ten years, I was convinced my stepbrother, Baron Tanhill, was dead. He led all of us to believe he was, but I recently discovered that he is alive."

The earl's lips twisted sardonically. "Yes, he is very much alive."

"Do you know him?"

"Yes, I know him." He took another swallow from his bottle. "That does not work to your advantage," he said when he lowered the bottle.

"I know," she whispered. "No one who ever met my stepbrother had a favorable impression of him. No one who ever dealt with him didn't come away from the experience without fearing him.

"Perhaps now you can understand why it's important that I marry before he comes back. Why I need to separate myself from him." She paused. "It's only your name I require, Lord Northcote. Nothing more."

"But if I give you my name, won't you lose your wealth to me?"

"I don't care about the money, sir."

"Ha!"

The earl threw his head back and laughed. His reaction startled her.

"You surely don't expect me to believe that, do you?" His dark gaze focused on her more intently. "I assure you, woman, I am not that big a fool. There is not a female alive who does not care about money. As you have probably heard, I am an expert on that subject."

"Actually, I have no idea what events in your past helped to form your ideas concerning female greed, nor do I care. Whatever reassurance you need, I will give it to you. The money is not important to me. The amount you saw on that paper will be yours once we marry. It's only your name I require."

He studied her more closely. "Why me? Why did you choose me?"

She held her ground. "I saw the way you intimidated all of society when you appeared at Lady Stratmore's ball. There was not one person there who was not in awe of you—and even a bit fearful."

The earl rubbed his fingers against his forehead as if that could ease his weariness. He looked so very tired. As if someone had placed the weight of the world upon his shoulders a very long time ago and had neglected to come back to help him carry it.

"I want you to leave. I'm far from sober, and I don't believe one word—"

"No. I will not go. At least not until you agree to consider my proposal." She could not back down until she'd given this her total effort. Somehow she had to convince him that saving his inheritance would be worth being married to her. "My father left me a great amount of wealth. It could all be yours. You would not lose Ravenscroft. You would not lose—"

"Damn you, woman. Stop your lies. I would rather watch every stone and timber of Ravenscroft fall down at my feet than marry you."

Jessica closed her eyes and fisted her hands in her lap. She should have known he wouldn't want her. After all, what man would want to have a wife who was deaf?

"Nor do I believe you are Baron Tanhill's stepsister. You probably don't have one pound to your name, other than the money someone sent you to offer me."

Jessica shook her head. "The money is mine. I am offering it to you in exchange for your name."

He bolted from the chair and crossed the space that separated them in one easy stride. Anger was blatant on his face, fury raging in his eyes. He did not believe her. In fact, he thought she'd been sent by someone who wanted to trick him.

He leaned down and pinned her shoulder against the back of the tall chair with his strong, muscular hand. The rugged contours of his face were so close she could see the black flecks in his eyes, his broad chest so near she could breathe in the masculine smell of the outdoors mixed with the strong tinge of liquor. Her flesh burned where he touched her. She was not at all used to such a feeling, and she knew she was in over her depths.

"Who sent you here tonight?"

"No one, Lord Northcote. I came on my own."

The smile on his face contained no friendship, but seemed an open wager of war.

The breath caught in her throat when he lifted his hand from the back of her chair to her neck. His touch sent a fiery warmth surging through her.

"So tell me," he said, moving his fingers. "Did you think when I stared into your big, sad eyes I would simply swallow my pride and hold out my hand for you to give me the money? Or did you expect to win me over first with your pretty looks and feminine charm so I would fall to my knees and believe your lies without question?"

"No," she said, hoping she'd said the word aloud. "I have not lied to you."

The lazy circles his thumb made at the base of her throat stopped. He arched his brows high on his forehead. Straight white teeth shone in contrast to the golden bronze of his handsome face, and she felt a strange stirring she didn't understand.

"You expect me to believe that until recently, you were completely unaware of your father's substantial wealth. That until recently you did not know your own stepbrother was alive?" He cupped her cheek in the palm of his hand. "I think not, woman."

"It's true." Her voice shook at the warm touch of his hand. "If you don't believe me, ask His Grace, the Duke of Collingsworth. I know you are friends. He will tell you."

He pulled his hand away from her as if her words had scalded him. He backed away as if each step near her was too close.

The air around them hung in complete stillness. The look on his face was a mask of incredulity.

"What does Collingsworth have to do with this?"

"Nothing. He will only verify that what I said is true."

Jessica looked into his face, trying to make out what he was thinking, but found his stony expression unreadable.

"He will verify your lies because he was the one who sent you with the money. Was it also his idea to offer marriage? Or was that your own?"

She shook her head, unable to say any words to defend herself.

He leaned forward and braced his arms against the back of the chair that separated them. "Did you honestly think I would marry you? Did you honestly think I was *that* desperate?"

Jessica flinched as if she'd been slapped. She should not have come here. She should have known better than to put her life and her future into the hands of a perfect stranger. She should have known it would be impossible for him to overlook her imperfection.

He took a step around to the side of the chair. "Did you truly think I would believe that you would willingly give up your wealth?"

"It did not occur to me you would not. I thought you would accept my offer because you were as desperate for my money as I was for your name."

His eyes narrowed. "Was becoming a countess that important to you?"

His accusation was like another slap across the face. He did not believe her. He was not going to help her. She should have known he wouldn't. An earl wouldn't want someone so flawed for his wife, even if she possessed such a huge sum of money.

His rejection destroyed her last hope of protecting herself from her stepbrother. Jessica reached for her reticule and rose to her feet.

"Where do you think you're going?"

"Home."

"No."

The earl's command halted the breath in her chest.

"Come here."

She didn't move.

"I said, come here."

Jessica took one shaky step toward him, then another. He would not see he had defeated her.

"Why did you come here tonight?" he voiced when she was close enough that he could touch her. "Weren't you the least bit frightened?" He reached out his hands and grasped her arms in a viselike grip and hauled her up against his chest. "After all, they say I killed my father because he wasted my inheritance."

What had she been thinking, coming to such a man? The Earl of Northcote had proved to be a more formidable match than she thought. He was angry and provoked, and the dark, hazy look in his eyes told her he was not thinking as a sober man. His unsteady movements and disheveled look only made him appear more menacing.

She tried to turn her gaze away from him but could not keep her eyes off the spot where his white lawn shirt gaped at his neck, revealing deeply tanned skin and wisps of black hair exposed beneath the loose lacing. He pulled her closer, and she braced her hands against his chest. Her fingers touched the corded muscles that ran across his shoulders and rippled beneath the soft material.

She closed her eyes to shut out the sight of his daunting masculinity. How naive to think she could convince a man capable of striking terror into all of London's nobility to consider giving her his name. How foolhardy to think she could survive a confrontation with one of the fiercest men in all of England. How impossible to think the Earl of Northcote would ever want to marry a woman so flawed.

She opened her eyes and stared into the blazing heat hidden behind his hooded frown. Her heart raced at a speed so incredible she feared it would leap from her breast. She had never been this close to a man before. Had never been touched by a man before.

"I think you don't realize how much more I could have demanded from you than just your money, woman."

He pulled her closer to him and brought her up against his chest.

Crashing into his body was like being thrown against a brick wall. He was hard and immovable.

To make sure she couldn't move, he wrapped a massive arm around her waist and clamped her against him. Then he cupped her cheek with his other hand. His thumb rubbed against her flesh, and she burned like he'd set her on fire.

"Is gaining a title worth the cost you would have had to pay?"

Her denial died in her throat.

His hands moved to her shoulders, his hold on her solid and firm. One roughened fingertip rubbed lazy little circles against the hollow spot at the base of her throat and then moved upward, stroking the callused pad of his thumb back and forth over her lips.

Jessica grasped his forearm and pushed at his arm to release his hold on her.

She needed to be free. She couldn't think. She couldn't breathe. His harsh, demanding touch confused her.

His fingers moved over her skin, creating a heat she could not understand. It wasn't right for him to touch her with such familiarity, and yet, a part of her wanted to keep his warmth and strength next to her.

She wasn't nearly as frightened as she should be. She wasn't nearly as embarrassed as she should be.

His fingers brushed against the sensitive skin at the back of her neck, then purposefully slid across her shoulders, then lower to her waist, and lower to the small of her back, and lower to—

She was on fire.

"Please, stop."

Jessica thought she'd spoken the words out loud, but she wasn't sure. She was sure of nothing right now. Her mind was a whirlwind of confusion that roared in her head until she couldn't think.

He cupped her cheek in the palm of his hand and lowered his head until he was inches from her face. "Surely you don't want me to stop, Miss Stanton. After all, didn't you come here tonight—alone, at this hour—to offer yourself to me? Isn't this what you really came here for?"

She shook her head and gasped for air. "No. I came to offer you the money you need to save your inheritance. I want your name."

"That's all, Miss Stanton? You want nothing more?"

"I...I..."

"You're not sure?"

He brought his face closer until his lips almost touched hers. Jessica could no longer see his lips to tell if he was talking. She did not want him to talk. She wanted him to…

He touched his lips to hers with such desperation it weakened her. His touch was not soft and gentle, but harsh and unyielding.

A thousand spikes of molten heat surged to every part of her body, then spiraled to one spot low in her stomach and swirled as a whirlpool even lower.

Never had she felt more afraid. Or confused.

Or as safe.

* * *

The last thing Simon had intended was to kiss her. Even as he reached for her, he had no idea why he was doing something so stupid. But when his lips touched hers, he could no more stop himself than he could stop the wind from blowing or the sun from rising. He was obviously drunker than he thought.

At first his only intent had been to frighten her into admitting she'd been following James's order to offer him the money he needed to save Ravenscroft. To admit she'd seen marriage to him as an opportunity to gain a title, and she'd made up her own rules as she went along.

That was before he'd kissed her.

Their first kiss had been short and harsh and unemotional. He'd hauled her up against him and ground his lips against her as if she were an overused doxy he'd found at a wayside inn. He'd wanted to make a point. Nothing more.

But when she looked up at him, her gaze portrayed such pleading and confusion that everything about her surpassed the realm of his understanding. She'd trembled at his touch as if she truly was an innocent. From that moment on he'd wanted nothing more than to believe that she was.

The rush of air that slammed against his chest was a hundred times more violent than he'd ever felt when he'd kissed a woman before. The heat where her delicate form pressed against him seared his flesh a thousand times hotter than he ever remembered being burned by a woman before. The need to deepen his kisses became an unconquerable force, a million times greater than anything he had ever experienced before.

Her lips at first remained tight and lifeless. As if she didn't know what to do. As if she truly hadn't expected him to kiss her. But as his mouth moved against hers she softened and accepted—almost welcomed—his assault.

At the first pressure of his mouth, she pressed her fisted hands against his chest, pushing him away. Finally, with a tiny moan and a sigh of resignation, she opened her clenched fists. Then, she touched him—tentatively at first, then with a much greater strength.

He drew his fingers through her hair, loosening the pins and letting her lustrous brown tresses fall to her waist. He tipped her head to the side to gain easier access to her mouth and tasted her hungrily.

Bloody hell. He couldn't get enough of her.

This was not supposed to happen.

He wrapped one arm around her back and held her tight. With his other hand, he cupped her cheek. Her skin was soft and smooth, like never-worn velvet. Again and again he drank from her sweetness. Sipping and tasting and relishing the feel of her against him. He needed to have more of her.

With slow deliberation, he moved his thumb along her jaw, stopping just beneath her bottom lip. He applied the slightest pressure, and she opened to him as if she'd waited a lifetime for him to discover her.

His tongue entered her honey-warmed cavern, searching for the treasure hidden there. She stiffened in his arms and pulled away, her small hands pushing against his shoulders.

He couldn't allow them to be separated and cradled the back of her head to hold her close. She muttered a quiet moan and pushed her fists against his chest once, twice, then stopped.

Heaven help him.

He found the treasure he'd been searching for. His tongue met hers. Touched. Withdrew. Touched again.

Her hands grabbed bits of his flesh along with the fabric of his shirt. He was in pain. But it was not from the grasp she had on his skin. His pain was a thousand times more consuming.

Trying to control a desperation that defied understanding, he lifted his mouth and stared into her eyes. They were glazed with emotion.

"Who are you?" he whispered, his voice hoarse and raspy. "Why are you doing this to me?" He took two gasping breaths of air before he covered her mouth again. He did not want to leave her.

He ground his mouth against hers, drinking deeply, sharing with her. Taking from her. And she did not deny him.

With each kiss, she gave more of herself. She wrapped her slender arms around his neck and held on with a fierceness that defied explanation. She opened to him and moved with him and asked more of him than he thought he had left to give.

With each kiss, he lost more of his self-control. More of the sturdy defenses he'd built to protect himself from emotions as strong as this.

Bloody hell. This was not supposed to happen.

A warning bell went off in his brain, exposing the lies and betrayal and deceit he'd experienced at the hands of a woman. A woman who had used him for her own gain. Just as this woman wanted to use him for her own gain.

Simon growled an agonizing moan and lifted his mouth from hers. He couldn't breathe. He couldn't think. His chest burned like someone had branded him with a hot poker and left the fiery tip inside to sear his heart. He opened his mouth as he struggled to take in huge gulps of air. He braved a look at the girl and saw only confusion.

This was all an act. It had to be.

He tried to push her away from him, but her knees buckled, forcing him to hold on to her until she regained her composure.

She gasped for air while her eyes darted from one side of his shoulders to the other, as if she was too frightened to face him. She looked as scared as a snared rabbit in a poacher's trap. Every inch of her body trembled in his arms.

"You still want to become my wife?" he said, tilting her face to look at him.

She didn't answer. Her look told him she realized she needed protection from him more than she needed his protection.

He dropped his hands from her and she stumbled, then grabbed for the edge of the wing chair and righted herself. She stood immobile for a moment, one hand clutching her stomach, the other fisted against her mouth. Her chest heaved, whether from fright or from his kisses he didn't know. He did not want to know. All he knew was that he wanted her out of his sight.

"Get out, woman."

She wasn't facing him. He realized she hadn't heard him.

He didn't want to touch her again, but he had to. Either touch her or wait for her to turn her frightened gaze to him, and he wasn't sure he had the strength to resist her.

He grasped her by the shoulders and turned her toward him. A muffled cry escaped from the back of her throat, and his heart lurched within his chest.

He didn't want to admit her reaction affected him. He didn't want to admit her kisses held any significance. He didn't want to admit there was a spot in his heart that wasn't hardened enough to keep her from entering.

"Get out, woman. Get out before I do something we will both regret."

She sucked in a harsh breath and twisted out of his arms. "I have already done something I regret, my lord." She wiped the back of her hand across her mouth.

With her chin raised, she rushed from the room.

Simon stood at the curtained window and watched her carry herself with the greatest aplomb through the darkness to a waiting carriage. He watched until she was safely inside.

"I didn't think it was possible for the little missy to leave more frightened than when she arrived," Sanjay said, from the doorway. "I was wrong."

"Frightened? Ha." Simon walked to the fireplace and leaned one arm against the mantle.

"I think when next I come back to serve you it will be as a small kitten. It will be my purpose to teach you gentleness and kindness. You are in great need of it."

Simon slammed his fist against the fireplace, then stumbled to his chair. "I don't need your opinion tonight, Sanjay. All I need is—"

"What you want is right here, master," Sanjay answered, setting a fresh bottle of whiskey and a clean glass on the table beside the chair. "I assume you will want to drink until you can no longer remember how badly you treated the missy."

Simon filled the glass and took a deep swallow. "I don't need you to be my conscience, Sanjay. Go to bed and leave me alone."

"Very well, master. I will go to bed, but I think you will not be alone. You will have many of your demons to keep you company tonight."

Simon heard the soft click of the door and knew he was finally alone.

He sank onto the soft leather of the wingback chair and dropped his head to the cushion behind him. He closed his eyes and tried to erase the sight of Jessica Stanton's long, curling tresses trailing behind her as she left the room, but it did no good. The repulsion and fear he'd seen in her eyes was one of the demons that refused to go away.

She'd been lying, of course. She couldn't be Baron Tanhill's stepsister.

Simon poured some whiskey into a glass and brought it to his mouth. His arm halted midway to his lips, and his fingers clenched the glass tightly. *She couldn't be Tanhill's sister*, he repeated a second time, then a third.

His heart raced at the possibility that she could. *If* she was, she had just offered him his most bitter enemy's head on a silver platter. Something he'd only dreamed of having.

Marriage to her would, according to her own admission, make Simon one of the wealthiest men in England and reduce Tanhill to an insignificant pauper. Not only could Simon use the money to pay his creditors and save his inheritance, but he could protect her from whatever mad scheme Tanhill had devised to take her money away.

If she was Tanhill's stepsister, he could save her. And this time he would not fail. He would not let Tanhill take another life he'd given his oath to protect. *If* she truly was Tanhill's stepsister, it would be possible to have every pound Tanhill thought to steal from the girl. And he could exact his revenge for what had happened in India.

Simon stared into the smoldering embers in the grate. *If* she'd told him the truth. She was, after all, a woman. No different from any other greedy, conniving woman God had placed on the face of the earth.

But she'd probably made up the whole story. She probably didn't have a pound to her name but had come only because James had sent her. She'd probably only thought of marriage when she saw the amount of money James was willing to offer him.

He'd kissed her because he'd meant to teach her how dangerous it was to play her treacherous games. He'd meant to show her how risky it could be to tempt him with the money to save Ravenscroft but at a price he was unwilling to pay. He'd meant to enlighten her on how disastrous it could be for her to give in to her greedy ambitions and seek more than what she'd been sent to offer.

Bloody hell. Why had he kissed her?

Simon thought of James. He did not doubt for one moment that James had been the one who'd sent this Jessica Stanton to him. *If* that was her real identity.

He took a deep breath and tried not to be angry with his friend. If James were the one about to lose everything, he would do the same if he thought it would help him.

But what did James think would be accomplished by sending her to him? Didn't James realize this woman held about as good a chance of becoming his wife as a snowball had of surviving in Hades?

Simon brought his glass closer, determined to drink until he could forget Jessica Stanton and the way he'd responded to their kisses.

It promised to be a very long night.

Chapter 5

Jessica paced the length of the Duchess of Collingsworth's bright, sunny morning room feeling as trapped as if Colin himself hovered outside the door waiting to have her committed to the asylum. She pushed a wayward strand of hair from her face and tried to make herself look more composed. It was hard. She'd never been more scared in her life.

She had five days until her twenty-fifth birthday. Five days until she became one of the wealthiest women in England. Five days to protect herself from her stepbrother's greed and hatred.

She clutched a hand to her breast to calm her breathing. She needed James and Melinda's help. She prayed to God they would give it to her.

Jessica clenched her fists in frustration. Never had she hated her deafness as she did right now. Never had she felt so helpless. So foolish.

Instead of pursuing a means of escape immediately, she'd wasted precious time and effort on her ludicrous plan to ask the Earl of Northcote to marry her.

How could she have been so blind? How could she have thought for a moment she could convince him that marrying her was the answer to his problems? Good Lord.

Half of London still believed he'd killed his father. What lapse of sanity had made her go to him in the first place?

Jessica remembered the liberties he'd taken last night—the liberties she'd allowed—and shuddered. He was a rogue of the worst kind. She hesitated to think what that made her. His only redeeming quality was that he did not seem offended by her deafness. Although his refusal made it plain he would never want the stigma of a deaf woman as his wife. How could she have embarrassed herself so?

She looked out onto the cobblestone street and watched a carriage ramble silently past the town house. With an impatient sigh, she smoothed the white lace collar at her neck, then touched her fingers to her lips. Lips that still tingled from his kisses.

She'd never dreamed a man's touch could cause such turmoil.

Her fingers touched the lips he'd kissed as she relived the emotions that had raced through her body. She tried to block out the image of him towering above her. But it was impossible to forget the muscled arms that had held her close; the lean, powerful hands that had caressed her skin; the rough, callused fingers that had seared her flesh with his touch.

Then, for the briefest moment, just before he'd pushed her away, she'd glimpsed the reason she would never doubt that he could protect her. She'd felt Northcote's impenetrable dominance, his unwavering courage. She'd sensed a strength about him that bordered on ruthlessness. A strength that would keep her safe from her stepbrother.

But it was too late now to think he could help her. She knew he would not.

Jessica looked at the clock on the mantel and paced from one end of the room to the other, praying Melinda would not be too much longer. It was well before the accepted hour for callers, but time was a precious commodity. Ever since she'd left the earl, some instinct had warned her she could not waste a moment of the time left to her.

She raised her hand to her forehead and rubbed her temples to ease the pounding. Her eyes still burned from the hours she'd spent staring blankly into the darkness after she'd run from the Earl of Northcote's town house. Then the tormented hours she'd spent pacing the floors until it was light enough that she could come to ask Melinda for help.

She leaned her shoulder against the frame beside the window and rubbed her eyes, hoping the dark circles had gone away. Heaven help her, but she was tired. She'd slept very little in the last two days. Eaten even less. She was weary with worry.

Small, gentle hands touched her shoulders, jolting her to her senses, bringing her back to the present. She turned to see Melinda's gaze go from mild curiosity to wide-open horror.

"Jessica?" Melinda gasped. "What has happened to you? Are you all right? Have you been hurt?"

"No. I haven't been hurt," Jessica answered, hoping she'd spoken loud enough for her voice to be heard. She shook her head just in case. "Is His Grace here?"

Melinda nodded, then pulled the bell rope and asked a servant to have James join them immediately. The frown that covered his face when he walked through the door told Jessica she'd failed at making herself look composed.

"What has happened, Jessica?" Collingsworth asked after he'd pulled a chair closer to the sofa where Melinda sat next to her. "What's wrong?"

Jessica lifted her chin and took a deep breath. "I need your help. Please, Your Grace," she said, looking at the Duke of Collingsworth. "I...I need to leave London immediately."

She felt Melinda's grip tighten on her fingers. The deep worry lines covering Collingsworth's forehead deepened. She hated herself for causing them so much distress, but she was desperate. "It's imperative that I leave London as soon as possible."

"Leave? Why?"

Jessica took a deep breath. It was difficult to put the words into the open. Speaking them would make her nightmare more real. "My stepbrother is alive."

James's shoulders rose as he sucked in a sharp breath, and then he released a long, slow sigh.

"How do you know?" he asked, his face mirroring the dread she felt deep in the pit of her stomach.

"One of Ira's sources told him. Colin has been in India all this time, and he's on his way back. I must leave before he gets here."

"Perhaps you don't have to leave. Perhaps I can—"

"No. There's nothing you can do. I need to leave. Now."

"Where do you intend to go?"

"I don't know. I don't care. France, perhaps. Or...the American colonies. It matters little, as long as it's someplace where he can't find me."

Jessica stared at the shocked look on her friends' faces. "I'm sorry to put you in the middle of this, but I need you to make the arrangements for me. I'm not sure I can handle them. Especially since time is of the essence."

Melinda put a trembling finger to Jessica's cheek and turned her head back toward her. "Listen to me, Jessica. James is very powerful. I'm sure he can help you."

Jessica shook her head. "I'm afraid even His Grace's powerful connections cannot save me. Here," she said, seeing the disbelief on their faces. She reached into her reticule and handed Collingsworth the paper Ira had given her—the same paper the Earl of Northcote had crumpled and thrown to the floor. "This is what I will be worth on my twenty-fifth birthday. My father left all of this to me."

Collingsworth smoothed the sheet, then scanned the figures, halting at the bottom of the page. "Bloody hell," he whispered.

He lifted his gaze from the paper to her face, then back again. The look in his eyes was an open book. There was no misunderstanding his thoughts. He knew the danger she faced as well as she did.

She sat back, pale and exhausted. "My birthday is Friday."

The duke stood. "Oh, Jessica…" The frown on his forehead deepened as he looked back at the figure at the bottom of the page.

"There's nothing anyone can do," Jessica said, trying to calm the fears screaming deep inside her. "Colin will never give up until he has control of the money. He intends to put me in an asylum. Ira found out he's already started the proceedings."

Melinda's grip tightened on her fingers, and Jessica turned her head, unable to look at either of them. "I must leave," she repeated. "It's the only way. Even you cannot guarantee that the courts will not grant my stepbrother control over me. He is family, after all, the obvious choice to control Father's wealth."

No one spoke. Finally, the Duke of Collingsworth touched her arm again.

"Perhaps there is another way," His Grace said. "Perhaps if you were to marry—"

Jessica emitted a small, choked laugh. "No. I have already exhausted that possibility." She saw the question in their eyes, but could not admit to them that even a man who was desperate for a dowry and about to lose all had refused her.

Melinda squeezed Jessica's fingers as she often did to indicate she needed Jessica to look at her.

"But—" she started, then stopped.

Her rounded mouth opened in surprise, and Collingsworth rose to his feet. He assumed a warrior's stance as he faced the door, as if he thought he might need to protect them.

Melinda's expression of concern deepened. Whatever disturbed them was cause for alarm. Times like this made her hate her deafness even more.

"What is it?" Jessica clutched Mel's hands. "Has something happened?"

Jessica's heart pounded in her throat. Something was wrong, she could see it on both of their faces. Feel the danger surround her.

"Someone is here," Melinda said as her husband took one step toward the door.

The Earl of Northcote burst through the doorway with a very flustered doorman on his heels. Jessica couldn't catch all the servant's words, but she knew he was apologizing profusely for allowing the uninvited guest to invade their portals.

"What the hell have you done, Collingsworth?" Northcote bellowed as he entered the room. He came to an abrupt halt when he spied Jessica.

She couldn't breathe. Her heart slammed against her ribs and then raced with the speed of a runaway horse and carriage.

The hooded scowl on his face deepened, and his piercing glare shot angry daggers meant to do harm.

From his look, Jessica could tell he'd spent as restless a night as she. In fact, she wasn't quite sure it had not been worse. His disheveled appearance made him look more like a pirate on the open seas than a member of London's elite. From the scorching look in his bloodshot eyes, Jessica was thankful there wasn't a sword hanging at his side. She did not doubt he was angry enough to use it. Nor did she question on whom.

The two-day growth on his face and the errant lock of dark hair that curled on his forehead gave him a foreboding look. His white lawn shirt gaped open at the neck, showing that same triangle of golden-brown skin that had drawn her attention last night. It still exposed the same curling wisps of black hair. There was no gleaming white cravat at his neck, nor was there a waistcoat beneath the unbuttoned tailcoat. He was most improperly dressed for making a call.

High boots stretched to his knees, covering tight black breeches that hugged thick, muscular thighs. He looked ready to attack, but it was the knotted muscle in his jaw and the predatory expression on his face that caused her the most alarm. She could not tear her eyes from him.

"I wish I could say I'm surprised to find you here, Miss Stanton," he said, taking a step closer. "But of course, we both know I am not."

Collingsworth reached out his hand to grasp Northcote's arm. "What is the meaning of this, Simon?" The earl twisted away and continued across the room until he stood in front of her.

"How easily the lies tripped off your tongue last night. Did you think me such a fool that I would believe even one word that spilled from your deceiving mouth?"

"Simon!" Collingsworth yelled. "Bloody hell, man. What is wrong with you?"

"There is nothing wrong with me, James. It's the plan you and this pretty little liar concocted that has gone wrong."

Jessica's gaze darted from one face to the other, frantic to catch all that was being said. Heaven help her. They were talking too fast. And the Duke of Collingsworth didn't look at her when he spoke.

"Melinda, take Jessica to my study. Simon and I have—"

"No!" Simon interrupted. "She will stay here." He spun around to level His Grace a harsh look. "Why? Why did you send her to me last night when you knew I would not take your money?"

"Last night? Where did you see Jessica last night?"

Simon shook his head. His lips curled upward to form a bitter smile. "Don't, James. Don't play me for an ignorant fool. I'm wise to your scheme."

"You're not making sense, Simon. I have no idea what you're talking about."

Simon leaned down, his face just inches from hers. "You haven't told him yet, my dear? He doesn't know you've failed?"

Jessica looked into his eyes filled with anger and opened her mouth to speak. "Please, my lord," she whispered. She was so tired and confused, she couldn't think.

He reached out to her. He lifted his muscular hand from his side and touched her cheek. Dear God, she'd dreamt of that touch all night. She'd prayed to feel that strength again.

But she did not want to see the disgust and revulsion she saw in his eyes.

"Would you like me to tell His Grace that his plan went for naught? Would you like me to explain that even though I found you physically attractive and I truly enjoyed our passionate, yet all too brief, exchange, I would not play the beggar just to provide you with a husband?"

The room suddenly turned terribly warm. She couldn't breathe. She couldn't force the air into her body. The roar in her head and the bright lights that darted behind her eyes made her dizzy. She pushed his hand away and wiped the dampness from her forehead. She needed to get away from him.

From the corner of her eye, she knew Collingsworth was yelling. He grabbed Simon's arm and tried to pull him away from her, but the earl twisted out of the duke's grasp and continued to level his accusations.

"Or perhaps His Grace doesn't know that you offered to sell yourself to me. Perhaps he doesn't realize how desperate you are to trap a husband. Could it be he still thinks you came only to offer the money and not your body?"

Everything around her spun in dizzying circles. She felt strange—disoriented. She sprang from the sofa and rushed across the room, heedless of the obstacles in her path or the small table she knocked over in her escape. She had to get out.

But before she could reach the door, a strong arm reached out for her, bringing her to a halt. The viselike grip twisted her about and pulled her up against him. It was the same hard chest she'd struggled against last night. The same unyielding arms from which she had not been able to free herself.

Dear God. She could not let him humiliate her again.

She had no idea if her deafening cry was successful in escaping her body. She clamped her hands over her ears as her scream echoed inside her head. Then Jessica welcomed the blessed darkness that consumed her.

And she knew no more.

* * *

Simon caught her slender body just before she hit the floor and picked her up in his arms and held her. She weighed almost nothing. Her face was as white as the lace collar around her neck, and even the rosy lips he'd kissed last night had lost their color.

"Bloody hell!" he exclaimed.

She seemed so small and fragile. So helpless. Nothing like the proud woman who'd stormed from his house last night.

Simon laid her gently on the sofa against the wall and then raked his hand over his two-day stubble. "I didn't mean to scare her," he said to no one in particular.

Melinda gave Simon an angry glare as she raced past him toward Jessica.

Hell! Bloody hell!

Simon squeezed his eyes shut and ground the palms of his hands against his aching sockets.

"What did you mean when you referred to the lies Jessica had told you last night?" his friend said quietly from behind him. The tone of his voice was as deadly as a double-edged sword. Simon chose to ignore the danger.

"You should know. You're the one who sent her."

Simon heard the air hiss through James's clenched teeth.

"Humor me, Simon. What happened between you two last night? Where could you have seen Jessica? She never leaves her home."

"Well, she did last night. She came to see me at my town house. Where you sent her."

Simon looked over at her. The color had not returned to her cheeks, but her breathing seemed a little more normal.

"What did she want with you?" James asked.

"She came to offer me the money you had given her. She showed me a piece of paper with an astronomical amount on it and told me it was all mine if I would only marry her."

Simon lifted his head and faced his friend. The angry frown on James's face punched him in the gut, but Simon refused to let it deter him. "When you told me you were as rich as Croesus you were not exaggerating, James. Did you honestly think it would take that much money to get me out of debt?"

"I had no idea how much it would take. I still do not. Did Jessica happen to tell you why it was so important that she have your name?"

"She claimed my name would protect her. A highly unlikely story about her stepbrother coming to claim the money."

Melinda sent him a withering look. "I need to get another blanket," she said, stomping past him.

James stood with his arms crossed over his chest. "My wife is very protective of her friends," he said. The glare in his eyes leveled Simon with a dangerous look. "Do you know she's deaf?"

"Yes. She was at least honest about that."

A long moment of silence stretched between them as Simon turned back to the sofa and the girl who'd caused him such a restless night. "Why did you choose her, James? Could you find no one else?" Simon turned to face his friend. "Did you think I wouldn't find out that you had sent her?" He braced his shoulders and filled his lungs with air. "Did you have to pay her much to sell her body and offer to become my wife?"

Before Simon knew what had happened, James's fist careened into his jaw. The impact of the blow sent him flying through the air, coming to a stop only when his large frame crashed against the sturdy wall on the opposite side of the room.

Simon slid to the floor, his legs sprawled out before him. He rubbed his hand over his jaw, then moved it from side to side to make sure it still worked. Before he was steady enough to rise to his feet, the Duchess of Collingsworth walked through the door, carrying a blanket. She stepped over his feet without even a glance, then paused when she reached her husband and gave him a tender kiss on the cheek.

"Thank you, James," she whispered, lowering a sideways glance to Simon's prone body.

James shook his head as he looked at Simon, then held out his hand to help him up.

Simon reluctantly took his proffered help and crawled to his feet. He shook his head and walked over to the couch, still rubbing his sore jaw. "Which part of this story have I gotten wrong?"

"The whole bloody thing, Simon," James answered, taking a cup of tea one of the servants had brought in and handing it to him.

"You mean you didn't send her to me?"

"No. I did not send her."

Simon stared at the tea swirling in his cup. "And her inheritance?"

James nodded. "She will receive every pound of it on Friday."

Simon raked his fingers through his hair. "Bloody hell, James. What made her ask a complete stranger to marry her? Once word reached society's ears, there would be no end to the line of suitors vying for her hand. Why did she come to me?"

"I think she had this misplaced idea you could protect her."

"Protect her from…?" A fist of painful reality punched Simon in the gut. "Tanhill is really her stepbrother?"

James nodded once, then breathed a heavy sigh.

A reaction as severe as any Simon had ever experienced slammed through his body. He looked at the pale girl just beginning to stir. "Heaven help her."

"No, Simon. I think heaven intends for you to help her. Perhaps heaven even intends for her to help you."

Chapter 6

*B*loody hell. The girl had told him the truth. She *was* Tanhill's stepsister.

Simon ignored the knot twisting in his gut and stared out the window of the study while he waited for James to return. Tanhill's stepsister was still in the drawing room. The duchess thought it best if he weren't there when she revived.

He stared out the window overlooking the garden and watched a pair of nightingales that sat on a thick branch of the budding alder tree. *Tanhill's stepsister.* The implication of what that meant registered in his mind with startling reality.

The pale color of her cheeks when she faced him last night, the desperate look in her eyes. He couldn't forget the brave front she'd exhibited. He couldn't forget the way he'd talked to her, accused her of being little more than a common whore. He closed his eyes to block out the memory.

Outside, the male nightingale's melodious tune soared above the normal sounds of the morning as if the tiny thrush had something significant to celebrate. He looked at the smaller bird nestled on the branch beside him. Perhaps he did.

Perhaps they both did.

The door opened behind him. "Is she all right?" he asked without turning. He kept his voice deliberately bland.

"Yes. She and Melinda will join us in a few minutes." Collingsworth walked across the room and poured two cups of tea. He handed one to Simon. "Would you like something stronger?" he asked, nodding to the brandy decanter sitting on a table next to his mammoth oak desk.

"Poison?" Simon said, his lips twisting cynically.

His friend's laughter echoed in the silence. "Excuse me for saying so, but you look like hell."

Simon raked his fingers though his disheveled hair. "I hope I never have the opportunity to return the compliment."

James sat in one of the two cushioned chairs flanking the fireplace. "Sit down, Simon. Let's look at this rationally."

"Bloody hell. There is no rational way to look at this. I have before me the opportunity to save Ravenscroft. The manor, the fields, the forests and ponds. I have the chance of a lifetime to care for and repair the homes of every Northcote tenant who has gone without since my father and his extravagant wife squandered the money. And repair the church and…" Simon breathed a sigh.

"…then begin to care for the other five Northcote estates. All I have to do is marry Tanhill's stepsister, and pray she won't run off with the gardener and humiliate me worse than my previous fiancée. Is that a rational view of the situation?"

James did not answer him. When he spoke, his voice was soft, tinged with a hint of concern. "Perhaps there is another solution."

Simon set his empty cup on the corner of the desk and sat to face his friend.

"The reason she came this morning was to enlist my help in arranging passage out of England. Perhaps she would be safe in the colonies."

Simon leaned forward in his chair and rested his elbows on his knees. "You know that will not assure her safety."

"She cannot stay here without protection, Simon," the Duke of Collingsworth said in a harsh tone. "She's worth a bloody fortune. Her stepbrother will move heaven and earth to take it away from her. You know him, Simon. He will not hesitate to get rid of her. He will either put her up before the courts to prove she's mentally incompetent and have her locked away, or..."

Simon breathed a heavy sigh. "Or he will simply kill her," he said. "As you and I know, torturing the helpless is second nature to him."

"It was never proved that he killed that barmaid, Simon. Perhaps—"

"I know." Simon sat back in his chair and touched the scar that angled from one side of his chest to the other. He tried to control the simmering rage building within him, but the torment on the faces of the people Tanhill had massacred in India refused to go away. He'd lost track of the times he'd wished Tanhill had been successful in his attempt to add his soul to the countless others who'd lost their lives in that faraway country.

James leaned forward. "Tell me what you intend to do, Simon."

A wave of indecision swelled within his chest. Every promise he'd made after his father had eloped with his fiancée paraded before him like a taunting curse, mocking and ridiculing him with its shrill laughter. He swore he would watch Ravenscroft fall to ruin rather than marry to save it. He swore he'd be content without a wife, home, and family rather than turn to another deceiving woman again.

But he'd also sworn to exact vengeance on Baron Tanhill.

Simon unconsciously fingered the scar on his chest. "I'll marry her, of course." A cold chill raced through his body when he said the words.

The look on James's face exposed a multitude of questions. "What do you think Tanhill will do when he finds out you've married his stepsister? When he finds out that you possess the wealth he thought to gain?"

"I do not doubt what he will do. He'll try to kill me. He must eliminate me before he can go after her."

"You'll be in danger, Simon."

"I'm counting on it." Simon closed his eyes and breathed in a harsh breath. He was being given the chance of a lifetime. And Tanhill would pay for everything he'd done. "I don't expect you to understand this, James, but I must have one more chance to conquer my ghosts."

"Destroying Tanhill is that important to you?"

"You have no idea. I would barter with the devil himself to see the bastard rot in hell."

"If you marry her, that is exactly what you will be doing."

"Perhaps."

James didn't move for several minutes. Simon could see his watchful gaze studying him. There was a look of genuine concern written on his face.

"What about Jessica, Simon? How will you handle her deafness?"

Simon stood and walked to the window. His vivid reflection stared back at him in the glass. "Her deafness will not affect me one way or the other," he answered. "Just as she will never affect me. Marriage to her will mean nothing to me. We will endure the union because it mutually benefits us both. Nothing more."

Simon braced one arm against the window frame. "I will provide her the protection she needs. In return, she will provide me the wealth I need to save Ravenscroft and make my estates profitable—"

"Simon," James interrupted. There was a warning in his voice.

Simon had not heard the door open, nor had he realized she'd entered the room.

Ignoring the unease he felt, he lifted his head. His gaze met Jessica Stanton's reflection in the window. She stood in the doorway with Melinda at her side. Her eyes focused on his reflection in the glass. He thought he saw a flash of pain in her eyes before she lifted her chin and raised her shoulders almost in defiance.

Bloody hell. How long had she been there? How much of what he'd said had she seen?

Simon looked at her eyes, her pale cheeks, and her lips. The lips he'd kissed last night.

Uncomfortable with the memories, he glowered, then turned his gaze from her face.

He stared at her hands fisted at her side. Hands that had touched him with a gentleness he'd never experienced before, then clung to him with a ferociousness he couldn't comprehend.

He pushed away the possibility that he cared what happened to her, one way or another. He did not. The last thing he wanted was emotional involvement with another deceiving woman.

James started across the room to escort both the women to a seat, but stopped short when Miss Stanton raised her hand in warning. "I cannot stay, Your Grace. I have only come to offer my apology and beg you will find a moment to visit with me when you are no longer occupied."

Collingsworth shook his head. "No, Jessica. Please, stay. Together we will work out a solution to your problem." He glanced at Simon for help.

Simon said nothing.

"No," she answered, the glare in her eyes lethal. The tone of her voice deadly. "There is nothing more to be said. Everything I had to say to the earl was said last night."

Simon took a step toward her. "I think there is a great deal left, Miss Stanton." He noticed the slight lift to her shoulders and the determined gleam in her eyes. "You came to me last night with an offer of marriage. I have reconsidered your offer."

"I, too, have reconsidered my offer," she said. There was a pleasing expression on her face, but when she spoke, her words hissed through her teeth and spilled into the room like venom. "It will be a cold day in hell, my lord, before I will marry you."

He held her icy glare for a long moment, and then he smiled. "Then you'd best ring for another wrap, my lady. Because the temperature is dropping even as we speak."

* * *

For a long time, no one moved. Not even to breathe. Jessica stood in a haze of confusion, trying to assimilate what he'd said.

"I have changed my mind, sir," she said firmly, her voice stiff and cold. "I no longer wish to marry you."

He kept his gaze leveled at her. He looked every inch the ruffian—a pirate on the high seas—a man more dangerous than any she had ever seen. He was in need of a good night's sleep, a shave, and a clean set of clothing. Yet, for some unfathomable reason, Jessica thought he was the most handsome man she had ever seen.

"James," he said to the Duke of Collingsworth, yet keeping his gaze locked with hers.

She refused to look away.

He met her challenge. "Leave us alone for a while and send someone after my solicitor."

Jessica panicked at the thought of being alone with him. "No. I don't want—" He was not listening, but talking through her words. She stomped her foot.

"And James," he continued, "stand ready. The marriage must be binding. We cannot make one mistake or overlook even the smallest detail, or our lives could be forfeit in the end."

Jessica could feel the blood rush to her head and thunder against her ears. She stared at his mouth to make sense of the words and commands he issued. He intended to make her his bride.

Heaven help her.

Even though a husband was exactly what she'd been desperate to find last night, it was something she was just as desperate to avoid today. Last night her actions had been impulsive, borne from desperation. She'd realized it during the sleepless hours after she'd left him. It had been a blessing he'd turned her down. She would not chance making the same mistake twice.

She stared at his lips. He instructed James as if he were his commander, and James hung on his every word. Even Melinda listened with wide-eyed attentiveness as they discussed the plans for her future. They acted as if she weren't there.

Twice his gaze left her and then returned, and each time her heart flew to her throat. She was torn between anger and relief.

She wanted to turn on her heel and race across the room, but she didn't. She held her ground. The man issuing orders and taking control of her life was a power to be reckoned with. As much as she feared him, he was all that stood between her and an asylum.

She stared at the overwhelming mastery he exhibited and dispelled a shudder. Although he seemed cruel and uncaring, she needed him. He towered before her as an unconquerable force, equal to the task of protecting her from Colin.

Her chest tightened as she struggled to take her next breath. He closed the distance between them and drilled her with a gaze so penetrating her heart leaped in her breast.

He turned her so she could see each of them and then touched a finger to her chin and tilted her face upward to make sure she could see his lips. His touch was so opposite the harsh look he leveled at her. Almost gentle.

"Could you give us a moment alone?" he said to the Duke and Duchess of Collingsworth. "Miss Stanton and I have some important details to discuss." He looked over at Melinda and then back to her. "I promise she will be safe."

Jessica's world stopped.

I promise she will be safe.

A warmth wrapped around her heart, and the heat it caused seeped ever so slowly through her chest and down to the very pit of her stomach where it swirled as a boiling pool.

I promise she will be safe.

The breath caught in her throat. How she'd longed to have those words spoken. Not since the fever had cast her into her solitary, terrifying world of silence had she dared to dream that someone would give her such a beautiful promise.

He touched his finger to her chin, making sure she was watching him. "James, do you know the name of Miss Stanton's solicitor?"

"Yes."

"Good. Send someone for him immediately, then send someone to contact my solicitor."

Melinda reached for her hand and held it tight. "Call if you need me." She gave her a gentle hug. "Don't worry. Everything will be all right."

Jessica nodded and then stepped back.

His tall, immovable frame stood next to her, his nearness so consuming, he sent a scorching warmth through her. She pulled in a shallow breath and held it.

He pinned her with a determined glare that only intensified when the duke closed the door and left them alone.

She knew that from this day on her life would never be the same.

* * *

Simon walked to the fireplace and stared into the flames. He grasped the six-foot-plus span of the mantle, and he held his grip until his knuckles turned white. The muscles across his shoulders burned, and the tight cords following the back of his neck ached. He lowered his pounding head between his arms and took a deep breath.

He listened for the rustling of her navy muslin dress to tell him she'd moved from the spot where he'd left her, but there was no sound.

No doubt she was so frightened she couldn't find the courage to move.

He didn't blame her. He knew he must look a fright— his unruly and disheveled hair, the dark stubble on his face, the bloodshot look of his eyes. Hell, he hadn't even bothered to change his clothes from the night before.

He was hardly dressed to call on close friends, let alone meet with an innocent young woman to ask her to become his wife.

Wife.

Bloody hell.

He squeezed his eyes tight and slowly dragged fresh air into his body. Her soft voice interrupted, paralyzing his half-filled lungs.

"Why, my lord?"

He turned to face her. What torture he read on her face. "Why, what? Why have I decided to marry you now?"

"Yes." She took a step closer. "Nothing has changed." She hesitated. "I am still deaf."

"Like you said last night, you have what I need to save my birthright."

"You could have had the money last night. You could have agreed to the marriage last night. What changed your mind?"

His gaze locked with hers. How could he tell her he hadn't believed her last night? How could he tell her he hadn't wanted her enough last night to pretend she was telling the truth—that he still didn't want her?

He blinked away the guilt that threatened to consume him. How could he make her understand it was more than even the money? What he wanted was revenge.

He wanted her stepbrother. He wanted Tanhill to pay for the pain he'd caused. For the lives he'd taken.

He wanted Tanhill to pay for what he'd done to Sarai.

Simon rubbed the heels of his hands against his eyes and pointed to the sofa. "Sit down."

She sat on the cushion and clasped her hands in her lap. He moved to sit beside her.

"No. Please. Sit there." She pointed to a chair across from her.

He stopped short. "I won't bite. I promise."

"I wasn't afraid you would, Lord Northcote. It's easier for me to see what you're saying when you face me."

A deep blush covered her cheeks, and Simon released a sigh. "I'm sorry. I didn't think."

"You didn't know."

He sat on the sofa facing her and kept his gaze locked with hers. "You understand why we have no choice but to marry, don't you, Miss Stanton?"

"I know that you must marry me to save your inheritance, my lord, but I'm not sure marriage to you is my only choice. Perhaps if I left England and—"

Simon held up his hand and leaned forward. The sudden movement startled her. "You would never survive, Miss Stanton. You are deaf." He rested his elbows on his knees and fisted his hands into hard balls. He wanted to shake her. "It's hard enough for a young, single woman to survive on her own here in England where you have friends to help you and you are familiar with your surroundings. If you went to a strange country you would have no friends, and no one to protect you. You are too innocent and inexperienced."

"I'm not that innocent or inexperienced, my lord. I am capable of taking care of myself. You forget that I have managed on my own perfectly well for ten years without anyone's protection."

Simon stared at her without flinching and gave her his fiercest glower. She didn't back down. "You have avoided society and any involvement with people, Miss Stanton. That is how you have gotten along. And you did not have your stepbrother pounding at your door, determined to have you committed to an asylum to get your money."

Her eyes widened as if he'd slapped her.

He regretted his forwardness, but now was not the time to soften the truth. "I'm sorry, Miss Stanton, but you cannot escape from your stepbrother. Even a place halfway around the world is not far enough to hide you from Baron Tanhill. He's too desperate for your money."

She lowered her head and breathed a heavy sigh. "I know. Ira said the same."

"Ira who?"

She didn't answer. She hadn't been looking at him.

When she lifted her head to face him, Simon noticed that the spark in her eyes was no longer there. Neither was the look of independence and rebellion he'd seen on her face or the fight he'd sensed in her bearing. Resignation was the only expression he read on her face.

Resignation and submission.

"Perhaps it would be best if we laid out our requests and expectations here and now," she said, clenching her fists tighter. Her face seemed even paler than before. "So there will be no misunderstandings later."

Simon leaned back in his chair and regarded her with guarded openness. "Yes. Perhaps that would be best."

She leveled her gaze on him and took a deep breath. "Please, my lord. You go first."

Dear God, but it was hard to speak such blatant truths while looking someone directly in the eye. Especially truths he knew would hurt. Truths that would cause her pain.

"I do not mean to be cruel or hurt you intentionally," Simon said bluntly, "but my reason for marrying you is to save my inheritance. I can offer you no emotional attachment."

The proud, determined woman sitting opposite him lifted the corners of her mouth in a gentle smile. "You do not need to fear that I will ever expect there to be any emotional attachment from our marriage. I understand our union to be a marriage of convenience and nothing more. You will have my inheritance as a dowry, and I will have your name as protection. You have not offended me, my lord." She tipped her head to the side. "Is there anything more?"

"Yes. One other requirement."

"You will always be faithful to only me and will never bring disgrace to the name I give you."

Her gaze flew to her hands in her lap, and a blush flooded her cheeks. "Of course, my lord," she whispered.

Her head slowly lifted, and Simon could tell how hard it was to look him in the eyes. Her sigh quivered in the silence.

"Is there anything else?" she asked.

"No." Simon crossed his arms over his chest. "Do you have any demands?"

"Yes. I have three."

Simon raised his eyebrows. "And they are?"

He watched her take a deep breath. "I did not lie to you when I said the money means nothing to me," she said softly. "And I promise I will never make any undue demands on you. But I want your promise in writing that you will never have me committed to an asylum."

He sat forward. Fury erupted from deep within him. "Why the bloody hell do you think I would marry you if not to protect you from your stepbrother and keep you *out* of an asylum? Do you think I am equally as heartless?"

She did not blink an eye. "I would have your promise in writing before I agree to become your wife."

Dear God, she did. He could see her determination. "Then you will have it."

She breathed a sigh of relief. "I would also like there to be a small house somewhere nearby deeded in my name alone. Something simple. The size is not important."

Simon rose to his feet in front of her. "You will not live anywhere other than under my roof, Miss Stanton. I will not allow it. Is that understood?" Simon couldn't keep the anger out of his voice. Not that she'd notice, of course.

The defiant lift to her shoulders said she understood but did not like what he'd said. "I only want to own it as a guarantee that I will always have a place to call my own. Something no one can take from me."

Simon felt his anger abate. He could not imagine having the enormous wealth she had, yet feeling so vulnerable and insecure. "I know of three town houses in London that are currently available. They are all in good repair and located nearby. We will tour them in the next few days, and you can choose which house you would like put in your name. My solicitor will take care of all the details."

"Thank you, my lord."

"And the third request?"

"I would like a monthly allowance."

Simon could not stop the grin from covering his face. He knew the money would come in here somewhere. Even though she'd denied it meant anything to her, he'd known she'd been lying. There wasn't a woman alive who did not crave wealth. "Of course. And how much of your fortune would you like a month?"

She released a deep breath. "Fifteen pounds."

"What?" He hadn't heard her right. He thought she'd asked for only fifteen pounds.

She chewed her lower lip nervously and then lifted her chin defiantly. "Fifteen pounds," she repeated.

He stared at her and knew the confusion on his face was easy to read. The woman was worth more than the both of them would ever be able to spend, and she was bargaining with him for a paltry fifteen pounds a month.

"May I ask what you intend to do with such a vast amount of wealth?"

"I would feel better if I did not have to rely on your generosity. You made yourself quite clear last night, and I do not wish to inconvenience you or embarrass you with my presence or my needs. I'm used to my independence and taking care of myself. I wish to continue doing so."

Simon nodded in compliance. "Don't worry, Miss Stanton. You will get your allowance."

"Thank you, my lord. I promise I will make no further demands on you." She stopped and then lifted her wide-open gaze. "Except…"

"Except?" Simon looked at her indulgently.

"Would there be room in your employ for my servants? They are all extremely loyal and have been with me for years. Mrs. Graves is an excellent cook, and Mrs. Goodson…"

Simon closed his mouth, which hung open. "Yes. They can all come with you. Sanjay will be glad for their help."

"Sanjay?"

"My servant. He has been keeping the house by himself since we arrived. He will welcome their assistance."

"Thank you, my lord. I promise there will be nothing more."

Simon turned at the knock on the door, and Miss Stanton's gaze followed him. Collingsworth stood at the entry with Ira Cambden at his side. Ira walked into the room, and she leaped from the sofa and ran across the Turkish carpet into his outstretched arms.

"Oh, Ira," she cried out, then buried her face against his chest.

"It's all right, Miss Jessica," he answered and held her for a long moment. The relieved look on his face was plain to see. He touched her cheek tenderly and then stood proudly at her side. "My lord," he said, bowing formally. "I pray I can be of service."

Simon narrowed his eyes. "You are acquainted with Miss Stanton?"

"Yes, my lord. I have been solicitor for the Stanton family even more years than I have represented the Northcotes."

"Yes, well…it seems that Miss Stanton is in need of a husband. For some reason beyond my realm of understanding, she has chosen me to fill that requirement."

Ira's eyes opened wide, his mouth dropping slightly, then lifting to an open grin. "Yes, my lord. That is correct. Miss Stanton is indeed in need of a husband." Ira reached for her hand and patted it softly. "Does my lord understand the full impact of the situation?"

"Yes, Mr. Cambden. Better than you realize."

"I'm afraid Baron Tanhill will not accept your marriage to Miss Jessica without some sort of repercussion."

"I know," Simon said, rubbing his hand across his face. He knew all too well. "Please. Bring your charge and sit down. We seem to have a great deal to discuss. James, join us. I fear it will take all of us to cover the details."

Ira Cambden sat on the sofa with Jessica at his side. Not once did she remove her hands from the older man's grasp.

Simon watched with a sense of something near envy because they were not his hands she wanted to hold. He sat opposite her and slid his chair so close their knees touched. He looked into eyes so blue he felt he could drown in them. Unfortunately, the hesitation he'd seen earlier was still there.

"How long do we have, Mr. Cambden?" he asked, making sure she knew what he was saying.

She turned her gaze to Ira. "Miss Jessica will turn twenty-five on Friday. According to the stipulation of the will, if there is no husband, all the money will go to her at that time."

"And if there is a husband?"

"The money will go directly to him."

Simon sat back in his chair. "Then she must be my wife by…"

"Thursday, my lord. At the latest. She will be safer if the money is never in her possession."

Simon reached out his hand and touched her beneath the chin. "We will wed on Thursday." He watched her swallow hard and noticed Ira Cambden pat her hand in a comforting way. "Do you understand, my lady?" Simon asked.

She nodded and answered a shaky yes.

"What are the stipulations of the will, Ira?" Simon asked, wanting to understand every detail so there would be no mistakes.

The solicitor produced a copy and explained item by item, not leaving out even the smallest detail.

When he finished, Simon sat back in his chair and breathed a deep sigh.

"Go home and pack your belongings, Miss Stanton. All your clothing and personal items, but nothing else."

A frown darkened her features. "There are some items that belonged to my mother. Could I possibly have just those?" Her expression was hopeful.

"They will stay with the house. You will take only the clothes in your closet and whatever personal items you have acquired since your stepbrother left." Simon turned to Ira. "Is that what the will stipulates, Ira?"

Ira nodded. "Miss Jessica is entitled to only the money. The home and contents are Tanhill's. Or will be on April twenty-fifth."

Simon lightly touched Miss Stanton's arms. "You will take nothing, my lady. Do you understand? No jewelry. No pictures. No mementos. Nothing. Only the clothes on your back and any items you have personally purchased since Tanhill left."

He thought he noticed a dampness in her eyes, but she quickly blinked away any sign of emotion and stiffened her shoulders. "Yes, my lord. Only my clothes and what is mine. Is there anything else?"

Simon shook his head.

With a quivering sigh she stood and moved away from the sofa. She kept her back to them, hugging her arms around her middle while she stared out into the garden.

Ira Cambden made a move to go to her, but Simon stopped him with a glance. Starting today, she would learn to rely only on him. Simon walked up behind her and put his hands on her shoulders. She stiffened at his touch.

He turned her around so she could read his lips. "I don't want her to be alone, James. Would it be possible for her to stay here until the wedding?"

Jessica started to protest, but Simon held up his hand to silence her.

"Of course," the Duke of Collingsworth answered.

"Do you have some men you can send with her while she packs? I don't want to take any chances."

Simon disregarded the stifled cry he heard from her throat. The look of alarm on her face was more difficult to ignore.

The Duke of Collingsworth walked to the door. Miss Stanton's gaze followed him. "I'll have a room made ready for you, Jessica," Collingsworth said to her. "And some men ready to go with her," he said to Simon, then left the room.

Simon placed his finger beneath her chin and turned her attention back to him. "Give the orders to your staff to pack their personal belongings and close the house. They are to remove nothing from the premises except the food in the pantry. Any leftover foodstuffs they will give away to the needy. They are to keep nothing for themselves. Do you understand?"

"Yes, my lord."

"I will trust you to take care of all the legal paperwork, Mr. Cambden," he said to the solicitor. "I will stop by later today to go over the details with you."

"Very good, my lord. I will have the paperwork in order to transfer Jessica's finances over to you as soon as you are legally married." The solicitor gathered his folder and walked to the door. "I will make sure that everything is documented so Tanhill will not be able to find anything we've missed."

"Very good, Mr. Cambden."

The door closed behind the solicitor, leaving Simon alone with his future bride. Her voice cut through the silence like a knife through warm butter.

"It's not too late, my lord. You do not have to do this. I will not hold you to our bargain."

He turned around to face her, expecting to see her tortured face gripped with fear and regret. What he saw twisted his heart in his chest. The look on her face was as stoic and resigned as if she had enabled herself to step outside her body to bravely accept whatever was expected of her.

"I have no desire to go back on our bargain, Miss Stanton. As you said, you are my only hope to save my inheritance and live a life free of financial worries. Without your money, I lose everything."

Simon wanted to ask her the same question but realized he didn't dare. He wasn't sure she would give the same answer. "We have struck a bargain. It's too late for either of us to change our minds."

The finality of his words left no doubt there was no turning back. For either of them.

Chapter 7

❧

Simon fastened the last button on his black waistcoat and studied his reflection in the mirror. He looked like hell. His face was pale, which made the dark circles beneath his eyes look even blacker. He'd slept no more last night than he had each of the nights since he'd made the rash decision to forfeit his freedom in exchange for Tanhill's death.

The room swam before him, and he rubbed his fingers against his temples to ease the pounding in his head. Every muscle in his body ached, but somehow he had to fight to keep this latest attack of malaria at bay until the day was over.

The clock in the entryway of his London town house chimed the hour. He braced his hand against the solid oak armoire and uttered a vile oath. In less than three hours, he'd be married. If he could still stand by then.

He wiped the perspiration from his face with a towel, then braced his arms against the new highboy and waited for the room to stop spinning. He'd sworn he would never offer his name to another woman again. Offering his name to Rosalind had been humiliating enough.

Simon slammed his fist against the dresser. If only the girl didn't need him so. If only she wasn't Baron Tanhill's stepsister. If only she was not the means to an end. An end to Tanhill.

A little voice hidden deep within him questioned his fairness in using her to exact revenge on his nemesis. He couldn't give an answer. He couldn't see past his hatred for the man who had taken so much from him.

Simon reached for his tailcoat and slipped it on. He was chilled to the very center of his bones. Damn! Why couldn't this accursed fever have waited until tomorrow? Until after he'd said his vows and signed his name to the papers?

He drank from the steaming potion Sanjay had fixed him earlier, and prayed it would keep away the worst of his weakness for a few hours more.

"His Grace, the Duke of Collingsworth, is downstairs, master," Sanjay said from behind him. "Mr. Ira Cambden is with him."

"Very well, Sanjay. Tell His Grace I'll be right down." Simon fastened the last button on his coat, then put the small box containing the ring he would put on her finger in his pocket. "Another shipment of furniture will arrive this morning, and Miss Stanton's staff should be here shortly. See to it the mistress's rooms are made ready and her staff gets settled properly."

"Yes, master."

A frown of concern covered his servant's face. Simon wiped his handkerchief over his face again and ignored the knowing look Sanjay gave him.

"Will you be all right, master?"

Simon ignored the question and walked across the room.

Sanjay followed him. "In my next life, I think I will come back as a gentle breeze. I will spend hours each day calming and comforting you. Then carry you away to a hillside far away where you can rest without worries. That is what I will come back as."

Simon stopped and gripped the doorframe to steady himself. "I think you would not make a very gentle breeze, friend. My disposition would be so disagreeable it would turn you into a raging gale before you could calm me." Simon dropped his hand to his side and prepared to leave for his wedding. When he reached the door, he stopped to issue a final instruction. "Have a room ready for me on the third floor. I will want to be well out of the way. If I am… indisposed when we return, be sure your new mistress has everything she needs."

"Yes, master. Do not worry. Sanjay will take very good care of the missy."

Simon walked to the top of the stairs and stood for a moment. What did it matter if he didn't love the woman he was going to marry? With very few exceptions, how many men in London had felt anything more than lust or a sense of obligation for the women they married?

He hissed the air through clenched teeth in an effort to block out the vivid reminder of how his body had betrayed him when he'd kissed her. There was no doubt that he'd reacted so outrageously only because he'd had too much to drink that night. He knew her body had licked at him like the flames of a raging fire only because it had been such a long time since he'd held a woman in his arms.

He made his way down the stairs and entered his study, where James and Ira waited for him. He refused to dwell on anything other than getting through this day.

The room was filled with beautiful new furniture—thanks to his future wife's money. A sardonic smile crossed his lips. God knew he hated using her for revenge, but he had no choice.

One vow he'd made, though. Never would he allow his feelings to soften toward her. Even if it was to be her money that would pay off his creditors and furnish his house, never would he let himself care for her. Never. He'd cared for a woman once before and had nearly been ruined. Such a weakness would not happen again.

Nor would he owe her for what she'd done. If it took every waking hour until his dying day, he would work his fingers to the bone to replace every pound he'd received from her.

Simon walked across the room to where a brandy decanter sat on the corner of the desk and poured himself two fingers. The brandy went down with a welcoming sting. Before he took his last breath, the slate would be wiped clean. He would not die as his father had. In debt. He would owe no one. Especially his wife.

"And a pleasant good-day to you, too, Simon," the Duke of Collingsworth said. "For a man about to be married, you look far from the expected picture of the happy groom."

Simon ignored James's barbed comment and refilled his glass. He raised his hand and stopped when the brandy touched his lips. Drinking would not help. He'd tried drinking before when he'd felt the symptoms coming on and it hadn't helped. It would only make the sickness worse.

"Is everything taken care of, James?"

"Yes. The arrangements have been made. I have the special license with me," James said, patting the inside pocket of his tailcoat.

"Is there anything else, Ira?"

"No, my lord. As soon as the marriage is over, I will take the court magistrates with me to the town house. They will attest that everything is in order and nothing has been removed from the premises. Then we will seal the house. No doubt it will take longer to sign all the papers after the ceremony than it will to perform the marriage."

Simon turned his attention to his solicitor. "We cannot afford to overlook even one detail, Ira. It could be fatal."

Ira worried his lower lip, then shook his head. "You forget," he said with a serious frown on his face, "I know Baron Tanhill, too. Never have I met someone so evil. It was as if the devil himself had a hand in raising him."

Simon turned to James and steadied his hand on the back of the wing chair. God, how he hated his weakness. He didn't want to, but he had to tell them. He would probably need their help before the day was over. "I am not well, James."

James rose to his feet and took a step closer. The worry was evident on his face. "Is there anything I can do?"

"No. There's nothing. It will pass in a few days. A remembrance from my time in India. While there I contracted malaria. I prayed my fever would stay away until after today, but I am not to be so fortunate. I will have to rely on you and Ira to make sure everything is as it should be."

"Of course," they both answered.

"Just be sure no one knows. Not the clergy or the magistrates or the witnesses. We cannot afford to have anyone question my health. Not even my new wife. Since she's marrying me because she requires my protection, I doubt she would be comforted to know she's married a man so weak."

"Begging your pardon, my lord," Ira interrupted, "but I doubt Jessica thinks she has married a weak man. She's a very strong woman, sir. Don't be afraid to trust her."

Simon laughed. His illness made him reckless. "Trust. I learned long ago, Ira, there is not a woman alive who can be trusted. Understand this here and now. I'm marrying Miss Stanton for two reasons alone. To pay off the creditors so I can keep what is mine. And to keep my promise to protect her from her stepbrother."

Simon walked to the other side of the room. He wanted to get this day over as soon as possible. "Are we ready to leave?"

Ira and James both followed him to the door. "Yes," James said from behind him. "Melinda has gone with Jessica to make sure everything is packed. I sent a small army with them. They will be safe."

"Good."

Simon fastened the buttons of his topcoat, then settled the black cape Sanjay threw across his chilled shoulders. There was another reason he was marrying Jessica. One he would not reveal to anyone. And it was the most important reason. Revenge.

Taking the inheritance Tanhill would steal from his stepsister was only the first step in his plan to destroy Baron Tanhill and make him pay for what he'd done to him.

And to Sarai.

* * *

Jessica smoothed the skirt of her simple ivory satin gown and stared at the three small chests that contained everything in the world she could take with her.

"Why don't you sit for a while, Jess," Melinda said, pulling back one of the protective covers that had been draped over the sofa. "James should be here with Simon shortly, and you can relax until they arrive."

"Relax?" Jessica smothered a shrill laugh. In just a few minutes she would leave her home for the last time and take a total stranger as her husband. A stranger who had made a point of telling her that the only reason he was marrying her was because he was as desperate for her money as she was for his name—and his protection. A stranger who had taken every opportunity to instruct her not to expect anything more from their union than the safety his name could offer.

Jessica paced the length of the room again, stopping only when Melinda grasped her shoulders. "Are you sure you want to go through with this, Jess? It's not too late to change your mind. Perhaps James could arrange—"

"No," Jessica said, not wanting to hear anything more. "I am doing the right thing. Marriage is my only choice."

She could not let herself think she had another option. She was too close to jumping at anything that might keep her from marrying the Earl of Northcote. She took a shaky breath. "I should check with Mrs. Goodson. I want to make sure—"

"Everything is done, Jess. We've already checked twice. Hodgekiss gave all the leftover food to the poor like you instructed. Every fire in the house is extinguished, and every piece of furniture is covered to protect it."

Jessica sank down on the sofa and let her weary shoulders drop. "He doesn't want me, Mel. Every look he gives me and every word he speaks tells me how disgusted he is to take me as his wife." Jessica brought her hands to her lips and covered the soft cry that wanted to escape. She turned her face away from her friend in case her eyes mirrored the hurt in her heart.

"When I was young, after my fever, I used to dream about getting married," Jessica said without facing her friend. "Of finding a knight in shining armor who would fall at my feet in adoration. Silly of me, wasn't it? Of course, in my dreams I wasn't deaf, nor was I plain and ordinary. I was always quite lovely. The belle of society."

Mel turned her by the shoulders. "You are not plain and ordinary, Jess. You are one of the most extraordinary people I have ever met. Much braver than I could ever hope to be."

Jessica shook her head and tried to breathe in deeply. "Have you noticed how domineering he is? He needs to control. I can't surrender that much of myself to him, Mel. I won't. I've been on my own since I was fifteen. I have had only myself to rely upon."

"What about your designs, Jess? How will you keep what you do from him? What if he will not allow it?"

The muscles in Jessica's entire body tensed with conviction. "Nothing will change, Mel. I doubt he will care enough one way or another. As long as society doesn't find out, I can't see where it will matter. I doubt that what I do with my time will be of any interest to him. I certainly will not let his opinion matter. I cannot trust him enough to allow him that much control over me."

"Give him time, Jess. Someday perhaps you will see his dominance as a strength, as a comforting support for you to lean upon."

Jessica lowered her gaze to the floor. She sincerely doubted it. "It doesn't matter, Mel. I am not what the Earl of Northcote wanted for his wife. What if society discovers I'm deaf? What if I cannot hide it? How will the earl ever survive the humiliation of society finding out?"

Jessica bolted from the sofa and walked to the two doors that led to the terrace. Beyond it was a lovely garden filled with flowers just coming to bloom. She stopped before exiting the room and placed her fingers on the small oval table that stood against the wall nearby. She gently lifted the dustcover that protected special items that had always been a part of her life and picked up the tiny miniature of a woman in a beautifully carved oak rocker holding a small baby in her arms. The baby was she. The woman was her mother.

She stared at the picture and let the heartache and longing swell within her. Her mother looked so happy. She had a husband who adored her and a baby to love. A future Jessica had only dreamed of having.

She knew Mel watched her, and she looked away, blinking rapidly to stop the tears from gathering in her eyes. She'd said good-bye to so many special memories during the last two days. How could she ever give up more? She was afraid she would shatter when she had to leave behind one more reminder of the only life she'd ever known. Even if that reminder was nothing more than the faded likeness of a woman who was at times little more than a distant memory.

The picture in the miniature swam before her, and she swallowed hard to keep the tears at bay as she held the picture to her breast. "Perhaps I could just take…"

Her words lodged in her throat when a shadow moved to her right. Her gaze locked onto the large figure darkening the doorway.

The Earl of Northcote took a few steps into the room, then halted.

The look in his eyes made him appear weary and tired. The expression on his face seemed frighteningly serious. It was evident he regretted this even more than she.

He crossed the room, his demeanor resolved and determined. He towered before her, as magnificently handsome as he had been the first night she'd seen him standing on the top step of the Stratmore ballroom. His broad shoulders filled out the perfectly tailored black tailcoat to perfection, and the white shirt and cravat glistened against his bronzed skin. His dark eyes pinned her with a penetrating glare, and she couldn't take her gaze from him as he loomed before her.

Jessica clutched the picture tighter for one more moment and then gave it up to his outstretched hand. His fingers touched hers, and he hesitated as if plagued with a twinge of regret.

He looked at the picture, then placed it back on the table. "You will take nothing but your clothes and the items that belong to you alone. We cannot give your stepbrother one excuse to cause trouble. The will states that everything in the house belongs to him. It's the way it must be."

Jessica swallowed hard and looked away. Sometimes the most difficult part of being deaf was staring into his face, reading the harshness and regret she saw in his eyes. She wondered if he realized how far into his soul she could see and how much of his hidden feelings were laid bare by just the look in his eyes? How much of the strength he'd honed to guard his emotions she could see? How much of the fear he tried to disguise as anger? She saw it all. She doubted he knew or he would have erected another barricade to defend himself. Another wall to separate himself from her.

She wondered how long he would keep her at bay, refusing to acknowledge or accept their relationship. Perhaps only a short time. Perhaps a lifetime.

He placed his hand on her arm, bringing her out of her daydream. His hand felt warm against her skin. Feverish.

Her heart jumped in her throat. The unique feel of fevered flesh sent a wave of panic rushing through her. Jessica lifted her gaze to his face. His face seemed flushed. His eyes were glazed with a hint of illness she hadn't noticed before. She placed her fingers against his hand again to make sure. Warm. Too warm. Then she moved to place her hand on his face.

Before she could touch him, he stepped out of her reach. He separated himself from her as if her touch was repulsive to him.

"It's time to leave. Are you ready?"

Jessica swallowed hard. "Yes, my lord. I am ready."

He extended his arm. She hesitated, then placed her hand upon his muscled forearm. She prayed he didn't notice how violently her fingers trembled when she touched him. If he did, he didn't show it. He kept her close as they followed the Duke and Duchess of Collingsworth from the room.

She'd promised herself she would be brave. That she would walk away without a backward glance. But before they took their final step over the threshold, Jessica turned to look at her home one last time. The home where she'd been born. Where she and her mother and father had talked and laughed and been happy. Where she could remember a time when she had still been a complete person.

The home where a raging fever had taken her mother from her. The home where she'd known the happiest days of her life. And the saddest. Where she'd learned what it was like to belong and be loved. Where she'd learned what it was like to be alone with no one to love.

The breath caught in her throat when the door closed behind her. She held on to the Earl of Northcote's arm and prayed she hadn't made the biggest mistake of her life.

* * *

Without flourish or fanfare, they were married in a quiet country church on the outskirts of London. With the queen's bishop and two high-ranking clergy of the church officiating, Jessica walked down the narrow aisle on legs that barely supported her. With Melinda at her side and Ira close by, she went through the motions, said the right words, smiled an adequate smile, and made the appropriate gestures to convince everyone she was willing to take the earl as her husband.

She stood before the legion of church and government officials Northcote had brought as witnesses and promised to love, honor, and obey a man who struck terror in her heart.

She knelt before the ornately carved wooden altar and vowed to trust completely a man who had yet to say his first kind word of greeting.

She held out her hand as he slipped onto her finger the ring symbolizing their union, then promised to submit to him in all things. To trust her life as well as her future to a man who had yet to grace her with his first smile.

With her hand nestled in his, she let his intense strength pour into every fiber of her body, then released a shuddering gasp when a strange molten fire surged to every part of her being, heating her with a warmth she couldn't understand.

Only once did he show any sign of tenderness. Of concern. Before he repeated his vows, he lifted his hand, and with his finger beneath her chin, he turned her head so she would face him. He held her gaze with unflinching steadiness and repeated the promise to protect her for all time. She imagined she had never seen a more somber look of commitment.

Then, the bishop pronounced them man and wife.

She felt the slight pressure as his fingers tightened around her hand and she lifted her gaze. If she lived to be a hundred years old she would never forget the uncertainty in his answering gaze. The look that said he questioned— doubted—his sanity for marrying her.

And then he kissed her. Despite the almost unnatural heat of his face, his kiss was the coldest, most unemotional kiss imaginable.

If only he had never kissed her before. If only she hadn't experienced the heat and fire of that other kiss as a comparison. Then she would not have known how lacking and unfeeling the slight pressure of his lips on hers truly was.

Then it was over.

Moments later they were seated in Northcote's coach on their way to her new home. Jessica leaned back against the maroon leather seat of the stylish black carriage and turned her head to stare out the window. She absently fingered the beautiful opal ring on her third finger and tried to squash the rising fears that ate away at her insides.

Four matching blacks pulled the carriage down one unfamiliar street after another as they wound their way through the quiet London residential district. She was now the Countess of Northcote and the man sitting beside her, legs outstretched, eyes staring blankly ahead, was her husband. Never had she felt more alone in her whole life.

Other than the vows he'd repeated that had bound them as husband and wife, the Earl of Northcote had not said another word to her. He'd protected her, buffering her from unexpected questions or comments spoken behind her back where she could not see the speaker's lips. He'd placed his arm around her shoulder and casually turned her to face anyone offering their congratulations as if he'd done so for years. But he had not spoken those same words of acknowledgment.

The Duke of Collingsworth had also hovered nearby. Watching. Keeping a wary eye focused on the bride and groom. Especially the groom. Jessica doubted if anyone besides herself noticed, but His Grace's concern was obvious. Something was not right with her husband.

He moved on the seat in the carriage. Straightened, then opened his eyes to look at her. "I know this day is probably not how you always dreamed your wedding day would be."

"I have never entertained dreams of my wedding day, my lord. I never thought I would marry."

"So, you are not disappointed?"

"No. I am not disappointed. You've fulfilled your part of the bargain. I have the protection of your name. I expect no more."

"Every woman expects more." He leaned his head back on the seat and closed his eyes. "Can you see to read my lips?"

"Yes, my lord."

"The name is Simon. Simon Warland, twelfth Earl of Northcote. You are now Lady Northcote. Countess of Northcote." He took in a deep breath and held it. Jessica thought she noticed his face grimace in pain.

"Are you all right, my lord?"

He lifted his head and focused his gaze on her. There was a glassy look to his eyes, and Jessica wasn't sure he really saw her.

"The name is Simon."

"Are you feeling well, Simon?"

"It's nothing that need concern you."

He leaned his head back and closed his eyes again, shutting her out. It was obvious he intended nothing about him to be her concern.

"Everything should be ready when we arrive. Your rooms have been prepared and your staff is in place. I have taken the liberty of furnishing your home. It was quite bare as you probably remember, and Her Grace informed me you are not accustomed to haggling with shopkeepers. It was amazing how eager the merchants were to advance me credit on my forthcoming marriage. If something is not to your liking, talk to Sanjay. He will take care of anything you need."

"You will not be there?"

"If you need something, talk to Sanjay."

"I'm sure everything will be in order," she answered, clutching her fingers in her lap. "What about you, my lord? Are you disappointed in your wedding day?"

"Don't worry about me. Your part of the bargain has also been fulfilled. I have your money and can now pay my father's debts and save my inheritance. What more could any two people ask from a marriage?"

Jessica felt as if a knife had been thrust through her heart.

As the carriage slowed to a halt she said a silent prayer of thanks. For the first time in her life, she was thankful for her deafness. At least she was spared hearing the bitterness she knew had been in her husband's voice.

When they reached the earl's town house, the door to the carriage opened and a small, dark-skinned man with a turban on his head greeted them. He bent over in the lowest bow Jessica had ever seen, and when he straightened his body, his face opened to a wide grin. Laughing black eyes looked up at her and held her captive. Jessica couldn't help but smile back.

"Come, missy," he said, helping her out of the carriage. "Sanjay will show you to your new home."

Before he spoke again, he turned to face her. Obviously, he'd been informed about her deafness.

"All your people are already settled and waiting for you to come. Hurry. Even your excellent cook is busy baking a cake to celebrate this happy day."

"Thank you, Sanjay." She turned around to see if Northcote was following.

"The master will come, missy," he said, turning his face close to hers. "Hurry. They are all waiting."

Jessica followed the exuberant servant up the walk and into the house. Hodgekiss opened the door for them.

"Welcome, my lady," he said, bowing formally.

Martha and Beatrice and Mrs. Goodson all stood in a line to congratulate the new bride, and even Mrs. Graves rushed out from the kitchen to join in the festivities. When Simon walked through the door they stood even taller, like little toy soldiers aiming to impress their new master.

Simon stopped before the short line of smiling faces. He graced them with a curt nod, then turned on his heel and marched up the winding staircase. His grip on the railing turned his knuckles white. She wondered if she and Sanjay were the only ones who noticed.

Jessica turned back to face her loyal servants and saw their looks of disappointment. A strong wave of protectiveness washed over her. She vowed she would become the buffer between her staff and her new husband. He would never intimidate them or make them feel unworthy.

Suddenly, every head turned to face him. He must have yelled for Sanjay to follow him because the small man bowed half a dozen times, then made his way up the stairs.

Jessica waited until her husband and his servant were out of sight, then painted a bright smile on her face and turned back to her friends. "Are you all settled in?" she asked, keeping her voice light.

"Yes, mistress," Hodgekiss answered for everyone. "Everything is perfect. 'Tis a fine house we've come to. A fine house, indeed."

"And such a beautiful suite of rooms for you, my lady," Beatrice added, twisting the ends of her starched white apron. Her attempt to cover their master's abrupt departure was obvious.

"Good," Jessica answered, blinking past the tears that stung the back of her eyes. "You wouldn't have a cup of tea ready, would you, Mrs. Graves?"

"Oh yes, my lady. And I've a pan of buttered scones just come out of the oven."

Mrs. Goodson took a quick step forward. "I'll have the tray ready before you're even seated on one of those new sofas the master had brought in this morning," she answered, following Mrs. Graves to the kitchen.

Jessica watched her staff quickly depart, all except Martha. She waited until they were alone before she spoke. "Where are my designs, Martha? Are they safe?"

"Yes, my lady. They are locked away in the last room at the end of the hall upstairs. Here is the key."

Martha reached in her pocket and handed Jessica a heavy brass key.

"The room is perfect for you to work, my lady. Large and spacious, with big windows to let in fresh air and light. We found an old desk and a few tables in storage and put them in there for you."

Jessica breathed a sigh of relief. She turned the key over in her hand, holding it tight. Everything that was important to her was locked behind that door.

"Thank you, Martha." Jessica placed the key in her pocket where it would be safe. "Is everything truly all right?" Jessica asked, knowing she would receive an honest answer.

"Yes, my lady. The master has seen to everything, and his manservant, Sanjay, has been more than helpful."

Jessica breathed a sigh of relief. "Then perhaps we can tour our new home after I've had a cup of tea and something to eat," she said, trying to sound more optimistic than she felt.

"It would be my pleasure. It is a beautiful home." Martha led the way to the drawing room with a broad smile on her face. She opened the door wide and stood back while Jessica entered.

Jessica took one step into the large, spacious room and stopped short. A lump formed in her throat that she could not swallow past. The room was an exact picture of her drawing room at home. If there were any differences, Jessica didn't see them. Not a misplaced chair or a missing table. It was as close a replica to the drawing room she had just left as Jessica had ever seen.

Two matching sofas faced each other on one side of the room with a large oval rug on the floor between them. The pattern on the rug even looked the same.

A cozy window seat nestled beneath the window that looked out onto the garden, and a small writing desk sat beside the double doors that led onto the terrace.

Even the flowers were identical to the ones she had in her home and were placed in the same spots as if someone had followed a map of her room.

"Who did this?" Jessica asked Martha.

"The master, my lady. It was already arranged like this when we arrived. Sanjay said Lord Northcote wanted you to feel at home. He gave strict instructions for the room to be exactly as what you had left."

Jessica walked from one side of the room to the other. She was oddly touched by his kindness. It was perfect.

"I'll get the tea, my lady," Martha said and quietly backed out of the room. Jessica was left alone with her thoughts.

She sat in the window seat as she often had at home and stared out into the garden. Heaven help her but he was a contradiction. Distant and aloof, yet gentle and considerate. He was such a confusion she couldn't figure him out. She didn't want to.

She knew there was a part of him calling to be understood. But she didn't want his voice to be the only one she heard. She couldn't let him become important. She would trust him to the extent she had to. She would rely on him to protect her from her stepbrother.

Trusting him to any further degree was a weakness she could not afford.

Chapter 8

❖

*J*essica pulled the hood of her cape over her head and ran through the black night and the biting rain to her waiting carriage. Hodgekiss held the carriage door open for her, and she clutched the package of material samples close to her to keep it dry as she climbed into the carriage. With a sigh of relief, she sank onto the soft leather seat and nestled her treasured package and the reticule containing payment for the two designs she'd just sold Madame Lamont.

The springtime weather had gone from a light mist to a torrential downpour since she'd entered the Black Boar Inn to meet with one of London's most famous dress designers. But that didn't matter. The inclement weather and the lateness of the hour made traveling even safer. The darkness cloaked her identity so she could secretly conduct her business without being discovered.

She closed her eyes and let her mind drift to all that had happened in the week since she'd first seen the Earl of Northcote standing at the entrance to the Stratmore ball. Her life had changed in ways she had never thought possible.

She fingered the large opal ring on her third finger, her only proof that the wedding had actually taken place. The stone felt unnatural and burdensome. Confining.

She tucked her hands into the folds of her gown. She didn't want to face the ugly truth about her marriage. She'd used her wealth to blackmail the earl into giving her his name. And because he was desperate for her money, he'd accepted what she offered, even though he had no intention of ever accepting her as his wife.

His aloofness after their wedding yesterday, plus the fact that he had yet to leave his third-floor sanctuary to seek her company, made his feelings perfectly clear.

Her husband obviously could not come to terms with the fact that he'd taken a deaf woman as his wife.

Jessica clenched her hand around her burgundy velvet reticule and thought of the two designs she'd sold tonight and the three new gowns she'd been commissioned to design. Her life would go on as it always had. She would have her designs and creations, freedom to attend the balls as she always had, opportunity to meet with Madame Lamont as she had tonight. And safety from her stepbrother.

Her heart skipped a beat. She would not let the knowledge that her husband wanted nothing to do with her matter. They would be two separate people sharing the space beneath the same roof, taking special care to avoid each other as much as possible, and being satisfied with maintaining a life that did not involve the other.

Jessica erased any hint of regret that threatened to surface and breathed in a healthy measure of resolve. She'd learned long ago not to expect anything more from life.

The carriage stopped in front of her new home, and Jessica gathered her packages, then ran beneath the umbrella Hodgekiss held for her until they reached the front door.

She removed her wet cloak and handed it to the servant, then stopped when Hodgekiss held out his arm.

Jessica turned her head toward him in confusion, then followed the wide-open, gaping alarm in his gaze as he looked upward toward the balcony.

Her husband glowered down on them, the ferocious glare in his eyes black and frightening. His face was pale, made even more ghostly by the faint glow of the candles in the chandelier. And a lock of dark hair fell across his forehead, making him appear even more dangerous. It was obvious he had just left his bed, and from his drawn features, he looked as if he needed to return there as soon as possible. Unfortunately, it was obvious he had other things on his mind.

She feared from the anger she saw in his eyes it would not take much incentive for him to storm down on them in a blaze of disapproving wrath.

"Where the hell have you been?"

Jessica knew he'd bellowed his question. His face turned a violent crimson, and the heavy sheen of perspiration covering his forehead was noticeable even from this far away.

"Where?" he demanded again.

"Out," she answered, irritated at his display of outrage.

"Do you have any idea what time it is?"

Jessica stared at him, the blood in her veins nearing the boiling point. The man had ignored her since he'd taken her as his wife, and now he interrogated her as if he had a right to care what she did. "Yes, my lord. It's a little past midnight."

"Who did you go to meet?"

Jessica thought quickly what she should say. She couldn't tell him the truth. He could never know of her meetings with Madame Lamont.

"Who was he?"

Jessica watched his white-knuckled grip tighten around the wooden railing. She could not believe he had asked her such a question. "He? I only wanted to go for a ride."

"At this hour?"

He swayed again and caught himself just before Jessica thought he might stumble over the railing.

"Yes. I do not go out during the day."

"Good God, woman. Are you insane, too?"

Jessica swallowed hard and fought the urge to rush up the stairs and slap him. "Perhaps, my lord. But your rough-hewn attitude and demanding inquisition allows little assurance concerning your own sanity, should I wish to question it."

She could see the tightening of the muscles in his jaw, and was thankful he was so far away from her.

"Don't you realize what could have happened to you? You are not safe out alone at this time of night."

Jessica stopped short. How dare he try to tell her what she could and could not do. "I'm perfectly capable of taking care of myself. I have done so for years."

"Bloody hell, wife. You are a fool." He took a deep breath, then swayed again. "You will not leave this house again without my permission. I forbid it. Is that clear?"

Jessica glared at him, unable to believe he had just made such a demand. She would not allow it. She could not. No one, not even her husband, was going to refuse to let her leave her home. She braced her shoulders and spoke her words with distinction and clarity. "Perfectly, my lord. Unfortunately, such a demand is not acceptable."

He slammed his fist against the wooden railing, and Jessica noticed Hodgekiss jump beside her.

"Hodgekiss, show your mistress to her room, and make sure she does not leave the house again tonight."

Jessica turned her face toward her butler just in time to see his lips form a very obedient, "Yes, my lord."

She looked back toward the balcony. He was not finished with his demands.

"Sanjay. Sanjay!"

The small, dark-skinned man, who had seen to her every need for the last two days, ran from the shadows and bowed twice, then waited for his instructions.

"I don't care if you have to lock her in her room. My wife is not to leave the house again without my permission. See to it."

"Yes, master," he answered.

Before Jessica had time to voice her objections, her husband dismissed her with a turn of his back. He walked across the open balcony, keeping his hand braced on the railing for support, then disappeared up the stairway that led to the third floor. Sanjay followed, reaching for his master once when he hesitated against the railing and again when Northcote's footsteps faltered on the first step, but he did not touch him.

Jessica noticed a look of concern on Sanjay's face, but he pulled back his hands when Northcote swayed and let him go the rest of the way unaided.

A few minutes later, Sanjay hurried down the stairs and rushed to one side of her. Hodgekiss stood on the other. Damn him!

Jessica stomped her foot on the floor and turned first to Simon's servant. "He will not lock me away," she fumed. "No one will tell me whether or not I can leave my own home. No one."

"The master does not want to lock you away, missy. He is only concerned for your safety."

"No, he isn't. He doesn't trust me."

"The master does not want anything to happen to you. That is all."

Sanjay backed toward the stairs, making sure she could see his face.

"Let me show you to your room, missy. Everything will be better in the morning."

Jessica grabbed the package of material samples from Sanjay's hands and stormed past him. She would go to bed. Not because she was following his orders, but because she was so angry and frustrated and tired that she was on the verge of saying something she would wish she could take back in the morning—like shouting out loud how much she regretted marrying the earl in front of his servant.

When she reached her bedroom, she slammed the door behind her as hard as she could. Even though she could not hear the loud noise when it closed, at least her husband could. He would know he'd made her angry.

Jessica readied herself for bed and crawled between the covers. She slammed her fist against the pillow, wishing his face was there.

She would not be a prisoner in her own home. He would not stop her from going where she wanted and meeting with whomever she wished.

She would not let him.

* * *

Jessica tossed and turned in her bed, trying to forget the scene earlier with Northcote. Who did he think he was, ordering her to stay in the house? She'd be damned if she'd allow him to make such demands. That wasn't the reason she'd married him. She only wanted his name, not his dominating hand controlling her.

She closed her eyes again, but knew it would do no good. With an exasperated sigh, she threw back the covers and gave up trying to sleep. Grabbing her robe, she crossed the room and walked out into the hall. Perhaps a glass of warm milk might help calm her nerves.

She could not dispel the uncomfortable realization that her marriage was not turning out at all the way she'd planned. Being confined in this house by her husband would not be much different than having her stepbrother lock her away in an asylum. She could not allow either to happen.

She lifted her taper high and stepped out into the open hallway that overlooked the large foyer below. An ornately sculptured chandelier, larger than any Jessica had ever seen, hung high above her from the center of the domed ceiling. Narrow slits of lead-paned glass, reminding her of lightning bolts, allowed the sun to brighten the room in the daytime and the stars to twinkle above her at night. The view tonight was magnificent.

Two matching staircases curved upward to the second floor, the stairway on the left continuing to a third floor, unused as far as she knew, except for her husband's rooms, since the staff stayed on the first floor behind the kitchen.

She looked up, then took several steps down the stairs, keeping a tight hold of her candle with one hand and a steadying grip on the sturdy oak banister with the other.

Before she reached the foyer below, a flickering candle outlined a moving shadow, and she stopped. She braced her shoulders and prepared for another round of heated words. Her husband needed to know she would not allow him to order her around like one of his servants. He needed to know from the start that she would live her life as she pleased.

Jessica stood her ground midstairs with unwavering determination, watching as the light grew brighter. The air left her chest in a rush when Sanjay walked into the open carrying a tray laden with several steaming mugs of hot liquid and a pitcher of water. Unaware that she was there, he muttered something as he climbed the stairs and Jessica stared at him, trying to make out some of the words. The few words she understood caused the breath to catch in her throat.

"Fever. Demon fever."

A part of her wanted to run. She knew what a fever could do. How it could destroy a person's life. The knot in the pit of her stomach slammed against her ribs, and she remembered the fevered flesh she'd touched when her fingers had brushed against her husband's hands. She closed her eyes and let the murky darkness pound against her ears. It was Simon's voice she heard. She shook her head, wishing away his silent cry for help.

Sanjay looked up as he climbed the stairs and came to an abrupt halt. The tray wobbled in his arms.

"Oh, missy," he said, clearly startled. "I did not know you were there. I was thinking of many other things."

Jessica couldn't hide the frown on her face. "Is that for your master?"

"Yes, missy."

"What is in the mugs, Sanjay?"

Sanjay's eyes darted from side to side as he searched for words. "The master needs something to warm him, missy. He is chilled."

She took one look at the mugs and basin of cool water. "He's sick, isn't he?"

"Nothing for you to worry, missy. Sanjay will take care of everything."

Jessica stared at Northcote's faithful servant as he shifted the tray in his hands. The worry was evident on his face.

"I must go now, missy. You go back to bed now. Sanjay will take care of the master."

Jessica watched Sanjay rush past her and go up the stairs that led to the third floor. A picture of Northcote's pale face, his trembling hands, his fevered flesh flashed before her, and another silent cry for help echoed in her head. It was his voice. His pain. She could hear it deep inside her. She didn't want to, but she wouldn't sleep until she knew what was wrong.

She cautiously made her way up the stairs, then down the hall until she came to a room with a faint glow beneath the door. Slowly, carefully, she lifted the latch and looked in. Sanjay sat on a small stool beside a bed, rinsing a cloth in the cool water he'd just brought up. Jessica knew without looking that the man tossing fitfully on the bed was her husband.

For a moment she couldn't move. She couldn't even breathe. As if Sanjay felt her presence, he turned around to face her.

"Oh, missy. You should not have come here. The master would not want you to see him like this."

Jessica stepped inside the room and shut the door. She closed the distance to where Sanjay sat and stared down at the man lying on the bed.

Every inch of his body was drenched in sweat, the streams of water running like raging rivers down his face and neck and soaking through the light sheet he kept pulling from his naked chest. A lock of thick hair lay plastered to his forehead while the dark hair on his arms and torso stuck to his flesh.

Back and forth he thrashed on the bed, flailing his arms, fighting the invisible demons Jessica remembered from her own fever. She took the cloth from Sanjay's hands and rinsed it in the cool water, then placed it on Northcote's burning forehead. She touched her hand against his cheek, then reached for his hand. "How long has he been like this?"

"He has been getting worse since he returned home yesterday."

"We should send for a doctor," she said, wondering why he hadn't said anything. "He's burning up."

"No, missy. The doctor can do no more than we can."

"How do you know? Has a doctor been to see the master?"

"Yes, missy. Many times."

Jessica rinsed the cloth again and laid it back on his forehead, then took another cool cloth and wiped the wetness from his exposed skin. "And there's nothing he can do?" She looked up, making sure she could see Sanjay's face when he answered.

Sanjay shook his head. "He has the malaria. Most all the time he is strong and can keep the fever away, but sometimes the demon spirits are too powerful and he cannot fight them."

"How long does the sickness last?"

"Three days. Maybe four. This time very bad."

Jessica touched her fingers to his cheek. He was so hot. So very hot. "What can we do for him?"

"We must make him drink plenty water, missy. Plenty, plenty. And the special liquid in this cup. He must drink it all."

"What is it?"

"The English doctor calls it quinine. He says it will make the master much better."

Jessica picked up the cup. "Help me."

Sanjay ran to the other side of the bed and raised Northcote's head. "The master would not want you to do this, missy."

"The master will never know. Besides, he's too sick to stop me."

"I think he will not like it."

"Don't worry about that. Just help me."

Sanjay held Simon's head, and when Jessica pushed on Northcote's chin, he opened his mouth and drank a little of the liquid. It took four more tries before the cup was empty. As soon as they lowered his head to the pillow, he reached for the cover and ripped it away. Sanjay caught it before it exposed the lower half of his body, but what Jessica saw was enough to take away her breath.

A large, ugly scar crossed his chest, from under his arm on one side to below his waist on the other. Sanjay tried to pull the cover back up to hide it from her, but Jessica put out her hand and stopped him.

"How did this happen?" she whispered, looking into Sanjay's face.

"It happened in India, missy. Long time ago. The master almost died from it. That is when he got his fever."

"But…how? Who did this to him?"

Sanjay pulled the cover back over the Earl of Northcote's chest and then looked at her. The expression on his face was unreadable. "I will let the master tell you when he is ready."

Jessica took another look, then turned to rinse another cloth.

She had just wiped the drops of sweat from his face when the chills began. Wild, violent shivers that wracked his body, causing the whole bed to tremble.

Jessica threw one after another of the heavy blankets Sanjay handed her over Northcote, tucking the edges as tightly as possible around his broad shoulders and long torso, beneath his narrow waist and hips and then down his muscled legs. She barely had one spot tucked in before he'd thrash about, ripping the covers from his body and pushing them to the floor.

Jessica sat at his side for what seemed an eternity, the endless hours running into each other.

The sun rose, then sank behind a wall of clouds. For all of one day and through the night of the next, she bathed him in cool, wet cloths when the fever drenched his body, then covered him with as many warm blankets as Sanjay handed her when the chills overtook him. While she battled to cool Northcote's fever and warm his chills, Sanjay struggled to keep his flailing arms from doing either of them any harm. Northcote repeatedly mumbled thoughts and fragmented sentences that, except for an isolated word here and there, Jessica could not begin to make out.

Not until the sun was high in the sky on the second day did Simon breathe a heavy sigh and fall into a peaceful sleep.

Jessica put her hand to his forehead and felt his cool flesh, then brought her fisted hand to her mouth to stop the cry of relief that wanted to soar from somewhere deep within her.

She stood at his bedside and wiped the lone tear that spilled down her cheek. Every inch of her body hurt, and she rolled her shoulders to ease the burning muscles across her back, then looked into Sanjay's emotion-filled eyes. "The fever has broken, Sanjay. I think the master will sleep now."

"The fever very bad this time, missy. I was much worried."

Jessica straightened the covers that lay across Northcote's chest, then looked up into the deep worry lines that covered Sanjay's face. "You need to rest, Sanjay. I'll sit with him while you get some sleep."

"I cannot let you, missy. The master would not like knowing that you have come to take care of him."

"The master will never find out. Besides, I would like to stay with him for a while. It is my place. If he shows any signs of waking, I will send for you immediately."

A slight smile covered Sanjay's face. "Very well, missy. You can sit with the master while I rest. I will not be long."

"And have Mrs. Graves prepare you something to eat."

"Yes, missy. Thank you, missy."

Sanjay made several low bows and then walked behind her. Jessica turned in her chair to follow him. "Who is Sarah, Sanjay?"

Jessica waited a long time for him to answer. "It is Sarai, missy."

"Was she someone the master knew in India?"

"Yes."

"Was the master fond of her?" she asked before she could stop herself.

"Yes, missy. The master was very fond of her."

"I see," Jessica whispered and then looked at the man sleeping peacefully on the bed. When Jessica turned back, she was alone in the room. Alone with the man she'd taken as her husband just three days ago. The man who, even weak as a kitten, caused her heart to pound in her chest and her flesh to tingle. The man who had loved and lost someone in India by the name of Sarai.

Jessica lowered her weary body to the chair beside his bed and studied his chiseled features. With trembling fingers she reached out and lifted the errant lock of hair that fell to his forehead. Then, with hesitant moves, she worked her way downward, across his high, angled cheekbones, over the thick, coarse stubble that prickled the soft pads of her fingers, then against the strong, rigid contours of his jaw.

Touching him caused a thousand fiery shooting stars to soar through her body, igniting a strange heat that swelled and burned deep in her stomach. Touching him while he slept caused a myriad of confusing sensations. She had never touched a man before. She could not believe the feel of his flesh against hers could cause such intense heat to spread to every part of her body.

Jessica lifted her hand from Simon's face, then moved it lower, to the dark wisps of hair that covered his chest. How many times had she stared at that bronzed triangle peeking out beneath his shirt, wanting to touch it? More than she cared to remember.

Several trembling breaths later, Jessica pressed her hand against his chest again. With deliberate caution, she slowly moved her fingers upward, resting the pads of her two fingers in the hollow of his neck, feeling the steady beating of his heart.

She lightly skimmed her hands across the hard lines of his shoulders and down the bulging muscles of his arms. He was beautiful to look upon. Her hand finally rested atop his hand lying flat on the covers.

She compared his dark skin to her pale flesh, then shifted her hand beneath his. Palm to palm, flesh to flesh, warmth radiating warmth. She twined her fingers within his and marveled at the feel of him. His mammoth grasp dwarfed her smaller one, and a strange and powerful strength seeped through her body. A strength she'd never felt before. A force she didn't want to be without.

He moved, tossing his head to the side, holding her hand in a crushing grip. "Sarai? Sarai! Oh Lord, no."

"Shh," she whispered in his ear, pressing her cheek against his face. "Everything's all right, Simon. Everything's fine."

He relaxed beneath her, his grip on her hand loosening, his harsh breathing slowing. For a little while, he was at peace.

Jessica bathed his face and chest again and then sat on the edge of the bed, her slippered feet tucked beneath her to keep them warm and Simon's hand nestled in her lap because she could not let go of him. She stared into the rigid contours of his face. He was indeed incredible. And asleep he did not seem nearly so angry with her. Not nearly so disappointed in her.

She brought his fingers to her mouth and pressed her lips to his flesh, remembering the one kiss they'd shared before.

"Cold…so…cold."

He shivered violently, and Jessica tucked the covers closer around him. She had to keep him warm. Jessica hesitated, then stretched out beside him and held his hand to her breast while he slept.

* * *

The sun was high in the sky when she opened her eyes. A heavy blue blanket had been draped across them both, and Simon's arm was wrapped around her shoulder holding her close. Her head rested upon his chest in a most unseemly fashion while her hand angled down over his bare stomach. The steady rise and fall of his chest soothed her entire body.

Jessica cautiously slid from the bed, making sure not to disturb him, then tucked the covers back around him. She placed her hand on his forehead and sighed with relief when she found it cool to her touch. When she turned, she saw Sanjay sitting in the corner, watching her. She put her finger to her lips and tiptoed to the door.

"I think he will be all right now, Sanjay."

"Missy very brave. Demon fever very strong this time. I am very glad you were not afraid. The master had much need of you. Even if he did not really know you were here."

"I must go," she said, facing the dark-skinned man. There was much understanding in his eyes—too much understanding. "Come for me if you need anything."

"Yes, missy. And for this time we will not let the master know you were here."

Jessica shook her head. "There is no need for him to know."

She took a deep breath and quickly went back to her room. She would never let Simon know she had seen his sickness. He was so proud; he would not want to know she'd seen him like that. Nor would he want to know she'd slept beside him and held him with such familiarity. That would be equally as embarrassing. For them both.

Chapter 9

❧

Jessica placed the light peach-patterned chiffon sample next to the willow-green silk and stood back. No. It still wasn't right. It needed more color.

She threw the material on a growing pile of discarded samples and reached for a scrap of emerald-green satin. After laying the fabrics next to each other, she stepped back to see the results. An unexpected burst of excitement raced through her body. Yes. Oh yes! The familiar rush of elation she felt whenever she completed that perfect design or found that perfect match made her want to dance around the room.

With quick steps she raced to her cluttered work desk and searched for a charcoal pencil. She shoved the design she'd been working onto the floor and began again. The dress was all wrong. The skirt too narrow and plain. It needed to be more elegant. More voluminous. She outlined the shape. Rounder. Fuller. At least three flounces. No, four. A foot deep, one layered atop the next.

Jessica drew the lines of each layer. Each flounce would be trimmed with yards of the loosely rolled peach chiffon hung in soft scallops and gathered at one-foot intervals. Each tuck would then be fastened with a large rosette made from the emerald-green satin and accented with deep maroon tufts around each flower.

The skirt alone would require at least one hundred and fifty of the smaller flowers, three inches in diameter. No, four. And the bodice...

Oh, the bodice. Jessica sketched the tiny waist made to look even smaller by the full gathers of the skirt, then drew the lines upward. The shoulders would be bare. A décolletage so low and daring it would turn every eye in the room. A covering of the loosely rolled peach chiffon would follow the top of the gown, barely concealing the rise of creamy flesh. And the center of the bodice would dip lower still.

A large emerald-green rosette would adorn the front of the gown, making the dip between the breasts a focal point that could not be ignored. A matching flower would be placed in the slight V at the waist and another in the back.

Jessica couldn't sketch the design fast enough. She showed each tuck and gather with the greatest precision and outlined each decorative rosette with infinite detail.

The Duchess of Hawthorn had commissioned a special gown to be designed for the queen's birthday celebration in June. Madame Lamont had given it to her when she'd been to see her five days ago. The same evening her husband had displayed his anger, then forbade her to ever leave the house without his permission.

The same night she'd cooled his fevered face and held his chilled body close to hers.

Jessica breathed a sigh and then sat back in her chair. Her gaze fell to the note on the floor, and she went to open the door. "Good morning, Martha."

"Good afternoon, my lady. I'm afraid you've worked much longer than you thought. It's already the middle of the day."

"Oh." Jessica looked at the sun, far past its noontime place high in the sky. "It's almost finished," she said, holding out the design. "What do you think?"

Jessica waited while Martha perused the gown. She saw her servant's eyes widen and her brows rise. And then Martha beamed a broad smile.

"Oh, mistress. It's beautiful. And with the duchess's dark skin and golden hair it will be breathtaking."

"It is pretty, isn't it?" Jessica held the paper in her hands and looked at it once more. For a moment, she wondered what it might be like to be able to put on a gown this lovely and swirl around a ballroom in the arms of someone special. To be able to hear the music and the soft sighs of admiration when she walked into a room. To have every pair of eyes focus on her with a smile on their faces instead of a frown and a hushed comment no one realized she understood.

As soon as the thought materialized, Jessica dismissed it. She hadn't had these foolish dreams since she'd been young. Before she realized how much her deafness would change her life. She couldn't imagine why she was having them now.

"Perhaps you can bring me a tray, Martha. I still need to make a few adjustments to the sleeves."

"Begging your pardon, my lady, but the master is waiting for you in his study."

"The master? Lord Northcote?"

Martha's lips lifted to form a shy smile. "Yes, my lady."

"Did he say what he wanted?"

"No, my lady. He only asked that you join him in his study at your earliest convenience."

Jessica tried to look relaxed. "Thank you, Martha." She tried to pretend that being summoned to her husband's side for the first time since her marriage did not alarm her. "Tell Lord Northcote I will be right down."

"Yes, my lady."

Martha opened the door and left Jessica alone with her thoughts. She took a deep breath and stood, then smoothed the gathers of her green-and-white striped day dress, taking special care to tuck under the worn edges on the cuffs of her sleeves. How she wished she'd put on her navy gown, but it was too late now.

After she washed the charcoal smudges from her fingers, she patted the chignon at the back of her neck to make sure most of her hair was still in place. Only a few uncontrollable wisps outlined her face, but there was nothing she could do about that now. With a nervousness that surprised her, she walked down the stairs until she reached the study.

The door was open. Her husband stood with his back to her, his arms braced on either side of the large mullioned window. Thick, dark hair fell in deep waves just below the top of his collar at the back.

Jessica knew what it felt like to rake her fingers through his hair and push it back from his face. She also knew when he turned around there would be one errant lock that rested on his furrowed brow.

He wore no jacket. Nothing but a snow-white, loose-fitting lawn shirt that contrasted sharply with his bronzed skin, and black breeches that hugged his muscled thighs much too tightly by far. Dear God. She knew the disturbing feel of his taut, muscled flesh. An uncomfortable heat warmed her cheeks.

She hadn't moved a muscle, but as if he sensed her presence, he turned. Their gazes locked.

His face was close shaven, displaying his handsome features just as she remembered them. His skin still seemed slightly pale, and the haunted look in his eyes gave her cause for concern, but that same familiar air of command she'd struggled against since she'd first met him was as strong as ever.

Despite her promise to remain relaxed and poised, she fidgeted nervously. She thought she'd rehearsed the way she would act and the words she would speak when they had their first conversation, but she wasn't prepared for the expression on his face or the look in his eyes. All her well-laid plans flew out the window and were replaced with a gust of warm spring air.

With a forceful show of control, she cleared her throat. "You wanted to see me?"

He didn't take his eyes from her, and the evaluative look on his face studied her with more intensity than she could hold up under. He braced his hands behind his back, focusing his dark gaze on her, and she did not have to wonder what he thought. It was obvious from the look he gave her faded gown and disheveled hair. Her plain, high-necked day dress, noticeably out of fashion and frayed around the cuffs, suddenly seemed even worse for wear.

"Won't you sit down," he said, pointing to a chair facing the large oak desk where he'd met her that first night.

He took a step toward her but stopped when she pulled back. This was the room where she'd first met him, where she'd kissed him that first time.

Her cheeks grew hot when she remembered how he'd taken her in his arms and kissed her at this very spot. A wave of heat burned a path through her body. When she looked back at him, she knew from the deeper frown on his face he remembered it, too. She couldn't sit there. She slowly walked to another chair on the other side of the desk and sat. He smiled, then walked around the desk and sat down.

"I must first apologize for neglecting you so," he said, leaning back in his chair. "I regret you have had to accustom yourself to your new home alone, but my absence was unavoidable."

"It's not necessary for you to explain your whereabouts to me."

His eyebrows shot upward in an accusatory arch. "Just as you thought it was not necessary to explain your whereabouts to me the other night?"

She lifted her chin in defiance. "I did not think you would care."

The look on his face didn't hide his bewilderment. "You didn't think I would care that you were out, alone, after midnight?"

"There was no reason why I thought you might." Jessica lifted her shoulders and sat straighter.

"I see."

She cleared her throat. "It's no secret that we have entered into a marriage of convenience. We are both mature adults and know to expect nothing idealistic from our union. Your comings and goings are totally unrelated to me, as mine are totally unrelated to you. I therefore think it's best to take care of all the unpleasant details right now."

"And what details would those be, wife?"

"Schedules. Routines. Habits. Small details so we can best share the same house without inconveniencing each other in the extreme."

His lips thinned. "Are you suggesting we make a schedule to avoid each other?"

"I'm only suggesting that we do whatever is necessary to complicate our lives as little as possible." She looked at his tightly clenched fists resting on top of the desk and the firm set of his jaw, and couldn't help the feeling of dread that washed over her. "Does this upset you? I thought you would approve of my idea."

"Approve? Why would you think I would approve?"

"Because you've made it perfectly clear that you do not wish to have an association with me. We are both used to living our separate lives, and I see no reason to let anything change just because we are man and wife. Our marriage is, after all, little more than a business agreement."

He slid his chair back with a surprising amount of force and shot to his feet. He placed his hands palm-down on the top of the desk. "It may be nothing more than a business arrangement to you," he said, leaning forward, "but taking you for my wife was no little matter where I was concerned. We may never learn to care for each other in an intimate way, but you are the Countess of Northcote, and..."

He pushed himself away from her and paced before the window. She didn't know what he was saying.

"...Do you understand?" he finished.

Her cheeks burned. "Excuse me, my lord, but unless you face me when you speak, I don't know what you're saying."

He closed his eyes and dropped his chin to his chest. "Forgive me," he said, facing her once more. "It will take me time to remember."

He swallowed and began again. "I suggest we give our marriage a few days before we start making rules, wife. Perhaps we'll find we're perfectly suited to living together without any preconceived restrictions."

Her gaze fell to the floor, and when she looked up he was before her.

"Martha tells me you've missed your noon meal. What were you doing that occupied so much of your time that you forgot to eat?"

She swallowed hard. "I…I was…looking at material for a new gown."

His gaze flew to her frayed collar and cuffs. "Good. From the looks of what I've seen of your gowns thus far, you are in dire need of a new wardrobe."

Jessica's cheeks burned even warmer as she worried her lower lip.

"I stopped by your rooms on my way down but you were not there. I thought perhaps you had gone out."

She shook her head. "I do not go out in the daytime."

"So I seem to remember." He clasped his hands behind his back and lifted his shoulders. "Then it's time we change that habit. I will give you time to eat a light lunch, and after you change into something more suitable, we will go for a ride."

"A ride?"

"Yes. A ride in the park. In a carriage. The two of us."

Something frightening and uncontrollable flashed like a brilliant light behind her eyes. She knew it was raw fear. She shook her head, then lifted her chin defiantly. "No. I prefer to stay here."

Jessica clasped onto a fold of her green-and-white skirt and twisted. "If you'd like to go for a ride, I'll tell Hodgekiss to have the carriage sent round—"

"You misunderstand me. I wish for both of us to go for a ride together."

She did not lower her gaze. "I'm sorry, my lord, but I'm not accustomed to going out in the afternoon."

"Then it's a custom we will have to change." He jabbed his hands in the pockets of his breeches, displaying a growing irritation she couldn't miss.

Jessica took a step closer and held her ground. "No. I do not go out in public. Besides, we cannot go for a ride now. It's the peak hour for all of society to be out. There is no telling who we will meet."

A wide grin of satisfaction covered his face. "I know exactly who we will meet. The cream of society's elite, some of her most influential members. It's time they were introduced to the Countess of Northcote."

"I cannot!"

He leaned closer toward her. "You will. You cannot hide away forever, wife. You are now the Countess of Northcote, and I have decided it's time you played the role."

"But society will find out I'm deaf."

Simon frowned. "Why do you insist on making your deafness such an issue?" he said, glaring at her.

"Because it is."

"Only to you."

Jessica slapped her fist against her thigh and let her words carry the fury she felt. "You will wish you had not desired to put me on display once society discovers my deafness. There will be no end to your regret when I am shunned and you are ridiculed for marrying someone who will never hear the sound of your voice."

He brushed her fears away with a wave of his hand. "They will not find out yet. You are much too clever."

"And you are much too foolish."

He bowed in acquiescence and opened his face to a wide grin. "Foolish to a fault, my lady. I have a wife I swore I would never have. It's only fitting that you take a ride you swore you would never take."

He stepped around his desk and held out his hand to lead her from the room. She ignored his offered arm and walked ahead on her own. When she reached the doorway, she turned to face him. "You will not always have your way, my lord," she warned, trying to control the fear threatening to suffocate her. "The day will come when you will wish you had listened to my words."

"I consider myself duly warned, my lady."

She turned away from him, unable to battle his fierce opposition any longer.

When they reached the dining room, he gave Sanjay more orders. "Have Mrs. Graves prepare a cold platter, then have Mrs. Franklin pick out something festive for the mistress to wear."

"Yes, master," Sanjay answered with a broad grin on his face. "Right away, master."

He waited until they were alone, then turned and touched a hand to her chin. "Trust me, Jessica. I've taken a vow to protect you, and I swear you will always be safe with me."

Jessica was so frightened she could not find any relief in his words. "You will fare no better than I the day society finds out that you've married a deaf woman. You'll be ridiculed and taunted and—"

He grabbed her firmly by the shoulders. "Stop it. You think I care one bloody whit what society thinks of me? It's you who should be concerned, wife. Society thinks you have married a murderer."

She held his gaze. "Society is always eager to believe the worst."

"And you don't?" He held up his hand to halt her answer. "Never mind," he interrupted before she could say more. He pulled out a chair from the table. "Sit down. We will at least face the lions on a full stomach."

Jessica sat at the table and took a swallow of the wine sitting at her plate. She could tell from his words he'd be damned if he'd let anything stop him from getting what he wanted. Including the fears he saw on her face. She knew she didn't stand a chance. The knot inside her stomach twisted harder. Society at its best could destroy them both and not care a whit what they had done.

Though he'd sworn he would not let anything happen to her, even the ferocious Earl of Northcote would not be able to stop society once they turned against them.

Chapter 10

❧

*J*essica sat regal and straight on the seat of the open carriage, holding her look of controlled resignation until she thought her face would break. Damn him. She'd taken every care to keep her deafness hidden from the *ton*, and in a few short minutes, the man she'd married for protection was going to ruin everything.

He beamed as if he didn't have a care in the world, and Jessica inwardly fumed at the risk he was willing to take with her future.

She looked at the smile on his face and fought to control her temper. She wasn't aware that he even knew how to smile. He'd certainly never shown her he could before. He'd done nothing but scowl and frown and glare at her from the minute she'd met him. Now he wore a heart-stopping grin as if it were a part of his true nature.

She stared at their liveried driver's back rather than at the unending line of carriages and phaetons and landaus traveling over the smooth paths of Hyde Park. Didn't he know they were bound to pass by someone who would want to stop to talk?

Icy fingers touched deep inside her.

She wanted to be away from here. She wanted to be where it was safe. "I was thinking, perhaps we should go back now. There is a bit of a chill in the air."

His grin widened. "It's a glorious spring day, my lady. Hardly cool enough for even a shawl."

She looked up at him hopefully. "Perhaps tomorrow will be warmer?"

"Perhaps." Without warning he reached for her hand and looped it through his arm, pulling her closer to him. "Until then, you will just have to rely on me to keep you warm."

The blood roared in her head. She'd never been held like this by a man before. "This is hardly proper, my lord. Whatever will people think if they see us?"

He touched the back of his fingers to her cheek. "They will think we are newly married and cannot stand to be separated."

He blessed her with a grin Jessica was sure tilted the earth on its axis, then lowered his head and loomed over her until he was much too close for her to even think. If only he would not look at her like he did.

"They will think our marriage is a love match, and that we've each found the perfect partner."

He lifted his hand and cupped her cheek in his palm. Her face burned like it was on fire. She couldn't breathe. He'd stolen all the air in London.

"And they'll think we're so contented with each other we hardly know the rest of the world even exists."

He traced his thumb against her lips while his gaze locked with hers, refusing to release her from his spell.

He tilted her head slightly, bringing her lips closer, then stopped. He slowly raised his gaze to a spot just behind her left shoulder and lifted his brows. Jessica stared at his lips, waiting to feel the warm pressure against her mouth. Praying he would kiss her and terrified he would not.

"Good day, Covingsworth."

Jessica saw Simon's mouth move to say the words, but could not comprehend what they meant until he leaned back, lifting himself away from her. She turned her head to the left and saw the Marquess and Marchioness of Covingsworth riding next to them in their carriage. The grins on their faces said they knew exactly what Simon had been about to do. Jessica wished to die.

"Allow me to introduce my wife," Simon said, sliding his arm around Jessica's shoulder.

Simon made the introductions as effortlessly as he did everything else, and it was more than she could do to watch the words being spoken so she could answer at the appropriate time.

"It is a pleasure to meet you, my lady," the marquess said, and the look on his face was genuine. "I can't tell you what an honor it is to make your acquaintance."

"Thank you," Jessica answered, sure her face was a brilliant red. She wanted to die of mortification. She'd almost allowed Simon to kiss her in the middle of Hyde Park in broad daylight, and two of society's most influential members had seen them. Her head pounded. Heaven only knows what else she would have let Simon do if the marquess and marchioness had not arrived. Jessica berated herself again for her weakness.

The marchioness leaned forward and graced Jessica with the most contagious smile she had ever seen. "Congratulations, Lady Northcote. Your husband and mine have always been close friends, and I know you and I will soon be able to boast the same closeness."

"Thank you, Lady Covingsworth," Jessica said, moved that Simon's friends wanted to include her so easily. Or would until they found out about her impairment.

"I've been wanting to welcome you back, Simon," the marquess said, and Jessica watched his lips. "It's time you returned."

"Yes. I've stayed away long enough."

"If there's anything I can do, don't hesitate to ask."

"I appreciate the offer, Covey."

"That's what friends are for." The two men exchanged knowing glances, and then the marquess sat back in his seat. "And I can't tell you how pleased I was to hear you'd married. How fortunate for you. Your wife is enchanting." He looked at her and smiled.

"Thank you, my lord," Jessica answered, knowing her face was even redder than before. She wasn't used to receiving such open compliments. No one had dared to even speak to her until today. Until Simon had taken her into the public and forced her to become a part of his world.

"I am very fortunate," Simon answered. "I've found the most amazing woman in all of London. If I'd known she was here all this time, I would have rushed to come back sooner."

Simon reached for her hand. When he twined his fingers through hers, a raging heat surged throughout her body. Even though Jessica had no choice but to focus her gaze on what was being said, all she wanted to do was lower her eyes and slink away in confusion. How could he distract her so easily? What would happen if she were ever alone with him? She didn't even want to think of it.

"Well, I can see this is not the most opportune time to keep you, Northcote," the marquess said, lifting his lips in a knowing smile, "but I didn't want to miss this chance to welcome you home. I will be in touch shortly."

The marchioness leaned forward in her seat and smiled openly. "We are hosting a small gathering next week, Lady Northcote. Perhaps you and your husband will honor us with your presence?"

"I—" Jessica's eyes darted to her husband. She expected him to make their excuses. His words shocked her.

"We would be honored, Lady Covingsworth. Thank you."

"Until next week then." The marquess gave them a parting nod, then motioned to his driver.

Jessica watched the marquess's carriage move away, wishing to have them return so she could refuse their offer. She gave her husband a look of disbelief, but the expression on his face reflected none of her doubts or fears. "Do you realize what you have just done?"

He raised his brows in a most disconcerting manner. "I had a quick conversation with a dear friend, then said good-bye so we could be alone again. Now, where were we? Oh yes." He leaned closer and turned his body inward until he was as near as before.

Jessica pushed him away with a hard shove. Damn him. He was taking too many risks. She couldn't do it. "I do not attend small gatherings. I do not go where people expect me to talk to them. I do not—"

"Did you know," he said, lifting her hand from her lap and twining his fingers through hers, "your hair is the most amazing color I have ever seen. It's not brown, yet it is not quite black, either. In the sunlight it shimmers in a kaleidoscope of remarkable shades. It's like burnished brass mixed with deep chocolate and…"

"It's the same color as charred grass after a fire," she said, fighting the effect of his warm flesh holding her hand. Why did being near him cause such turmoil inside her?

"Hardly, my lady. Hardly charred grass."

"Listen to me, my lord. We cannot attend the Covingsworth affair. You must—"

"I wonder what it would look like loose and flowing across your shoulders. Or in soft curls around your face. I've only seen it in that silly knot at the back of your neck."

He touched her hair. Jessica lifted her hands to keep him from removing the pins. "Simon, don't. We must come up with a suitable excuse so that—"

"And your eyes. At first I thought they were brown, but they are not. They're the most unusual shade of gold I have ever seen. Like the riches of Egypt. Deep and gold and—"

"Now you are being ridiculous. My eyes are the most common shade in the world. You're not listening. I will not allow you to ruin my life. I cannot attend…"

"And your lips…"

His gaze dropped to her mouth. She couldn't breathe. Not with his hand holding hers, and his face so close, and his lips nearly touching her. Dear God. She was letting him affect her again. "Simon, I…I think I would like to go home now."

His gaze didn't leave her face. "You have the most enticing mouth I have ever seen. So full and lush and…"

"That is absurd. You could just as easily be describing a cow standing in the field, my lord."

Simon lifted his mouth in a smile so open and innocent even his eyes crinkled at the corners. "I have never had the urge to kiss a cow, my lady."

The air caught in her throat, and Jessica laughed. It was the first time in days—no, weeks—she'd found something funny to laugh at. And she didn't want to stop. She found his remark so hilarious, even a tear trickled from her eye.

"I would not want to imagine you kissing a cow, either, my lord," she said, stifling another giggle. "I'm sure you would not find it at all to your liking."

His expression changed in the blink of an eye, and she studied him more closely. "What is it, Simon? Is something wrong?"

There was surprise in his expression mixed with a degree of regret, and she wondered what she'd said or done to bring about such a marked change. She must have said or done something to cause such remorse.

He cupped her face with his hand, then wiped away the wetness from her cheek with his thumb. A frown furrowed his brow, and his gaze did not leave hers. There was such tenderness in his actions, such exposed sensitivity in his touch, Jessica feared for him.

"What's wrong, Simon? Have I said or done something to offend you?"

He shook his head. "Far from it. You've given me something I can never return to you—the sound of your laughter. I would give the world to be able to describe the sound to you. Of all the things I wish for you, it would be that you could hear the pure elation in it."

She turned her face away from him. This was not the way she wanted him to be. She could battle his gruffness, she could challenge his temper, but it was impossible to be unaffected by such kindness. Didn't he know what he was doing to her? He was forcing her to go out in public where her disability would eventually be discovered. He was forcing her to leave her world of seclusion and safety. He was making her wish for things that were impossible to have.

He touched her chin and turned her face toward him. "Jessica, I didn't mean—"

"Please, don't. I learned long ago it did no good to wish for things that could never be."

She tried to separate herself from him, but he wouldn't let her move away. Instead he held her close and brushed his fingers along the side of her face.

Why was he doing this to her? Why did he pretend he cared? She knew he couldn't keep up the pretense for long. It was only a matter of time until her deafness became too great an embarrassment to him. It was only a matter of time before he would no longer wish to be seen with her, when he would want to keep her hidden so people wouldn't find out about her deafness. Just as her father had.

"Are there birds singing today, Simon?"

He stopped to listen. "Yes, there are birds singing."

"That's what I would wish to hear first," she said, looking into the trees, knowing the sound came from above.

Then she lifted her face toward the sun. It had been so long since she'd been anywhere other than just her garden in the daylight. It was suddenly as if she couldn't take in enough of what was there. And yet…She didn't know if she was strong enough to live with the consequences if she failed. Every experience was another risk Simon intended her to take.

He squeezed her fingers gently, and she turned to him. She'd become used to the pressure on her hand when he wanted her to look at him.

"See, Jesse, you have to admit the outside is not as bad as you feared. There is a whole world waiting for you, and I will be here to—"

Simon's words stopped, his gaze focusing on a spot far away. His body stiffened, every muscle as tense as an archer's bow, coiled to strike. The expression on his face hardened, his look determined and unyielding.

"Driver, turn here," he ordered, and the carriage took a sharp turn to the right.

Jessica looked ahead and saw a carriage coming toward them. "Who is it, Simon?"

Simon spoke without looking at her, and although Jessica could see his lips to read what he'd said, she knew he was more interested in the approaching carriage than in her.

"Something is wrong, Simon. What is it?"

"Nothing is wrong. I would like to see a smile on your face, though."

Jessica lifted her lips in an upward curve that seemed stilted even to her.

He glanced at her, his look distant and changed. "That is a pathetic smile, wife," he said, touching one corner of her mouth. His touch was tender. The look in his eyes was not. "Perhaps you would care to practice a bit before we greet the Earl and Countess of Milebanke." Simon indicated the approaching carriage with a nod of his head. "They will no doubt want to visit with us and extend their congratulations."

Jessica's heart leaped to her throat. The Countess of Milebanke was the last person she wanted to see today. "Surely you don't intend to stop?"

Simon's lips curved in an even more sardonic smile as he leveled a hostile gaze straight ahead. "Of course we must stop. Unless Lady Milebanke has changed while I've been gone, she's one of the biggest gossips in all of London. To ignore her would be unthinkable."

"Simon, no. You don't know what she's like. She has a reputation for being brash and cruel. If she even suspects that I am—"

"She will suspect nothing, wife, except that you are the most beautiful woman in all of London and wonder how I was lucky enough to convince you to marry me."

"Simon…"

Jessica watched the shiny curricle come toward them pulled by a pair of matching blacks, and a knot tightened in her stomach.

"Smile, Jesse. I promise you'll be safe."

He cradled her hand securely, then turned his concentrated gaze on the two people in the carriage stopping beside them. "Good afternoon, Milebanke. Lady Milebanke."

Jessica wondered if the sound of his voice was as volatile as the glare in his eyes. He leaned back in the seat and looped her arm through his in a secure and possessive grasp. On the outside, he looked as if he did not have a care in the world, as if there was not the slightest possibility that his wife's disability might be found out. Jessica fought the rise of panic in her chest. Sitting close to him, she could feel the tension that seemed ready to snap.

"Good afternoon, Northcote," the earl said, glancing around uncomfortably, as if he wasn't sure he wanted to be seen with the tainted Earl of Northcote. "I hear congratulations are in order."

"Yes," Simon answered, turning toward Jessica. "May I present my wife, Lady Northcote. Jessica, Lord and Lady Milebanke."

"How do you do, Lord Milebanke. Lady Milebanke."

"Our best wishes to you, Lady Northcote," Milebanke said. "You cannot imagine our surprise when we heard Northcote had taken himself a wife."

Jessica reminded herself to smile. "I'm sure our marriage took most of London by surprise, my lord. The looks we've received today confirm it."

The countess leveled Simon a most derisive glare, then lifted her lips, her smile as venomous as the kiss of death. It was obvious to Jessica that all the players except she knew the rules to the game they were playing. At that moment she was as angry with Simon as she'd ever been.

Lady Milebanke turned her attention back to Simon. "Although most of your peers understand your...rush to take a wife, my lord, none of us were even aware you and the lady were acquainted."

"Then I feel complimented," Simon said, patting the hand that rested on his arm. "You cannot imagine how gratifying it is to know I was able to court my wife in private without all of society wagering on the outcome at White's. I consider discretion of the utmost importance."

Lady Milebanke snapped open the delicate lace fan in her hand and thoughtfully fingered the intricate design. "Some thought that when you returned, you would look to more familiar quarters for a wife." A forced smile lifted the corners of her mouth. "You surprised us all. Especially your dear stepmother. She is extremely interested in your happiness, as you know."

The countess's eyes glazed cold and taunting, even hateful, and Jessica felt Simon's muscles tighten beneath her hand.

"I doubt my...*stepmother* has ever been interested in anyone's happiness except her own. You forget, no one knows her better than I."

The countess looked adequately shocked by Simon's words, as did Jessica. Even the earl shifted uncomfortably in his seat before filling the gap in the conversation with inoffensive trivia.

"Since you and your new bride are out and about, may we assume you are ready to make the social rounds?"

"You may," Simon answered. "We have already accepted an invitation for next week."

"Excellent. We are hosting a ball this Friday evening," the earl commented. "Perhaps you and your wife would care to attend?"

Jessica watched Lady Milebanke bristle with discomfort. Her words confirmed it.

"I'm sure it is far too soon for Lady Northcote to feel comfortable in public. Perhaps—"

Simon held up his hand. "Nonsense. We wouldn't miss it for the world."

"Perfect," the earl answered, oblivious to his wife's irritation. "I demand a dance, my lady," he said, smiling at Jessica. "I am especially fond of the waltz."

"As is my wife," Simon encouraged. "She will look forward to the evening. And the dance."

"Good. Good. Well, congratulations again, Lady Northcote," Milebanke said, issuing the order for his driver to go.

Jessica kept the smile on her face and her eyes focused on the unfriendly glare on Lady Milebanke's face until the couple was out of sight.

With a decided jerk, she faced her husband with enough anger to start a war. She attempted to speak, but couldn't at first. Her whole body was numb with terror. What had he done to her?

In the span of a few short hours, he'd disrupted her life more than she could handle. He had charmed her, cajoled her, and said words that left her dizzy with wanting. The minute she let down her guard, he turned on her with lightning speed, putting her in situations he knew she could not handle.

A lump formed deep in her throat. He'd used her. She knew it now as blatantly as if he admitted it. That was why they were here. That was why he'd taken her out for a ride. He'd used her to gain an invitation to Lady Milebanke's ball without a care one way or another if she would suffer in the end. He only cared that he got what he wanted.

She slid as far away from him as she could, the smug grin on his face painful to see. "I would like to go home now."

"Yes. We can go now."

Jessica refused to drop her gaze from his face. The look in his eyes revealed more than she'd seen before. It was determined and possessive and ruthless. A man obsessed, and nothing would stop him. Especially a woman. Even his wife.

"I hope you are satisfied, my lord."

He leaned back in his seat, the vengeful look on his face obvious. "Yes, wife. I am very satisfied."

Chapter 11

❦

Jessica paced her bedroom and let her anger heighten to the boiling point. How could Simon display her so to the public? How could he risk her meeting his peers where someone would find out what she'd been keeping secret since she was a child? How could he expect her to play the role of his wife when they both knew she was not? How typically arrogant of him.

Jessica pulled her wrapper closer around her shoulders and paced from one side of the room to the other another time. Why on earth was he forcing her do this? Didn't he know she could never become involved in society? Didn't he know she only ever attended a ball for a very brief time, then left? Didn't he realize that while she was there she never spoke to anyone except Mel?

Heaven help her. He expected her to dance a waltz with the Earl of Milebanke.

Jessica fisted her hands at her sides and marched the length of the room. She couldn't do it. She *wouldn't* do it. She wanted to be left alone with her creations and her designs. She didn't care what he said or how angry he became, she would not allow him to take such control of her life.

The taper on the bedside stand flickered, and her hands shook as she lit another candle to replace it. She needed light. Lots of light. It was bad enough she couldn't hear. She couldn't abide not being able to see either. She lit another candle and thought about the ball he expected her to attend.

If she went, she would go as she always had. Alone. She would sit off to the side and wait for the women who wore her creations to arrive. Then she would go home. Let society think what they wished. Let her husband say what he would. If he were here right now she would…

But he was not here.

Simon had not come to her bed again tonight.

Jessica picked up a pillow and hugged it to her breast. She tried not to let his absence bother her, but it hurt to know he did not want her. It hurt even more to know she cared.

Why couldn't he have stayed distant and unapproachable? Instead, he'd showed her a different side to his personality this afternoon. He'd been charming and witty and irresistible. He'd stirred a thousand emotions inside her she thought no one would ever make her feel. The way he looked at her, talked to her, and held her close to him caused an ache she could not explain.

She hadn't glimpsed that side of him again after they came back from their ride this afternoon. Even though he'd held her hand so possessively and smiled at her with such affection while they were in public, his endearments had all been for show, to dupe all of society into thinking he cared for his new wife.

He went to his study immediately after they returned home, with a package that had come from Ira. For the rest of the day he'd closeted himself with the papers, coming out only to eat. He stayed at the dining table long enough to be polite, then shut himself away with his papers again. For all she knew, he was still downstairs.

Well, let him stay there. She wanted nothing to do with him. He could rot down there for all she cared.

He'd done nothing but issue orders and make decisions for her since he'd recovered from his illness. *He* had decided they'd go for a ride in the park. *He* had decided they'd attend the Covingsworths' dinner party. *He* had decided they'd go to the Milebankes' ball Friday night.

He had made every decision, but she was the one who would have to take all the risks. Well, she would see about that.

Jessica wadded the pillow in her arms and threw it across the room. She missed the bed by a yard but hit a gilt-framed painting on the wall—a very ornate, expensive-looking painting. The picture fell to the floor, the frame splintering into fragmented pieces. Jessica covered her mouth with her fist and stifled a groan. What had she done?

She stared at the shattered pieces. This was all his fault. Oh, how she wished the pillow had hit her husband instead of the beautiful painting. He deserved it. He was the one who'd created such chaos in her life.

Jessica rushed over to the painting, bent down, and touched the splintered pieces lying on the floor. The canvas itself was still in one piece, but the frame wasn't. Maybe it wasn't a valuable painting. Maybe he would never notice she'd ruined it.

She had to pick up the pieces. She rose to find something in which to put the shattered frame and stopped.

Her husband stood in the open doorway with his arms folded across his chest and one booted foot crossed over the other. His shoulder rested against the doorframe, his tall, massive figure blocking the entrance in a casual pose.

"I…" She swallowed past the lump in her throat. "I… it broke."

"So I see."

He pushed himself away from the doorway and took several calculated steps across the room until he stood beside her, staring down at the broken picture frame.

He slowly turned his head until he faced her. "You disliked the painting that much?"

She gasped. "No. It was very beautiful, but…"

He tilted his head to the side to get a better view of the skewed piece of canvas and then returned his gaze to her. "Did you really think it was beautiful?"

"Well, perhaps not beautiful, but it was a nice painting."

"I suppose so. I'm afraid I had never really noticed before." He picked up the limp canvas and looked at it. Then looked at her. "Perhaps it was only because my grandmother painted it that I never evaluated it too critically."

A tiny gasp escaped her mouth. "Oh," she moaned. "Your grandmother." Jessica knelt down and picked up a few of the larger pieces of the frame. She handed them to him with the greatest care. "I didn't mean to break it. Truly. It just…happened."

He laid the pieces on a nearby table and leaned down to pick up the crumpled pillow. He held it out to her. "Is this what caused the accident?"

She swallowed. "Yes."

"Can I assume that if it was not the painting you were trying to break, then there was something else you intended to hit? Something that upset you?"

Jessica turned her face away from him. This was all his fault. If he had not insisted she go for a ride in the park, then they would not have met the Milebankes. And if she had not met the Milebankes, then she would not be expected to go to a ball Friday night.

Every muscle in her body stiffened when he placed his finger beneath her chin and turned her gaze back to him.

"Could it be you were thinking about *someone* when you threw the pillow? Someone in particular?"

His dark eyebrows arched high, and the tilt to his head said he was waiting for her answer.

Jessica folded her arms across her middle and stepped away from him.

He was too close. Every place he touched tingled and grew warm. Every time she stood so close to him, a thousand butterflies fluttered in her stomach. She had to get away. She had to put a halt to these feelings before it was too late.

"Has something upset you, Jessica?"

She took a deep breath. Of course she was upset. Did he think she was the type who threw things for no apparent reason? What kind of woman did he think he'd married? "You ask me that after what happened today?" She twisted away from him and paced the length of the room. She stopped and looked him straight in the eyes. "I am angry."

"Why?"

"Why?" She couldn't believe it. He didn't even realize what he was doing to her. How unreasonable he was. What he expected of her. The risks he expected her to take. "Since the moment I met you, you have done nothing but turn my life inside out."

"And how have I done that?"

He walked across the room and closed the door. Her heart skipped a beat. "Why did you close the door?"

He came closer, standing before her so she couldn't miss one word. "Because you are screaming like a harpy, wife, and I do not care to have the servants hear our conversation, let alone every neighbor on Old Cherry Lane."

Jessica pursed her mouth shut and stomped her bare foot. How dare he! "I doubt very much if I'm screaming like a harpy, *husband*, and if I am, you deserve it."

He leaned against the tall bedpost and stared at her. He looked so casual and relaxed she wanted to hit him.

"Would you mind explaining why I deserve to be the object of your tirade?" he said.

"Because of everything you have done today."

"And that would be?"

"First, you insisted I go for a ride."

"Which I thought turned out to be a very pleasant experience."

She rolled her eyes. "Then, you deliberately risked both our futures by stopping to talk to the Marquess and Marchioness of Covingsworth."

"Which I thought went very well."

"But you didn't know it would when you stopped."

"Didn't I?"

Jessica glared at the smug expression on his face. He was so sure of himself. "Next, you used me to get an invitation to a ball Friday evening, even though you know I cannot go."

"I know no such thing, Jessica."

"You cannot make me, Simon. I'm not ready to take that chance."

"You will be fine. I promise I will not leave your side for one moment."

Jessica slammed her fists against her hips and took a confrontational step closer. "You promise not to leave my side?" She gave a harsh laugh. "I can't wait to see that, Simon. I'm sure the Earl of Milebanke will enjoy dancing with the two of us."

A smile broke out on her husband's face, and Jessica had the biggest urge to wipe it off his handsome face.

"Well, perhaps I will let the earl dance with you alone."

"No!"

"Have no fear, Jesse. Poor Milebanke is so overweight and out of shape he'll be lucky if he can finish the dance, let alone carry on a conversation while he maneuvers the steps."

Jessica gritted her teeth. "I don't care about that. I cannot dance with him."

"Yes, you can. And you will. You'll be facing him the entire time. You will not miss one word he says."

"But…"

"You'll be fine."

"No!" she cried. "No, I will not be fine!"

"Why?"

"I do not know how to dance."

The shock on his face was evident. Jessica had never been more ashamed in her life. She'd never felt more exposed. More deficient. She fought the tightness in her chest and glared at him with all the hostility she could put in her gaze.

Damn him.

"You did not marry a pampered debutante, Simon. Someone who spent her younger years learning how to pour tea and carry on polite conversation." She couldn't look at him any longer. "Or dance."

Damn him.

She turned her back and held on to the corner of the new wardrobe he'd purchased for all the party dresses she didn't own. "You did not marry a proper somebody who spent years learning to organize parties and balls and entertain the *ton*. But an impaired nobody who spent every waking hour of her youth watching people move their mouths, studying their lips, trying to guess what they were saying. Someone who couldn't carry on even the smallest intelligible conversation until she was seventeen years old. A flawed, less-than-perfect—"

He clamped his hands around her arms and spun her around to face him. "Stop it. I will not have you talking like that."

Every muscle in her body froze, and Jessica stared unblinking at the angry look she saw on his face. "Please, leave me alone. I don't want you to touch me."

Jessica fisted her hands at her sides and stiffened against him. She would not give in to her body's desperate cry to be held. She would not allow herself to lean on his strength. She'd had only herself to rely on since she was fifteen years old, and she was not about to let her traitorous body ruin everything now.

Even though he'd given her his name and promised to protect her, she would never be foolish enough to think that Simon Warland, twelfth Earl of Northcote, could ever really care about her. When society found out about her deafness, she would see how quickly he turned his back on her. And she would have only herself to rely upon again.

Jessica swallowed past the lump in her throat. "Please leave. It's late and I'm tired."

His grasp loosened, but he didn't remove his hands from her arms. He applied a gentle pressure, rubbing up and down, easing away the tenseness. Her knees trembled beneath her, and she squeezed shut her eyes. Please, let him leave, she prayed.

He turned her in his arms and held her. Jessica could not bring herself to look at his face. She didn't want to read one excuse that came from his mouth.

In one fluid movement, he ran his hands down her arms and grasped her by the fingers.

A white-hot bolt of lightning raced from the tips of her fingers where he touched her, warming her whole body with an uncontrollable shudder. He placed her right hand sideways in his, palm to palm, and wrapped his fingers around hers. With practiced grace, he lifted her left hand to his shoulder, wrapped his arm around her waist, and pulled her toward him.

"What are you doing?" Her naked body tingled beneath her thin muslin nightgown, and the loose-flowing robe was not barrier enough to protect her from the fire his touch burned on her skin. His hand rested against her back, searing her flesh, robbing her lungs of the air she needed to breathe.

"Don't, Simon." Jessica pulled back, trying to escape his grasp. "It will do no good. I cannot dance. I cannot hear the music."

"You don't need to hear it."

"Yes, I do. This is not like reading lips." She pulled at her hand and swallowed past the breath that caught in her throat. He had no intention of letting her go. "You don't know what it's like. I cannot hear the music."

Blood pounded in her head, crashing in waves against her ears. He could not expect more from her. She refused to attempt the impossible.

"I will hear the music for you."

Jessica clamped her teeth on her lower lip and turned her head away from him. Didn't he know? Didn't he realize she could never be normal? Didn't he see that no matter how much he forced her to do what was easy for everyone else, he couldn't change the facts?

His wife could not hear.

Her heart slammed in her breast when she felt his finger beneath her chin, raising her gaze until it locked with his. The determined look in his eyes bound her to him. "Trust me, Jesse. Follow where I lead you." He moved. Slowly to the right. Then back to the left. Again to the right. Then back to the left.

Jessica tightened her grip and shifted her startled gaze to her feet. His finger raised her chin.

"Look at my face, Jesse. Move with me. Follow my lead."

Jessica moved her right foot, then her left. Every muscle in her body trembled. She couldn't do this. But she was. And heaven help her, what an amazing feeling.

To be held securely in his arms. To move with him as if they were one. Her gaze drifted back to her feet, but Simon's fingers tightened on her hand in warning and she quickly looked up.

"Relax. I will lead and you must follow. To dance, you must rely on your partner to show you where to go."

He pulled her closer and executed another series of simple steps—first to the right, then to the left.

His hand wrapped around her waist like a tightened vise. Each movement caused her to brush against his muscled chest until her breasts ached. A consuming heat swirled deep within her stomach and moved lower.

Jessica breathed a fluttering breath and tried to let her shoulders drop. How could she relax with his arms around her? How could she relax with a whirlpool of turbulence spiraling to her stomach? How could she relax when she couldn't even think?

Right. Left. Right. Turn, left. She closed her eyes and let her body do whatever he led it to do. Right. Left. Turn, right.

Who would have thought moving around the room in a man's arms would be such a wondrous experience? Surely it was not at all proper to feel this way.

His fingers tightened around her hand again, and she looked up. His lips parted. A gentle smile lit his face. "You are a fast learner, wife."

Jessica swallowed and then took a deep breath. For some reason her breathing was much more labored than usual. "It's only because you're holding me. You leave me little choice but to move as if my body is one with yours. I doubt if Lord Milebanke will hold me so."

"He won't live to see dawn if he does."

Jessica frowned at him. She must have misunderstood what he said.

Simon cleared his throat. She could feel his chest rumble beneath her hand.

"To waltz, you will execute a series of similar steps. Start with your right foot, and the pattern is slow-quick-quick, slow-quick-quick. Like this." Simon demonstrated the steps and then pulled her into his arms and moved across the room.

Jessica stumbled on the first two quick steps, and he stopped and began again.

His patience gave her confidence. The second time was better, and by the time they'd done the series a few more times, she was moving in his arms as if she'd danced forever.

A slight pressure to her hand brought her gaze upward. He greeted her gaze with a brilliant smile. "Don't look down. Keep your eyes open and a smile on your face."

Around and around the room they twirled, her one arm resting on the bulging muscles across his shoulder, the other outstretched with her fingers nestled securely in the palm of his hand.

Jessica held on to him as they moved across the floor, unable to take her gaze from his face. Her husband had such a beautiful face. He could make her feel things she did not want to feel. Ache for things she did not understand. Suddenly, an explosion of shivers raced through her body.

She let her hand roam over his shoulder. His thin lawn shirt hid very little. The open lacing down the front revealed much. Never before had she experienced such power. Such overwhelming strength. The breath caught in her throat.

She brought her gaze back to his mouth. The same mouth that had kissed her until she could barely breathe. A kiss that still lingered in her memory. That still caused her to shudder.

"I'm dancing, aren't I?"

"Yes, Jesse, and you are dancing beautifully."

He held her tight and circled with her around the room again.

This wasn't dancing. This was heaven. On a real dance floor, being held in someone else's arms, it would not be like this. She would make a fool of herself, and the whole world would know she couldn't hear.

She closed her eyes and pressed her body hard against him. A blast of heat raced over every inch of her skin. The chilly night air no longer seemed cool but hot, as if it were the middle of summer. And they were barely moving.

Jessica opened her eyes. "Simon?" She struggled to find the strength to speak.

"Yes?"

"Do all waltzes move this slowly?"

"The one I'm listening to does."

"But there's no music."

"I told you, we don't need music."

They barely moved. Only swayed back and forth. Back and forth. They stood in one spot and moved back and forth while his hand…Oh, God. His hand. Jessica bit her lower lip.

His hand moved over her back, blazing a path wherever his fingers touched her. Up to her shoulders. Cupping her head. Threading his fingers through the loose waves. Then moving down again to the small of her back. And lower.

She wanted to look away from him, but she could not. The penetrating gaze in his eyes bound her to him while his hands worked a strange magic on her flesh. She couldn't breathe. Every inch of her body tingled in response to his touch.

In a single movement, he pushed the robe from her shoulders.

It fell to the floor at her feet. Only her thin muslin gown separated them. It seemed far too revealing—yet far too confining. A violent churning swirled deep in her stomach, and she could not make it stop.

What was happening to her? She wanted nothing, except his hands to touch her. His lips to kiss her.

He rested his hands on her hips and moved upward ever so slowly. He touched the side of her breasts and moved inward.

She should make him stop. She'd die if he did.

The room suddenly darkened and she blinked. "One of the candles went out."

"We do not need light, Jesse."

"I will not be able to see what you're saying in the dark."

"It doesn't matter, wife. I will not be talking."

Simon blew out another candle, then pulled her to him and covered her mouth with his own.

She was drowning. This kiss was nothing like the first kiss. Before, only his mouth had turned her weak-kneed and helpless. Now she could not even begin to describe the chaos his hands caused.

She wanted him closer. She wrapped her arms around his neck and held on as if she were in danger of falling. Heaven help her, she was. Simon had taken her to the precipice of a tall mountain and leaped with her in his arms. He had flown with her high into the sky as if they both had wings, then soared back to earth. Only they had yet to land. Their feet were nowhere near the ground.

He kissed her again. Deep. Hard. Completely. His mouth opened atop hers, and Jessica followed his lead. She knew what he wanted, and she welcomed him. The moment his tongue touched hers a thousand tiny fireballs exploded inside her.

She'd been lonely for so long, ached for something so long and never understood what it was. Now she knew, but wasn't sure she could live with the knowing.

It was Simon. She ached to have his arms around her, his lips against hers, his hands touching her.

She couldn't understand what was happening to her. She couldn't stand on her own. The sensations he caused with his touch, with his kiss, were a thousand times greater than anything she had ever imagined.

She dug her fingers into the corded muscles of his shoulders and held on.

His mouth lifted from hers, and he framed her face with his hands. A glazed look stared down at her. "This was not supposed to happen yet, Jesse. I promised myself it would not."

He brought his mouth down on hers again, his kiss even more intense than before. More demanding. When he blazed a trail of kisses down her throat, Jessica tilted her head, amazed at the raging fire spreading through her limbs.

He touched his lips to the hollow spot at the base of her throat, then kissed a path over the rise of her breasts while his fingers worked at the ribbons of her gown. The material parted, and he pushed it off her shoulders until she stood naked before him.

She shuddered a sigh. Oh, the feel of his mouth against her skin. Jessica squeezed her eyes shut tight and held him close as he moved his kisses lower on her breast. The sensation was tantalizing. She was powerless to do anything but anchor her hands on his shoulders and hold him to her.

She had never experienced anything so wonderful. So agonizing. She was positive she could stand no more. She wrapped her arms around Simon's neck and nestled her head against his chest as he carried her across the room. He laid her down in the center of the bed, and she opened her arms to welcome him.

Chapter 12

❦

*S*imon lifted a handful of Jessica's satiny-brown hair from her shoulder and let it sift through his fingers. He'd been awake for hours, watching as muted shades of purple and pink and blue gave way to the sun's vibrant rays. He was waiting for his wife to open her eyes and berating himself because he knew when she did, he would want to kiss her again.

For hours he'd watched her sleep in his arms, her head resting on his chest, a look of contentment on her face. That look tested every ounce of willpower he possessed.

He did not want to feel a softness toward her. He'd learned his lesson long ago. Rosalind had been an excellent teacher.

A disturbing heaviness pressed against his chest when he remembered the way Jessica had opened her arms to take him to her. The way she'd given herself to him, even though she didn't understand what was happening to her.

Simon brushed a wisp of hair from her cheek and pulled the covers closer around her shoulders. In her sleep, she lifted her hand and rubbed the side of her face where he touched her, then breathed a deep sigh and settled back again with her arm draped across his body.

He filled his lungs with air and closed his eyes. He was not displeased with her. Not at all. Even though he would never allow himself to care for her more than necessary, on the whole, he considered himself lucky. She was more than pleasing to look at. Even beautiful, if he'd take the time to notice, which he would not. And her quick wit and intelligence did not cease to amaze him.

But it was her courage that impressed him most. An inner fortitude that gave her the strength to protect herself and her secret. A strength that would not allow her to admit defeat, no matter how many impossible situations he put in her path.

In less than twenty-four hours she had—for the first time ever—gone for a ride during the daylight where people could see her, conversed with members of the *ton* without making one blunder or giving away the fact that she could not hear what they were saying, accepted two invitations to mingle with society, learned to waltz, and had given her body to him.

Although she'd tried not to show it, Simon knew each experience had terrified her. Watching her stand up to him and question his every demand made his guilt that much more consuming.

He wasn't proud of the way he'd used her, but she was a means to an end. He needed her wealth to make possible his dream of saving his inheritance. He'd married her to impose the vengeance he'd waited three years to exact. He would take every pound Tanhill thought to steal from Jessica and destroy him with it. He would see Tanhill beg for his life like he'd made Sarai beg for hers.

Simon looked at what was left of his grandmother's mediocre painting. His courageous wife was also a bit of a spitfire with a better than passable temper.

He leaned his head back against the headboard and chuckled. He liked that about her, too.

"What is so funny?"

Her voice startled him, and he looked down. He didn't realize she'd woken, and wondered how long she'd been watching him. "Did I wake you?" he asked, sitting up so she could see his lips.

"No."

She tried to pull away, but he wouldn't let her. He wasn't ready to give up the feel of her body next to his. He touched her cheek and then let his fingers trace a line across her determined jaw. "Are you all right? Did I hurt you?"

Her face turned the most alluring shade of crimson, and she lowered her gaze. "No," she answered, shaking her head. "I'm fine."

She relaxed when he wrapped his arm around her shoulder and held her close. He'd seen the confusion on her face last night just before he'd taken her. He knew how much it required for her to trust him.

He also saw the passion that blazed in her eyes, but he was more startled by his own reaction.

He'd always been a master at controlling every physical situation. Until last night. Until her.

And he'd seen the astonishment in her gaze when she'd soared over the edge. Her explosive release mirrored his own.

Her fingers touched his skin lightly, then moved to the scar on his chest. "I didn't know what it would be like between a man and a woman. No one told me." She leaned up on her elbows to see him.

He breathed a deep sigh. "I know." He brushed his fingers over her cheek and then cupped her chin to tilt her face upward. "It's early yet. Go back to sleep."

"I'm not tired. I'm ready to rise."

"No. Stay here." She didn't move for a moment and then placed her hand back on the scar that angled across his chest. His muscles rippled beneath her fingers.

"How did you get this?" she asked, running a finger along the length of the jagged scar.

He saw concern in her gaze and tried to ignore it. "It's not important. It happened a long time ago."

"In India?"

"Yes."

"It was a very deep wound. You could have died."

"Does that bother you?"

A frown deepened across her forehead. "Death always bothers me. It would bother anyone."

"It did not bother the man who did it. He watched the life flow from my body with a smile on his face."

"He must have hated you very much."

Even though he tried not to relive the horrors of that day, there were times when his mind refused to obey. How could he tell Jessica that her stepbrother did not need a reason to kill? He enjoyed causing pain.

"Simon?"

"Yes."

"Will you have an heir now?"

The breath caught in Simon's throat. "I don't know."

"Isn't that why you came to me last night?"

Simon hesitated. "Yes. But it's still too early to tell. It often takes time." He looked at the pretty pink blush coloring her cheeks, and his body hardened in response.

"Melinda said it's important that you have an heir."

He told himself he would not take her again. That he was strong enough to fight his desire for her.

He locked his gaze with hers and knew he was losing his battle. Even though he'd had her twice already last night, it hadn't been enough. His body reacted as if it had been years since he'd last had a woman. As if he were starving for something only the woman beside him could give.

He lowered his head and kissed her, moving from her lips to the sensitive spot behind her ear, then trailing a path down her throat. She was beautiful.

He kissed her mouth once more and held her cheeks in the palms of his hands. "Look at me, Jesse. Open your eyes and look at me."

She stared at him, the dark look in her eyes glazed with passion, the feel of her hands on him desperate. With a need that totally consumed him, he made love to her again.

Their journey was magnificent, their release violent and earth-shattering.

Simon collapsed against her and buried his face against her neck while he gasped for air. Loving her was incredible. Like never before.

He lifted himself up and looked into her eyes. Hopeful anticipation stared back at him, and he knew she was waiting for some sort of declaration from him of...what? Love? Hardly.

"Go to sleep, Jesse."

Simon pulled away from her and rolled to the other side of the bed. With his arm beneath his head, he stared at the panels in the ceiling and cursed the way his body had betrayed him. He didn't want it to be this way. Never thought it would be.

He kept his gaze from finding hers again. He knew if he looked, he'd see her hurt and confusion. He let the old barriers surround his heart and told himself he didn't care. He would not let himself care. No woman would have that power over him ever again.

When he was sure she was asleep, he crawled out of bed and tiptoed across the room, careful not to disturb her. He stopped in midstride. What did it matter how much noise he made? She would never know.

Why did he keep forgetting she couldn't hear?

* * *

Simon opened the door to the last wardrobe. Empty. He looked back to his sleeping wife on the bed and stuffed his hands into the pockets of his breeches. He'd been up and dressed for nearly an hour, but evidently his wife needed more rest. He didn't bother to hide his smile of satisfaction while he resumed the search of his wife's wardrobe.

He found three very worn day dresses with frayed collars and cuffs, and three more better dresses in dark, lifeless colors. He recognized the dark dress he'd seen her in the first time she came to him. And the striped dress she'd worn yesterday to the park. And the pretty, yet plain, dress in which she'd been married.

Where were the rest of her clothes? The party gowns? The fancy clothes she would wear when they went out?

Simon left the wardrobe doors ajar and walked out to the hall.

"Beatrice," he said to the maid coming up the stairs. "Where does your mistress keep her ball gowns?"

"Her ball gowns?" The puzzled look on her face was almost comical.

"Yes. Her gowns. The gowns she wears when she goes out."

"Oh." The maid clasped her hands at her waist. "The mistress hardly ever goes out."

"I know," Simon admitted in frustration, "but surely she has something else to wear other than what is hanging in her room. Every woman has spare closets filled with useless clothing."

"Not the mistress, my lord. She is very frugal."

"She does not have another room where she stores her gowns?"

The maid shook her head.

Simon looked down the hall and saw only rooms with doors standing open. He knew what was in each. All except the room at the end of the hall. He walked down the long corridor and lifted the latch. It was locked.

"What does your mistress keep in this room?"

Beatrice's eyes opened wide, and she twisted her hands in her apron. "Things, my lord. Just the mistress's things."

"Things?" Simon raised his brows and leveled the nervous maid with an icy glare. "What sort of things, Beatrice?"

"Oh, I'm not at liberty to say, my lord. They're the mistress's personal things."

"Do you have a key?"

"Oh no, my lord. Only the mistress has a key." Beatrice twisted her apron tighter. "But the mistress keeps none of her gowns in the room. Just her personal things."

"No gowns?"

"No, my lord."

Simon turned on his heel and walked back to his room. Where did his wife keep the rest of her clothes? Surely she had some. And exactly what sort of personal things did she have that had to be kept under lock and key?

Simon turned back to face the wide-eyed maid. "Beatrice. Have a hot bath sent up for your mistress and a cup of chocolate."

"Yes, my lord. Right away."

Before Simon could tell the flighty maid to have the cook make Jessica a slice of toast, she was halfway down the stairs, well out of earshot.

Simon walked back to his wife. When he entered the room, Jessica was just waking. She stretched her arms above her head like a lazy cat stirring after a long nap, then rolled to the other side of the bed. The sunlight shone on her coffee-colored hair that was fanned out on the pillow like it had been last night. Simon held the breath that caught in his chest and pushed away the urge to pull off his clothes and climb back in bed with her.

Bloody hell. She was a sight to wake up to.

"Are you looking for something?" Her gaze scanned the open wardrobe doors as she covered her mouth to hide a yawn. She modestly pulled the covers under her chin and sat up in bed.

She looked irresistible. "Yes. I'm looking for your gowns."

She pointed to the other wardrobe. The one with the six dresses hanging in it.

"No. Your good gowns. The ones that might be appropriate to wear to the Milebankes' on Friday."

"Those are the only gowns I own." She sat straighter and tucked her knees close to her chest. She looked back at the wardrobe containing the pathetic collection of gowns at the same time he did.

Simon stared at her in disbelief. He remembered her request for a monthly allowance of fifteen pounds to purchase a new gown upon occasion. Jessica Warland, Countess of Northcote, one of the richest women in England, had six dresses to her name, none of which were appropriate to wear out of the house.

The temper he usually kept well under control threatened to show itself. "What do you plan to wear to the Milebankes' on Friday, Jessica?"

Her eyes sparked with a hint of anger. "*If* I go, I will wear the navy gown. It's the newest."

"That is your best gown?"

"Yes. When I go out in public, I sit where I'm not noticed and stay only a little while. I hardly need an expensive gown to sit off to the side."

Simon raised his gaze to the ceiling. He locked his jaw and took a breath of air that hissed through his clenched teeth. "That is what you intend to wear when I introduce you to society?"

She hesitated. "I have not decided whether or not I will go."

"You have not decided?" A flash of anger exploded in him as violent as a shot from a cannon. "The decision is not yours to make, my lady. I have decided you will go, and by God, you will."

She stared at him, the gleam in her eyes dangerous. "Be careful how much you demand, my lord. You seem to be making all the decisions concerning our future, and I do not appreciate the double intent of your actions."

"I don't know what you're talking about."

"Really? Do you think I do not know the real reason we took that ride in the park yesterday?"

She fisted her hands at her side in a show of anger. "And you accomplished your goal, didn't you, my lord? You acquired a number of invitations yesterday and will undoubtedly receive more before the day is over. You may accept as many of them as you wish." She lifted her chin in defiance, but Simon saw her hands tremble at her sides. "But I do not plan to go with you. Surely you do not expect me to?"

Simon raised his brows and stared at her. Bloody hell. "You did not think I would expect you to go with me?"

"No. I thought you would see how foolish it was to risk the *ton* finding out you had married a—"

"You are my wife!"

"I'm deaf!" She slammed her fist on the bed at her side. "I cannot take the risk. I will go as I always have, alone and unnoticed."

"Bloody hell, woman! You are the Countess of Northcote. You will no longer go anywhere alone and unnoticed."

With one hand, she anchored the sheet beneath her chin. She slammed her other fist down again at her side.

"You cannot expect me to change the way I have lived just because we're married. That is not what I thought you wanted in a wife." Her cheeks flushed a deep shade of crimson.

"Then you misunderstood." Simon paced back and forth at the foot of the bed, stopping only when he had his temper under control. "On Friday evening, you and I will take our rightful place in society. Our entrance will be well marked by the *ton*, and we will be afforded the respect and honor due an earl and his countess."

Simon ignored the pale coloring of his wife's face and the white-knuckled fists clenching the covers on the bed. "You will be adorned in a stunning new gown that will cause a remarkable sensation. We will dance each dance together, save the one waltz you promised Lord Milebanke, and mingle with the other guests as if neither of our pasts had ever been in question."

Her face paled even more.

Simon took a step closer to the bed and towered over her with daunting ferocity. He clenched his teeth and took a deep breath. He had always been proud of who he was. Even when his father and the greedy wife he married squandered and gambled away what was rightfully his, it was never the Northcote name that caused him embarrassment.

He leveled his gaze and made sure his wife could understand each word he said. "I will not stop until I have restored the Earl and Countess of Northcote to their rightful places in society. Our presence at the Milebankes' on Friday is the first step in attaining that goal."

Simon stared at her. She had three days to outfit herself in a gown. A gown that would set London on its heels.

He fought the wave of concern and frustration that washed over him. They would be accepted by society. He would flaunt his wife and his riches before the *ton* so that when Tanhill came back, his and Jessica's acceptance would be so solid he would not be able to touch either of them.

Without Jessica's wealth, Tanhill's hands would be tied. He would be nothing more than a pauper sporting a title—and a lesser one at that.

His wife was the key to his plan. Simon intended to use her wealth to destroy her stepbrother. He owed it to himself and to the son he would someday have. He owed it to Sarai.

After Friday, the *ton* would know he had returned to take his rightful place. And Jessica would realize the life he offered her was a damn sight better than the reclusive existence she'd lived the last few years.

Simon took a few deep, calming breaths and tried to hold his temper in check. "Do you know the identity of this elusive dress designer everyone is talking about?"

Her eyes opened wide. "What?" Her voice sounded strained.

"Do you know who she is?"

She wrapped her arms around her knees and tightened her grip. She was obviously nervous about even searching out a dress designer. "No one knows her name. She is very secretive."

"I don't care how closely she guards her identity," Simon bellowed. "You will have one of her creations. You are the Countess of Northcote. Who is the best dressmaker in London?"

"Madame Lamont."

Simon turned from her and paced the room, his mind racing to find the most expedient way to proceed. "How long does it take to make a gown?" He was prepared to hire as many seamstresses as necessary. "Do you have a style you like? A color?" Although he didn't know a lot about women's clothing, he obviously knew a damn sight more than his wife. It was important that she have a stunning gown by Friday night.

"Simon?"

Her voice cut through his rambling, and he turned to face her.

"Are you talking?" she asked.

"Yes."

"Then look at me."

Simon hissed a rude expletive and then sat down on the bed and faced her. "I'm sorry. I will learn in time." He took her hand in his. It was chilled. He held it close and looked into her eyes. "Ira and Collingsworth will be here shortly. We have some important business to discuss that cannot wait. As soon as we are finished, I will take you to this Madame Lamont."

She pulled her hands out of his grasp, her wide eyes filled with terror. "No."

"Why? You said she was good. Is there some reason—"

"No. She is the best, but…"

"But what?"

"I…I don't want to bother you when you're so busy. I can attend to this myself."

Simon looked again at the pathetic dresses hanging in her wardrobe and shuddered. He really could not afford to take time out of his busy day to sit in a dressmaker's shop and pick out material, but he sure as hell wasn't about to let his wife go by herself. If the six ugly dresses she already owned were any example of her taste in clothing, he could never allow her to choose a gown by herself.

Simon stood. "I will let you go without me only if you promise to take the Duchess of Collingsworth with you. You obviously have a lot to learn about what is fashionable, a talent with which Her Grace is already quite proficient."

Jessica nodded. "Very well. I will take the duchess with me."

"You will learn about fashion in time, Jesse. It's only because you have gone out so little that you lack the sense to know what is in style."

Simon clasped his hands behind his back. "Spare no expense. Trust Her Grace's judgment on the design and instruct this Madame Lamont to hire as many seamstresses as necessary. The gown must be ready by Friday night."

Jessica nodded again. "I will find the perfect ball gown. Don't worry that you'll be embarrassed, Simon."

The breath caught in his throat. "It's not just for me that this is important, Jesse. Society will not turn their backs on the Northcote name. They will not turn their backs on you. I will not let them."

"And when society finds out I'm deaf?"

"You are my wife. The Countess of Northcote. Society has no choice but to accept you."

The panic-stricken look in her eyes stopped him from releasing his breath. He turned before he could see more doubt on her face and walked to the door just as someone knocked softly from the other side.

"The water is ready for the mistress's bath," Martha said, carrying a tray over to the table beside Jessica's bed. "It's in the next room. The Duke of Collingsworth and Mr. Ira Cambden are waiting for you downstairs, my lord."

"Thank you, Martha. Tell them I will be right down."

"Yes, my lord." Martha turned to Jessica. "I'll return shortly to help you with your bath, my lady."

Simon watched the servant leave the room and then turned back to Jessica. "Are you sure you don't need my help selecting a gown? I'd be more than willing to postpone my meeting to help you."

"No. That's not necessary. Her Grace will go with me. She can no doubt teach me which designs are best."

Simon looked at the somber expression on her face, and a twinge of guilt slammed him in the gut. She sat on the bed, the inflexible stiffness of her back regally straight, the dignified lift of her head high, and the determined look in her eyes hardened and level. With a slow nod she acquiesced to his demands. Only the hands she clenched tightly in the covers around her knees indicated her trepidation.

"You have nothing to fear, my lady."

"If you say so, my lord." The tone of her voice lacked conviction.

A gnarled fist twisted around his heart. Simon held her gaze for a long time, refusing to admit he was the least bit nervous about the *ton*'s initial reaction to them. He slapped his fist on his thigh and released the breath trapped in his chest. "Stop by the study before you leave," he said, facing her from the doorway. "Ira will undoubtedly be anxious to see you."

The look in her eyes was flat. "Of course."

He turned away before the expression on her face could bother him more than it already did. His wife would have a stunning gown for their entrance into society, and the Duchess of Collingsworth would go to help her select something to wear, or he would.

Obviously, his wife did not know the first thing about fashion.

Chapter 13

❧

*J*essica stood before the door to Simon's study and smoothed the pleats to her navy gown. She was ready to go to Madame Lamont's.

She thought of the look on her husband's face when he'd insisted she present herself to society, and another tremor of anger swelled within her. He'd done nothing but turn her life upside down since he'd recovered from his illness. Now he expected her to go to Madame Lamont's where half the women of the *ton* might be.

Jessica fought the urge to run back upstairs and hide in her room.

She patted the folded paper in her pocket, satisfied that her design was well hidden. The design was a special gown she'd created weeks ago, one she hadn't been able to part with. Now it would be hers.

It was magnificent. As she'd drawn the lines, she'd envisioned someone special wearing her gown. Someone elegant and graceful, like Melinda. Someone who would do her creation justice.

Never had she dreamt she would wear the gown herself.

She breathed a heavy sigh. Perhaps the beauty of the design would overshadow some of her many faults.

She patted her pocket again. Somehow, she would have to find a way to secretly give Madame Lamont the design. At least her husband wouldn't be there.

She didn't want to think what might happen if Simon found out that his wife, the Countess of Northcote, designed gowns like a common laborer. Without a doubt, he would forbid her to sketch another design ever again.

She wouldn't do it. She *couldn't*. Creating beautiful gowns was all that gave meaning to her life. She couldn't give up that part of herself.

A cold shiver shattered her resolve. Life before Simon had been so simple. So uncomplicated.

So empty.

Jessica thought of the night she'd spent in his arms, and a rush of warmth surged through her veins. She stubbornly brushed the feeling aside. She could never let herself forget the reason he'd married her. He already had her money. If all went well, after Friday night he would be repositioned in society, and once he was certain she carried his child, it was likely he would never come to her bed again. Once that happened, she would eventually be left with only her talent to create. She would always find comfort in her designs.

She touched the drawing hidden in her pocket and reached for the latch to the study door. She didn't think to knock. It would do no good. She couldn't hear the command to enter, and she didn't want to disturb her husband from his business.

She stepped inside the room. Both Simon and Ira were behind the massive oak desk, Simon sitting in his chair and Ira standing behind his shoulder, pointing to some papers spread out in front of them.

The Duke of Collingsworth sat in a chair in front of the desk with his back to Jessica. All three were so engrossed in their discussion that none of them heard her enter.

Rather than disturb them, she sat in a chair against the near wall and waited for them to notice her.

She watched her husband, unable to keep her gaze away from the long, sturdy fingers that held his pen. The same fingers that had held her and stroked her flesh. She looked at his shoulders, unmistakably broad beneath his snow-white shirt and forest-green jacket. Her hands could still feel the warmth of his flesh atop hers.

She closed her eyes and turned away from his powerful physique. Just the sight of him made her remember what they'd shared last night, and a torrid sensation revived deep within her stomach. She took a long, slow breath and focused on his face.

He seemed angry. A muscle at the side of his jaw twitched as he listened to Ira talk. His teeth remained clenched when he breathed.

"These are the only notes you've been able to acquire?" he asked, holding two pieces of paper in his left hand. "The deed to this town house and the creditors' notes to Northcote Shipping?"

"Yes." Ira shifted to the side and moved another paper in front of Simon. "And they didn't come cheaply." He pointed to the bottom of the paper on the desk. "Mottley is buying up every company with a ship that can sail."

"I don't give a bloody fig how much it costs. I can recoup the money once Northcote Shipping becomes profitable. But I can do nothing if I don't have a company to run." Simon lifted another paper and then handed it to James.

"What about Ravenscroft, Ira? Who has acquired the notes to Ravenscroft and the other Northcote estates?"

"I'm not sure," Ira said. "I've traced them through three bogus companies so far, and the last lending office I contacted informed me they didn't know who had acquired the notes."

"Something is wrong here, Ira," Simon interrupted, flipping through the pages. "Surely someone knows who bought the notes from the creditors."

"It's very strange, my lord. No one knows anything, yet everything leads back to Mottley and this new shipping company he's forming, Great Northern Shipping."

"Why would Mottley want Ravenscroft and the estates? They are of no value to him. To shipping."

"Perhaps Mottley is not alone in the creation of Great Northern Shipping," Ira said, thumbing through the papers as if searching for something that would help Simon.

"What are you saying, Ira?"

"I don't know. It's just a thought. A very scary thought."

The Duke of Collingsworth was talking, but Jessica could not see what he was saying. From the frown on Simon's face, it was not good.

"I'm afraid I have to agree with His Grace," Ira said, laying a piece of paper in front of Simon. "Here is a list of all the properties Mottley has purchased or attempted to purchase since he arrived in London two months ago. Don't ask where I got this information. Just trust that it's correct."

Simon stared at the paper on the desk in front of him, and Jessica watched his eyes grow wide. He leveled his gaze at Ira and then looked back to the paper in his hand. "What the hell is going on?"

Ira shook his head. "I don't know, my lord."

Simon stared at the papers before him again. "Everything Mottley has purchased so far is mine. The two town houses in London. Ridgeway Estate. Parkland House in East Sussex. Sutterland Manor. The iron mines near Southampton. He intends to destroy me."

Ira reached for another paper in his folder. Simon looked at it and let it fall to the desk. Ira picked up the paper and handed it to Collingsworth.

"Damn him, Ira," Simon said. "Damn him to hell."

"It's only by luck that I was able to pay the creditors for Northcote Shipping and this town house on Old Cherry Lane. The old Duke of Wellmont loaned your father the money against them five years ago. When the duke died last year, he left everything to a distant relative in France. Fortunately for you, the young scamp did not want anything in England, so he sold the notes to the first person who offered for them. Luckily, that was me."

"Bloody hell," Simon said, raking his fingers through his dark hair. "I could have lost the house and the ships, too."

Jessica clenched her hands in her lap. It didn't take a genius to realize that someone intended to take everything that was Simon's and leave him with nothing. A knot twisted deep in her stomach.

"What do you know about Mottley?" Simon asked. "And this Great Northern Shipping Company? Who is backing him? Where is he getting his finances? What are they shipping that is so profitable?"

Jessica stirred in her chair, and Simon's eyes darted to where she sat. The Duke of Collingsworth turned with a look of surprise on his face, and Ira stepped to the side of the desk.

Jessica faced the three men staring at her. "Opium. Mottley is shipping opium."

Simon came around the desk and stood in front of her. "How long have you been here?"

"Long enough."

"How do you know what Great Northern ships?"

"Alexander Mottley was at Lord Stratmore's ball last week, and I saw him speaking to Baron Carver's youngest son, Sydney. He is involved somehow."

"Sydney?" Collingsworth questioned, stepping to the other side of Simon's desk so he could face her. "He's always had a reputation for being on the wild side, but I can't believe he would become involved in smuggling opium. Why?"

"For the money," Jessica said, clenching her hands tightly. "Baron Carver is bankrupt. They are in danger of losing their estate. It's not entailed."

Simon wiped his hand across his face. "It's amazing what one will do for money."

A cold shiver raced along Jessica's spine. *Yes.* It was amazing what one would do for money. Hadn't Simon taken a deaf woman as his wife for her money?

"What else can you tell us, Jesse?" Simon asked as he stepped to her and lifted her chin with his finger.

She shook her head. "Not much. The company is headquartered in India—"

Jessica stopped short when she saw Simon's reaction. His shoulders rose, and the frown on his forehead deepened. "What's wrong, Simon?"

"Nothing," he answered. "Go on."

"Well, they said that most of the opium would be sold to China in exchange for tea, which they will bring here to England. Although there will be one shipment of opium that will come to England."

"Did they say when?"

"No."

"Anything else?"

"Only that the owner of Great Northern Shipping is still in India. He's expected soon, but neither Mottley nor Carver are looking forward to his return."

"Bloody hell, Simon," the Duke of Collingsworth said. The worry on his face was evident. "How did he find out already that you had married—"

"That's enough, James."

Jessica looked from James to Ira and then back to Simon. "What's wrong, Simon?"

"Nothing, Jesse." Simon placed his hands on her shoulders. "Are you on your way to pick up the duchess and visit Madame Lamont?"

"Yes."

"Good. Spare no expense, Jessica. Make arrangements for at least a dozen gowns."

"But if money is—"

"Money is not a problem." Simon turned to Ira. "Tell her, Mr. Cambden."

The moment Jessica looked into Ira's familiar face, something inside her breast tightened. She took one step toward her friend, and when he raised his arms to her, as was his habit, she stepped into his embrace.

Ira held her longer than was proper, but Jessica was glad. She hesitated to leave his embrace.

Finally, he pulled her away from him and held her by the shoulders. "Money will never be a problem for your husband, my lady. You can order a hundred gowns if it pleases you to do so."

Jessica forced a laugh. "I think one gown will be enough for today, Ira."

Jessica felt a touch on her shoulder. She knew it was Simon. "I think no less than a dozen will be enough for today."

She started to protest and stopped when she saw the determination in his gaze. "Very well."

He nodded his approval. "Are you ready to leave then?"

"Yes."

"Sanjay will go with you."

"Very well." Jessica said good-bye to His Grace and Ira, and then Simon walked her to the door.

"Simon?" She turned and spoke quickly before he closed the door behind her. "Does my stepbrother have anything to do with this?"

Simon placed a finger against her lips and shook his head. "Don't worry about a thing, Jesse. This involves only me. You have nothing to fear."

"But—"

"You have nothing to fear. Take care of the dozen gowns you are required to purchase, and I will take care of the rest."

He didn't give her time to respond but turned his back and closed the door to the study. Sanjay stood there with a ready smile on his face.

An uneasy feeling gnawed inside her. She didn't know how he'd found out she'd married Simon, but she was convinced Colin had already started his campaign to destroy them. His plan was clear. He would destroy Simon first.

Chapter 14

❦

Jessica placed a shaky foot onto the cobblestone walk in front of Madame Lamont's dress shop, praying the smile on her face made her appear more confident than she felt. She crossed the narrow walk and took her first step through the open doorway. Even though Melinda walked close at her side, Jessica had never felt more alone.

With head held high and shoulders straight, she made her way through the crowded room. All eyes turned in her direction, the shocked expressions obvious. She'd expected as much.

She followed one step with another until she reached a large oval table displaying fine laces and netting. She stopped, pretending to peruse the fabrics. She absently picked up a width of canary-yellow netting.

Melinda touched her arm, and Jessica looked up.

"That is a beautiful color, isn't it, Jess?"

"What?"

"The netting you have wadded in your hand. It's a very pretty color."

Jessica loosened her grip around the netting and noticed the material and the color for the first time. "Yes. It's very pretty. It would go perfectly with your coloring."

"And yours," Melinda said with a smile.

Jessica lifted the corners of her mouth. "I will have to keep it in mind."

She turned her head to look at the women who crowded Madame Lamont's dress shop. She'd hoped business would be slow this afternoon. It wasn't. All eyes watched her, the awareness evident in their wide-open gazes. Their curiosity was obvious as dainty gloved hands cupped the sides of their mouths.

In one corner, three young debutantes stood before a velvet-covered table admiring a display of fine Irish laces. On the other side of the spacious room, a middle-aged woman with two younger girls, perhaps her daughters, sifted through samples of ribbons and frills of chiffon and velvet piping. Three or four more groups of women milled about, shifting from one display to another. Most of the women she recognized from the balls she'd attended. A few she did not. All seemed to recognize her. Each gave her a cursory glance and then huddled closer to make whispered comments.

A number of Madame Lamont's shop assistants, each attired in a white ruffled shirt and a gray and maroon-striped skirt, moved busily from one group to the other. At a table nearby, one of the assistants held up a beautiful shade of apricot voile for the Marchioness of Crestwall. The Countess of Burnhaven stood beside her, and although Jessica had never spoken to either of them before, she recognized them. They were both very influential ladies in society. Influential enough that they could make or destroy a reputation with a single word or a turn of their heads.

Jessica wished there was a way to avoid them. But there was not. She and Melinda would have to pass beside them on their way across the room. To ignore them would be inexcusable.

She braced her shoulders and matched steps with Melinda, walking around a cushioned divan near a table set with small cakes and hot tea, then past a counter with parasols of every imaginable color and material. The marchioness and the countess both ceased talking as she and Melinda neared, the apricot voile in Lady Crestwall's hand drifting unnoticed to the table. Melinda stopped.

Jessica couldn't help but concentrate on the gown Lady Crestwall wore. The fabric was the richest shade of emerald-green satin, the full overskirt edged in wide scallops draped from a narrow, gathered waist, exposing an underskirt made of the palest yellow satin Jessica had ever seen. She could not find words that would do justice to the stunning picture Lady Crestwall presented.

She was a beautiful woman. Ebony hair, perfectly coiffed, a flawless complexion the color of fine porcelain, and a figure rounded in all the right places. Without a doubt she was one of the most gorgeous women Jessica had ever seen.

Rumor had it, however, that her beauty did not reach to the inside. She was known to be noticeably unapproachable, and Jessica could see that every fiber of her bearing exuded a chilling aloofness.

Lady Crestwall's evaluative look studied Jessica, appraising her from the top of her head to the hem of her skirt. She did not look like she was impressed with what she saw. Her gaze halted first on Jessica's out-of-fashion bonnet. She raised her brows in disdain. Then she focused on Jessica's worn gown. Her eyes widened in horror, giving both Jessica and her gown a most disapproving glare. With a regal lift of her chin, Lady Crestwall turned her attention back to Melinda.

"Good afternoon, Your Grace," Lady Crestwall said, making it apparent that the new Countess of Northcote didn't warrant further notice.

"Lady Crestwall. Lady Burnhaven," Melinda returned. "What a pleasant surprise." Melinda turned toward Jessica. "Have you and Lady Burnhaven had the pleasure of meeting the Countess of Northcote?"

Thankfully, the Countess of Burnhaven stepped forward, not giving Lady Crestwall an opportunity to snub her. "No, we have not met," Lady Burnhaven said. "It is a pleasure to meet you, my dear."

Jessica smiled. "The pleasure is mine," Jessica answered, not taking her gaze from Lady Burnhaven's smiling eyes. Her expression was kind and gentle, her easy manner cordial and open.

She was older, perhaps in her midfifties or more. She carried a pleasingly plump figure that suited her well, her roundness adding to the friendly, comfortable picture she conveyed.

"May I congratulate you on your recent marriage, my lady," Lady Burnhaven added, her wishes made sincere by the smile on her face. "The earl is indeed a fortunate man."

"Thank you, my lady," Jessica answered. "I will tell the earl you said so. He will no doubt need reminding upon occasion."

Lady Burnhaven laughed politely and nodded in agreement. "You are so right. All husbands need reminding on occasion." She reached for Jessica's hand again. "I can tell you have a sense of humor. It is undoubtedly an attribute the earl finds charming."

"I'm not sure. There are times when I'm certain it is a confusion to him."

Lady Burnhaven patted the top of Jessica's hand. "I would keep it that way if I were you, my dear. A little confusion is always an advantage."

Jessica could not help but smile. "I will remember you said so."

Lady Crestwall made a slight movement, and Jessica turned her attention to her. The cool smile on her face appeared haughty and judgmental, her wary scrutiny visible. She stiffened her demeanor and graced Jessica with a most condescending look. "You cannot imagine our surprise, my lady," she said, hardening the fixed look on her face. "Your marriage to the earl came as a shock to the entire *ton*."

An uncomfortable pause followed. Finally, Lady Crestwall lifted her pert, patrician nose and continued. "Considering your husband's past disastrous relationship, we did not think he would ever marry."

Jessica stiffened. Melinda's hand lightly touched her in warning.

Lady Crestwall was not content to stop there. The malicious glint in her eyes told how much she enjoyed causing such agitation. "You are, of course, aware of the scandal surrounding his last attempt at marriage. Those of us who know him are surprised he took a wife so rashly."

Jessica met Lady Crestwall's malevolent glare. "I doubt Northcote considers our decision to marry rash," she said, raising her chin. "As you know, choosing a woman…or man…with whom you intend to spend the rest of your life is not a decision one would make without careful consideration."

The slight curve of Lady Crestwall's lips threatened to crack her face. "Of course."

Lady Burnhaven may have said something. Jessica chose to ignore any comment she might have made because she didn't want to look in her direction. She would not be the first to shift her gaze from her adversary. The Marchioness of Crestwall would have to look away first.

She did.

She lowered her gaze, giving Jessica's outdated gown a scathing look. Her perusal was meant to intimidate and embarrass her.

As Jessica watched the cold, haughty glare, she realized that even the most beautiful outside covering could not hide or change such ugliness on the inside.

"Have you come to see Madame Lamont?" Lady Crestwall asked.

"Yes," Jessica answered, bringing a small smile to her lips—a smile she far from felt. "My husband is not overly fond of my wardrobe."

Lady Burnhaven laughed. The movement turned Jessica's attention to the elderly lady. "Do you have an appointment?" the countess asked.

Jessica shook her head.

"Oh my. I wouldn't be too disappointed then if you are not able to see Madame today. It's nearly impossible to see her without an appointment. Lady Crestwall has had to wait two weeks to see Madame. Haven't you, Lillian?"

A deep color darkened Lady Crestwall's cheeks as she struggled with an excuse to the question. "Our schedules did not match. That was the problem."

Lady Burnhaven spotted an assistant coming toward them. "You had best inquire, then, my dear," she said to Jessica.

Jessica watched a young shop clerk make her way to where they were standing and steeled herself for another confrontation. Lord, but she was growing tired of this. Simon was demanding too much of her. She only wanted to sit in her room with her sketch pad and pencil and get lost in her creations. She only wanted to live a quiet, peaceful life without having to watch every face to see who might be speaking to her. She only wanted to escape to someplace where she would not be subjected to such constant scrutiny.

Jessica looked at Melinda and lifted her chin proudly. "We should go—"

"Oh, miss," Melinda said, raising a graceful hand to gain the girl's attention. "Would you tell Madame Lamont that the Countess of Northcote is here to see her?"

"Does the countess have an appointment?" the girl asked, looking at Jessica.

"Please, tell Madame Lamont that the Countess of Northcote is here and requests a moment of her time," Melinda repeated.

"Yes, my lady."

The assistant turned away, and the lift of Lady Crestwall's shoulders drew Jessica's attention. "I'm afraid you are in for a disappointment, Lady Northcote," she said, curling her lips sardonically. "Madame Lamont will not see you without an appointment. Perhaps she would make an exception for the duchess," she said, nodding in Melinda's direction, "but she will hardly give up her time for—"

"Lady Northcote," Madame Lamont said, rushing across the storeroom floor. When she reached them she clasped her hands together as if elated to see her. "What a surprise. It is indeed a pleasure to welcome you to my humble dress shop." She clasped her hands together again and bowed her head. "Have you found everything to your satisfaction? Is there anything I can show you? I am, of course, completely at your disposal."

Jessica smiled. "I'm in need of a gown, Madame Lamont. In fact, I need several gowns."

Madame Lamont clapped enthusiastically. "Oh yes."

Jessica leaned closer to the dressmaker. "Perhaps you have something by that new designer all of London is talking about?" she said, keeping her voice loud enough to be heard.

Madame Lamont bowed slightly. "I think I have just the gown for you, my lady. If you will follow me?"

Jessica turned to the other ladies. "If you will excuse me."

"Of course," the countess answered, a pleased look on her face.

The marchioness, however, only gaped at her in astonishment.

"Close your mouth, Lady Crestwall," the countess said, tapping her lightly on the arm with the tip of her parasol. "It is most unbecoming."

Without another word, Jessica turned her back and followed Madame Lamont across the wide room and through a door marked *PRIVATE*. She wanted to turn around and relish the stunned look on Lady Crestwall's face once more, but she didn't. She couldn't. Her legs trembled so violently she was lucky they had enough strength to carry her across the room. If she stopped, she would more than likely fall flat on her face.

"Thank you, Madame," Jessica said as soon as the door had closed behind her. She released a huge sigh and leaned a hand against the back of the floral divan that sat in the middle of the room. "I was afraid I wasn't going to last another minute out there. There were so many people. I didn't know who would be speaking next."

Melinda rushed to her side. "You were wonderful, Jess. No one suspected a thing. Did you see the look on poor Lady Crestwall's face when Madame Lamont greeted you? We're lucky she didn't swoon on the spot."

Jessica fisted her hand against her mouth. "She was so angry, she'll never speak to me again."

"She was about to give you the cut before Madame came out. Your reception gave her second thought."

The room swam before her, and Jessica closed her eyes and gripped the cushions of the divan tighter.

Madame Lamont put her arm around her shoulder. "Come, sit down, my friend. I can tell it has been a most exhausting day for you."

Jessica sat down on the end of the divan and Melinda sat next to her. Jessica gripped her hands in her lap and pressed her knees together to keep them from shaking.

"I am so proud of you, Jessica," Madame Lamont said with a clap of her hands. "You can't imagine my surprise when Corrine told me you were here."

"I had little choice," Jessica said, taking a deep breath. "My husband insisted I come. In fact, if it had not been for pressing business, he would be sitting here with me instead of Melinda. He is quite determined I improve my wardrobe."

"Your new husband obviously has excellent taste. From what I see," she said, staring at Jessica's navy gown, "your wardrobe is in dire need of improvement. I cannot wait to meet him to tell him how much I agree with his decision."

Madame Lamont moved a chair in front of Jessica and grinned a broad smile. "At first I could not believe the wonderful news. That my dear, dear friend, Jessica Stanton, had become the Countess of Northcote. How very lucky the earl is that he married you."

Jessica smiled. "It all happened so fast I've barely had time to adjust to the change myself."

"Have you told him you cannot...I mean, does he know...?"

"Yes," Jessica answered. "Northcote knows I cannot hear. It's hardly something I could keep from him for very long."

Madame Lamont laughed. "My dear, dear friend. If you wanted, I do not doubt you would be able to hide your deafness forever. You are that good at reading what people say. I had met with you in secret for more than two years before I realized. And only then because the breeze from the window blew out the candle and we were in the dark."

Jessica nodded, remembering that night. She hated the dark. Not being able to see or hear terrified her. It was as close to being totally helpless as she ever wanted to find herself. "But you did not seem surprised when I told you," Jessica said.

"The knowledge was like a door that opened to answer all the questions that puzzled me. Why we had to meet in secret. Why the room was always so brightly lit. Why I always had to sit facing you."

"I was afraid you would not want my designs if you found out I was deaf."

Madame Lamont laughed. "It's not necessary to hear to create. Your fabulous gowns come from in here." The dressmaker pointed to her heart. "Such talent has nothing to do with here." She pointed to her ears. "But you did not come here to talk of when we first met. What can I do for you?"

"I need your help," Jessica said, leaning forward. "I must have a special gown made for this Friday. Is it possible?"

"For you, my lady, anything is possible." Madame Lamont leaned closer. "Have you brought me anything special?" she asked. There was a twinkle in her eyes.

Jessica reached her hand to her pocket and pulled out one of the papers hidden there. She handed it to Madame Lamont, and Melinda stood to look over the dressmaker's shoulder.

"By all the saints," Madame Lamont said, clasping a hand over her mouth. "This is the most beautiful gown I have ever seen. Oh, what perfection. What exquisite detail."

"It is remarkable, Jess," Melinda said, sitting down beside her and reaching for her hands. "What color do you see for your gown?"

Jessica cleared her throat. "White. A creamy white with an underskirt of the softest shade of apricot satin."

Madame Lamont bobbed her head up and down, clapping her hands in front of her. "Yes. Oh yes. The overskirt will be beaded with thousands of tiny pearls and the only other color on the gown will be an apricot velvet ribbon entwined through the lace. It will be magnificent!"

Melinda turned Jessica's head so she would not miss her words. "Very special, Jess," she agreed.

"Do you think Simon will be pleased, Mel?"

"I'm sure he will. You will be the most beautiful woman at the ball."

The emotion in Melinda's eyes forced Jessica to lower her gaze. "I hardly think I will be the most beautiful, but it's important that I do not embarrass him."

Melinda placed her finger beneath Jessica's chin and lifted. "You will not embarrass him, Jess. You could never embarrass Northcote."

Madame Lamont gained Jessica's attention when she tapped her on the arm. "When I heard you had married, I was not sure I could look for any more creations from you. The Countess of Northcote, after all, may not have the need to create more designs."

The breath caught in Jessica's throat. "I will always have the need to create gowns, Madame. My designs are who I am. It's what I do. Except now, it's more important than ever that I keep what I do a secret."

Madame Lamont smiled widely and bowed slightly. "Your secret is safe with me, my lady."

Jessica took a deep breath just as the door opened and a girl in a gray and maroon-striped skirt stepped into the room.

"Excuse me, Madame. But the Duchess of Stratmore is here to inquire about her gown, and you said when she came you wanted to speak with her."

"Yes. Oh yes." Madame Lamont rose from her chair. "I will only be a moment," she said, nodding to Jessica and to Melinda. "Explain to Mary which fabrics and colors you want, and she will bring them to you. I'm sure you already have your gown pictured in your mind's eye," she said with a twinkle and a bright grin.

"I do," Jessica answered, fingering the design for her gown.

Madame Lamont turned when she reached the door. "I will be back as soon as I take care of the duchess, and then I had best meet with Lady Crestwall. She is a most frustrating and impatient woman, as you have probably already surmised." She motioned for the assistant to come closer. "Mary is completely at your disposal until I return to you."

When Madame Lamont exited the room, Jessica selected the material and accessories for her ball gown. Then she pored through volumes of Madame Lamont's private gallery. She recognized many of the creations she had designed and picked out a few of her favorites, making notes to alter them with a few minor changes so no one would recognize having seen them before. A neckline here. A collar and sleeves there. Epaulets of lace and ruffles replacing netting and gauze.

The simplest of the designs would be made into day dresses or gowns she would wear when she spent quiet evenings at home. The more elaborate of the designs would be changed into the special gowns Simon would expect the Countess of Northcote to wear when they went out.

After an hour of looking, Jessica had found eleven designs she would have Madame Lamont make for her. The twelfth was her special design of white silk moiré and soft apricot satin. She sighed gently when she looked at it again. It would indeed be very special.

With loving gentleness, she placed it to the side and turned back to her other gowns, losing herself in the kaleidoscope of fabrics and designs and colors placed before her. She set samples of finished satins and smooth silks and soft velvets beside the picture of each gown. Mixing and matching and comparing some of the finest materials she had ever seen, from rich brocades to versatile linens to exquisite laces, nothing skipped her notice. She hardly realized she was not alone. Each time a clerk brought more bolts of fabric into the room, she sifted through them with the enthusiasm of a child in a candy store.

Finally, she stepped back and looked at her finished selections. She rolled her shoulders to ease the burning stiffness and breathed a deep sigh. Done. Each pattern with the materials selected for it lay in a nice, neat row, waiting for a seamstress to begin work.

Jessica turned around. "What do you think?" she asked Melinda.

Melinda rose from the divan where she'd been observing for the last hour and more, and walked to the table. The expression on her face beamed with open adoration. "I think I will never again select a gown or decide what color to make it without you at my side. There is not one thing I would change on any of them." Melinda placed her hand on Jess's arm. "You love doing this, don't you, Jess?"

"Yes. I cannot imagine doing anything else. I cannot imagine not being able to create. It's something I can't explain, Mel, but the designs and colors and fabrics are in here," she said, pointing to her chest, "waiting to come out."

"You are a marvel to watch. Truly, a wonder."

"I don't think that. I fear most people would think I'm crazed." Jessica swallowed past the lump in her throat. "Or worse."

The door opened behind them, and Melinda motioned for her to turn. Madame Lamont bustled through the door carrying a small bag. "Here," she said, closing the door and turning the lock to make sure they were not interrupted. "I have brought payment for the design you delivered today. Do not think anything has changed, my lady. I have no intention of paying more for your designs just because you are titled."

A bright smile covered Madame Lamont's face, and both Jessica and Melinda laughed at her humor.

"I'm shocked, Madame," Jessica said in mock surprise. "I was certain you would double my payment because of my new title."

"I would double your coins only because of your talent, my friend. Never because of your title."

They all laughed again as Madame Lamont placed the tiny velvet bag in Jessica's hand. "I assume you do not want the money applied to the exorbitant bill your husband will receive."

Jessica held the bag tight. "No. The money from the designs is mine. Lord Northcote will never know about it."

"He will never discover your talent from me. But be sure to warn him of my bill."

"Do not worry. Northcote ordered me to spare no expense. The ball we will attend Friday is far too important for him to worry about a paltry few hundred pounds in dressmaker's fees."

"Paltry?" Madame Lamont said with a shocked look on her face. "I will remind you of your words, my lady, when you have to explain my bill to your husband."

They all laughed, then Jessica and Melinda moved to the door. "The gown will be ready by Friday, Madame?" Jessica asked to make sure.

"Yes. It shall be ready. My seamstresses are sewing tiny pearls on the silk already. They will work on nothing else until it is finished."

"Thank you, Madame."

Madame Lamont reached for Jessica's hands and held them in her own. "No, Lady Northcote. I thank you. If not for you, I would be nothing. Your designs have made me famous. Your creations have gained me entrance to not only the cream of society, but to the queen herself. And your friendship is more valuable than the most precious gem in the world. I am rich beyond measure."

Jessica was past words. When Madame Lamont opened her arms, Jessica took one step and held the dressmaker close. Jessica had such few friends, but those she had were so very special. "I must go now," she said, fighting the emotion that wanted to dampen her eyes. "Thank you again for your help."

"The pleasure is mine," Madame Lamont answered, walking them to the door.

Every pair of eyes followed them, the gaping looks of shock and surprise still there.

Chapter 15

❦

*W*hen they exited Madame Lamont's shop, Sanjay stood beside the carriage waiting for them. "Did you have a good day, missy?" he asked, first helping Melinda into the carriage, then Jessica.

"Yes, Sanjay. A very good day." She sat in the seat opposite Melinda and smoothed her skirt. "I'm afraid your master will think I had an outlandishly good day when he receives the bill."

Sanjay laughed. "That will be the master's worry, then," he answered, making sure she could see his face. "Are we ready to go home, missy?"

"Yes," Jessica answered, but Melinda jumped forward and reached for her hand.

"No. Wait. I forgot my reticule. I left it in Madame Lamont's office."

Jessica looked at Sanjay. "Would you mind returning for Lady Collingsworth's reticule, Sanjay?"

Sanjay bowed low with a smile on his face. "Yes, missy. I will be right back."

Jessica watched Sanjay turn away, and when he disappeared into the shop, her gaze moved to three men sitting on a wooden bench in a little shaded area Madame Lamont had for bored husbands and those not inclined to mingle amongst a gaggle of gossiping women discussing fashion and finery.

She recognized two of the men—Baron Farley and Viscount Reddington. Farley was a plump, middle-aged gentleman with a shiny bald crown gleaming in the bright sunshine. Jessica thought his head would soon be deep red if he didn't put on the hat he held in his hand.

Reddington sat in the middle, and Jessica recognized him immediately by his long mane of snow-white hair. Few elderly men were blessed with such beautiful white hair as the viscount had.

"Who is the man sitting on the bench beneath that big shade tree, Mel? The man holding the gold-handled walking stick?"

Melinda leaned forward in her seat and looked out the window. "That is the Earl of Chitwood. He's probably paying court to Lady Crestwall. Rumor has it that the earl is in dire need of the money the marchioness was left by her late husband."

Jessica watched their mouths as they discussed their surprise at seeing the Northcote carriage in public and the strange Indian servant who had been waiting in the sunshine for the past two hours.

"*Did you catch a glimpse of Northcote's new bride?*" Baron Farley asked, dabbing at the top of his head with a white lace handkerchief.

"*Only from the back as she left the dressmaker's.*" The earl turned his stick in front of him and then raised his hand to smooth the red satin cravat at his neck. "*Lillian says she is quite common. Wears the most atrocious gowns imaginable. She cannot fathom someone as well-bred and refined as Northcote marrying her of his own free will. She is sure there must have been pressure applied from some quarter."*

Reddington raised his shoulders, and both men turned to him. "*The talk at White's,*" he said, nodding his head, "*is that the shy little recluse came with a very large bank account. That would make even the most reluctant of men overlook a multitude of flaws in a wife. A large dowry often more than makes up for the lack of a title as well as a homely face and no personality.*"

"*And I cannot think of anyone more desperate for a dowry than Northcote,*" the earl said.

"*But so desperate that he would saddle himself with Tanhill's stepsister?*" the baron asked, twisting his hat in his hand.

The earl tapped his walking stick on the cobblestones a few times and then continued. "*I have it on good authority that Northcote had no choice. He either took her as his wife or he lost everything. Although, what he thinks when he compares her to Rosalind is far beyond me.*"

"*Perhaps he no longer thinks of Rosalind,*" Reddington said. The stunned looks both men gave him showed their disbelief.

"*Would you be able to wake up each morning facing another woman, and not think that you could be waking up next to the beautiful Rosalind?*" the earl said.

Baron Farley wiped the perspiration from his forehead again. "*Not a chance.*" He stopped in midmotion. "*What do you think will happen when Rosalind and Northcote come face-to-face? I'm surprised they haven't already. She's bound to want things to be as they were before.*"

"*But he is married now,*" the earl said.

Baron Farley lifted his head and laughed. "*Do you think a wedding band will cause Rosalind a moment's hesitation? If it does, it will be the first time.*"

The Earl of Chitwood gripped his outstretched hands on the gold handle of his walking stick and seriously contemplated the whole situation. "*I can only tell you what I would do if I were Northcote. As soon as I was assured of an heir, I would pack my wife off to the country so I would be free to set Rosalind up as my mistress. I can't imagine Northcote keeping his dowdy wife underfoot here in London while he is out having a gay time with the beautiful Rosalind. I doubt his lovely mistress would be adverse to spending the Northcote wealth for a second time.*"

Both men laughed. "*I should say not,*" Baron Farley said. "*And this time she could have it all without the boundaries of marriage.*"

The pressure in Jessica's chest tightened. She tried to swallow twice before she could make her throat work. Melinda tugged on her arm, trying to gain her attention, but she ignored her.

Simon was in love with another woman. Someone he intended to make his mistress.

Melinda tapped her arm again, and Jessica slowly turned toward her. Sanjay had returned and was waiting for permission to go home. He looked first at the three men now standing in front of the wooden bench, then looked back at her. There was a frown on his face.

"Is everything all right, missy?"

Jessica wanted to answer, but she could not make her voice work. She could only nod her head and sit back in the seat of the carriage with her hands clenched.

"Jessica. What is it?" Melinda said, reaching across the seat to hold Jessica's hands. "What were those three men saying?"

"Nothing. Nothing important." Jessica closed her eyes and swallowed hard. "Are we ready, Sanjay?"

"Yes, missy. I will take us home now."

Sanjay leaped to the top of the carriage with the driver, and Jessica leaned back against the soft maroon leather seats when the carriage lurched forward. Melinda asked twice more what was wrong, but how could Jessica tell her she'd just had her worst fears voiced out loud? How could she tell her she'd just seen three of Simon's peers confirm that there was another woman in her husband's life? And that Simon would probably send her away, or even worse, *put* her away so she would not find out about his mistress.

The tightness in her chest gripped harder. She'd told herself it wasn't safe to develop feelings for her husband, but how could she not care for him a little after the night she'd spent in his arms? How could she not care a little when she could still feel his strong, warm body covering hers, or relive the gentleness of his touch as he took her? How was it possible not to care just a little for someone with whom you shared something so special?

Jessica closed her eyes and worried her lower lip. It was far too late to stop herself from developing feelings for him. She already cared for him more than was wise.

They drove the short distance to Melinda's town house in silence. When they arrived, Jessica thanked her friend for all her help, then waited in the closed carriage while Sanjay escorted Melinda to the door. It didn't take long, and they were again on their way.

As the carriage rolled over the cobblestone streets, she played the conversation she'd seen over and over in her mind. Everything the three men had said was true. She was plain and ordinary to look at. Simon had only married her for her money. He had come to her bed only because he was obligated, because it was necessary for him to produce an heir. As soon as he was assured his seed grew within her, he would undoubtedly never touch her again.

Jessica tried to calm the fury building within her. How naive she had been to think there was not another woman in Simon's life. How naive she had been to think he could ever want her. How naive she had been to think he would be satisfied with a deaf woman as his wife.

Jessica fisted her hands in her lap. It was a known fact that many of Simon's peers kept mistresses. She'd thought this would not matter to her. As long as she was free to create her gowns, she could survive. As long as she could support herself with her creations, she would manage. But that was not the way it would be. He could not take the chance of running into his wife while escorting his mistress around London. He would want to send her away.

Jessica's fear grew greater, her determination more resolved. She would not last a week if she were relegated to some obscure country manor so her husband was free to be with someone he still loved.

She had to protect herself. She had to have the home he'd promised to give her before they had married. She had to have a place to call her own if—when—he left her for this Rosalind.

When the carriage pulled up in front of Simon's town house, Jessica almost jumped out before Sanjay had a chance to help her. The desperation she felt rushed through her veins as she raced up the walk and through the door Hodgekiss held open.

"Is the master in his study, Hodgekiss?" she asked.

"Yes, my lady. The Earl of Collingsworth and Mr. Cambden left a short while ago. The master is still working."

"Thank you," Jessica said, walking to the door. She knocked once and lifted the handle.

Simon looked up.

A look of concern replaced the smile on his face. "What is wrong, Jessica?"

He rose from his chair and took one step around the desk. Her raised hand stopped him. "I would like to speak to you. It's important."

The worry on his face deepened. "Has something happened?"

"No," she answered, shaking her head. "I only need to speak with you."

Jessica tried to relax her fingers when she saw his gaze focus on the tight fists she made at her side.

He took another step toward her, and she instinctively stepped back. She didn't know why. She wasn't afraid of him. She never had been.

She pushed aside her desire for him to put his arms around her and hold her. Something warned her she needed a certain amount of space to separate them.

"Very well," he said, stepping back behind the desk. He pointed to a chair in front of the desk where he intended for her to sit. "Now, what is so important that you could not even take time to remove your cloak and gloves before you came to speak to me?"

Jessica looked at the gloves still on her hands and pushed her fingers deeper into the folds of her cloak. She lifted her shoulders and took in a deep breath. "I would like to speak to you about the demand I made before I agreed to marry you."

"The demand?" The confusion on his face was obvious. So was the irritation.

"The house you promised you would provide for me."

"You have a house, Jesse. This house. Our house. You will not live anywhere but with me."

"You promised me a house that I could call my own."

"Bloody hell," he said, placing his palms flat on the top of the desk.

With a quick jerk, he shoved his chair away from the desk and stood. He braced his arms and glared down at her with the most menacing look Jessica had ever seen.

"What the hell has brought this on? What happened while you were out that made you think of demanding a house?"

She stood to face him. "Nothing. It's just that I need to know that I have a home of my own when…if I am no longer satisfied here."

"With what aren't you satisfied, Jessica? The house?"

"It's not the house," she answered, keeping a brave front.

"The furnishings? The servants?"

"No."

"With me?"

She couldn't answer.

Simon took three angry steps around the desk and stood directly in front of her. "Don't tell me you're not satisfied, wife. Not after what happened between us last night."

Jessica's face burned flaming hot. "That has nothing to do with anything. What happened wasn't real. It was—"

"Oh, it was real, wife. No amount of pretending can convince you it wasn't."

Jessica's heart beat faster. He could not go back on his word. She would not let him. "You promised. You promised I would have a house of my own."

"I bloody well know what I promised, wife. I have not forgotten. But I want to know what happened that made having your own house suddenly so damned important?"

"It just is," Jessica shouted.

Simon grabbed her by the shoulders and held her at arm's length. "What is behind this, dammit!"

Jessica wanted to strike the man who'd vowed to be her husband. "Who is Rosalind?"

Simon dropped his hands to his sides and took a step back from her. Fury blazed in his eyes, and anger tightened the muscles of his face. "Bloody hell."

* * *

Jessica watched Simon's reaction to Rosalind's name with a sense of devastation. Spikes of black anger flashed in his eyes before he turned his back to her.

A knot twisted in the pit of her stomach. She'd prayed what she'd heard had been nothing more than idle gossip, male boasting. Now she knew it was not. Now she knew the comments linking Simon to a beautiful woman he had loved in the past—probably still loved today—were true.

She took several deep breaths. She'd known from the beginning there was little chance he could ever love her, but she'd hoped that in time their relationship would develop. Perhaps even into affection. Now she knew that would never happen. Simon was in love with someone else. A woman named Rosalind.

He braced one hand against the window frame while he stared out into the sunshine. The sunshine didn't reach them. Instead, an ominous darkness engulfed the space that separated them.

She focused on the ramrod straight line of his spine; his taut, muscular legs; and the white-knuckled fist clenched behind his back. He did not move. She assumed he was formulating an acceptable explanation. After all, how many men found it easy to explain the woman they intended to take as a mistress to their wife?

She could see each heaving breath he took. His shoulders broadened and the smooth material of his white lawn shirt stretched across the rippling muscles of his shoulders and upper arms. When he turned around, the determined fierceness she saw frightened her.

"Who told you about Rosalind?"

"Her name was mentioned."

The hostility in his eyes turned harsher. "You will never speak of her again. Do you understand?"

The severe look on Simon's face wrapped her heart in a blanket of dread.

He turned away from her and stared out the window again as if looking the other way would put a halt to their conversation.

"Do you still love her?"

Simon spun around to face her, his hooded eyes dark and angry. "Do not enter that part of my life, Jessica. She has nothing to do with us."

"Doesn't she?"

Simon pounded a fist on the top of the desk. "No! She was part of my disastrous past. You are my wife now. That is all that should matter."

Heaven help her, she could not let it die. She could not pretend it didn't matter. Her whole future rested on the woman named Rosalind and whether or not Simon still loved her.

"What is Rosalind to you, Simon?"

He stood before her, his body rigid and tall, resignedly stoic in stature. For a long moment he didn't answer. When he did, his straightforward gaze pierced her to her very soul.

"Nothing. She is nothing to me."

Simon's words were as bleak as the look in his eyes. If only he would answer her outright. If only he would explain what Rosalind meant to him. His evasiveness had only one meaning. It was an admission that he loved her, but something had happened to stop him from marrying her. Perhaps the loss of his money.

Jessica struggled to keep her emotions from running wild. She tried to keep her fears at bay. Money was no longer a problem for Simon. Only an unwanted wife. Heaven help her.

She prepared herself to battle him further, to challenge him and the lies he wanted her to believe, but suddenly he changed. The rigid bearing of his stern carriage slackened, then yielded in relaxed resignation. For the first time ever, he looked defeated. With tentative footsteps, he crossed the room and stood before her.

His look was softer, more conciliatory. She braced her shoulders, refusing to let his nearness affect her. She could not trust him, or herself. She could not fall prey to his charms.

He lifted her chin with his fingers. "I will not let Rosalind come between us. I want you to forget you ever heard her name. Whatever was between us died a long time ago."

"But—"

"No, Jessica. You must trust me in this. Anything you read on anyone's lips is nothing but vicious gossip and speculation. Do you understand?"

Jessica nodded, ignoring the first cold tremor that traversed her spine.

"Rosalind belongs in the past, and that is where she will stay. You need not concern yourself with her ever again."

Jessica fought to control the voice that screamed in her head. She fought to control the devastation that threatened to consume her. She thought Colin was her only threat. She'd prayed Simon would be her salvation. Now she knew she could rely only on herself.

Simon reached for her and grasped her by the shoulders. There was a look of desperation in his eyes, a tenacious bond in the way he held her. "You shall have your house, Jessica. I will send for Ira first thing in the morning, and you can discuss the details with him to your satisfaction. But you will never leave me."

He cupped her face between his hands and tilted her head so she could see every word he spoke. "If a house of your own will make you feel safer, you will have what you want. But I will hear no more talk of separate homes, or separate lives, or separate beds. You are my wife. You must trust me to look after you and keep you safe."

He pulled her close to him and then lowered his head and covered her lips with his own. His kiss was harsh and demanding. Passionate and consuming.

No matter how hard she tried to fight the effect of his hands caressing her and his lips touching hers, she could not. His mastery over her was too complete. Her need to be held by him too overpowering.

Her husband had already awakened needs she thought were forever dead. He'd aroused passions she ached to have assuaged.

Heaven help her. She was doomed if she allowed herself to care for him.

She was on a course with certain disaster because she already did.

Chapter 16

Simon paced back and forth the length of the drawing room, then turned and paced the room again, waiting for Jessica to come downstairs so they could go to the ball. Out of the corner of his eye, he caught James watching him. The amused grin on the Duke of Collingsworth's face broadened, and Simon leveled him the most ferocious scowl he could muster. To his abject frustration, his longtime friend answered with a burst of laughter.

"Heavens, Northcote. Just watching you is exhausting. By the time we get to the ball, I'll be too tired to even dance one dance with my wife." Collingsworth crossed one ankle atop his other knee and curved his arm over the back of the sofa. "Surely you aren't concerned with the *ton*'s reaction as to how Jessica will look?"

"What kind of arrogant fool do you think I am? I have never cared one whit what the *ton* thinks about looks. I only want to introduce the Countess of Northcote into society and assure my peers that my wife and I intend to take our rightful places among them."

"And you do not trust that your wife will look the part?"

Simon poured a very small amount of brandy into a snifter and stared at the golden liquid swirling in the glass. "I would be proud of her even if she were barefooted and garbed in homespun cloth." A picture of Jessica garbed just that way flashed before his eyes. A picture of her standing in the middle of their bedroom, as she had last night, her bare toes curled beneath the simple, homemade nightdress that hung to her narrow ankles, and long chestnut-brown hair cascading over her shoulders and past her waist. A warm heat coursed through his veins as he remembered the way she'd opened her arms to him and held him close to her. The way she'd given herself to him.

"I have little to fear concerning her looks," he said, mentally shaking himself. "That famous dressmaker, Madame Lamont, arrived early this morning, sporting a whole entourage of fitters and seamstresses. Before they were finished, your wife's lady's maid arrived, armed with hair irons and sweet-smelling soaps and face powders. She was ready to 'face the difficult challenge,' as she so bluntly put it.

"All day long, servants rushed up and down the stairs carrying armloads of towels and hot water and feminine things to be pressed, and more hot water and more frilly things to be pressed."

"And this has you worried?"

Simon threw the brandy down his throat and let the liquid blaze a path all the way down. "Hell yes. What are they doing to her? Other than her outdated clothing, she is perfect. She doesn't need to be painted up like a phony actress on a stage or made up to be a fake china doll everyone is afraid to touch. She needs to stay exactly as she is. I don't want her changed."

Simon gave his friend a most severe glare when the Duke of Collingsworth roared with laughter. "I swear,

Simon. I can see that marriage to Jessica has already changed you."

"I have not changed in the least," he said, rubbing his hand over his smooth jaw. "I just don't want her altered. And I don't want her to be put through any more than she already has been. Attending the ball tonight will demand enough from her."

Simon did not wait for his friend to comment. He walked to the far window and looked out onto the terrace and the garden beyond. "I have not seen a lot of kindness in my life. My mother died too soon for me to remember much of a female's tenderness. Very seldom could Father tear himself away from his gaming and carousing and endless round of parties and balls to show me much more interest than he showed the butler or his valet."

Simon locked his hands behind his back and filled his lungs with a deep breath. "I would be lying if I told you I didn't resent him and the way he lived. At times I even hated him. Especially after Rosalind."

Simon turned. "That's why tonight is so important. It's important that I face the *ton* and stand proudly before them as I was unable to do the whole time while my father was alive." Simon fisted his hands. "But I know how terrified Jessica is. She's only doing this because I'm forcing her. She's terrified that someone will find out she cannot hear and she'll be labeled the freak she thinks she is."

Simon sat in the chair opposite James. "You've known her for some time, James. She went to the balls, did she not?"

"Yes. But she didn't stay long. She sat off to the side, well out of the way, and never talked to anyone but Melinda.

She stayed only until most of the guests had arrived, then quietly exited a side door. Usually, most in attendance didn't even realize she was there."

"Why did she go? It wasn't to meet people. It wasn't because she felt the need to belong. And heaven only knows, it wasn't to have someplace to wear her fancy gowns. Until now, she didn't own a gown worth wearing in public."

His Grace smiled at that. "No. It wasn't because of her gowns."

Simon lifted his gaze. "Why, James? Why did she go, when facing people terrifies her so?"

"I don't know. I've often asked Melinda that same question, but she never gives me an answer. Perhaps she went only to see the people. To see who danced with whom, and how the women wore their hair, and their beautiful gowns. And pretend."

"Pretend?" Simon asked.

"Yes, pretend. Pretend that she was the one in the pretty gown, dancing in the arms of a handsome man. I don't know. Far be it from me to try to understand women. Even my wife still confuses me."

Simon smiled at Collingsworth's honesty, then leaned his head against the back of the chair. "Something happened the day Jessica went with Melinda to see Madame Lamont."

"I know. Melinda said Farley, Reddington, and Chitwood were sitting on a bench outside Madame Lamont's shop. Jessica was totally absorbed in their conversation."

"Is that who it was?" Simon said, rubbing the heel of his hand against his eye. "I asked Sanjay what had happened, and he only knew she'd watched three men talk."

"Melinda said after they left, your wife was clearly upset, but she wouldn't talk about it. Did she tell you what they'd said?"

Simon fought to breathe past the knot that hammered in his chest. "She asked me about Rosalind."

A lingering silence hung in the room, and finally Collingsworth released a long breath that hissed through his teeth. "What did you say?"

"I'm afraid I didn't handle it well at all. In the first place, her question took me totally by surprise. I didn't think she knew about Rosalind. And I was not in the best of moods, as you probably remember. This happened right after my meeting with you and Ira. The more I pored over the papers Ira had left, the angrier I became. I'm afraid I didn't need much of a spark to set me off, and nothing sets me off faster than being reminded of Rosalind."

"So, what did you tell her?"

Simon shoved himself out of the chair and gripped the cushions at the back. "I told her Rosalind did not matter and that I never wanted her name mentioned again."

His Grace leaned back in the chair and stared at Simon. "Did she understand?"

"What do you think? You are married. Would Melinda have understood?"

"Not a chance," His Grace answered on a humorless laugh.

"Well, neither did Jessica. I don't know what the three men said, but I can only guess. I was hoping I could be the one to tell my wife about my...stepmother." Simon could not keep the bitterness out of his voice.

"Perhaps she feels threatened by Rosalind? You were engaged to marry her, you know."

"Don't remind me," Simon said. "But I don't think Rosalind is the only person by whom she feels threatened."

"Then who?"

Simon stared at his reflection in the mirror on the wall. "Me. I'm the one forcing her to face every one of her worst nightmares while I'm getting everything I always dreamed of having. More money than I ever thought to have at my disposal, my rightful place in society, and the assurance that the Northcote name will never be outcast. What has she gained from our marriage?"

The Duke of Collingsworth sat straight in his chair. "Protection from Tanhill."

Simon steadied his gaze until it locked with James's serious expression. "Do you know what she asked from me when she returned from Madame Lamont's?"

James shook his head.

"She asked for a house of her own. A safe haven where she could go should she ever need to escape from…" Simon paused. "From whom, James? From Colin? Or from me?"

"Surely she doesn't think she needs protection from you, Simon?"

"No." Simon lowered his head to his hands and breathed a heavy sigh. "Surely not me." A stab of guilt punched him in the gut. Since the day he'd realized who Jessica was and how much she was worth, every move he'd made had been calculated with one goal in mind.

To destroy Tanhill.

He had not married Jessica just to protect her from her stepbrother. Or to save his inheritance. He'd married her to take possession of the money Tanhill would steal from her as soon as he locked her away in an asylum. Money that would give his enemy more power than he or the rest of England could afford to let him have.

Simon leaned his head back against the cushion. He'd tried to convince himself that, in part, his actions were necessary to accomplish a greater cause—to save the vast Northcote estate. And to a point that was true.

The money had been necessary to pay his debts, necessary to rebuild his inheritance. But he'd resigned himself to losing everything before Jessica came with her offer. Marriage to her meant he could have everything—the money necessary to protect what was rightfully his, the level of respect and position of distinction he'd enjoyed before his father had ruined them, the ability to use the power associated with the Northcote name.

But those benefits were secondary when faced with the knowledge that Jessica's wealth gave him the capability to destroy Tanhill. Financially. Then, physically.

And what had he given his wife in return? Nothing except the promise of his name, which she now doubted he would use to protect her, a notoriety she did not want, and a dependence on him she refused to accept. And he was forcing her to risk exposing her deafness.

"Excuse me, Your Grace. My lord," Melinda interrupted from the doorway, "but I have come in search of two gallant and noble young gentlemen who would like to escort two charming and enchanting ladies to a ball."

The Duke of Collingsworth stood and executed a very low bow. "You happen to be in luck, Your Grace. It just so happens that my friend and I have gotten dressed for just such an occasion and are in need of two ravishingly beautiful females. And you, my dear, just happen to complete the order to perfection."

"Oh, how fortunate," Melinda said, accepting her husband's most improper embrace with no sign of embarrassment.

Simon turned to the doorway. His wife was nowhere in sight. "Did Lady Northcote come down with you?"

"No. I came down first to give her a moment to herself. She's nervous, as you might well imagine."

Simon walked to the door. Perhaps it would be best if he had a word with her before they left. He hadn't been able to see her all day. Twice he'd tried to breach the barrage of servants attending his wife, but Madame Lamont had taken over the role of commander in chief, and would not let him near her.

"Lord Northcote?"

He turned back to Melinda. She was still nestled in her husband's arms. "She will be all right, won't she? I mean, no one will find out that she cannot hear, will they?"

"No." Simon shook his head. "No one will find out she cannot hear."

The duchess nodded rapidly, then brought her folded hands up to her mouth. "I pray they won't. She is so proud."

Simon turned on his heel and walked out of the room. When he reached the center of the large foyer, he lifted his gaze upward.

The breath caught in his throat. Jessica stood on the balcony above wearing the gown Madame Lamont had promised would steal his breath.

The dressmaker had lied. Her description did not come close to preparing him for such a stunning sight.

A scattering of tiny pearls covered the wide overskirt, giving the gown the distinction of simple elegance. Her thick, coffee-rich hair was gathered upward on the crown of her head, allowing the mass of loose ringlets to tumble in layers away from her face and down her back. Only the faintest wisps of curls outlined her face, accented by thin apricot velvet ribbons the hairdresser had threaded in and out among the tendrils. The style was ever so simple, yet ever so elegant.

Swallowing past the lump in his throat, Simon moved to the bottom of the stairs and waited. His heart pounded in his ears as he watched her descend the stairs, one hand resting on the railing, the other clutching a delicate lace handkerchief that matched the apricot of her gown.

Her gaze locked with his, not moving, not wavering. It was as if the approval she saw in his eyes and the look of appreciation on his face gave her strength.

When she neared, he reached out his hand. Only when her warm flesh touched his did he remember to breathe.

He held both her hands in his for a moment, then brought them to his lips. "You, my dear," he said, lifting his head so she would not miss his words, "will, without a doubt, be the most beautiful woman at the ball tonight."

"I will not embarrass you?"

Simon touched his fingers to her cheeks. There was no thick, heavy powder on her face. No bright, gaudy colors on her cheeks and lips. "I should be the one worried that you will be embarrassed to be seen in the company of someone so ordinary looking as myself."

She shook her head and gave him a shy smile. Simon placed a finger beneath her chin and raised her gaze until she could see him. "Nothing will happen, Jesse. I will make certain that nothing happens."

She nodded, and Simon leaned down and kissed her forehead softly. "You are truly beautiful, Countess," he said, looking at her again. "Not one woman at the ball will be half so lovely."

When they turned around, the look he saw on the Duke and Duchess of Collingsworth's faces confirmed his opinion. His wife was perfect.

He wanted this night to be perfect, too. He didn't care what it took, he would make sure it was.

Tonight he would take the first step to bringing about everything he'd dreamed of accomplishing. He would introduce his wife into society and face his stepmother for the first time since his father's death. His blood raced at the thought of seeing Rosalind again.

* * *

Jessica clutched the glass of punch Simon handed her and prayed she could hold it steady when she brought it to her lips. She lifted it to her mouth and managed to take only a small, delicate sip instead of downing the entire glass to quench her dry throat.

Somehow, she had survived thus far.

How often had she dreamed of standing on the top of the stairs and having her name read aloud as she entered a brightly lit, beautifully decorated ballroom? How often had she fantasized about walking through a crowd of society's finest on the arm of the most handsome man in London? How often had she imagined herself standing in the midst of a crowd of people as if she belonged? Tonight it had actually happened.

She knew the exact moment their name was announced. The whole room turned in unison to stare at Simon and her, the looks of curiosity obvious. Simon stood at the top of the stairs with his hand covering hers and did not make a move. For the longest time, he let the *ton* drink its fill, evaluate the two of them. Then, he gently squeezed her hand, a signal for her to look at him. When she turned her head, the slow, seductive smile on his face warmed her to her very core.

She could not help but return his smile. Before they took their first step down the stairs to meet their host and hostess, he brought her hand to his lips and kissed her fingers. It was like a dream come true, and she indeed felt like a fairy princess on the arm of her Prince Charming.

Meeting the Earl and Countess of Milebanke had been a puzzling experience. The earl seemed pleased at their presence, but the countess greeted Simon with a chilly demeanor. The underlying glint in Lady Milebanke's eyes almost seemed malicious. Perhaps she and Simon had not always been on the best of terms? Perhaps she thought his presence would cause a catastrophe that would affect the success of her ball? Perhaps to have as her guests the couple foremost on the lips of society's greatest gossips was not worth the risk? Whatever the reason, Simon seemed to revel in the discomfort he caused.

All eyes in the room focused on them as they made their way to where the Duke and Duchess of Collingsworth waited for them.

"You seem to have a habit of bringing a room to a halt when you enter, my lord," Jessica said to her husband after they passed a small group who parted for them.

Simon smiled. "I think this time I'm not the one stopping the ball, wife. Very few eyes are upon me. And if Baron Cargille doesn't remove that lecherous grin from his face when he looks at you, he and I will have to have words before long."

She laughed. A heated warmth spread all through her when Simon covered her hand on his arm and pulled it closer to his body. She felt very secure and smiled confidently as they made their way over to the duke and duchess, near the terrace door.

"You look absolutely ravishing, Countess," His Grace said, bowing slightly. "Everyone here is in awe."

"Oh, Jessica," Melinda said, the look of excitement evident on her face. "All the women are green with envy over your gown. Lillian Crestwall informed Lady Stratmore that she knows for a fact your gown is an exclusive creation by that elusive designer who Madame Lamont has at her disposal. Now everyone is more anxious than ever to find out how to get a design from her."

Jessica held her breath, praying Simon would not question how she got her design in such short order.

Thankfully, he did not, and talk changed to other, less dangerous topics. As they visited, Jessica noticed Simon made sure he was never more than a hairbreadth away from her. Soon, the Earl and Countess of Burnhaven came to join them, and Jessica smiled as the conversation progressed easily between the six of them.

It was not long, however, before Lord and Lady Pepperlaine joined them, then a Lord Barkley, and the Duke and Duchess of Westlawn, all friends of Simon's or of His Grace's. Each, of course, made a point of including her in their conversation, and Jessica was grateful her gloves concealed her damp palms as she glanced from person to person, struggling not to miss anything.

Their group had grown too large. Jessica could not keep up with each mouth that moved. A wave of insecurity washed over her, and she took several deep breaths to steady her nerves.

As if Simon felt her growing panic, he reached for her hand and twined his fingers through hers. She looked up at him.

"They are playing a waltz, my lady," he said with a warm smile lighting his face. "I'm certain you recall promising the first waltz to me."

Jessica placed her hand on Simon's outstretched arm as he excused himself and his wife, then led her out onto the dance floor. He took her in his arms, as he had each night when they'd practiced in the darkness, and with a gentle smile, he led her in the steps that were by now so familiar she could do them without thinking.

She felt the warmth of his hand on her back and marveled at the security that enveloped her. Her hand tightened on the steel muscles spanning his shoulder, and she was engulfed by his strength. She felt safe as long as she was with Simon.

"You seemed uncomfortable just now," Simon said as they moved across the dance floor. "Why?"

Jessica kept her gaze focused on the easy smile on Simon's face and followed his lead. It was no different than when they danced at home in the privacy of their own bedroom. "The crowd. There were too many mouths to watch. I couldn't tell which ones were talking to me."

He held her a little closer. "I see. I didn't think of that. I will not let it happen again. Smile, Jesse," he said, squeezing her hand reassuringly. "The whole of society is watching us, and we wouldn't want to disappoint them."

She forced her lips upward. "No, my lord. We wouldn't want to disappoint them."

Simon turned her on the dance floor. "Do you know what? I think I prefer dancing with you in our bedroom to dancing here on a crowded dance floor. There are not nearly so many clothes separating us, and I can choose to end the dance whenever I like."

Jessica looked around to make sure no one was dancing close enough to have overheard her husband.

"Admit it, wife. Don't you wish the very same thing?"

Jessica felt her cheeks burn with embarrassment. How could he think such thoughts when they were but one mistake away from all of London finding out she could not hear?

"You loved it," he said, pulling her even closer to him. "I know you did."

Jessica held her breath while Simon's touch sent a spattering of tingling pulses racing through her. She knew the look in her eyes mirrored the passion they'd shared last night. "I think you are getting quite bold, my husband."

"If you don't want me to kiss you right here, my lovely little wife, with all these people watching, you had better stop looking at my mouth with such longing in your eyes."

Jessica quickly glanced to the side and swallowed past the lump in her throat. How was it possible for him to read her so well?

She looked up when his hand touched her chin and turned her face. "You shouldn't touch me so, Simon. Everyone is staring at us."

"Of course they're staring. You're the most beautiful woman in the room."

"That's not true. Most of the women are not half so interested in me as they are in you."

"Really? Do you think so?"

The innocent look on his face was as unexpected as the teasing gleam in his eyes. Both were unfamiliar to her. "Yes. I think when they look at me they wonder what you saw in me to marry me."

"No, wife. They know exactly what I saw in you, and they are envious because they do not possess it."

The breath caught in her throat. Did he really mean that? Jessica shook herself. No, she could not let herself think such thoughts for even a moment. She would only get hurt if she did.

Northcote swirled her around one final time and then stopped. The music must have ended, for all the other couples had stepped off the floor. As he led her back to where the Duke and Duchess of Collingsworth waited, Jessica thought that if nothing else, Simon had given her this one fairy-tale evening.

For these few hours, he'd allowed her to feel beautiful and desired and accepted. And he'd not only forced her to face society, he'd demanded that she become a part of it. She could not deny that it was something that still scared her to death. Something she would never have had the courage to do on her own.

She also could not deny that every time he held her, or kissed her, or made love to her, she cared for him a little more.

The power that gave him over her frightened her most.

Chapter 17

*S*imon stood to the side, watching Jessica dance the promised waltz with the Earl of Milebanke. Good Lord, but she was lovely. She seemed to float across the dance floor even though the plump, out-of-breath toad holding her in his arms seemed to have a difficult time just keeping step to the music.

An unfamiliar warmth surged through his body, starting deep within his chest and traveling to the tips of his fingers and toes. Blatant desire worked its way to the pit of his stomach and lower, where it swirled to an all-too-familiar ache of need Simon had sworn no woman would ever make him feel again.

He watched the smile on her face broaden at something Milebanke said, and then Simon moved his gaze to where the earl's beefy hand rested against the graceful curve of Jessica's slender waist. A violent wave of jealousy smacked him square in the chest.

He'd done nothing all night except fight off randy young bucks and middle-aged philanderers wanting to dance with the radiant young Countess of Northcote. Jessica was like the proverbial ugly duckling who had blossomed into a beautiful swan right before everyone's eyes. Simon cursed himself for showing the world what was hiding beneath that drab finery.

"She's doing splendidly, don't you think?" the Duke of Collingsworth said, handing Simon a glass of brandy.

"I think if the good earl moves his hand one inch lower on her waist, I'm going to call him out."

Collingsworth answered Simon's comment with a laugh, then glanced around with a more serious look on his face. "Is she here yet?"

"No."

"Perhaps she will not come."

Simon shook his head. "She'll be here. When have you known Rosalind to pass up an opportunity to set the *ton* on its ear?"

Collingsworth lifted his mouth in a cryptic grin. "You can almost feel the excitement, can't you? There's not a soul in the room who hasn't spent most of his or her time watching you and Jessica to make sure they haven't missed Rosalind's arrival."

Simon's gaze returned to Jessica. "I haven't noticed. I've been too busy watching that overfed windbag manhandle my wife."

Collingsworth laughed. "You have nothing to fear, Simon. The dance is over and Milebanke is bringing your wife back to you. Look. He's so winded he can hardly make it across the floor."

"By Jove, Northcote," a puffing Milebanke said, returning Jessica to Simon's side. "Your wife is the best partner I've had for a dance in years. Didn't stumble over her toes once."

Simon placed his arm around his wife's waist and pulled her to him.

"My wife should take lessons from her," Milebanke continued, wiping big beads of perspiration from his forehead. "She always complains that I cannot follow the beat, but the countess here had no trouble. Just goes to prove, it's my wife who has no ear for music and not me."

The Duchess of Collingsworth soon joined them, then Parker Waite, the Marquess of Bedford, and his lovely fiancée, Lady Linquist. Bedford had been a childhood friend of Simon's and was most eager to offer his congratulations on his recent marriage.

It seemed most of the *ton* was again curious to talk to him and meet his beautiful bride. Before long, the circle of well-wishers surrounding them had grown to a crowd. Simon looked down on Jessica's pale features and knew it was time to take her away. He reached for her hand and realized from the frightened look in her eyes when she looked at him it was almost too late.

"If you would please excuse us," he said loud enough for everyone to hear, "I think I would like to have another dance with my wife."

Simon wrapped his arm around Jessica's waist and led her to the dance floor without a backward glance. "I almost waited too long, didn't I?" he asked, holding her close.

He loved the feel of her in his arms. He loved looking into her eyes and seeing the emotions she tried to hide. He loved being this close to her. Sometimes that scared him to death.

"Almost," she replied, breathing a sigh that shuddered beneath his hand at her back. "You have a great many friends who want to welcome you back. You must have been well liked before you left."

"As well as most, I suppose," he answered, shrugging away the compliment.

"That's not what people say."

Simon raised his eyebrows and gave her a questioning look. "And just what do you see, Jesse? What new information and tales of scandal are you reading on people's lips tonight?"

"Much, my lord," she said with a smile on her face. "The *ton* is busy talking about both of us."

Simon laughed. "And what are they saying about you, my lady?"

She lowered her gaze, and Simon watched with interest the warm, rosy glow that covered her cheeks.

"Well, for the most part," she said, "they are impressed with my gown. I dare say, I have passed their scrutiny according to fashion, but I'm sure it's mostly because I'm dressed so differently from how they are used to seeing me."

"No, my lady. They are impressed because you are beautiful and there is no one who can compare to you."

Simon smiled when her cheeks glowed even brighter.

"I think, however, I will *not* repeat much of what I have read on people's lips concerning you, husband. I fear your head is far too large already, and I would not want to give you a false sense of greatness that I would just have to deflate later on."

Simon threw his head back and laughed. "What a saucy little wench you have become."

"I beg your pardon, sir, but I have always been the picture of politeness and decorum. Hardly saucy."

"Very well, my perfectly decorous little wench. What else have they said about us? I would like to know."

"Very well. If you insist. According to Lady Andover, you have always been far too serious, even when you were young, and she cannot get over that she has seen you smile at least half a dozen times already tonight."

"Oh, really?" he said with a chuckle.

"Yes. And dear Lady Dewitt, who hears hardly more than I, thinks you a besotted young fool and that the looks you are giving me are simply scandalous."

"Does she?" Simon looked over at the dowager countess sitting in a chair against the wall and graced her with one of his most magnificent smiles. "The poor old woman must be all of ninety years old. I wonder what she'd think if I kissed you right here on the dance floor?"

"Don't you dare. We have caused enough talk for one evening. I do not want to add to their natter."

"I think we have not given the *ton* nearly enough excitement, wife. I think I would like nothing more than to hold you close and kiss you."

Simon turned with her in his arms. They were close enough to the double French doors that led to the terrace that he could waltz her out into the cool night air. He led her to a quiet corner and stood with her beneath an orange-colored paper lantern. This is what he'd wanted to do all night.

The longer he'd looked at her this evening, the more he'd wanted to hold her. The more he'd wanted to press his mouth against hers and touch her in places he should not. The more he'd wanted to make love to her.

Before she had time to be shocked by his intentions, he pulled her close and lowered his mouth until their lips met. The fireball of passion that soared through his body was intense enough to pull a harsh moan from deep in his throat. He could not think of anything but holding and touching and taking her.

He tilted her head to the side and deepened his kiss. He pressed his lips to hers and drank from her sweetness. He ravaged the warm, moist cavern she opened to him, taking what she offered. He could not get enough of her.

She wrapped her arms around his neck, and he tightened his hold to keep her steady. He kissed her again, deeper, taking even more of her until neither of them could breathe. He wanted her so badly. He kissed her again, telling himself he had to stop.

Now.

With an agonizing moan, he lifted his head and pulled her up against him when her knees buckled beneath her.

She leaned her forehead against his chest, and he held her close to him while they gasped for air. For a long time, they both stood in the cool night air beneath the flickering orange lantern, waiting for their breathing to return to normal.

Finally, he tilted her chin upward and looked into her eyes, still glazed with passion. "I have wanted to do that, and more, all night. Ever since I saw you standing at the top of the staircase in your beautiful gown. Ever since I held you in my arms and danced that first waltz with you."

"I know," Jessica answered.

Simon heard the hoarseness in her voice. He traced her swollen lips with his index finger. "You do?"

"Yes. Lady Dewitt said so. She told Lady Andover she was surprised you had not taken me out into the garden long before now."

Simon lifted his gaze to the twinkling stars above and laughed. "I'm not sure I like that you can read what everyone says," he said when he lowered his head so Jessica could see what he was saying. "You may read something you will wish you had not seen or believe some gossip that is false, and I won't be able to set you straight."

Jessica stiffened in his arms. "You mean, you won't be able to censor what I discover, my lord?"

"No. I would never censor what you can or cannot see, wife. I would only advise you to realize that not all you read on people's lips is anything more than gossip."

"Don't you think I already know that, Simon? I have been watching what people have said for years, and it's usually fairly easy to tell what is based on fact and what is simply a vicious rumor."

"And what fact can you dispel as vicious rumor tonight?"

She looked at him in all seriousness and breathed a sigh as if debating whether or not to trust him with a vital bit of information. "I can dispel the rumor that Lord Cardwell is going to ask for the Duke of Dunford's eldest daughter's hand in marriage."

"But of course he is, Jessica. The match has been understood for years, and I heard just tonight all that is left to finalize are the last few details before the engagement is announced."

"No, Simon. The match was called off just this afternoon and no one knows it yet."

"How do you know this?"

257

"I saw a conversation between Lord Dunford's youngest daughter and another friend. She said her sister is so distraught she doubts she will ever be well enough to leave the house again."

"But Cardwell needs that match. Everyone knows he's desperate and needs the dowry that Dunford will provide. Why has he bolted?"

"I cannot say."

"I think you can. Don't leave me hanging now, wife."

Jessica looked around, and when she was satisfied there was no one about who could hear them, she continued. "He's in love with someone else."

"Someone else? Who?"

"Lady Belmont. But he cannot reveal his feelings yet. She has been widowed less than a year. It's too soon."

"But she's penniless."

"It will cause quite a scandal, won't it? The son of a penniless earl giving up a sizable fortune to marry a penniless widow, all in the name of love. You think it's a mistake?"

Simon looked at her. "I think there are times when duty, obligation, and responsibility leave no room for love. There are times when we have no choice but to ignore what our hearts want us to do and let our heads rule our actions."

"Is that what you did when you married me?"

Jessica's question stopped him short. "No. I was not in love with anyone else when I married you."

The look in her eyes told him she wanted to believe what he said, but the rumors she'd heard about Rosalind wouldn't let her.

"My heart belongs to no one save myself, Jessica. I told you from the beginning it never would. My reasons for

marrying you were never a secret, and I sacrificed no unre-
quited love to achieve what I needed. If you need a reason
why I took you as my wife, you have three. Duty, obligation,
and responsibility. Nothing more." Simon paused. The spell
had been broken. "We should go in now."

He wanted to turn away from the hurt he saw on her
face, but he didn't. It was best if she never let herself entertain any romantic notions about their marriage.

"Yes. Perhaps we should go in," she said, turning away.
She took two steps and then stopped. "One more thing,
Simon," she said, turning back.

"And what is that?"

"The owner of Great Northern Shipping has arrived
from India."

The air left Simon's lungs. "Are you sure?"

"Yes. Sydney Carver was here for a short time earlier and
said he could not stay long because he had an important
meeting he dare not miss."

"Perhaps he has another meeting? Perhaps—"

"No. He said he had to go down to the Great
Northern Shipping office, and he wished the bast—
He wished the man he was going to meet would have
stayed in India."

A blast of icy dread chilled him to his bones. "Did he
call him by name?"

"No." There was a confused look on her face when she
looked up at him. "I thought you knew his name?"

"I do. And it's not important."

That was a lie. His name was as important to Simon as
it would be to his wife. Simon closed his eyes and blocked
out the innocent expression he saw on her face.

He was not ready yet. He had not had enough time. Not enough time to prove to Jessica that she could trust him. Not enough time to convince her she would be safe with him.

Especially after she found out the reason he had married her was to destroy her stepbrother.

Chapter 18

$\mathscr{S}$imon felt the change in the crowd the moment he and Jessica stepped into the ballroom. Every breath of air seemed charged with the hint of impending excitement.

She was here. He felt it.

He'd waited three years for this night. He'd traveled thousands of miles and been haunted by scores of unanswered questions. Rosalind was not going to go unchallenged one more day.

The blood roared in his head. He would finally know what had happened the night of his father's death. And when he forced the truth from her, the entire *ton* would be here to witness her confession. And he would be cleared of any connection with his father's death.

Simon led Jessica through the room. With each step, his gaze scanned the throngs of gaping people.

"Is it too soon to go home, Simon?"

Simon looked down at Jessica. He could tell from the uneasy look on her face she felt the change, too. She worried her lower lip while the frown on her forehead deepened.

"In a little while, Jesse. It won't be long now."

He clasped his arm around her waist as one by one the couples stepped aside. Like the parting of the Red Sea, they opened to let them through, leaving a path down the center of the room.

Men in tailcoats and women in voluminous skirts fanned out as if petals falling from a rose to reveal the hidden center.

Simon wanted to jeer at the crowd. They anticipated the revealing of a priceless treasure. Of a love lost yet still alive and blooming. Little did they know that he could not put into words how he felt about Rosalind. There were not words vile enough.

The crowd parted to reveal the hidden treasure.

Rosalind, Lady Northcote, posed before them, her beauty as magnificent as he remembered, her regal bearing befitting royalty reigning over her subjects.

Her red satin gown shimmered with every move of her hourglass figure. Tiny streamers of glistening diamonds glittered in her mass of jet-black curls that hung down nearly to her waist.

He'd forgotten how stunning a picture she presented. He'd forgotten how absolutely beautiful she was. He'd forgotten everything except how much he detested her.

"Hello, Simon." With brazen aplomb, Rosalind stepped toward them, flashing a smile so seductive only a blind person could miss it.

From the hesitation in Jessica's step, Simon knew his wife had not.

The look in Rosalind's eyes showed not a hint of trepidation. Not a glimmer of remorse. But blatant aggression.

The crowd of onlookers gathered closer around them. Circling them. Making them the central attraction.

This was what he wanted—to meet her face-to-face. He would explain everything to his wife later. After Rosalind admitted what happened the night his father died. When he finally knew of her involvement.

"Lady Northcote." Simon acknowledged her with a bow, too slight to be considered polite.

His blood boiled when she turned her flirtatious wiles on him.

"What a pleasant surprise, my lord."

"Is it?"

"Why of course. You can't imagine how much I have missed you."

Simon arched his eyebrows. The pouty protrusion of her lips sickened him. "I wasn't sure you would actually come tonight."

"Really? Why not?"

"We hardly parted on the best of circumstances. The night my father died was—"

She lifted a gloved hand. "Let's not speak of such unpleasantness now." Rosalind whipped open her fan and waved it in front of her face. In front of her mouth.

From the way Jessica stiffened beside him, he knew she could no longer see what was being said.

"You look wonderful, my lord. Even more handsome than when I last saw you." Rosalind placed her black-gloved hand on his arm as if she had a right to touch him.

Simon had to force himself not to recoil. He didn't have to look down to see Jessica's reaction. He could feel her hand clench tighter around his arm.

"Aren't you going to tell me I look wonderful, too?" she said, lowering her lashes seductively.

"My approval has never been important to you. I hardly think it's warranted now."

"Dear me," she said, snapping her fan closed and slapping it against the palm of her hand. "A bit owlish tonight, aren't we? Not at all how I would prefer you to be after all this time." Rosalind skimmed her tongue slowly across her ruby-red lips, then puckered them in a seductive pout. "Would it be possible to speak with you in private, my lord? It's so terribly crowded here."

Simon smiled. "I hardly think so, my lady. I prefer an audience when I am with you."

"Do you?" She laughed. "Then an audience you shall have. But I'm quite thirsty. I'm going to get a drink from the refreshment table. We can continue our conversation there."

Simon was left with no choice but to follow Rosalind to the refreshment table in a remote alcove of the ballroom. They were no longer surrounded by a crowd of eavesdroppers, but only a few couples who were getting something to drink. None of them made a move to leave, but stayed to overhear whatever they could.

Rosalind took a glass of punch a servant handed her, then turned to face him. "Have you missed me, my lord?" she asked after she took her first small sip. "I have to admit that I have missed you."

"No, Rosalind. I haven't missed you at all."

Simon stepped to the side, in hopes that Jessica would be able to see Rosalind's mouth. But Rosalind moved further away. Realizing there was nothing he could do to gain his wife the advantage, he gave up and stood his ground.

"Have you been to your husband's grave lately?" he said. "Placed even a flower there in remembrance?"

Rosalind shot him a harsh glare, her face a decidedly paler shade. "How unkind to bring up something so painful at such a festive occasion. You have no idea how devastated I was. It took me forever to recover from my loss."

"More than a few hours? I can hardly believe such sentiment." Simon straightened his shoulders. "Perhaps guilt made your recovery more difficult. Tell me, Lady Northcote. I have never quite understood what occurred that night. I have never been able to picture in my mind how my father's accident could possibly have happened."

The uncomfortable look on Rosalind's face quickly faded. She banished her unease with a laugh. When it came to acting, she was a professional.

She glanced around at the couples scattered nearby who could undoubtedly hear at least fragments of what they said. "Now is hardly the time to discuss something so unpleasant, my lord. I would much prefer being introduced to your lovely wife."

Rosalind gave Jessica a brief glance, as cold as a chilling wind, then turned her back again so Jessica could not see her face.

Simon knew his wife had no idea what Rosalind was saying. But more than that, it galled him to see the cursory glance she gave Jessica. The speed with which she dismissed her.

He focused his gaze on Jessica. He saw the intimidation in her eyes. Felt her terror. She stiffened in his arms, the look in her eyes revealing her confusion—her fear.

Rosalind curved her lips upward to a full, knowing smile. "I was most distressed you took a wife without first consulting me, Simon." She leaned closer and spoke so softly the crowd around them couldn't hear her. "I was even more distressed to find you had chosen such a renowned little wallflower to be your countess."

Simon bristled. "It will be a cold day in hell before I consult you on anything I do. As for my wife—"

Jessica's hand grasped his arm firmer, and he glanced down. The air froze in his chest. She looked at him with the most trusting smile on her face, but the look in her eyes bespoke pure terror.

Rosalind cupped her hand to her mouth and whispered again, always averting her face so Jessica couldn't see her mouth. "How unfortunate, Simon. If I had known how desperate you were for a wife, I could have helped you find someone more suitable."

Bright lights exploded in Simon's head. How could he ever have cared for such a vile creature? She wasn't worthy to even be in the same room with the woman he'd married.

"My father deserved you," he hissed, keeping a protective arm fastened firmly around Jessica's waist. "Did you ever care for him at all, Rosalind? Or was it only his money you were after?"

Rosalind bristled, the glint of defiance glaring in her eyes. She swirled her red satin skirt and opened her black lace fan with a flick of her wrist. "Be careful, Simon. Two can play this game of yours."

"I'm hardly playing a game, Rosalind. I am talking about my father's death. Were you there when he died?"

Rosalind's glare turned deadly. "I am sure such a topic does not interest your wife in the least. Does it, Lady Northcote?"

Rosalind asked the question loud enough for everyone to hear, but she did not face Jessica when she asked it.

"Does it?" she asked again, turning to openly face Jessica. Rosalind waited a second, then lifted the corners of her mouth. "Perhaps she couldn't hear my question?" she said, smiling the most malicious grin imaginable.

The blood raced to Simon's head, crashing against his ears like the waves of a wild, uncontrollable ocean.

Rosalind knew Jessica's secret. Somehow she'd discovered the secret Jessica had kept from society for more than a dozen years.

A chilling fear paralyzed every nerve in his body and stole the breath from his lungs. He didn't doubt for a moment that she would expose her to the *ton* if he questioned her further about his father's death.

Jessica stared at Rosalind in confusion and then turned to him. Simon saw the open pleading in her eyes. How could she answer when she had not seen what had been said?

Simon clenched his teeth until every muscle in his jaw ached. He could feel Jessica shudder against him, feel her trembling hand clench around his forearm.

She kept her head high and her features composed. But he knew she was terrified on the inside.

He couldn't do this to her. Having her deafness exposed was Jessica's worst nightmare, and Rosalind was threatening to do just that with half of London society watching.

Jessica looked around to each of the couples standing near them, then back to him. She opened her mouth to speak, but no words came out. Only a ragged gasp of air.

"It wasn't important, Jesse," Simon interrupted. "If you will excuse us," he said, looking at Rosalind with cold disdain, "my wife and I were just leaving."

Simon made a move to lead Jessica toward the door, but Rosalind stepped in front of them. Her hand rested on his forearm, and she did not even try to hide the satisfaction on her face.

"You must call on me, Simon. Soon. We have so much to catch up on."

Simon put a protective arm around Jessica's shoulder and ushered her from the room. He had to get her out of here. He had to take her where she would be safe.

* * *

Rosalind.

Jessica could still see the invitation in her seductive grin as Simon walked away from her.

The air caught in her throat. She didn't think Simon's mistress would have the nerve to accost them in front of such a large crowd. She didn't think Simon would publicly acknowledge her before all of society.

She'd been wrong.

Jessica kept the forced smile on her face as they issued the expected words of appreciation, then bade their host and hostess a pleasant farewell. When they reached the door, Simon took the apricot satin wrap Madame Lamont had made to go with her gown and placed it around her shoulders.

His fingers barely touched her before he pulled his hands away to grab his black cape from the butler. With a powerful swish, he wrapped the black satin around his shoulders and fastened the clasp beneath his chin.

Jessica placed her hand atop his offered arm, and a rush of trepidation raced through her. The muscles beneath her fingers bulged like hardened bands of steel, strung taut and ready to snap.

A breath caught in her throat, and Jessica swallowed past the lump that refused to move.

They walked out the door and down the stairs to where their driver waited for them.

Simon did not speak one word. Neither did she. Nor did she brave a look at his face until he turned to help her up the two wooden steps into the carriage. What she saw squeezed painfully around her heart.

His exposed emotions lay close to the surface, and Jessica tried to interpret what he felt.

There was a hard set to his jaw as the muscles on either side of his face clenched tightly. She looked into his eyes, but the furor she saw frightened her. She wanted him to say something. She wanted to discover to whom his anger was directed—at her, or at the woman they'd just left. But he said nothing.

Gnarled fingers of dread twisted around her heart, threatening to suffocate her. Never before had she seen such anger in another person. And it was an anger she didn't understand.

A picture of the breathtakingly beautiful Rosalind flashed before her eyes.

Was he angry because the woman he'd hoped to keep secret possessed such incredible nerve as to flaunt herself in front of not only the whole of society, but also his wife? A wife he'd thought to keep in ignorance until he was assured of an heir?

Or was he angry because his wife was such a stark disappointment when compared to his mistress? And now all of society knew it.

Jessica couldn't think, she couldn't breathe. She'd known this would happen. She'd known she wouldn't be able to hide her deafness. She'd known when she couldn't read the lips of the person talking to her, she'd look the fool. A crazy, addle-headed fool.

By the saints, no wonder Simon didn't want her. Even dressed in the most beautiful gown she had ever created, Jessica had paled in comparison to the dark-haired beauty.

A picture of the woman in the red satin gown swam before her eyes. The seductive look in her eyes seemed burned in her memory for all time. Had her action been a challenge for him to acknowledge her before the *ton*? Or his wife? Or both?

Her face burned with embarrassment. How dare Simon put her through this. She stopped on the top step of the carriage and spun around to face him. "Tonight will be the only laugh you and Rosalind will have at my expense, Simon. Ever."

Her husband reached out to turn her to him. He intended to counter her demand with a demand of his own. But she would not let him. Not this time.

She turned away from him, refusing to read what his lips said.

With that, she stepped into the carriage and leaned back against the soft maroon leather seat.

Simon sat in the seat across from her, not next to her as he had on their way to the ball. He moved his long, muscular legs to one side as if to touch her was painful.

She turned her face away from him, focusing her gaze on the darkness outside as they sped down the empty London streets. Hadn't Simon asked enough of her since their marriage? Did he have to add a public confrontation with his mistress to the list? She cursed the lump that formed in her throat and swallowed hard.

Damn him. He would not make her care. Even flaunting his mistress in front of her before all of society would not make her care.

From the moment he had agreed to give her his name in exchange for her money, she had known he could never love her. He had told her as much. Love had never been part of the bargain. Why hadn't she remembered that vow all the nights he'd held her in his arms, the times he'd kissed her, and taught her to dance? All the nights he'd lain with her beneath him, giving her pleasure—taking in return? All the nights he'd made love to her, pretending to care for her?

What a fool she'd been to think if she put on a pretty gown and threaded ribbons in her hair, she would be like all the other women.

A pain tightened in her chest. Lord, she hurt. Facing the truth was painful, but she could no longer ignore it.

All the fashions and finery and frills in the world would not change the fact that she was flawed.

Jessica didn't flinch when Simon placed his fingers beneath her chin. She was too numb to care.

He wanted her to look at him. Perhaps he'd come up with an excuse he thought she would believe. Perhaps an apology he thought she deserved. Perhaps some well-rehearsed lies to smooth over the situation. Well, she didn't want to see it.

Jessica resorted to a trick she'd learned over the years. She closed her eyes. She closed her eyes and locked herself in her private world of silence. A world where no one could intrude. What she couldn't see, she couldn't read. She couldn't hear.

He placed his fingers beneath her chin again.

She kept her eyes shut and turned her face farther away.

The third time, Simon grabbed her by the shoulders and shook her. It wasn't a hard shake. Not hard enough to hurt her. Only hard enough to demonstrate his frustration.

When Jessica still refused to open her eyes, he released her arms and let her sink back against the leather seat.

In a move that caught her off guard, Simon cupped the palm of his hand against her cheek and moved his thumb along the sensitive skin just beneath her closed eyes.

Jessica stifled a gasp and jerked her head away from him.

Damn him. He would not make her yield. Her deafness was her only defense against him.

She leaned her head back against the cushion and rode the rest of the way home in dark silence. Her stomach knotted in a tight ball and lurched with every bounce along the cobblestone streets. Only when the carriage came to a halt did she open her eyes, but even then she didn't look at Simon. He would not have the satisfaction of knowing how much he had hurt her.

She didn't wait to be helped from the carriage, nor did she take his offered arm. She walked the short distance to the town house, knowing he was close behind her. Before she reached the entrance, Sanjay opened the front door, flashing her a broad smile that was the antithesis to her dark mood.

"Did you and the master have a good time, missy?" Sanjay said, taking the cloak from her shoulders.

Jessica laughed. "Wonderful, Sanjay," she answered, choking on the words.

She spun around and looked at Simon. His black look impaled her with a violent fury. "Didn't we, my lord?" she said, then turned toward the steps and forced herself to take them one by one instead of running away from him like she wanted.

Damn him. He would not make her cry.

She swiped at the wetness that dampened her cheeks. He would not make her cry.

Chapter 19

The door to their bedroom opened, and his massive figure filled the lighted space.

Jessica stared at the entrance, the light from behind him making his shadowed form appear larger, more impressive. She knew he'd come to her eventually. She'd lain in her bed for hours, waiting. She knew him well enough to know he would not let what had happened tonight rest, that he would face the turmoil head-on.

She breathed a heavy sigh. Yes, it was best to get it out in the open. Best to learn about the mistress he refused to give up and know where their marriage was headed.

He took several steps into the room, closing the distance between them. He no longer wore his tailcoat, his waistcoat, or his white satin cravat. His gleaming white dress shirt hung open almost to his waist, exposing a good portion of the dark hair on his chest. In his hands he cradled at least a half-dozen candles and holders. One was lit. As he walked to her bedside, the flame flickered, casting the features of his face in a glowing light.

"Have you finished with your pouting?" he asked, making sure she could see his face.

She refused to answer. She hadn't been pouting. She could not believe he saw it that way.

He shrugged his shoulders as if it did not matter one way or another, then took the one lighted candle and reached out to light the taper Jessica had at her bedside. He put another beside it. One by one, he lit each candle he'd brought with him plus the other candles already in the room. He placed them in a circle around the bed, on stands, on chairs, on the desk, on anything nearby. Candle added to candle and the room glowed with a brightness that equaled daylight. He lit the last candle and set it on the trunk at the foot of the bed.

"What are you doing?" Jessica sat up in bed and leaned her back against the headboard.

Simon moved to her side, propped a pillow behind her back, and pulled the covers under her chin.

"I am making sure you can see every word I speak." Then he closed and locked the door. "Can you?"

"Yes."

"Good."

Simon stood beside the trunk. He clasped his hands behind his back and braced his feet apart as if he were prepared for battle. The look in his eyes indicated he was ready for more than just a minor skirmish.

"Have you calmed, wife?"

The breath caught in her throat. "You are asking if I have calmed?" She laughed. "I'm not the one who stormed to the carriage without speaking a word."

Or the one who could not bear to touch his wife after he'd seen his mistress.

He stepped closer and grasped the tall posters at the foot of the bed. He lifted his chin ever so slowly and impaled her with a look that sent a shiver down her spine. "I'm not the one who shut her eyes and closed her husband out, Jessica. I'm not the one who built a barrier impossible for anyone to penetrate. I'm not the one who used her deafness to take the coward's retreat and fight unfairly."

The hooded darkness of his eyes and the vein that stood out in his neck evidenced his anger. She could only imagine how loud his voice must be.

He took another step. "You will never again do to me what you did tonight, wife. Do you understand? No matter how angry either of us becomes with the other, you will not shut your eyes to close me out."

The air caught in her throat as the temper she very seldom experienced exploded within her chest. She threw the covers back and jumped from her bed, standing less than an arm's length away from him.

She couldn't believe this. "You are angry because I closed my eyes and refused to read your lips?"

"You will never shut me out like that again, Jesse. I won't have it."

"You won't have it?" Jessica stomped her foot in frustration. "You won't have it! It's perfectly acceptable for you to ignore my inquiries whenever you feel like it, but when the slipper is on the other foot and I ignore you, you will not have it? Well, you can bloody well think on that again, my lord."

"Mind your tongue, wife."

"I have only learned such language from you, my lord. It seems to be all that comes from your mouth."

Jessica saw his anger.

He stared at her with the blackest look of foreboding while he clenched his fists at his sides. His brows furrowed so deeply she thought she could hide a farthing in the creases. And he locked his jaw so tightly the knots on either side of his face jumped in agitation.

"With whom are you angry, Simon? Me or your mistress?"

The air hung heavy between them. His eyes opened wide, and he stared at her with the most flagrant look of astonishment she had ever seen.

She would not back down. "Are you upset with me because I refused to sit quietly at your side and listen obediently while you made up lies to convince me that your mistress's appearance at the ball tonight was an accident?"

Jessica ignored the crude expletives she read on Simon's lips. She was not even familiar with some of the words, but she was not about to stop now and have him explain their meaning.

"Or are you angry with your mistress because she embarrassed you by so brazenly showing herself at the same ball as your wife?"

Jessica bit her bottom lip to keep it from trembling. And to keep the tears from forming in her eyes.

"How dare you expect me to come face-to-face with the woman all of London knows you would have married but did not because she did not come with the dowry I brought you."

Her husband cursed again, and this time she understood all the words.

"There is no need to use such language with me, Simon. I'm not at all impressed or intimidated by it."

"I do not expect you to be impressed by anything I have to tell you, wife. Obviously, you already think the worst of me."

Jessica bit back the emotion that threatened to spill from her eyes. Her chest tightened painfully. "Did you know she was coming to the ball? Did you plan it that way?"

"Saints help us, Jesse. Is that what you think?"

"I know what I saw." She wrapped her arms around her middle to stop the ache. "I know what the people around us said."

"Of course. And you chose to believe every word of gossip you heard. You will take even a stranger's word over mine."

"Please, Simon. Don't make up any lies. Let's get all this out into the open and deal with it there."

"Very well, Jessica. Let's do get this all out into the open and deal with it." Simon pulled out a chair and sat down, crossing his arms over his chest as if he sat in judgment. "Who told you the woman you saw tonight was my mistress?"

Jessica sat on the edge of the bed, then rose to her feet again. She preferred the slight advantage standing gave her. "I read the Earl of Chitwood's lips, and he said everyone knows you're in love with her, but you were forced to marry me because of the money."

"And you believe him?"

Jessica placed her fingers at her temples and rubbed. "I don't know."

"Have I given you cause to think I have a mistress? Have I committed one indiscretion that makes you think I have been unfaithful?"

Jessica shook her head. "No. The earl said you would probably be discreet until I had given you an heir."

Simon bolted to his feet and slammed his hand against the back of the chair. It fell over backward, but he didn't bother to pick it up. "Bloody hell, Jessica. Your curse is not that you are deaf, but that you hear too much. And not all of it is worth hearing."

Simon raked his fingers through his hair, then took a step closer to her. "Watch my lips, wife. And understand every word I speak, for I will say this to you only once." He grasped her by the shoulders and held her. "The woman you saw tonight is not my mistress."

Jessica turned her head away from him and knew the cry of anguish buried deep in her breast had escaped. "Oh, Simon," she moaned. "Don't—"

Before she could continue, he cupped her face with his hands and turned her toward him. That telltale vein stood out on his neck. "She is *not* my mistress."

An ache tightened in her chest. "That's not what I saw. That's not how she looked at you, Simon."

"It doesn't matter how she looked at me. I married you. You are my wife." Simon grasped her by the shoulders. "Rosalind was in the past, Jessica. She is no longer important."

"How can you say that? She is important, Simon. She is very important."

"Not to me!"

Simon's dark brows knitted together in a harsh line, and spikes of blatant anger flashed from his black eyes. She didn't care. All she could think of was the beautiful woman in the red satin gown with the sultry look in her eyes that had issued the challenge to have him as her own.

Jessica twisted out of his arms. Torrential waves of panic washed over her, robbing her senses of all calmness. "It was a mistake to go tonight," she said, hugging her arms around her middle. "I knew it would be a disaster. I wish I had never listened to you."

Jessica wasn't sure she had said her words aloud, but when Simon's hands clamped around her upper arms and turned her around to face him, she knew she had.

"Tonight went perfectly," he said through clenched teeth, the look in his eyes as focused as any she'd ever seen. "You took your rightful place in society, both as my wife and as the Countess of Northcote. The evening was perfect."

"No. It was not perfect," she argued, wadding the open material of his shirt in her hands. She tried to take a deep breath, but the air caught in her throat, escaping in a ragged shudder. "She knows I can't hear. She saw I couldn't answer her when she spoke behind her fan. She knows," Jessica cried, "and now everyone will know you've married someone who is deaf."

Every fear Jessica had ever envisioned swirled in her head, reminding her of all the reasons she should not have tried to pass herself off as normal.

Simon lifted her chin so she could see his lips. "Rosalind will tell them nothing. She will not dare."

"Yes, she will." The hungry look she saw in Rosalind's eyes flashed before her like the warning of a tragedy to come. Jessica fought the overwhelming fear that slammed her heart against her ribs. What had she been thinking?

She pushed her hands against Simon's chest, struggling to free herself from his grasp. She wanted to run away. She wanted to be somewhere safe. Someplace where the outside world could not hurt her.

She twisted to escape, but his arms clamped around her like two bands of hardened steel. "Let me go, Simon," she cried, turning her face so he wouldn't see the moisture welling in her eyes. "There is no need for you to pretend anymore."

She pushed hard against his chest, but with a hard jerk he brought her around to face him squarely. "You are my wife. There is no way to pretend you are not."

"How long can you pretend you care for me? How long can you pretend you would rather have me at your side than…?" A lump formed in her throat, and Jessica fought to swallow past it. "How long, Simon?"

Her breaths came out short and ragged. The ache in her chest tightened painfully. The open, undisguised look in his eyes caused her heart to beat wildly. Her skin tingled when he cupped her cheeks in his strong hands, forcing her to look directly at him.

"You are my wife." He rubbed his thumb over her lips. "Neither of us will ever forget it."

Before she had time to catch her breath, Simon brought his mouth down on hers, crushing her against him. His kiss was not tender and loving, but harsh and possessive. He ground his lips against hers, controlling her movements, demanding her submission. She fought him with all her strength, but his demands forced her to yield to his dominance.

"Give over to me," he said, holding her gaze. "Give over at least in this."

She struggled as long as possible, but in the end she gave up. This was what she wanted, what she thought she would never have. A man whose strength she could lean on, whose power she could count on to protect her, whose arms she could rely on to hold her.

Jessica wrapped her arms around Simon's neck and held him to her. The moment he invaded her mouth an explosion of fevered emotions erupted within her. No matter how much he gave, she needed more. She needed to touch him and hold him to her and have him within her. She needed to pretend he'd made his vow to never love her because he feared losing his heart.

Not that he had already lost his heart and it belonged to Rosalind.

Jessica drew her fingers through Simon's thick, dark hair, holding him close as he kissed her deeply. Heaven help her but she wanted him. A painful thought tugged at her heart. She'd come to care for him too much. An image of the beautiful Rosalind flashed in Jessica's mind, a sultry smile on the temptress's face as she lifted her glass and beckoned Simon with a beguiling look.

His hands raked across her flesh, blazing a path wherever he touched. He wanted her as much as she wanted him. She could tell by his kisses, by the way he ravished every inch of her skin, by the tenseness of his flesh as it knotted beneath her fingers.

The frantic need to make him hers became more intense. Jessica flattened her palms on Simon's chest beneath his open shirt and moved her hands over his shoulders, atop each corded muscle that rippled beneath her fingers. A huge gasp of air rushed from her lungs when he lifted his mouth from hers and blazed a path with his lips down the side of her neck to the base of her throat.

With expert ease, he pushed her soft muslin gown from her shoulders, then carried her to the bed.

Jessica wanted to think only of Simon and the pleasure they could give each other, but in a flashing glint behind her eyes, a beautiful woman with gleaming black hair and a red satin gown crooked a seductive finger and smiled a sultry smile. Jessica tried to block it out, but Rosalind's image wouldn't go away.

"She intends to have you for her own," Jessica gasped, not realizing she'd spoken the words out loud. With an abrupt halt, his movements stopped and he cupped her face in his hands and stared down at her. The look in his eyes depicted a strange and uncontrolled fury.

"You will not speak of her, Jesse. Rosalind has no place between us."

Jessica wanted to tell Simon what she feared. She wanted to tell him what everyone at the ball had seen. That Rosalind intended to take him away from her. And deep in her heart, Jessica knew Rosalind would not give up until she had him.

"Love me, Simon."

Jessica didn't want tenderness or compassion. Their lovemaking was a battle to prove possession. She met and matched every thrust as she struggled to maintain a hold on her husband.

Higher and higher they soared until Jessica leaped from the highest pinnacle, spiraling through the air into a vast abyss of weightless abandon. With a violent shudder, Simon arched his back and followed her over the edge.

He remained atop her for several long minutes, his panting body wonderfully heavy, amazingly secure. When he moved to leave her, she tightened her grip and refused to let him go.

With one arm anchored around her shoulders and the other around her waist, Simon rolled to his back, keeping her against him all the while.

Jessica draped an arm across his chest and snuggled her face into the crook of his neck. She matched each breath Simon took with one of her own until she was positive he had fallen asleep.

"I will not give you up without a fight," she whispered against his neck as he slept.

A painful tug pulled at her heart, and she blinked back the tears that threatened to roll from her eyes. "Please, do not want to give me up either."

* * *

Rosalind climbed the stairs that led to her bedroom and swung open the door to the sitting room. Her startled lady's maid jumped in her chair and fluttered open her eyes, then bolted from her seat. She did not react quickly enough to reach the wrap Rosalind dropped before it hit the floor.

Without giving the half-asleep servant time to retrieve the cloak, Rosalind lifted a mass of shiny, black hair from her shoulders and waited impatiently while the slow-wit fumbled with the row of buttons down the back of her gown. When the last button was open and the laces undone, she dismissed the servant with a wave of her hand and went into her bedroom.

A candle was lit beside her bed and the covers turned down as she'd demanded. Even though the temperature was not overly cold, a fire blazed in the fireplace. Rosalind could not abide being chilled.

With undeniable grace, she sauntered to her dressing table and dropped her jewelry, piece by piece, onto a china tray. Then she pushed her black and red satin gown from her shoulders and let it fall to the floor. Each piece of red satin underclothing slowly, seductively, joined the gown.

When she was gloriously naked, Rosalind lifted a long, tapered leg and stepped over the puddle of satin around her ankles. She stretched her arms above her head and purred like a relaxed, satisfied alley cat. She slowly lowered her arms and skimmed over each vivacious curve of her body.

She smiled. Not a bulge or an extra ounce of flesh anywhere. She ran her hands over the full, hard mounds of her breasts and down to the narrow dip of her waist, then over the perfectly rounded curve of her hips. Her body was still as youthful as ever. More desirable than ever.

With a loud sigh of satisfaction, she reached into her wardrobe and pulled out a robe made of the sheerest fuchsia mesh imaginable. She belted the satin tie around her middle and glanced at herself in the mirror. She could not keep the grin of approval off her face. This gown was so transparent she'd be just as covered if she wore nothing.

"Well, did you see her?"

Rosalind slowly turned her head and gazed over her shoulder at the blond Adonis lounging in a soft chair near the bed. "Have you had an enjoyable evening, my lord?" she asked, lifting her mouth in a smooth, seductive smile.

"You certainly took your time. I thought perhaps you didn't intend to return home tonight." The man shifted in his chair. "Did you see her?"

"Yes, I saw her."

"And?"

Rosalind sauntered closer, concentrating on her lover's long, muscular legs. He'd stretched them out before him and crossed his ankles in a relaxed pose while slowly turning a half-empty glass of brandy in his fingers.

Rosalind took the glass from his hand. "She's not at all how you described her," she said over the rim of the glass. "She's not the gangly, unattractive freak you remembered before you left." Rosalind took a sip from his glass and handed it back to him.

"Northcote had her out in public?"

Rosalind remembered the young thing hanging on Simon's arm, and a violent wave of jealousy heated her blood. She thought Simon's wife would resemble the wild animal she'd been given to believe she was, but she didn't. She'd looked whole. Innocent.

Perfect.

"Did she say anything? Did you hear her speak?"

"No. She couldn't hear a word I said. She stood at Simon's side and left with him as soon as I arrived."

He drained his glass, then reached for the crystal decanter and filled it again. "That explains it. I doubt she's much more than a trained animal. Even bears on a leash can be taught to walk at their master's side."

Rosalind lifted her foot and straddled his legs, feeling the heat from his thighs. She reached for his glass and held it to her lips, letting him feast on her breasts, then smiled when his gaze moved lower.

His white satin shirt gaped open to his waist while long tapered fingers clenched on the arm of the burgundy-striped chair.

She loved the effect she had on men. She loved to watch their breathing grow heavy and labored with lust and their eyes turn black with passion. It was a power so few females realized they possessed. So few knew how to use. The knowledge was as heady as anything she could imagine. His voice pulled her back.

"What about Northcote? Did your blood boil when you saw him, Rosalind?"

She smiled a slow, easy smile. She would not let him know just how much she had warmed at seeing Simon again. But she would not let him think she was unaffected. "The earl has not lost his appeal," she said, slowly running her tongue up the side of the glass to catch a drip. "But London is full of men who have not lost their appeal."

He leaned his head back against the cushion and laughed. He was in a good mood tonight. As of late, such moods were rare. It was no doubt due to the amount of liquor he'd consumed and the fact that he was already celebrating because he was so close to getting what he wanted.

She knew it would be in her best interest to take advantage of his rare good humor. "How soon before we have the money?"

"Your greed is showing again, Rosalind," he said, the laughter in his voice harsh. "Don't worry, there is more than enough. Even you couldn't spend so much money in a hundred lifetimes." He took a sip of brandy, his gaze far away as if he were deep in thought. "It will take a little time. I have to make sure everything is perfect. I want to enjoy every second of this."

She put her hand on his shoulder and ran a long fingernail down his chest. "It's not just the money. You know that," she said with a pout on her lips.

He pulled her down, straddling her on his lap, and gripped a hand at her waist. "Be patient, Rosalind. Everything must be in place before Northcote realizes what I've done. He has not suffered enough yet."

"Why does he have to suffer? He hasn't done anything."

"You don't know half of what he's done."

She looked into his eyes. There was a strange, evil look there she had never seen before. A glimpse of hatred so strong it frightened her. "All he has done is marry your stepsister to get her money. That's not so uncommon. Numerous marriages occur for the very same reason."

Colin dropped his head back against the chair and laughed. "You fool. He didn't marry Jessica for the money. He married her for revenge."

Rosalind pushed away from him. "I don't believe that."

"Do you think my stepsister was the only marriageable woman in England who came with a dowry? Do you think that the Earl of Northcote wasn't able to find anyone but a deaf freak to marry to save his precious Ravenscroft? Hardly." He laughed, and even his laughter sounded strange.

He moved his hand up her body, cupping her breast. He squeezed hard and Rosalind winced. Damn. She would be bruised again tomorrow.

"I'm going to make his life hell. I want him to feel the frustration of knowing he'll never get back what used to belong to him. I want him to know I own everything that should be his, just like he has everything that should be mine. I want knowing he's lost everything to eat away at his insides until he cannot eat or sleep or work. I want him to know that all the money in the world will not get him what he wants most—Ravenscroft."

He moved his hand to her other breast and kneaded it painfully. She sucked in her breath and tried to lift his fingers. Instead, he lowered his mouth and bit her. Rosalind held her breath and waited. He'd done worse.

"When he realizes there's no hope left, when he realizes he has lost all, only then will I kill him. I'll put my deformed stepsister away where she belongs, then put a bullet in Northcote's back and watch the flesh rot from his bones."

Tanhill loosened his grip on Rosalind's breast and smiled. "Only then will I be satisfied."

A cold shiver ran up her spine. Heaven help her, he intended to kill Simon. "Don't you think perhaps it would be a mistake to harm Northcote? He is, after all, nobility. His death would surely be questioned."

"My mistake was not making sure he was dead the first time I had the chance."

Rosalind leaned back, swatting his hand from her breast. "You tried to kill Simon before?"

Tanhill laughed. "Yes. In India. Your noble earl took offense when I raped one of the locals. I didn't realize she was a member of his household, the youngest of the family that took care of him. Quite a pretty piece, about fourteen or so, and a virgin. That made her quite a prize."

"What happened?"

"The girl's screams brought Northcote running. He would have killed me if I wouldn't have had my sword hidden beside me. Just as he was about to attack, I turned around and slit him open from shoulder to waist. I don't know how he lived."

Tanhill closed his eyes and leaned his head back against the cushion. "All this could have been avoided if I had made sure he was dead. I won't make that mistake again."

The hair stood up on the back of Rosalind's neck. The game she was playing was terribly risky, but as long as she stayed a step ahead of him, she would be fine. In the end, she would have Simon for a lover and more money than she could ever spend. That's the way it should have been from the beginning. Simon should have been hers years ago. Marrying his father had been a mistake.

"What's our next move?" Rosalind asked, ignoring his hands moving over her body.

"You'll make sure you're invited to every social event where the earl and his wife are in attendance. There will no doubt be an attempt to prevent me from having her committed, and it may be necessary for you to testify as to her peculiarities."

"But she didn't seem peculiar when I saw her."

"Then you'll have to make up some instances. We will not worry about that until the time comes."

"I'm not sure it's wise to confront Simon again so soon," Rosalind said, remembering the violent anger she saw in his eyes. "He still carries some absurd suspicions regarding his father's death."

Tanhill grasped her chin between his thumb and forefinger and held tight. "I trust you can take care of him. Nothing can get in our way now. I will not rest until Northcote is dead and my dear stepsister is locked away where no one will ever find her."

Rosalind thought about the pretty young girl locked in an asylum. She shuddered. But there was no other choice. If she was to have Simon for her own, it could not be helped.

"If I'm to attend all these functions, it will be necessary for me to improve my wardrobe," Rosalind said, ignoring the rough way his hands touched her flesh. "I hardly have anything to wear."

"Of course." He clasped his hands at the neck of her robe and rent the filmy material in two. "You have talked enough," he said, freeing himself from his breeches. "It's time you paid for all those gowns you expect me to purchase for you."

His hands grabbed her around the waist, lifted her, and then brought her down hard.

Rosalind sucked in a deep breath, then closed her eyes and pictured in her mind Simon's handsome face.

Chapter 20

$\mathcal{S}$imon climbed into the ducal carriage sporting the gold emblazoned *C* on the door and sank back against the maroon leather seat across from the Duke of Collingsworth. With an audible sigh, he closed his eyes and let the wave of exhaustion he'd held at bay for the last two months creep into every weary bone in his body.

"I appreciate your help tonight, James," Simon said to his friend. They'd just spent a long evening going over some papers with Ira Cambden. The information all pointed to the same frightening conclusion.

Simon breathed a heavy sigh. The pain reached deep into his chest. "Damn him, James. How did he do it? How did Tanhill managed to acquire so many of my father's notes without leaving a trail? Jessica's money makes me one of the richest men in London, yet all I hold free and clear is the town house and Northcote Shipping—and every day he comes closer to taking even those away from me."

Simon dropped his head back against the seat and fought the wave of anger, knowing how close he was to losing everything. For weeks he'd battled the constant threat of someone trying to destroy Northcote Shipping. He'd spent endless hours struggling to get the ships ready to set sail and loaded with their first cargo only to have one small disaster after another hinder his progress—a fire purposely set on one ship, weevils planted in the flour on another, torn sails on a third. Yesterday he'd had to stop a rebellious crew from walking off because someone had convinced them they would never get paid.

Storm clouds continuously gathered, and he knew it was only a matter of time until the worst hit.

Seeing to the constant repairs of the damaged ships, hiring honest supervisors and reputable workers, and checking on the shipping manifests and cargo inventories took an insurmountable amount of time. Time he would rather have used in finding a way to get his properties away from whoever controlled the notes.

"Even though I have no proof," Simon said, fisting his hands at his side, "I know Tanhill holds the notes. Deep in my gut I know it."

The Duke of Collingsworth crossed one leg over the other. "I don't understand how he acquired the notes so quickly. You have only been married to Jessica for two months. How has he accomplished so much in such a short amount of time?"

Simon hesitated, then answered. "Tanhill set out to destroy me long before I married Jessica. His vendetta to take everything away from me started before I met Jessica."

Collingsworth lowered his foot and sat forward in his seat. "Perhaps you'd like to explain?"

Simon kept his gaze focused on the houses that passed outside the carriage window. "It's a long story, and it goes back to my time in India."

"You knew Tanhill there?"

Simon nodded. "Not well. I had little association with him. He was deeply entrenched in a group with whom few wanted to associate.

"One day I was called before my commanding officer and shown a list of names. The list contained soldiers the army believed were involved in illegal activities. Tanhill's name was on the list." Simon breathed a heavy sigh. "I was ordered to discover what I could about their activities."

"What did you find out?"

"The men on the list were smuggling opium to England and China. Tanhill was the leader of this group."

"Did you report him?"

Simon shook his head. "I intended to, but my commanding officer was on patrol. This was just before the fiercest of the uprisings, and patrols went out daily. I was afraid Tanhill suspected I knew what he was involved in, but wasn't sure. Before I could report my findings, the worst of the uprisings reached Cawnpore. Tanhill used the revolt to silence me before I could tell anyone what I knew."

Simon sat forward and rested his elbows on his thighs. "Tanhill and several of his group broke into my house. I wasn't home at the time, but returned shortly after they arrived to find Sanjay fighting them off as best he could. They intended to rape Sanjay's mother and sisters. He saved all of them but one. Tanhill raped her, then killed her."

Simon swallowed hard. He could still hear Sarai's screams. "She was only fourteen." Simon sank back against the cushion. "I tried to save her, but Tanhill had a sword. I didn't see it until it was too late."

"Hell, Simon," the Duke of Collingsworth hissed through clenched teeth.

"By the time I healed enough to tell my commanding officer what I'd discovered, I was told they weren't looking for Tanhill any longer. He was dead."

"Dead?"

"Yes, he'd faked his death. They recovered a body after the massacre with his papers on it. Of course, the soldier was too mutilated to recognize, but the papers identified the corpse as Captain Tanhill."

"Do you think it's possible Tanhill's still involved in the opium trade?"

"I'd wager every pound I have that he is." Simon looked at his friend. "There's no middle ground in this, James. He won't give up until he has it all and I am destroyed. That's why it's so important that I protect Jessica's inheritance. He'll do whatever it takes to get it."

Simon raked his fingers through his hair. The fear that Tanhill could get to Jessica punched him in the gut like a doubled fist. A picture of Sarai's bloody, lifeless body flashed before his eyes. Jessica's happy, smiling face appeared in contrast. He knew how quickly those smiles could fade, and he'd do everything in his power to prevent that from happening.

He didn't know when it had happened or how. He certainly hadn't wanted it to, but he had come to care for her—more than care. They were comfortable with each other, and the hours away from her were torture. Empty and lacking.

He missed her easy laughter and quiet patience. He missed her gentle touch and the way her gaze held him captive each time she looked at him. Perhaps the day would even come when there were no longer secrets between them. Secrets that neither of them were willing to share.

A wave of warning raced down his spine. She still did not know the real reason he'd married her. That was the most dangerous secret of all.

The carriage turned the corner to his street, and Simon sat forward. "I can't thank you enough, James," he said as the carriage stopped in front of his town house. "Rest well. You deserve it."

"You too, my friend."

Simon prepared to dismount, but the Duke of Collingsworth's fingers tightened around his arm.

"We'll stop him, Simon. I know how worried you are for Jessica, but we won't let anything happen to her. She'll be safe."

Simon nodded, then jumped to the ground and sprinted up the walk as the carriage pulled away. He pictured Jessica curled in the big chair in his study, waiting for him. She always was. It was her habit. He longed to hold her close and keep her next to him where their secrets could no longer intrude.

His steps quickened. She would probably be asleep, but as soon as he kissed her cheek she would moan softly and turn toward him. Before she was even awake, she would hold out her arms and—

A movement in the bushes to the left of the town house caught Simon's attention. He turned just in time to see an arm lift, then heard the muffled pop of gunfire in his ear.

He hadn't moved fast enough. A sharp jolt pelted him in the shoulder, knocking him off balance. Instinct and years of training on the battlefields of India caused him to dive to the ground.

He rolled to the side behind a large oak tree in front of the steps. He carefully looked to the spot from where the shot had come and saw his assailant running to another hiding place even closer. Simon angled behind another tree. It would not be long before he was trapped with nowhere to hide.

The gunman moved again, his tall, broad physique moving gracefully in the shadows, his overly long blond hair shimmering in the moonlight. Fury more violent than the pain in his shoulder consumed him to his very soul. It did not take a genius to figure out the man holding the gun was Tanhill.

Simon crouched low and dived toward a row of azalea bushes. He rolled beneath the low branches just as another shot rang out, the bullet hitting something just above his head. His shoulder burned like the fires of hell, but he ignored it.

Tanhill moved again, but stopped when the door to the town house opened and Sanjay and Hodgekiss both ran out onto the front steps holding lanterns high above their heads.

"Help is on the way, master," Sanjay hollered. "Stay where you are."

Simon rolled back under the bushes and listened to the sound of retreating footsteps racing over the lawn and down the cobblestone street. When he was sure Tanhill was gone, he got to his feet and wiped the perspiration from his face.

"Are you all right, master?" Sanjay asked, running down the steps to help Simon into the house.

Simon ignored Sanjay's help, cursing himself with every step he took. Why hadn't he realized an ambush was exactly the tactic Tanhill would use?

Hodgekiss held the door, and Simon stormed through the entrance as furious as he'd ever been in his life. Furious because his shoulder hurt like hell. Furious because he'd been such a fool not to anticipate such a cowardly move by Tanhill. And furious because he'd almost failed Jessica.

He walked to his study, barely glancing at the stunned look on his wife's face. The look that said until now she hadn't considered that one of them could be in mortal danger.

His anger rose to another level. His stupidity could have left her to face her stepbrother on her own.

At that moment he was angry with everyone. Especially himself.

He made his way across the room, stopping next to a full crystal decanter of brandy. Instead of pouring the liquor into a glass, he lifted the bottle to his lips. The liquid burned a path down his throat, and Simon welcomed the warm relief. Without looking, he knew Jessica stood behind him, waiting. If he could find a way to send her away without looking into her face he would. But he couldn't. He took another long swallow and turned to face her.

"Go up to bed. It's late."

She glanced at the blood on his jacket. "You're hurt."

"It's nothing. Just leave me alone." Simon braced himself against the corner of the desk. The wound wasn't bad, just a graze. Painful enough to remind him what could have happened.

"But you—"

"Go to bed, Jesse. Sanjay will take care of it."

She shook her head, the stunned disbelief obvious. "Why? Why would Colin want to kill you?"

Simon's world froze. "How do you know it was your stepbrother?"

"I saw him from the window."

"Hell."

"I don't understand. Why would he want to hurt *you*?"

"Why do you think? For the money."

"But he can't get the money. I don't have it any longer."

"No. I have it now," he whispered.

Simon held her gaze and waited. He knew it would not take her long to decipher his meaning.

Her eyes opened wide. He knew the moment she understood.

"Oh, dear God," she moaned, covering her mouth with her hands. "Give him the money, Simon."

"No."

"What good is it to either of us if you're dead?"

Simon gripped her by the shoulder. "Don't, Jesse—"

She twisted out of his grasp. "You knew what my stepbrother would do before you married me, didn't you?"

He ignored the tremor in her voice, the shocked look of guilt on her pale face.

"Didn't you?"

"Yes."

"Why did you marry me? If you knew, why did you—"

"My reasons have never been secret. I needed the money. It was worth the risk."

He regretted the words as soon as they left his mouth, but it was too late to take them back. He lifted his head and gazed into her pale face. A fierce knot twisted in his gut. "Go to bed. It's late. Tomorrow you will send our regrets for any obligations we have accepted for the rest of the week. You will not leave the house until this is settled."

"And when, pray tell, will that be? When you are dead and Colin has found a way to lock me in an asylum?"

Before he could assure her she would always be safe from her stepbrother, she turned and left the room, her chin as high and her shoulders as rigid as they'd been the night she'd come to him to propose marriage. The only difference was her gown was no longer drab with a frayed collar and cuffs, her hair was not pulled tight in that hideous knot at the back of her neck, and she was no longer a stranger to him. His life would have no meaning if something happened to her.

He'd do whatever he must to protect her.

Chapter 21

Rosalind stormed past the timid servant who held the door to her town house and threw her cloak and gloves in a heap on the floor. She marched into the drawing room and swirled around as Colin closed the door behind him. God, she hated him.

"You bastard! You stupid, ignorant bastard! You could have killed him!"

Colin arrogantly shrugged his shoulders and folded his arms across his chest. "What did you think I intended to do, darling? Pay him a social call?"

"You said you only wanted to threaten him."

Colin smiled. "I did. Unfortunately, he survived."

"That was not our agreement."

"I don't give a bloody damn what we agreed to. I want Northcote dead, and I won't give up until there's six feet of dirt on top of him."

"No!"

Before Rosalind could protect herself, Colin had her in his clutches. His fingers grasped her arms with a force that made her cry out.

"Don't you tell me what I can and cannot do, bitch. You are *not* the one who makes the decisions. I am."

Rosalind stood up to him with as much bravado as she could gather. She hadn't gotten this far by cowering before this maniac. She'd be damned if she'd show him any weakness now. "You are in control of nothing, Colin." She twisted out of his grasp. "You're deluding yourself if you think you are. Without me you can accomplish nothing. Simon has so many runners watching your every move, you can't even visit that filthy trollop at the Boar's Head Inn without him knowing exactly how many times you use her."

"Shut up!" He raised his hand to hit her.

Rosalind lifted her chin and laughed at him.

His hand halted in midair.

"What's the matter, Lord Tanhill? Are you finally tiring of Northcote besting you at every turn?"

"Shut up!"

"You can no longer make a move without Northcote knowing about it first. And you're so desperate to get your hands on your stepsister's inheritance you're starting to make mistakes."

He slapped her hard, then pulled her up against him. "That money should have been mine." His face contorted with rage. "I should have had it when the old man died."

Colin pushed her away from him, and she stumbled against the corner of the desk. He stormed from one side of the room to the other. "I can't wait any longer. I need capital and I need it now."

He stopped to fill a glass with brandy and threw it down the back of his throat. "The men I borrowed the money from want a down payment on the notes or they will offer them to that little weasel who is Northcote's solicitor." He filled his glass again.

Rosalind straightened the sleeves on her gown, then reached for the glass in his hand. "That is why you need me."

Colin was not a patient man. Unfortunately, Simon had toyed with him longer than he could stand. He was becoming more desperate and more violent each day. It would not be long before he snapped. He had almost gone too far tonight.

"Tomorrow I will take care of your problems like I did before." She rubbed her hand down the front of his shirt, then took a drink and handed the glass back to him. "Your notes can be extended for a price, Colin. I'll make sure of it."

Colin threw back his head and laughed. "You're nothing more than a titled whore, Rosalind."

Rosalind slapped him. The stunned look on his face was worth the risk she took. She was not a whore. She was a survivor. She did whatever she had to do to survive. She always had.

"You need me," she hissed. "And don't you forget it. Without me you will lose every one of your notes." Rosalind lifted her lips in a smile of satisfaction. She had Tanhill over a barrel and he knew it. "I'm the only one who can save you."

"That money is mine, and don't *you* forget it."

"You have no money, Colin. You only have debts."

Colin bristled. "It won't be long and I will. My opium shipment will come in soon. It was supposed to be here before now." He took a swallow from his glass. "And I've made some investments in a new company that everyone guarantees will show a profit. Between the profits from the opium and the new company I've invested in, I'll have enough money to clear every one of the notes and take care of that demented stepsister of mine forever."

Colin stepped closer to her and cupped his hand against her cheek. "Then, you'd better watch out, my sweet," he said, squeezing her chin between his thumb and forefinger. "You won't be nearly as valuable to me then."

He moved his hand to her neck, wrapping his fingers around her throat.

Rosalind grabbed his arm and tried to pull him away from her, but he only smiled a sinister grin. "And Northcote will be six feet under, while my dear stepsister languishes in an asylum. I will have every pound of her inheritance to do with whatever I want."

He moved his hand up and down the narrow column of her neck, and then with the unsuspected violence of a man demented, he grabbed the neckline of her gown and tore the material in two, baring her breasts.

Rosalind tried to cover herself, but she was not strong enough to push his hands away. He shoved her against the desk, then with one hand, grabbed her wrist and twisted her arm behind her back. The look in his eyes was vile, evil—insane. She had reason to be afraid of him.

"Let me go, Colin. You're hurting me."

"Northcote is a dead man. If you ever even think of taking his side against me, you won't live long enough to enjoy any of the money I'm going to take from my dear stepsister."

Rosalind pushed against his chest, trying to free herself from his grasp. Every day she feared him more. She was not afraid he would kill her—yet. He needed her. But when she no longer had a use…

Rosalind was as frightened as she'd ever been in her life.

Chapter 22

❧

Simon stood out in the garden, alone, contemplating the attempt on his life the night before. Tanhill had almost triumphed again.

He rubbed his shoulder, the ache a bitter reminder of how close he had come to losing his life.

The bastard would die.

A picture of Jessica's pale face flashed before him, the look of stunned shock when she realized that neither of them was safe. He could not believe she hadn't realized before now that her stepbrother had no intention of letting either of them live.

She knew it now.

Simon recalled how pale she was when she rose this morning. Dark circles rimmed her eyes as if she hadn't slept all night. She'd shied away as if what happened had been her fault. As if she'd pulled the trigger herself.

More than once he'd caught her staring at him, her eyes brimming with self-condemnation and regret. Bloody hell, what had she thought her stepbrother would do when she married him?

He'd tried to make up for his short temper and thought-less words last night. He'd gone to their bed after Sanjay had taken care of his shoulder and reached for her. He needed to hold her, to have her lie beside him and wrap her arms around him as if she needed him to be close to her.

Her reaction had startled him.

She came to him willingly enough, but the stiffness did not leave her body. The coldness he felt when she lay in his arms was unmistakable. As unmistakable as the wall she'd erected to separate herself from him.

Damn Tanhill. Simon wouldn't rest until he was dead.

At the sound of footsteps, Simon turned. The Duke of Collingsworth walked toward him with Ira on his heels.

James began his interrogation even before he reached the stone bench where Simon sat. There was a look of concern on his face.

"Are you all right? Ira came to me because he'd heard you'd been shot."

"I'll live."

Both men stared at him in worried silence.

"It seems Tanhill has taken exception to my actions of late."

"What actions?" James asked, sitting on a bench opposite him.

"It's a game he and I have been playing. He has obviously tired of it."

"What have you done, Northcote?"

Simon clenched his hands. "I have men watching him. He hasn't made a move that I don't know about. He's scrambling to come up with enough capital to make payment on his outstanding notes and is running out of people to whom he can turn. A simple word in the right places discourages even the most indiscriminate lender." Simon took a deep breath. "I've also set up a bogus company and let it be known that any investor will double their capital almost immediately. Colin has invested every pound he could lay his hands on into it. When it fails, he will be destitute."

"Why haven't you said anything?" Collingsworth asked. "I could have helped. We both could have," he said, looking at Ira.

Simon shook his head. "It's too dangerous."

"I don't give a bloody damn about danger. You can't handle this by yourself any longer. You need our help."

Simon hesitated, then pounded a fist against his thigh. "He has to be stopped, James. He puts himself deeper in debt every day, but it's not enough. He's borrowed money against my holdings in East Sussex and Ridgeway Estate and Sutterland Manor. They will fall first."

"What about Ravenscroft?" James asked.

Simon shook his head. "Ravenscroft will fall, too."

"Rumor has it," Ira said, "financially, Baron Tanhill is already ruined. He can borrow no more money from any quarter. He has left a string of debts all over London. No one knows how he's managed to hang on as long as he has."

"He's got someone working with him, someone who manages to get his loans extended whenever the holder gets nervous about receiving their money," Simon said.

Both men lifted their heads and frowned. "Maybe Sydney Carver or Mottley?" Collingsworth said.

"No. I've had men watching them, too. It's someone else. Someone who has secretly gone to his creditors to negotiate the terms of his loans. Every time I think I should be able to get my hands on some of my notes, Tanhill receives an extension."

"He can't do that indefinitely. Just be patient, Lord Northcote," Ira said. "He's on the brink of ruination."

"Only if I can stop his opium shipment from coming in. If that shipment arrives before he goes under, I'm done. With the money he receives from the sale of the drugs, he'll have the power to fight me God only knows how much longer. Long enough to try to kill me again. Long enough to get at Jessica."

Simon raked his hand through his hair. "I married her to make sure Colin could never touch her or her money, but if that shipment comes in…" He ran a worried hand across his jaw. "He will not stop until I'm dead and Jessica is locked away. She's not safe."

"Do you have any idea when the shipment is due?"

"I've had informants working the docks for weeks now, and no one has heard even a hint about an opium shipment arriving."

The Duke of Collingsworth leaned forward. "I'll see what I can do on that score. Ira will delve deeper into Colin's finances. Maybe we can come up with something to help you."

The three men held silent for a moment, and then James questioned Simon with a worried look on his face. "Is there anything else, Simon?"

"Tanhill is supporting a mistress."

Collingsworth smiled. "Let him. It will further deplete his cash flow."

"It's Rosalind."

Collingsworth's eyes opened wide. "Bloody hell. Are you sure?"

Simon prayed he was wrong. It was one thing to exact vengeance on Colin. That had been his plan from the beginning. Tanhill would pay for what he'd done to him. What he'd done to Sarai. What he'd do to Jessica if he wasn't stopped.

But involving Rosalind was another matter.

All of society would assume he'd exacted his revenge because of their relationship in the past. Because he was a lover scorned. Because Rosalind had chosen his father over him.

Simon straightened, resigned with what he must do. She'd made her bed. He could not do anything to help her now.

"We have to hurry," Simon said. "I'm running out of time. Last night was but his first attempt. Heaven help us if he goes after Jessica."

Simon knew he could stand anything but that. He wouldn't survive if anything happened to her.

James looked toward the house. "Where is she?"

"She hasn't slept well of late. I made sure she went to her room to rest before I came out here. There is too much I don't want her to know yet."

"Like what?"

The words burned in his throat, and saying them didn't make them any less painful to admit. "That I did not marry her for her money but because she was Tanhill's sister. My hatred for him runs so deep I would have married her even if she was demented as well as deaf."

Simon knew how harsh his words sounded, but they were true. Neither he nor Jessica would survive as long as Tanhill was alive.

Chapter 23

❦

*J*essica twisted the key in the lock to her private room and then turned—and came face-to-face with her husband.

Simon slowly lifted his arm and opened his fist. "Give me the key, wife."

Jessica tightened her fingers around the key in her hand and swallowed past the lump in her throat. "Why?" she asked, tucking the key into the folds of her gown.

"Because I will not have you lock yourself away in a room where I cannot reach you. What if you were in danger?"

She turned her face away from him and closed her eyes. She was so tired. She was so worried about what would happen to him, she was past finding the courage to stand up to him. Past finding the courage to care if he found out about her designs. What did she care if he opened the door? It was too late now.

She slowly raised her arm from her side and held out the key.

Simon put it in his pocket and then placed his hand around her waist and led her to the room they shared each night. When he'd closed the door behind them, he stepped close to her and cupped her cheeks in his hands. "What's wrong, Jessica? Talk to me."

Welcome heat spread from where he touched her skin and melted to a place low in her stomach. His touch always did that to her. She cursed her traitorous body for letting him have such an effect on her.

She tried to turn away from him, but he held her firmly in his grasp. "You will not turn away. Talk to me. Tell me what's wrong."

Every nerve in her body prickled in defense. She stepped away, stopping when her back pressed against the wall. "What would you like to know, Simon? What is it you want me to say?"

"I want you to tell me why you've been acting this way. Why you've avoided me. Why you stiffen in my arms each time I hold you. You can start by enlightening me on those few mysteries."

She looked down at the floor. "I'm tired. That's all."

Simon touched her beneath the chin and raised her face until she faced him squarely. "That's not it. Please, Jess. Talk to me."

The words of regret she'd kept unsaid since the night Simon had been shot formed in her mind, threatening to squeeze the breath from her body. She could not face him. She could not be this close to him, knowing what had happened was her fault. Knowing every second she'd spent as his wife put him in danger. Knowing their marriage was a sham.

A wave of dizziness washed over her. Jessica raised her arm and leaned against the wall to support herself. Dear God, she hurt.

She ignored the strong hands she felt around her shoulders and walked away from him, taking refuge in the room they'd shared since they married. "I would like to be alone, Simon."

She turned and focused on where he stood.

"No."

The room that had always seemed huge now closed in around her like a small, explosive tinderbox. Her precarious world, which for months she'd struggled to hold on to, crumbled around her, leaving her vulnerable and exposed.

She stared into the unyielding expression on his face. He left her no choice.

"Very well. Perhaps it's best we get everything into the open before…"

She couldn't face him. She didn't want to see anything he had to say. She went to the window and kept her back to him.

"Believe me, Simon. If I could undo what I have done, I would. If I could relive the night I came to you, I would. What is happening is my fault, and it's too late for me to change it."

Strong hands clamped around her shoulders and turned her toward him. The shadowed look on his face startled her. "Nothing is your fault, Jesse."

She shook herself free from his grasp and laughed. "I was a fool, Simon. From the very beginning I was so naive I didn't even suspect. I thought I was giving you something special, making a noble sacrifice. I thought you would not mind taking a deaf woman for your wife if there was enough money. But it was never really the money. Was it? You only married me because I was Baron Tanhill's stepsister. You intended to use me and the money to destroy my stepbrother. That was always your intention."

He gaped at her, his eyes gleaming as she revealed every word he'd spoken. "Bloody hell! You were watching. You saw Collingsworth and Ira with me in the garden."

Jessica laughed, knowing it came out as a demented cackle. "At least I like to think I'm not demented. You were spared that embarrassment."

"Bloody hell, Jesse. I—"

Jessica raised her hand. "It's just as well, Simon. I would have discovered it sooner or later."

She walked to the window and then turned to face him. "How long did you intend to put up this public charade of our blissful marriage? How much longer did you intend to suffer presenting me to your peers as if you were proud to have me at your side? How much longer could you have pretended it was me you wanted instead of…"

She couldn't finish her question. Jessica warded off the stabs of regret. "I didn't know my stepbrother would try to kill you, Simon. If you can believe nothing else, believe that."

She lifted her gaze, but Simon no longer stood behind her. He'd walked to the fireplace and stood with his head lowered between his outstretched arms.

The ache inside her breast hurt more. Dear Lord, she'd come to love him.

She swallowed the lump in her throat. "I thought if I took your name, it would solve everything. You would have the money to save your inheritance. I would have your protection. My stepbrother could never bother us again. I didn't know what I was asking you to give up. I didn't know about Rosalind."

"No!"

Simon spun to face her, knocking an oriental hand-painted vase from the mantel to the floor. It shattered at his feet. "Leave Rosalind out of this!" he said, the hostile glare in his eyes frightening. "Rosalind will not come between you and me."

"She already has, Simon. She loves you."

"Rosalind loves no one. She only wants what she cannot have."

"And she wants you. I saw it the first time she looked at you."

"She could have had me once, but she chose my father instead. Rosalind and I were engaged to be married until the memorable afternoon I caught her in bed with my father and the two of them were forced to do what was honorable and marry."

Jessica clamped her hand over her mouth.

"Don't look so shocked, Jesse. All of society has known about it since it happened. All but finding them in bed. Except for Collingsworth, I was thankfully spared an audience for that little scene. Society is content to think Rosalind simply preferred my father. That she didn't want to wait to inherit the money and title. They prefer to think of me as the scorned lover."

"And now Rosalind has chosen my stepbrother."

Jessica knew her words would cause a response. She was not prepared for the magnitude of Simon's reaction.

"Bloody hell, Jesse. I don't give a tinker's damn about Rosalind." He paced the room, stopping only to glare at her and open his mouth as if to speak, then close it and pace some more. "But no matter what I say, you will not believe me, will you?"

"I don't know. I don't know what to believe. Your heart is so filled with hatred for my stepbrother, there's no room for any other emotion to grow. You told me as much before we were married, but I thought perhaps in time…"

Every nerve and emotion in Jessica's body was numb. She no longer felt anything other than the empty void left by Simon's confession. Her knees buckled beneath her, and she sat on the edge of the bed with her hands clenched in her lap.

"I would like to know why you hate Tanhill so, Simon. What he did to you that caused you to sacrifice everything to destroy him. Did you know him here in London?"

Simon shook his head. "No. I barely knew your stepbrother before I left. I certainly didn't know he had a stepsister."

"Not many did," she admitted.

"After Rosalind married my father, I struggled to keep everything afloat, but father and his new wife spent money faster than I could bring it in. The day came when I could take no more, so I bought a commission in Her Majesty's Army and went to India."

"Is that where you met him?"

Simon nodded. "I arrived in India the year before the uprising. I'd met Tanhill a few times informally, but didn't have too much association with him."

Simon raked his fingers through his hair, then paced the floor in front of her. He stopped to continue. "I was stationed at the outpost in Cawnpore. That's where I met Sanjay. He and his mother and three sisters took care of the house the army provided for me. About a year after I arrived, all hell broke loose. The Indian uprising started in Meerut, and by June it had reached Cawnpore. The fighting was fierce and the atrocities horrendous on both sides. But none was worse than the innocent slaughter of women and children."

Jessica watched Simon's face pale and knew he had tried to bury all this with his past.

"For Tanhill, the massacre was an excuse to rid the world of as many of the heathen Indians as he could, and to satisfy his thirst to kill. Men, women, young, old, children…babies, he didn't care."

Jessica's stomach recoiled in horror. Simon stood with his arm braced against the tall poster at the foot of the bed. The anguish on his face tore at her heart, and she wanted to put her arms around him to comfort him. She didn't.

Instead, he faced her with a black determination she found staggering.

"Tanhill and his drunken band of miscreants went from house to house, raping and torturing and murdering in their quest to purge the world of the enemy. I came home just after they'd broken into my home. Sanjay had protected his family the best he could, hiding his mother and two of his sisters in a small chest. With nothing but a hoe from the garden, he held off the three men intent on raping his oldest sister. When I arrived, it was not difficult to take care of the men downstairs. They were already drunk and easy to handle."

An unreadable darkness filled Simon's eyes, masking his face with a hard set.

"Sanjay's youngest sister was upstairs when they broke in, and she didn't get to safety quickly enough. Tanhill found her. He raped her and beat her and…"

Simon jabbed his hand through his hair and slammed his fist against the post of the bed. "I can still hear her screams. I ran down the long hallway like a man possessed. All I could think of was to get him away from her. I didn't see the weapon he had at his side. Before I could protect myself, he raised his sword and swung."

Jessica couldn't breathe. She looked at his chest to the scar that would not go away. "And Sanjay's sister?"

"Her name was Sarai. She was only fourteen years old. Just a child." Simon stared at nothing for a long time, then slowly turned his gaze to Jessica. The look in his eyes was filled with torment. "Tanhill killed her. I lay helpless on the floor, and Tanhill laughed in my face. Then he put his sword to her throat and killed her."

Jessica clamped her hands over her mouth. *Dear God.* It was Sarai.

"When I found out you were Tanhill's sister, I knew what I had to do. You were my answer, the pawn I needed to destroy my enemy."

Simon touched his hand to Jessica's cheek and rubbed his thumb over her lips. "I just didn't think you would ever become so important to me. Don't you see? I had to marry you so Tanhill would never get the money. Marrying you was the only way I could protect you from him. It's no different than the reason you came to me."

The truth hurt. Simon was right. She'd gone to him to blackmail him into marrying her without telling him the real reason. Without considering that her stepbrother would kill the man she'd married to get the money.

What she had done to Simon was no worse than what he had done to her.

"We've made a bargain between us. You cannot back away from it," Simon said, touching her face.

"I have kept my part of the bargain. I have—"

"No. You have not. You are my wife. How much longer do you intend to keep yourself from me?"

Every muscle in her body went rigid. "I'm not sure I can share you. I know you want—"

"No! I only want you! I am what I am because you have made me so. You looked beyond my hatred and vengeance and gave me your heart for safekeeping. I want nothing but to spend the rest of my life loving you."

He held her by the shoulders and looked into her eyes. "I want no one but you," he repeated, then brought his mouth down on hers.

He held her with a desperation that startled her, his lips pressing firmly against hers, warm and insistent, fiery and possessive.

His mouth opened atop hers, urging her compliance, demanding her acceptance. How could she deny him? She'd waited a lifetime to find the man holding her in his arms, and she could not give enough of herself to him. She followed his lead, and when he tipped her head to gain easier access, she moved with him, waiting for his invasion.

His tongue skimmed her lips, teasing, tormenting until she moaned in frustration. Every nerve anticipated the silky feel of his tongue touching hers, the never-ending battle for dominance and control.

She couldn't wait any longer. She wanted him so badly she pressed herself against him, urging him to share his passion with her. She wrapped her arms tighter around his neck and let the feel of his soft woolen jacket rub through the thin material of her gown. She wanted him now with a desperation that was unequaled. She needed him more today than ever. She would die if he would not take her.

Jessica said the words out loud, pleading for him to want her, begging for him to kiss her. When his tongue entered her warm, waiting cavern, she moaned a low, keening sound that vibrated in her head.

He deepened his kiss, then pulled away, then kissed her again until she was weak with desire.

Her hands clutched the fabric of his jacket, holding on to it for support, pulling at it to touch the hardened muscles she knew rippled beneath it. She needed to touch him, know the feel of his flesh touching hers, of his warmth radiating through her.

He kissed her again. Then again. And again until their breathing seemed to be one. Until her harsh, ragged gasps matched the violence of his own breathing. She could not take a breath unless he allowed it.

Without lifting his lips, he moved his hands to the buttons on her gown, popping them free, ripping what did not yield to his frantic movements. He pushed the material from her shoulders, letting it pool at her feet.

Cool air kissed her flesh, heightening her desire. Then he picked her up in his arms and placed her in the center of the bed.

Wild currents raced to every part of her body, burning a path to the pit of her stomach, then lower.

His hands moved over her, touching her, caressing her, causing a fire to rage within her. He kissed her again, hard, passionate, demanding. His tongue mated with hers, invading her warmth, taking what she gave freely. He raised his head and looked at her, the glazed look in his eyes dark with passion.

With a desperation that robbed her of every ounce of control, she pulled him to her, twining her arms around his neck to hold him close.

She clung to him while he carried her high atop their world of human frailties, until she shuddered in his arms.

He followed her over the edge, trembling violently above her, then collapsing against her while his breathing came in harsh, ragged gasps.

She held him close, never wanting to lose him.

She traced her fingertips over the rippling muscles across his shoulders and down his arms, over his smooth skin, damp from their lovemaking. She waited until his breathing slowed, then moved with him when he rolled to the side.

"Promise me my stepbrother will not harm you," she said, looking into his face. "Promise me."

He cupped his hand to her cheek and touched her gently. "I promise. As soon as the authorities have the opium shipment, this will all be over."

"Do you know when it will arrive?"

"No. There's probably only one other person besides Colin who knows the date and time of the opium shipment."

"Do you know who that is?"

Her husband shook his head. "I'm still trying to discover who Tanhill trusts enough to negotiate for him."

Jessica laid her head back on his chest and felt the soft thumping of his heart against her cheek. She wrapped her arms around his middle and held on tightly.

She had to do something. She could not afford to lose Simon now. She would die if she did.

A plan began to formulate. She knew exactly what she would do because she knew who was working with Colin. She'd seen her face in the carriage the night Simon had been shot.

Jessica carefully listed every detail so she would not make one mistake. Underestimating her stepbrother would be deadly.

She concentrated on when she would make her first move, but lost her train of thought when Simon's hands moved over her.

When he came over her and lowered his mouth to hers, she twined her arms around his neck and pulled him to her.

Tonight she would love him.

Tomorrow she would find a way to save him.

Chapter 24

❦

Jessica stood in Rosalind's drawing room, surrounded by a wealth of treasures—priceless paintings, costly Chinese vases, expensive French furniture. Each item bespoke an extravagance that hinted that its mistress had at her fingertips an inexhaustible supply of wealth. Jessica knew she did not.

Careful not to touch anything, she walked around the room, mindful of the delicate crystal and fragile porcelain. It was not a house in which she felt at ease, and as she perused the formidable opulence, she wondered if Simon would be happy in such surroundings had he married Rosalind.

A sigh of contentment escaped her. The satisfaction she felt knowing he would not be at all comfortable filled her with a strange sense of peace and gave her a confidence she'd not felt before.

She walked to a window that overlooked the garden. The view was breathtaking. Rosalind's penchant for extravagance extended even beyond her house. Stone walkways, marble benches and tables, and naked statues crowded the perfectly tended gardens bedecked with rare flowering bushes. Jessica turned away from such lavish extravagance.

Rosalind stood in the doorway, watching her.

The emerald-green silk moiré of her fashionable gown accented her ebony hair and porcelain complexion even more than the red satin had done. The vivid green of her emerald eyes shone in stark brilliance behind long, dark lashes that fluttered softly.

For an eternity they both stared at each other. Evaluating. Judging. Disliking.

Rosalind spoke first. "You cannot imagine my surprise when I was informed that you had come to call, Lady Northcote. What an interesting scenario. Simon's wife with his former fiancé. What the *ton* wouldn't give to see this."

Rosalind swept through the doorway, brushing past Jessica in a flashy show meant to intimidate. She stopped and leveled Jessica with a look that revealed the beautiful siren intended to dominate.

"Can you understand what I'm saying?"

Jessica studied her thoughtfully. "Yes. I know what you are saying," she answered calmly.

Rosalind smiled. "Tanhill thinks you're an idiot. He thinks you don't know what's going on around you and have to be led around like an animal." She swished her full skirt as if emphasizing her presence, then stepped around the plush maroon velvet divan. "But I don't." She leaned one graceful hand against the mantel of the lit fireplace in pose. The picture she presented was magnificent. "I think you are quite intelligent. A perfect match for Simon. Am I right?"

Jessica held Rosalind's gaze and lifted the corners of her mouth ever so slightly. "Perhaps."

Long seconds dragged by. A slight flush started from beneath Rosalind's low-cut bodice and crept up her neck, coloring her cheeks. From the repeated clenching of her hands, Jessica knew the tense silence in the room bothered her hostess more than it bothered her.

"Please, sit down." Rosalind pointed to the velvet settee and then poured two cups of tea from the ornate china tea service a maid had placed on a lace-covered table. She handed one to Jessica. With indescribable grace, she moved to the delicate Louis XIV chair facing her.

"Imagine," she said, smoothing the lines of her gown. "Your stepbrother thinks you a deaf-mute with little more intelligence than an animal, and here you are, the epitome of grace and perfection. I knew he was wrong, of course. When I saw you at the Westawalds' ball with Simon, you didn't look the uncultured savage Tanhill would have me believe."

Jessica cradled the fragile cup and saucer. It was strange. She thought she would be terrified facing the woman she believed was Simon's mistress, but she was not. If anything, she pitied her.

Tiny lines appeared around Rosalind's eyes and mouth, and on close inspection, Jessica noticed the small blemishes on Rosalind's skin that powder failed to conceal. For a woman who relied on her beauty to gain wealth and popularity, it must be terrifying to watch your youthfulness fade.

"Your stepbrother thinks Simon virtually kidnapped you and made you his wife without your consent. It wasn't that way at all, was it?"

"Hardly," Jessica answered without dropping her gaze from Rosalind's face.

"Do you love him?"

Jessica was too surprised to answer.

Rosalind smiled. "Of course you do. It's impossible not to, isn't it?" She sipped her tea. "Since my return, I've been most distressed that you elected to attend none of the same functions as I," Rosalind said. "Rumor even has it that you inquire if my name is on the guest list and decline all invitations if I have also been invited."

"You will have to take that up with Lord Northcote. That was his choice."

Rosalind shook her head. "What a pity. He and I were quite close at one time, you know."

"I think perhaps he does not want to be reminded of that...closeness."

The glare in Rosalind's eyes sharpened to a deadly attack, and she raised her curved eyebrows in disdain. Jessica placed her saucer firmly on the table and sat back. "I think it's time we dispensed with the small talk and I explained my purpose for coming."

"By all means." Rosalind set her saucer down beside Jessica's and lifted the corners of her mouth in a snide grin. "I cannot imagine why you're here."

"I have come to warn you."

"Warn me?"

"Your scheme has been exposed. Yours and Tanhill's. The authorities are closing in on my stepbrother's illegal drug operation."

Rosalind stiffened. "I have no idea what you're talking about."

"They know about the opium shipment, and they know about Tanhill's involvement with Great Northern Shipping and Lord Mottley and Sydney Carver."

To Rosalind's credit, she showed the perfect expression of surprise. "I can't imagine what this has to do with me."

"What they don't know is the name of his operative. The person my stepbrother has working with him to do what he cannot openly do himself."

Rosalind paused, her eyes narrowing. "How dare you."

"I saw you in the carriage the night my stepbrother tried to kill Simon. I know you are his mistress and you are helping him make the arrangements he cannot publicly make himself."

Rosalind clenched her hands in her lap and glared at Jessica. The malicious look on her face made her quite ugly. "What do you want?"

"I want to know when the opium shipment will arrive."

Rosalind lifted her head and laughed. "What kind of fool do you take me for? Do you know what Colin would do to me if he found out I gave you that information?"

Jessica fired her answer right back. "Do you know what will happen to you when the authorities arrest you? Do you know the penalty for smuggling opiates?"

"How dare you!" Rosalind jumped from the sofa and swept across the room to the window. She stared out into the garden for a long time before she turned. "Why are you telling me this?"

"Because if Tanhill is not stopped, he will destroy all of us."

"Perhaps you will not survive, but I—"

"None of us will survive! You forget, I grew up with him. I know him. He does not share. You'll be lucky if you escape with your life."

"No."

Jessica refused to give up. Rosalind was her only chance to protect Simon. "You have the most to fear, Rosalind, because you know too much and you demand too much. Look around you. Do you honestly think my stepbrother will give you free rein with his purse to keep spending like this?"

Rosalind stared at her, then sat down on the sofa. She kept her head high and her shoulders erect in a show of composure, but she wasn't composed. She was scared. Even though she was a survivor, what Tanhill might do to her frightened her.

"What will I get out of this if I give you the information you want?"

"Fifty thousand pounds. Help me and I'll make sure you never lack for money. Give me the date and time of the opium shipment, and you will live the rest of your life as you are accustomed."

Rosalind paced the floor, obviously contemplating her dilemma. "What's stopping me from going to Simon myself and offering him the same deal? Perhaps I could even convince him that I am more suited to him than you."

Jessica smiled. "You are welcome to try."

"You're pretty sure of yourself, aren't you?"

Jessica lifted her eyebrows and tipped her head slightly. "Excuse me for being so blunt, but you are too late. You would have Simon now if you had stayed out of his father's bed."

"My, my. The bite of your tongue can be wicked. And so unexpected." Rosalind's face turned as red as if Jessica had slapped her. "I see you and Simon have shared all our dirty little secrets."

"This is your only chance to save yourself, Rosalind. You can give Simon the information he needs, or you can take your chances with Tanhill."

Jessica's heart hammered in her chest. For a moment she feared Rosalind would not make the right choice.

With a swish of her emerald-green silk skirt, Rosalind turned and stood before Jessica as proudly as a queen. "Colin is expecting a messenger today informing him of the date and time the shipment will arrive. The message is to be delivered here, and I am to inform Colin of its arrival. Come back tonight at eight o'clock and you will get your information."

Jessica breathed a sigh of relief.

"Once you receive the information, Simon will have to act fast. Colin is anticipating the shipment anytime now."

Jessica nodded and rose.

"He loved me, you know," Rosalind said, a look of pride on her face, "but I was young and foolish. I thought only of living the lifestyle Simon's father lived and spending money like he spent it." She paused. "And being a countess. I was afraid Simon's father would live forever, and if I didn't marry him, he would marry someone else and there would be no inheritance left for Simon and me to enjoy."

The look in her eyes softened. "It's amazing how quickly the money was gone. When all is said and done, you realize your title cannot fill your closets with beautiful gowns. It was a mistake to let Simon go."

As quickly as she'd shown a hint of remorse, she squared her shoulders and wiped any softness from her face. "A mistake it is too late to do anything about." She lifted her chin. "You will have the information you want tonight at eight. Tomorrow morning, I expect a bank draft for fifty thousand pounds deposited in my name."

She hesitated. "Don't let anyone see you come here. You are not the only one who is afraid of Colin. I have lived with him. I know how evil he is."

Jessica stared at Rosalind and almost felt sorry for her. What must it be like to be so desperate for wealth you would prostitute yourself to a man like Tanhill?

"Are you sure you will have the information by tonight?"

"Yes. The messenger should arrive sometime this afternoon. Whether you believe it or not, I still have feelings for Simon. I don't think it would be in anyone's best interest if Colin were to win. Especially yours, Lady Northcote. Now go, before anyone knows you were here, and make sure no one sees you come tonight."

Rosalind turned to look out the window facing the garden, dismissing Jessica with unapproachable finality.

Jessica left her without saying anything more. She walked across the black-and-white marble entryway and out the door a frowning butler held for her.

She walked down the narrow walk to her waiting carriage.

"The master not like it that you come here," Sanjay said, opening the carriage door.

"You must not tell him, Sanjay. Simon cannot know I was here." A rush of panic raged within her. "It would be too dangerous for him."

"But not dangerous for you?"

"No. I am not in danger, but if Simon found out I came here, he would be." Jessica took a step closer. "Promise you will not tell him."

Sanjay put a finger to his cheek and studied her. Jessica didn't trust the look in his eyes.

"Maybe just this once I do not tell him. Maybe."

Jessica breathed a sigh of relief. Rosalind could have the money. Jessica didn't care if she gave up every pound of it. But she could not lose Simon. She would not let Colin kill him.

Tonight she would get the information Simon had spent the last two months trying to find. She would pay him back for risking his life to protect her.

* * *

Jessica didn't feel nearly as confident as she made her way back to Rosalind's town house later that evening. With a bravado she did not feel, she pounded the brass knocker and jumped when the heavy oak door swung open on its own. Her hand trembled as she tentatively pushed it open, then walked inside.

The house was empty. No butler stood there to take her cloak. No maid came to show her to the drawing room. Only the faded flickering of half-burned candles in the chandelier showed the way.

Jessica walked across the foyer, the gooseflesh rising on her arms with each step she took. Something was wrong. She could feel it.

She took a candle from the table beside the drawing room door and lifted it high. Upon entering, she noticed that the room looked much like it had the last time she'd been here except there was no warm fire blazing in the fireplace, and no candles lighting the darkness.

And Rosalind was not here waiting for her.

Jessica rubbed the back of her neck, easing the tiny prickles that bit into her skin. In a quick second, she made the decision to leave and take the hackney coach she'd hired home.

She turned to run from the room but came to a halt when a man stepped out in front of her.

It was Colin.

He hadn't changed in the ten years since she'd last seen him. He was still as broad-shouldered and menacing as the day he'd left, with the same loathing repulsion carved on his face when he looked at her.

He stepped forward and blocked her exit. There was no way to get past him. The blood pounded in her head.

"It's been a long time, freak. Aren't you glad to see me?"

The light from her candle cast a shadowed glow on his face. It was frightening.

He took one step toward her, and Jessica retreated until the wall would let her go no farther. From this angle she noticed a broken vase on the floor and an overturned chair behind the writing desk.

There'd been a struggle here. Raw fear erupted within her like an active volcano. She stared at him like the deaf-mute he thought she was.

"Rosalind sends her regrets, but she is unable to meet with you."

Jessica felt another wave of real fear. Where was Rosalind? Thousands of voices screamed in her head, telling her to run, warning her to get away from him, but her legs would not move. Why had she come alone? Why hadn't she at least told someone where she was going?

"Do you know what I'm saying?"

Her stepbrother looked at her like she was a trained animal and he expected her to perform a trick. "Rosalind said you would be able to understand everything I said, but you can't, can you?" His eyes narrowed with contempt. "Can you understand me?"

Jessica lifted her chin. "Yes, I can understand you."

The startled expression on his face showed his surprise as well as his horror. Jessica could tell he thought she was still the same as when he'd left.

"I don't believe it," he said, dropping his head back onto his shoulders and laughing. "What a fool I've been. I should have known even revenge would not have made Northcote marry you if you were truly as repulsive as I believed."

"Let me pass, Colin," she said, putting on a brave front. "You are too late. I'm Lord Northcote's wife, and you have no right to—"

Her stepbrother grabbed her arm. "Right? What do you know about rights? What is right about a deaf freak inheriting all that money?"

Jessica twisted out of his arms. "The money was my father's," she said defensively. "It did not belong to you."

"The money should have been mine. The plan was perfect. Your father was to die in the carriage accident, and his money was to go to my mother."

Jessica's heart skipped a beat. "You killed my father?" She stared at his mouth, unable to believe what he'd said. "Why, Colin? What did Father ever do to you?"

The incredulous look on his face darkened with unmasked hatred. "What did he do? He was going to let them ruin me. I needed money to pay my debts, and he refused to give it to me. He made me a pariah in society. Creditors hounded me day and night, demanding money I didn't have. Your father was going to let them throw me into debtor's prison."

Colin fisted one hand and slammed it against the palm of the other. He shook his head as if he remembered something he would rather forget. "And there was the unfortunate incident with that barmaid. I didn't think anyone had seen me leave her room, but someone must have. I was being blackmailed, and your father refused to pay the money."

He stepped back and smiled. But it wasn't a smile Jessica wanted to remember.

"I couldn't have that, so I arranged for your father to have a little accident."

"But that accident killed your mother, too."

He shook his head. "That wasn't how I had it planned. I thought she had gone to the country for the weekend. I didn't intend for her to die. I needed her alive to inherit the money."

Jessica choked on the words. "You killed them both."

He glared at her with more vehemence than Jessica had ever seen anyone express. "She was not supposed to die," he repeated. The veins stood out on his neck. "I don't know why she went with him. She couldn't stand to be around him any more than I. She hated him. She only married him for his money. Everyone knew that."

Jessica shook her head.

Colin laughed again. "You are such a fool. Your father didn't care for my mother any more than she cared for him. The stupid man thought his darling little girl needed a woman's tender, loving care, and that my mother, Lady Tanhill, would actually use her title and influence to introduce a freak into society.

"Then the money went to you. In a trust, until you were twenty-five years old. To be given to your husband when you married."

Colin reached out again and laughed when Jessica twisted away from him. He was playing with her like a cat with a frightened mouse, tormenting her until he came in for the kill.

"You cannot imagine how disappointed I was to hear you had married Northcote. I was terribly upset to learn you'd given him my inheritance. We are enemies, you know. I almost killed him in India. Pity I didn't finish the job. He has caused me nothing but trouble since that day."

Colin reached out. Jessica twisted, but could not move out of his reach in time. He clamped her face between his thumb and forefinger and jerked her toward him. He squeezed her cheeks until she thought her jaw might break.

"Did you actually think I would let you keep all that money? Did you think I would stand by and watch all that wealth slip past me and go to you?"

He smiled at her, a frightening sneer, his lips curling upward in disdain. In the candlelight, the look in his eyes shone with a demented glare, and Jessica's heart leaped to her throat, consumed by a fear as cold as ice. She had to get away from him.

"You gave Northcote my inheritance without even knowing what you had done. You stupid bitch. I suppose you gave him your body, too?"

Jessica shook her head to clear it. She needed to think.

"Has he come to your bed yet?"

Jessica didn't react. She couldn't let Colin know Simon had.

"Well, it doesn't matter now." Colin curled his lips in disdain. "Where you're going, there will never be a chance you'll give him an heir."

Jessica opened her mouth to speak. Perhaps she could reason with him. Perhaps she could convince him to let her go. To her utter horror, she found no words would come out.

"Oh, God. How pathetic," he said, turning his head as if he could not abide to even look at her. "It's good I'm here." His lips curved upward maliciously. "It's good I have come to help you…*sister.*"

Waves of panic pounded in Jessica's ears. Every spot where he touched her hurt. He enjoyed causing pain, she could see it in his eyes, tell it in the look of pleasure on his face. She tried to pull away, but his grip on her arms tightened.

"I've come to take care of you. I'm going to put you away so society will not have to look on you any longer. I'm going to lock you away; then I am going to find the man who stole my inheritance and kill him."

Jessica fought with all her might, but he was too strong. His arms came up beneath her chin and pinned her to the wall.

"It's almost finished," he said, glaring at her, the repulsion and hatred so obvious it sent chills down her spine. "Before the night is over, both of you will get exactly what you deserve and I will have more money than I will ever be able to spend. Quite fitting, don't you think?"

Jessica clamped her hands around his arms. Her finger-nails dug into his flesh as she tried to pull him away from her, but Colin pressed his arm tighter against her throat. God help her, she couldn't breathe.

"It's no use fighting me, sister. No one even knows you're here. Except Rosalind." His lips curled upward, the look in his eyes gleaming with self-satisfaction. "Poor Rosalind. She should have known better than to betray me." His grip tightened. "She'll never deceive me again."

Jessica gasped for air. Rosalind was dead. Colin had killed her.

He held her in his grip and turned to the door and hollered. "Frish."

A burly giant appeared from the darkness and walked to where Colin had Jessica pressed against the wall. He reeked of body odor and strong garlic, and stared at her like he had more to fear from her than she did from him.

"You know what to do with her, Frish," Colin said, starting to push her forward. He stopped when the repulsive giant held out his hand.

"Where's the money, bloke? You said you'd have the money with you. I ain't takin' her 'til I get paid."

"No! You can't do this, Colin!"

He was going to put her in an asylum. Colin was going to give her to this big bully and have her locked away.

Frish gave Colin a scowl that would have frightened most men. "That was our deal. I ain't goin' nowhere 'til I been paid."

"Don't worry, Frish. You'll get your money. I'll bring it with me tomorrow."

"You said you'd have it tonight."

Colin's temper exploded. "Something came up. I'll have your money tomorrow."

"You'd better, Mr. High and Mighty. Or someone else will be knowin' where the little lady is hid. There's more that's got money than just you. If you want to keep where we're takin' her a secret, you won't try to cheat us."

Colin glared at the man. "You're getting paid well, Frish. Don't even think of double-crossing me. The day you do will be your last day on this earth."

"No!" Jessica screamed, swallowing the panic in her throat. "You can't do this, Colin."

"Who's going to stop me, freak? Northcote?" Colin laughed. "He'll be dead by morning."

Jessica struggled harder to get away from him. The hatred inside him was so powerful she had trouble breathing.

"Now get going," he said, shoving her forward. "Take her to Mrs. Broadly and tell her to lock her up and forget she's there. I don't want anyone to know who she is. Is that understood?"

"Sure, mate."

The man called Frish grabbed her from behind and pulled her up against him.

Jessica struggled harder, twisting until she had at least one arm free. "Please," she said, turning in his arms until she could see his face. "Don't listen to him. I am the Countess of Northcote. I will double whatever Colin has promised you if you'll let me go."

"Well, blow me over. She claims to be the Countess of Northcote."

"I am," Jessica insisted. "I'm the Countess of Northcote."

"Don't listen to her," Colin interrupted. "She's insane. Why do you think her family wants her put away?"

"No! Colin, please. Don't do this!" Jessica fought Frish with every breath she took, but he was too strong.

"You always were too proud for your own good," Colin said, watching her struggle. "Even as a child you thought you were better than anyone else. Always sticking your nose in the air like you were somebody when you were nothing." Colin leaned close and yelled in her face. "Nothing! The closest your father could come to giving you a title was to marry one."

He stepped away from her. "Get her out of here!" he yelled.

Jessica knew this was her last chance to get away. She brought her foot up and stomped down on Frish's instep, then turned around and lifted her knee as hard as she could. Frish dropped his arms from around her and clutched his crotch, but before she could get away, Colin had her in his grasp.

Without hesitation, she brought her arms up as hard as she could, pushing against Colin's chest, fighting to free herself. She struggled with all her might, and when he raised his arm to push against her throat, Jessica opened her mouth and sank her teeth into the thin material of his silk shirt.

Colin reared back and pulled himself away from her, holding his injured arm in front of him. Jessica didn't wait to see what he would do next, but ran across the room as fast as she could. She reached the drawing room door, then raced through the entryway toward the door that would lead her to freedom.

Just as she reached the entryway, Colin's hand clamped down on her shoulder, spinning her around to face him. A growing circle of blood dotted the pristine sleeve of his shirt, and when she looked up at him, his eyes glowered with madness. "You bitch!"

She saw his arm move before she felt the blow, and his fist struck her face. Jessica staggered, and then blessed darkness consumed her and she knew no more.

Chapter 25

Simon jumped from the carriage and took the steps to his town house three at a time. The two husky men he'd brought with him stayed close on his heels. They knew what they were to do.

The first man stopped outside, taking his place next to the steps, prepared to guard the entrance from any unwanted intruders. The second man followed Simon through the door Sanjay held open for them, almost jerking the door from Sanjay's hands in his attempt to close and bolt the thick oak slab behind them.

"Where is your mistress?" Simon charged into the drawing room, hoping he'd find Jessica waiting up for him. The room was empty.

"Missy is in her room resting," Sanjay answered. "She said she very tired."

Simon headed toward the stairs, stretching his long strides almost to a run. It was happening. One of the runners they'd hired to work for Great Northern Shipping had found out there was a very important shipment coming in during the night. Simon had no doubt this was the opium shipment. All signs pointed to it. His heart raced in his chest. It would be over soon.

Collingsworth and Ira had stayed at the docks. The authorities had been notified and were on their way, but Simon had to make sure Jessica would be safe. A wave of warring emotions rushed through him. He needed to be with her. Just in case.

He turned at the top of the stairs and glanced down at the man standing guard at the front door. Simon knew when the raid took place, Tanhill would seek him out. And if Simon could not stop him, Tanhill would come for Jessica next. The hatred that boiled between them had no boundaries.

Simon breathed a reassuring sigh and crossed the long hallway to their room. He fought the urge to call out to her even though he knew she would not hear him. He didn't care. The need to see her bordered on desperation. He just wanted to hold her one time.

Simon flung open the door and stepped into the room. Dark shadows danced on the walls, making strange and foreboding patterns. He walked to the bedside to light the lamp that sat on the small square table.

A soft glow illumined the area, and Simon held the lamp high. The bed was empty. He moved the light, searching every corner. She was nowhere.

"Are you sure your mistress came in here, Sanjay?"

"Yes, master. Martha even checked earlier and she was here. Maybe she went to her other room."

Simon did not set the lamp down, but carried it to the room at the end of the hall. The place he'd always found her. He swore softly under his breath, vowing that if she'd locked the door again, he'd break it down. He didn't have time to waste. He had to get back to the docks before Colin's shipment arrived.

He reached for the latch. It turned easily, and he pushed open the door. The blackness from inside brushed against him like a dangerous whisper of warning.

Simon lifted his lamp and scanned the room. What a strange room. There was no bed. No nightstand. No wardrobe containing her clothes. Only tables scattered throughout the room stacked high with scraps of material. Only squares of brightly colored cloth arranged on each table in an indiscernible order.

Simon lit a second and a third lamp. The room brightened to a warm glow, and he stepped to the center and looked around him. Lifting the lamp high, he turned in a complete circle. Each wall was cluttered with pencil drawings of gowns.

Although he could not remember who had worn each of them, he knew he had seen many of the gowns before. Why would Jessica have drawings of them? Why would she be so interested in what the other women wore that she would hang the designs on her wall?

Simon looked at the gowns again. He was sure these were gowns made by the famous dressmaker Madame Lamont. The ones created by the mysterious designer everyone was talking about. Why would Jessica have her…?

He looked at the material samples on the tables.

Bloody hell.

It couldn't be. Surely Jessica wasn't this mysterious person? The mysterious designer every woman in London wanted to design their gowns?

Simon walked over to the desk in search of an answer and picked up one of the many papers scattered haphazardly on top. It was a half-finished ball gown, the wide skirt trimmed with a mass of lace ruffles, while the bodice remained a series of fragmented lines, incomplete and undone.

The next paper was an unfinished skirt with samples of different materials attached at the corner. The next a finished design labeled "Day Dress for the Marchioness of Canterwall." Another labeled "Ball Gown for Lady Preston." Both clearly inscribed in Jessica's elegant hand.

Simon spun around. Where was she? He looked at the designs on the wall and fought the anger building within him. Why had she kept all this from him? Didn't she trust him enough to share her secret with him?

"Sanjay."

Where the hell was she?

"Sanjay!"

Sanjay appeared through the door at a run. "Yes, master."

"Where is your mistress?"

"I do not know, master. We have looked everywhere. She is not here."

"What do you mean, she's not here? She must be." Simon started toward the door. The anger he felt dissipated, replaced by an unexplainable fear that seeped to the very core of his being. "Search the house. Search every room and don't omit even the smallest corner."

"The servants are searching now, master, but I'm afraid it will do no good. I think the missy is not here."

Simon stopped in his tracks. "What do you mean?" The look on Sanjay's face caused his heart to skip a beat. "What has happened, Sanjay?"

Sanjay twisted his hands in front of him. "The missy went out this afternoon."

"Where?"

"To see Lady Rosalind."

Simon slammed his hand against the wall. "Bloody hell! Why didn't you tell me?"

"The missy made me promise I would not. She said Lady Rosalind knows when the opium shipment is coming. She went to find out for you."

Dear God, why hadn't Jessica come to him? Simon raced down the stairs and into his study. He opened a drawer and put an extra pistol in his pocket. "Sanjay, send someone to the docks with a message for the Duke of Collingsworth. Tell him to meet me at Rosalind's town house. I may need him."

"Right away, master."

Simon let his long, determined stride carry him out of the town house and into his waiting carriage. The two men he'd brought with him were already seated with the driver, and before Simon closed the door, he bellowed the address.

He had failed. He had failed to keep her safe.

An icy fear settled over him. The carriage rocked as it made its way across London's cobblestone streets, and Simon dropped his head back on his shoulders and closed his eyes. "Dear God," he prayed, "let me find her. Let her be all right."

He would not survive if he lost her. He would not be able to live with himself if something happened to her. If Tanhill found her. Like he'd found Sarai.

The carriage turned a corner and slowed. Before it came to a complete stop, Simon bolted out the door and raced up the front walk. The two men he'd brought with him were right behind, flanking him like an impenetrable wall. The door stood open, and Simon pushed at it before rushing through the opening.

"Jessica!"

He stepped to the center of the large entry and listened. Silence. A frightening silence. The front door wide open. Candles lit. Lamps glowing brightly in the study and the drawing room and the small salon beside it. But not a living soul came to see to them.

No butler rushed to see who was there. No downstairs maids ran in fright. No upstairs servants peeked out from hiding places above. Nothing.

"Jessica!"

Simon pulled the pistol from his coat and walked to the study. Tanhill would not catch him unaware again. Simon stepped inside the room and looked around. The air caught in his throat. There had been a struggle in this room.

The chair was not behind the desk as it should be, but overturned at the side. An unlit lamp lay broken on the floor with papers strewn around the desk. The curtains at one window had been torn down, pieces of glass from a broken pane shattered on the floor.

Simon ran from the room. Jessica's face appeared before him, the smile on her lips soft and gentle, the look in her eyes warm and trusting. Dear God. Where was she?

The drawing room door stood half open, a light shining brightly behind it. Simon kicked it open, his gaze searching the area for any sign of her. A broken crystal decanter, an overturned table, a woman's body…

"No!"

The roar that echoed in the room matched the roaring in his head. It must have come from him. He thought it had, although he wasn't sure. He raced across the room, pushing an overturned chair out of the way. She was lying on the floor behind the divan, her small slippered feet lying at an unnatural angle. Her green-and-white striped skirt bunched around her knees and…

She moaned.

Simon frantically moved to reach her while the two guards he'd brought with him shoved aside the divan. He looked down on the body on the floor.

It was not Jessica. It was Rosalind. The relief nearly paralyzed him.

Bruises had already blackened most of her face and arms, and a bloody stain darkened her gown in the front. She'd been stabbed and beaten. Simon didn't know how she was still alive.

He looked at the two men standing with him. The shock he saw etched on their faces matched the sickness churning in his gut. "Go for a doctor," he ordered, and one of the men left the room.

Simon knelt at her side, afraid to touch her. She was alive, although he wasn't sure for how long.

"Rosalind?" He lifted her hand and held it.

She stirred.

"Rosalind, can you hear me?"

She opened her swollen eyes. "Simon?"

"Yes, Rosalind. It's me. Where's Jessica?"

"Colin…found out. Oh…God."

"I know, Rosalind. Where's Jessica now?"

"Simon…don't…leave…"

A fit of coughing stopped her words, and Simon fought the panic that raged within him. Tanhill was out there, and so was Jessica. If he'd touched her…

A stab of cold fear slammed into his gut. "Where's Jessica, Rosalind?"

"Don't…leave me. I'm…afraid."

"I won't leave you. I'm right here. But you have to tell me where Jessica is."

He waited, but she said nothing. Her shallow breathing seemed even more labored, and he put his hand against her throat to feel if her heart was still beating. Barely.

"I should have…married you…Simon. I was a…fool… to marry your…father."

He bit back a sigh of impatience. "It doesn't matter anymore. The doctor will be here soon. He'll take care of you."

Simon heard the sound of footsteps behind him, and when he looked up, the Duke of Collingsworth came toward him.

"Oh God," Collingsworth whispered, staring at Rosalind's battered body.

Simon turned back to Rosalind. "Rosalind," he said, rubbing his thumb over the top of her hand. "Rosalind. Listen to me. I have to find Tanhill. He can't get away with this."

"I'm…sorry he's…dead, Simon. I…didn't mean to… do it."

"Who's dead, Rosalind?" Simon's heart beat faster in his chest. Was Colin dead? "Who's dead, Rosalind?"

"Your…father."

Simon's heart slammed against his ribs.

"We argued…and…I pushed him…He was…drunk…and…fell. I didn't…mean for him to…die."

Simon felt James's hand squeeze his shoulder, and he took a deep breath to hold himself together. He'd suspected for so long that Rosalind was behind his father's death, but had no proof. Now that he knew for sure, it no longer mattered. He only wanted to find Jessica and make sure she was alive.

"It's in the past, Rosalind. Just tell me where Jessica is."

Rosalind doubled in a fit of coughing, and Simon held her until she recovered. "Gone. Colin…has her."

Simon couldn't breathe. His heart pounded in his chest, fighting the loud voice of agony that screamed in his head. "Rosalind, please. Tell me where he's taken her."

"Simon…"

"I'm here, Rosalind."

"It's…too late."

"No."

Her body went limp in his arms, and Simon stared at her for a moment before laying her down. He couldn't think. He didn't want to remember Rosalind's last words.

He staggered to his feet and placed his hand against the wall to steady himself. He felt a terror unlike anything he'd ever experienced before. A fear that he had lost a part of himself he could not live without. The part that Jessica had silently claimed as her own.

Chapter 26

❧

$\mathcal{S}$imon had no idea where to look for her. He paced
the docks in the darkness, frantic with fear, waiting
for Tanhill to appear, or the shipment to come. He didn't
know if she was alive. He had no idea where Tanhill had
taken her.

Simon had never realized such devastating terror in his
life as when he'd left Rosalind's town house without Jessica.
She'd been there. Simon knew it as if he could still see
her. He could feel her presence. He could feel her terror.

He raked his fingers through his hair and struggled to
keep his worst fears at bay while he waited for Tanhill to
come. If he'd touched one hair on her head, he'd kill him.

Simon fisted his hands at his side and glared into the
blackness, waiting for the ship that would bring Tanhill
into the open.

"Tanhill's here," the Duke of Collingsworth whispered.
"His carriage just arrived." His Grace grasped Simon's
forearm. "Be careful." He tightened his grip on Simon's
arm. "They found Mottley's and Sydney Carver's bodies
floating in the river this morning. They'd both been shot
in the back."

Simon blocked out James's words. Two more people
were dead because of Tanhill. "Has the shipment arrived?"

"Not yet. Jackson's keeping watch from above." Collingsworth cast a glance to the crow's nest located near the top of the mast of one of the ships docked in the harbor. "He'll let us know as soon as he sees anything."

Simon nodded then released a heavy sigh. "Nothing can happen to Tanhill until we find out where he's taken Jessica. Make sure the authorities understand, James."

"They do, Simon. I've already explained everything to the officers. They know—"

James's words died on his lips.

Tanhill walked to the edge of the dock and watched the darkness for signs of his ship. The ship that would smuggle in the opium to be sold on the black market.

James tapped Simon's arm again and pointed to the crow's nest. The man stationed there waved his arms and pointed out to sea. He'd spotted the ship.

Simon touched the pistol in his coat and took his position to wait until the authorities made their move. He wouldn't let Tanhill out of his sight until then.

It seemed an eternity before Tanhill spotted the ship, and another eternity before the ship finally docked. Everything was in place. Dockhands in Colin's pay lowered the loading ramp, then scurried like rats foraging in the night, unloading their illegal cargo.

The blood thundered in Simon's head, buzzing in his ears while he waited for the signal. He had not lifted his gaze from Tanhill's blond head for a second. He knew exactly where he was.

Then the cry came for the authorities to converge. Voices from three angles bellowed the order to attack, and scores of uniformed men rushed from their hiding places to run up the wooden planks and overtake the smugglers on deck. The surprise on their faces was evident. The surprise on Tanhill's face was well worth the wait.

Simon moved closer as the authorities boarded the ship. James stayed at his side.

Even though the men in Tanhill's employ were markedly outnumbered, they refused to give up without a fight. Swords flashed, guns fired, and the first three men rushing up the gangway to board the ship didn't make it past halfway.

Cries of men injured and dying filled the air. Bodies fell to the deck of the ship or were tossed overboard.

Simon wasn't interested in the capture of smuggled contraband. He ignored the cries of human anguish and concentrated on Tanhill.

Tanhill moved to the side of the ship and scrambled down a rope ladder to a small boat tied at the bottom.

Simon followed him down the wharf with James at his side.

"Where will he go, Simon?"

"Inland until he can find a sheltered place to dock. Then he'll run like the worthless refuse he is."

They both crouched down behind a wide stack of crates and watched Tanhill maneuver his boat away from the violence and mayhem. In the darkness and the shadows, Simon and James kept close enough not to lose him, yet far enough away not to be seen.

Simon held up his hand and James stopped. "He's mine, James. I want him."

James nodded and stayed hidden in the shadows. "Be careful, Simon. He's dangerous."

"He's always been dangerous," Simon answered, watching Tanhill move his small boat between two docked ships. Simon moved closer, keeping his head down and his pistol in his hand. When Tanhill took the first step onto the dock, Simon lunged forward. "That's far enough, Tanhill."

Tanhill turned and lifted his hand. He aimed the barrel of his pistol at Simon's chest, but Simon ducked before Tanhill fired. He heard the bullet strike somewhere behind him. Before Tanhill had time to fire again, Simon leaped through the air, knocking him to the ground.

They rolled on the hard wooden boards. Tanhill kicked Simon hard in the stomach, then jumped to his feet. He swung his fist, connecting with Simon's jaw. Simon returned the punch, slamming his fist into Tanhill's face. The crunch of bones beneath Simon's hand helped to ease some of the loathing, but it did nothing to soothe the anger boiling within him. He was not absolved of any of the guilt and furor he felt, and his anger was soon replaced by a deeper hatred. Jessica's loving face flashed before his eyes, and he pummeled his fist into Tanhill's face again. Then again. And again. And again.

"Simon!"

James's voice snapped him to the present and he stopped. "Where have you taken her?" Simon bellowed, wrapping his hands around Tanhill's cravat and pulling him toward him.

Tanhill stumbled wearily when Simon let go and fell back against a large wooden barrel.

Simon lunged for him again, grabbing the front of his tailored topcoat and pulling him through the air. "Where have you taken her?"

Blood streamed from Tanhill's nose and a deep cut above his brow, but the glint in his eyes revealed a defiance that sent a wave of uncontrollable violence through Simon's body. "Where is she?!"

Tanhill dropped his head back on his shoulders and laughed. The laugh was cold, heartless. Evil. "She fights almost as well as you, Northcote," Tanhill said, wiping the blood from his nose on the sleeve of his coat. "Although, she doesn't have near your strength."

Blind, raging fury erupted within Simon. Blood thundered in his head, and a bright whiteness flashed before his eyes. He lost control. He'd lost Jessica. He hadn't protected her. He slammed his fist into Tanhill's face again. "Tell me where you've taken her," he hissed through clenched teeth, "or I'll kill you right here and now."

"No, you won't, Northcote. You won't kill me until you know what I've done with her. She's gone. I've got her hidden somewhere so remote you'll never find her."

"Where!"

"Where you'll never find her. She'll wallow in the filth and darkness until she no longer has the strength to survive while you search for her." Tanhill laughed his vile, evil laugh. "Do you know what else? I've left instructions that she's not to be given food or water until I give the order. Think of that while you're searching for her, Northcote."

Rage exploded within him, and Simon drew back his fist and struck Tanhill again and again. His blows were wild and damaging. Simon would have killed Tanhill if James hadn't stopped him.

"Where is she?" the Duke of Collingsworth demanded, pushing Simon away and supporting Tanhill's limp body himself. "You have nothing to gain by keeping Lady Northcote's whereabouts secret. The authorities know about your smuggling operation and have seized your drug shipment. It's all over. There is no need to add kidnapping to your list of crimes."

"Isn't there?" Tanhill said, lifting his swollen lip to form a malicious grin. "I should have made sure he was dead when I had the chance in India." Tanhill focused his gaze on Simon. "He married the freak just to get his hands on the money. It should have been mine. It would have been, too, if he hadn't interfered. All I had to do was have her committed, and any court in the land would have given me control of her wealth. He ruined it." Tanhill turned his gaze to Simon. The look in his eyes brimmed with hatred. "You'll pay. You'll both pay. And you can live with her death for the rest of your lives."

A long, deafening silence stretched in the darkness, and then Simon stepped over to Tanhill and grabbed him by the front of his bloodstained white shirt. He slammed him up against a stack of wooden crates and shoved the barrel of the pistol he carried in his pocket at Tanhill's head. When Simon spoke, his soft words held the sharpness of a sword. "Tell me where she is, or I'll kill you right now." A loud click echoed in the stillness as Simon cocked the pistol.

Tanhill choked out a strangled sound, fear and deliberation clearly written on his face. "Do you know how long I have hated her? Jessica with her stubborn pride and superior attitude. She doesn't deserve to live. You could be rid of her. Why would you want to save her?"

Simon tightened his grip. "Tell me where she is!"

Tanhill raised one brow, a sinister grin lifting the corners of his swollen mouth. "I don't believe it. You've fallen in love with her."

Simon stepped back and fisted his hands at his side, fighting to keep from slamming them into Tanhill's face again. The only emotion stronger than his hatred for Tanhill was his love for Jessica. "Tell me where you've taken her," he repeated, his voice menacing. "If you don't, I will take great pleasure in killing you now and finding her myself."

Tanhill lifted his shoulders and stood straight. He still had to anchor a hand against a nearby barrel, but the grin of satisfaction on his face belied any weakness. Simon wanted to strangle him.

Tanhill shrugged free. "Very well. I will tell you where she is—for a price."

Simon glared at his enemy, wishing he could put a bullet through his brain now. But he couldn't. He didn't know where to find Jessica.

"One hundred thousand pounds, Northcote, and my freedom."

"You bloody bastard," Simon hissed.

"Do you want to find her or not?"

Simon ground his teeth in anger. What choice did he have? "Where is she?"

"Your promise first."

Simon stepped back in concession, but kept his pistol aimed at Tanhill's head. "You have my promise. Now tell me where you took her."

A slight grin turned Tanhill's lips. "You will find your wife at—"

A loud explosion shattered the air around them. Simon turned toward the direction of the noise, to where Baron Carver stood with a gun in his hand, then back to Tanhill.

Tanhill's face opened in wide disbelief as a small crimson circle spread across his chest. In slow motion, he sank to his knees, then crumpled on the slabs of wood beneath him.

"No!" Simon reached for Tanhill, praying it was not too late. Praying he wasn't dead.

Simon lifted his enemy's head. A small trickle of blood ran from the side of his mouth, another from his nose. "Where is she, Tanhill? Where did you take Jessica?"

Tanhill opened his mouth to speak. He turned his head, choking on the blood in his mouth, then clutched his hands to his chest. His body stiffened. "It's...too...late."

"Damn you to hell, Tanhill. Don't you dare die!"

Simon looked at Tanhill's face. His lips curled into a sardonic grin, and he choked out a bitter laugh. "You'll never...find...her. Never."

Tanhill sighed, then turned his face to the side and went limp in Simon's arms.

Simon stared in horror at Tanhill's lifeless body. How was he going to find where he'd taken Jessica? How could he take care of her?

Every muscle in his body trembled. A part of him died. Jessica was locked in an asylum somewhere with orders not to be given food or water. God help him. Jessica was living her worst nightmare because he hadn't protected her.

Simon lifted his gaze as Baron Carver stepped forward. Simon wanted to kill him. He'd destroyed any chance of finding Jessica. He'd robbed him of any hope to get her out of the hellhole into which Tanhill had put her.

Simon bolted to his feet, his hands reaching out to wrap around the older man's neck. He stopped. The hollow look in the baron's eyes as he stared at Tanhill's inert body took the wind from Simon's lungs. "He killed my son, Northcote. My boy. He shot Sydney in the back and dumped his body in the river. They found him floating there this morning."

Simon dropped his head back on his shoulders and closed his eyes. How much more pain would Tanhill cause? How many more innocent people would suffer because of his cruelty?

Simon walked away from the gathering crowd. The authorities were there, and he had no desire to waste his time explaining anything to them. Let them conclude what they wanted. What the baron would tell them.

The tightness in his chest ached painfully. He'd failed to protect her.

"We'll find her, Simon." Collingsworth walked beside him, matching his long strides with equal determination. "We'll have her home by morning."

Simon made his way to his carriage, knowing this would be the longest night of his life.

Chapter 27

❖

The next day of searching without finding Jessica bordered on eternal. And the next day just short of sending him to the brink of madness.

He and James and Ira followed a dozen false leads and sent scores of runners looking for any clue that might lead them to where Jessica was.

They'd been to each hospital for the mentally insane in London—St. Luke's, Bedlam, and more—knowing the obvious places would leave them empty-handed. Tanhill would not have taken her where he could find her so easily.

Each institution they entered was crowded and frightening and depressing at best. Some they searched were harsh and inhumane. Filth and neglect and cruelty seemed the rule, the conditions a foul abomination to human decency. The blood thundered in Simon's head whenever he thought of the torture Jessica was enduring.

Day and night they searched, and still there were no solid leads. "Get some rest, Simon," James said when the carriage stopped in front of his town house. "And eat something, for heaven's sake. You're going to fall on your face if you don't take care of yourself. You won't do Jessica any good if you get sick."

Simon raked his fingers through his hair and then dismounted from the carriage with James beside him. He hesitated as a wave of defeat pummeled him. He didn't want to enter the house. He didn't want to stare into the hopeful, tear-stained faces of the staff as they waited expectantly for good news. He didn't want to see their expressions crumble when they realized he'd come home empty-handed.

"Where can she be, James? We've looked everywhere, and I'm out of leads. There are no more places for us to look." Simon fought the fear eating his gut. He didn't know it was possible to feel such terror.

"Something will come up, Simon. Perhaps we missed her. We can search the places here in London again tomorrow and—"

"No. She isn't in London. Tanhill took her somewhere out of the city. I know it. It took him too long to get back to the docks."

"Then maybe—"

"Master! Master!" Sanjay ran through the open front door waving a paper in his hand. "Come quick! Come quick!"

Simon raced up the stairs, his heart pounding in his chest. Maybe she'd come home. Maybe someone had found her. Maybe...

"A message. I found it slid under the door. No one there. Only the paper."

Simon grabbed the paper and ran to the nearest light. He unfolded it and quickly scanned the words. His heart stopped in his chest.

Yer lordship,

If you want to have your wife back, bring five thousand pounds tonight with you to Marberry's Park. Leave the money on the third stone bench from the front gate. The place where you can find her will be written on the paper you'll find under the rock.

This aren't no trick. I got proof.

A scrap of material fell to the table, and Simon picked it up. The air caught in his throat.

"I got your carriage waiting, Master," Sanjay said. "I think in my next life I will come back as an eagle so I can carry you where you need to go."

Simon handed James the note, then ran to his study. He opened the safe behind his desk and counted out five thousand pounds before putting the notes into a black leather bag.

"Are you sure, Simon?"

Simon handed him the scrap of material. "It's material from the dress Jessica was wearing the day Tanhill took her."

Collingsworth nodded. "What do you want me to do?"

"Follow me to the park and wait to see who picks up the money. Don't stop him. Just see where he goes. If it's a trick, we'll find him later."

Simon ran out the door with Collingsworth close behind and raced to his carriage. "Don't let him see you, James," Simon warned, then closed the door and raced to Marberry Park. His heart stuttered. This was it. He knew whatever he found would lead him to Jessica. In his heart he knew it would.

The carriage turned in the entrance to the park, and Simon fingered the leather bag with the money. He'd give a hundred times—no, every pound he had—to get her back and not regret it. He'd give his life to get her back and not regret it. A lump formed in his throat, and he tried to swallow past it, but failed. Dear God, he'd give anything to have her with him now. To hold her in his arms and feel her against him. To show her how much he loved her. Simon blinked back the wetness that threatened to fill his eyes. He wanted her with him always.

The carriage slowed, and Simon counted the stone benches along the path. One. Two. "Stop," he ordered his driver and jumped to the ground and ran to the stone bench. He set the leather bag on the slab and lifted the rock. He picked up the paper beneath it and ran back to the street to read the message beneath one of the lanterns that hung on the side of the carriage. It was the same writing.

Simon showed the note to his driver, and after his driver assured him he knew the location, Simon jumped back in the carriage and they left.

The night sky was starless with a light mist falling in the darkness, blanketing the night in an even gloomier cloak. Each mile stretched on forever, and with every drum of the horses' hooves, Simon thought of finding Jessica.

He prayed that Tanhill had not hurt her. That Tanhill had lied, and hadn't left orders for her not to be given food or water. His heart pounded against his ribs. It had been three days. He prayed that someone had been kind to her and had taken care of her.

He wiped his sweaty palms against his pants and suddenly stilled when the carriage slowed. Lights glowed from the windows of a massive stone mansion up ahead, its gloomy presence made even more oppressive by the drizzling rain.

The carriage stopped and Simon jumped to the ground. "Come with me, George," he said to the driver, and they ran to the door. Simon pounded on the rusted metal knocker in the center and waited.

A woman wearing a stained dress and an even filthier apron answered on the second knock.

"Where is she?" Simon roared.

The woman clamped her hand over her brown, rotted teeth in surprise when Simon and his driver burst uninvited through the door. She recovered soon enough, and found her voice.

"They're gone, my lord. Frish and the others took off this afternoon, leaving Frieda and me all alone to care for all these people."

Simon scanned the area. A score or more of the residents sat in squalor and their own refuse. His stomach turned.

"We didn't have nothin' to do with it. Frieda and me didn't know nothin' about the lady until they brought her."

"Where is she?" he demanded again, closing his senses to the filth and the stench and the atrocious human conditions all around him. This place was by far the worst of any he'd been forced to enter in the last three days. He willed his heart to keep beating. "Where is she!"

"In there, my lord. They put her down there." The woman pointed to a door at the far end of the room. "The key is here on this ring."

She held out her arm and handed him a ring with several large brass keys on it.

Simon took them and ran across the room. The second key fit, and the door opened to a set of steep stairs that seemed to be swallowed by pitch blackness. Simon reached around the corner and grabbed a lantern hanging from a hook on the wall. "Find another lantern and follow, George."

Simon held the light high and climbed down the stairs. The air was heavy and dank, and the odor was not as bad as above. But there was no light. Oh, how Jessica hated being in the dark.

Simon lifted the lantern and looked. There was no sign of her, only another locked door in this dungeon of horrors. He raced toward it and put the key in the lock. He turned and the loud click echoed in the darkness. He threw the door open and stepped inside.

There was nothing in the room—no cot, no bench, not even a chair to sit on. Only the cold, hard stone floor and the frantic scurrying of rats to their holes. A lump formed in Simon's throat that he couldn't work past. He lifted his lantern higher.

She was there.

Jessica's small, fragile body lay huddled in the corner. Her hair was a tangled mess around her face, and her knees were tucked tight against her chest. She kept her eyes closed to all around her as if she could close out the world by doing so.

Simon set the lantern on the floor and walked to her. He slowly reached out his trembling hand and touched her shoulder ever so softly.

"Jessica, sweetheart," Simon whispered, knowing she couldn't hear him. "It's me. I've come to take you home."

He touched her again, then reached up to brush the hair from her face. The air stuck in his throat, a gnarled hand twisting his heart in his chest. The bruises on her face were purple and green, the cuts on her hands and wrists and fingers caked with dried blood.

"Dear God! No!" he cried, knowing only he and God heard the anguish in his voice. Jessica heard nothing. She would not open her eyes to hear anything.

Simon fell to his knees and wrapped his arms around her, holding her close to him. "Jesse," he said again, brushing her forehead and cheeks with his lips. "Open your eyes for me, sweetheart." He heard only the slightest catch from her throat.

George came in with two lanterns burning brightly. He stood behind Simon, and when he lifted the lamps high in the air, the small room glowed like the middle of day. Simon ignored the vile curse the driver whispered when he saw Jessica's face.

"There are some blankets in the carriage. Get them. And some water."

"Right quick, my lord. Oh, right quick."

George ran out of the room, and Simon turned his attention back to Jessica. There was an icy feel to her flesh as well as a bluish tint to her lips. She'd been in this cold, damp cell for three days without a cover or blanket. Simon could tell she was chilled to her bones.

"Jesse, please. Open your eyes, sweetheart. Everything is fine now. I've come to take you home." Simon wrapped his hands around her fingers and lifted her hands to his face.

He gently kissed the palms of her skinned hands and the insides of her wrists where he could tell a rope had been tied. There was a slight moan from her lips, but when he looked, her eyes remained closed. Then he placed her hands to his cheeks and covered them with his own, letting the heat from his face warm her flesh.

He'd asked so much of her. He'd married her for revenge, and used her wealth to gain back his inheritance. He'd forced her to face the *ton*, and risk society finding out she was deaf. And…

A cold rush of devastation stole the breath from his lungs. He'd broken the only promise he'd made to her. His promise to always keep her safe. His promise to protect her from harm. From Tanhill.

Simon looked down at the cuts and scrapes and bruises and fought the agony tearing at his insides. He had failed. He hadn't kept her safe. Even though the marks on the outside would heal with time, Simon doubted the pain he'd caused on the inside would ever go away.

When he could hold back his emotions no longer, he buried his face in her bruised hands and wept. Rivers of tears, kept at bay for so long, rushed to the surface, flooding in torrents of grief and guilt and regret.

Violent sobs racked his body as Simon wept for all the pain and suffering he'd caused and seen and endured. For the bitter feelings he'd harbored against his father and the woman who'd been the cause of his father's death. He wrapped his arms around Jessica's fragile shoulders and held her to him while he wept for dear little Sarai, who'd given nothing but love to all around her during her short life.

And for the woman in his arms, who had loved him enough to put her faith and her trust in him, asking nothing in return except for his protection.

Simon's shoulders shook, and a heavy hand twisted his breaking heart. Hot, wet tears streamed down his face. He'd failed her. When she'd needed him most, he'd failed her. Tanhill had almost killed her because of him. If it hadn't been for the greed of a man called Frish, Simon still wouldn't know where Tanhill had taken her.

Simon barely heard her whimper in the small, confining cell, but when he lifted his tearstained face, her eyes were open.

She tried to speak, but she didn't have the strength.

"It's all right, Jesse. I'm here now. You're safe. Colin is dead. He can never hurt you again."

She moved her fingers to touch the tears streaming down his cheeks.

"I love you, Jesse. I love you so much. Please believe me. I love you."

Jessica moved her head slightly and leaned against him. He held her close until George came with blankets and water. Simon took the water first and held it to Jessica's lips. She tried to swallow, and the water came back up in a choking cough. Simon held her close until she could breathe again, then dipped his handkerchief in the water and held it to her lips.

Jessica sucked on the cloth, swallowing one drop of water at a time until she could speak. "I knew you would find me," she whispered, her eyes filled with tears.

Simon nodded, swallowing past the lump in his throat. "Yes. I found you."

"I was so afraid."

"I know, sweetheart. So was I. But everything's all right now."

Simon wrapped a blanket around Jessica's shoulders and then cupped her cheeks in the palms of his hands, tipping her face upward. "I love you, Jesse. I could not survive if anything happened to you."

Jessica nodded, and big, wet tears rolled down her cheeks. "I love you, Simon."

Simon pulled her to him and kissed her parched lips. He vowed he would never let anything happen to her again.

He picked her up in his arms, and George tucked another blanket around her before Simon carried her up the stairs. Jessica nestled her head beneath his chin, exactly where it belonged.

"Bathe and dress these people," Simon bellowed to the woman who had answered the door. "Someone will be here in the morning to get them. Pray the authorities do not file charges against either of you for their mistreatment."

Simon carried Jessica out of the hellhole where Tanhill had condemned her to die and sat with her on his lap while the carriage took them home. He remembered the hatred that had spurred him to take her as his wife. The need for revenge that had motivated his every action.

Vengeance against Tanhill had come with a terribly high price attached to it. Simon looked down at Jessica lying in his arms. He'd almost had to pay it.

Epilogue

$\mathcal{S}$imon walked into the room and sat in the huge wing chair he'd had brought up to Jessica's workroom. He still smelled of the sea and the outdoors, having just come from a long day at the docks, but he knew she wouldn't mind. She never did, but welcomed him as if she'd been waiting all day to greet him. No matter how hard his day had been, she could make him forget every worry.

It still amazed him she was the famous designer the *ton* clamored to have create their gowns. He could not believe she had been able to keep her secret from him.

He could not believe she was still able to keep her secret from the *ton*. They had been married more than a year, and no one even suspected. That was the only secret he didn't mind keeping from the world. That he loved his wife very much was something he wanted to shout to everyone in England.

There had been times right after he'd taken her out of that hellhole when he'd doubted she was strong enough to survive. Times he'd feared her stepbrother had the power to reach out from the grave and cause them more pain and suffering. But no longer.

"What are you working on?" he asked when she looked up from her drawings. He would never cease to be amazed by what one of her smiles did to him.

"It's a surprise."

Simon moved so he could look at his wife's newest creation.

"No, Simon. I don't want you to see it yet. Wait until it's finished."

Simon sat back in his chair and crossed the ankle of one leg over his other knee. "Very well, Jesse, but don't expect me to tell you I like it if I don't."

"When have you ever lied to spare my tender feelings?" she said, lifting her eyebrow in a teasing manner.

"Just last week." Simon tried to hide the smirk on his face and look serious. "When I saw the horrid purple gown you put on Lady Westawald. You should have been ashamed of yourself."

"That was not my fault, and you know it. I told Madame Lamont not to let the countess choose purple or pink, but she could not talk her out of it. There was nothing wrong with the gown, Simon. It was the color that made Lady Westawald look like a ship capsized at sea."

Simon laughed and looked at the growing number of designs hanging on the wall. She was truly a marvel.

He looked at her lush, ruby lips and held himself back from going over and kissing her. Their kisses were only the beginning to what usually happened when he came to watch her work. She complained that she couldn't create when he was here, but Simon only smiled and breathed a sigh of satisfaction. He thought he'd done some of his best work in this room.

She looked up at him, fidgeting with the pencil in her hand. "Melinda stopped by this morning. She and Collingsworth are having a special dinner next Friday and want us to attend."

Simon studied the frown on his wife's face. "And this has you concerned?"

Jessica looked down at the papers strewn on her desk and made a few more lines. "She is extremely excited. The famous pianist, Franz Liszt, will be there. He's in England on tour from Weimar, and has consented to perform a number of his Hungarian Rhapsodies."

Simon waited until she looked up. "And this bothers you?"

"All of society knows I cannot hear, Simon. Will they think me a fool if I attend?"

Simon held out his hand. "Come here."

He waited until she stood before him, then pulled her into his arms and nestled her on his lap. "No one will think you a fool, Jesse. They will admire you as they have from the moment they found out about your deafness. There is not one of them who is not impressed by your intelligence and ability to read lips."

"But I will not hear a sound the maestro makes."

"Then tell them you did not come for the music but to see Liszt in person. Rumor has it the Hungarian pianist is quite the ladies' man."

"Would you be jealous?"

Simon leaned down to kiss her. "Without a doubt," he said, tracing the satiny skin of her cheek with the back of his finger. "I had to wait far too long to find you, and I am not about to let some womanizer carry you off with a sweet song."

"I don't think you have anything to fear. What musician would want to compose beautiful songs for someone who could never hear one note of their music?"

"I would," Simon said, "if the someone in my heart were you."

"Oh, Simon. I would give back all the gowns I have ever created to hear the sound of your voice, or your laugh, or your sighs. I would give everything I have to hear you say you love me."

Simon cupped his hands around her cheeks. "Just because you cannot hear the words, doesn't make them any less real. I love you, Jesse. I will always love you."

Simon leaned down to kiss her. Their kisses were always passionate and giving, and the need they shared always went beyond touching. Tonight what they shared was even more demanding. Simon kissed her again, holding her close and touching her tenderly. This was the prelude to a wonderful symphony. Simon kissed her again. And again.

"No," Jessica gasped, the breath rushing from her body in gulps. "I want to finish my design first."

"Now?"

"Yes, now." Jessica jumped off Simon's lap and rushed to the desk.

Simon dropped his head back on the chair. Right now he would give anything if Jessica could hear the moan that came from his body when she left him like this. It was torturous agony, and she was the cause of it.

He gave her time, then walked over to the desk and stood there. "Are you done?" he asked when she looked up at him.

"Close enough," she said, making a few quick lines. "Here." She handed him her latest design. "What do you think?"

Simon stared at the paper. The emotions racing through him were hard to explain. Happiness. Pride. Love. None of them came close.

"Well?" Jessica asked, the look on her face taking on the slightest hint of doubt. "Do you like it?"

"Yes, I like it." He swallowed hard. "Did you have anyone in mind when you created this?"

"Actually, I thought I might have it made for myself."

Simon nodded. "You're sure you need a gown like this?"

Jessica smiled. "Yes. I'm quite sure."

Simon rushed around the desk and pulled Jessica into his arms. Their first kiss paled in comparison to the emotions they shared now. "I love you, Jesse."

"Those words are the most wonderful words I will ever hear, Simon. I love you too."

Simon kissed her again. Jessica's latest design drifted to the floor. A very pregnant woman wearing an elegant day dress and a broad smile on her face looked back at them.

About the Author

❀

𝓛aura Landon taught high school for ten years before leaving the classroom to open her own ice-cream shop. As much as she loved serving up sundaes and malts from behind the counter, she closed up shop after penning her first novel. Now she spends nearly every waking minute writing, guiding her heroes and heroines to happily ever after. She is the author of more than a dozen historical novels, and her books are enjoyed by readers around the world. She lives with her family in the rural Midwest, where she devotes what free time she has to volunteering in her community.